Praise for the Inspector Jack Oxby

The Cézanne Chase

"Readers will be drawn to the intrigue . . . steady action, looming suspense, and an appealing subject."
—*Library Journal*

"A fascinating look behind the scenes at those who deal, both licitly and illicitly, in the high-stakes art world. Intelligent and suspenseful, this engrossing tale of international intrigue will keep art lovers and non-art lovers alike pinned to their chairs." —Stefanie Matteson

"*The Cézanne Chase* is a virtual primer of the art world . . . It is also a marvelous travelogue that transports readers to dazzling museums and art capitals of the world. The dialogue and descriptive portraits of cities are first-rate . . . plenty of action and a plot that is terrifyingly plausible."
—*The Bergen Record*

"The beauty is in the technical details about fine art."
—*New York Times Book Review*

"Swan has created a page-turner . . . The stakes are high and so is the suspense . . . With quick, sure strokes our author leads us to a violent climax, [keeping] the action moving like the bursts from an AK-47."
—Bill Sweeney, KSRO Radio (CA)

"An action-packed, globetrotting thriller that will keep readers enthralled from start to finish. Thomas Swan paints an intriguing who-done-it . . . absorbing."
—Harriet Klausner

continued on next page . . .

The Final Fabergé

"Swan spins a taut tale . . . in a neat blend of art and crime."
—*San Antonio Express-News*

"Thomas Swan . . . is as knowledgeable as he is inventive."
—*Dallas Morning News*

"Oxby is charming and disarmingly intelligent."
—*Publishers Weekly*

"The excitement of the story is bound to send first-time readers of Thomas Swan in search of his previous books."
—*Sunday Star-Ledger*

"Plenty of fun facts about Fabergé [and] Russian architecture."
—*Kirkus Reviews*

"A pleasant diversion . . . Thomas Swan's research is meticulous."
—*Cleveland Plain Dealer*

The Da Vinci Deception

"Fans of Ian Pears's art mysteries will enjoy the lavish detail Swan provides on the minutiae of forgery. The captivating premise of *The Da Vinci Deception* will win over those who like their thrillers well decorated with objets d'art."
—*Booklist*

"A full cast of sharply etched characters, both villains and good guys, trace a twisting adventure."
—*Publishers Weekly*

The
Cézanne
Chase

———

Thomas Swan

AN ONYX BOOK

ONYX
Published by New American Library, a division of
Penguin Putnam Inc., 375 Hudson Street,
New York, New York 10014, U.S.A.
Penguin Books Ltd, 27 Wrights Lane,
London W8 5TZ, England
Penguin Books Australia Ltd, Ringwood,
Victoria, Australia
Penguin Books Canada Ltd, 10 Alcorn Avenue,
Toronto, Ontario, Canada M4V 3B2
Penguin Books (N.Z.) Ltd, 182–190 Wairau Road,
Auckland 10, New Zealand

Penguin Books Ltd, Registered Offices:
Harmondsworth, Middlesex, England

Published by Onyx, an imprint of New American Library,
a division of Penguin Putnam Inc.
This is an authorized reprint of a hardcover edition published by Newmarket Press.
For information address Permission Department, Newmarket Press,
18 East 48th Street, New York, New York 10017

First Onyx Printing, April 2001
10 9 8 7 6 5 4 3 2 1

PUBLISHER'S NOTE
This is a work of fiction. Names, characters, places, and incidents either are the
product of the author's imagination or are used fictitiously, and any resemblance to
actual persons, living or dead, events, or locales is entirely coincidental.

For Barbara.
And the grandchildren:
Sara, Michael, Josh, Cameron, Casey, and Dylan.
And as always, Steve.

Chapter 1

St. Petersburg, for all its frayed edges, has remained the jewel among Russian cities. The city and its people survived revolution, a nine-hundred-day siege in World War II in which nearly a million died, then a kind of benign neglect brought on by decades of Communist rule. It is a city of islands and bridges, built on the banks of the twisting Neva river. In spite of all, St. Petersburg's important institutions have survived, as has the spirit of the natives, who affectionately call their city "Pete" as they did during the years when it was known as Petrograd or Leningrad. In spite of decades of adversity, the university, the libraries, and the museums have held together with remarkable tenacity.

One museum in particular was enjoying a renaissance: the Hermitage. Catherine the Great decreed that the magnificent salons of the Winter Palace be made into its galleries. From Peter the Great until the Revolution, agents of the czars and empresses scoured the world for great art, until the royal collection bulged to eight thousand paintings and five times that many drawings. Four buildings compose the Hermitage, a giant sprawl in which there are a thousand rooms and 117 staircases.

It was early morning. Pigeons scavenged on the broad sidewalks then separated as a young woman walked with a purposeful stride to a door leading to the administration offices. Ilena Petrov came early to the museum every morning. It was this show of dedication and her recent completion of studies in European art history that had helped bring recognition and a recent promotion. She had been appointed assistant curator for European art and sculpture of the period 1850 to 1917, a position of immense responsibility. The collection of paintings in the Hermitage from those years was among the world's largest and, without question, of incalculable value.

Ilena carried a heavy cloth sack, in which were books and notepads and a thermos filled with strong tea as well as a thick slice of plushka, a sugary cinnamon blackbread baked by her grandmother. From a window in the reception office she could see the rising sun that reflected brilliantly off the spire above Peter and Paul Cathedral in the historic fortress across the river.

Each day, before the rest of the staff arrived, Ilena would go out into the long corridors and galleries, where she was alone in the silence. She went first to the Malachite Room to touch the carved figure of a cupid that had become her personal talisman then climbed the great Ambassador's Staircase up to the galleries that held her favorite artists. In room 318 were, among others, the works of Pissarro and Cézanne. Ilena had united their art by placing their paintings on the same wall, aware that the two men had been close friends and aware, too, that Paul Cézanne had not forged many long-lasting relationships.

Two windows in the small gallery room looked out to Palace Square and the Alexander Column, the pink granite of the ninety-foot high monument catching the early sun. Ilena entered slowly, her eyes taking in first a landscape by Corot then two village scenes by Pissarro. Beyond the doorway were two Cézannes. First was a landscape; next to it was a portrait of the artist titled *Self-Portrait in a Beret*.

She approached the portrait then was suddenly jolted by an awareness that something was terribly wrong. Drawing closer, she saw that Cézanne's face seemed to have been painted over. Now she could touch it and saw that the paint where the head had been was a jellied mass, sagging away from the canvas. It was the canvas she had seen, bleached to a ghostly white.

Ilena screamed, a long, pitiful cry. She brought her hands to her face and stared in shock and disbelief. For minutes she stood, trembling, as if rooted to the spot in front of the canvas. Anger overwhelmed her. Who could be so cruel, she asked aloud. She backed away then turned and ran. Not until she had reached the head of the magnificent stairway did she stop. She sat on the top step, her body bent forward, her head lowered and resting on arms crossed over her legs.

She began to weep.

Chapter 2

Christie's salesrooms were on the second floor of the building on New York's Park Avenue and 59th Street, space the two-hundred-year-old London-based auction house had occupied since coming to America in 1977. Christie's, like its fierce competitor, Sotheby's, was one of those places where an obscure painting could be given the imprimatur of greatness by dint of someone paying many times more than it was worth, and where art-world insiders set prices by helping to establish the reserve, the confidential minimum price agreed upon by the seller and the auction house below which the painting will not be sold. The presale price is higher than the reserve and is generally publicized in advance of the auction so that the auction house can encourage the bidders to accept the presale price as an arbitrary minimum.

The auction at hand had been widely advertised in the media and through special mailings to known buyers and had attracted an overflow of the serious and curious. They were jammed into the square, high-ceilinged main gallery. An adjacent, smaller gallery was also filled to standing room an hour before the auction began. Serious bidders were in view of the auctioneer, but others, who wanted anonymity, were represented by a surrogate or a member of Christie's staff, several of whom were positioned at a bank of telephones at the side of the auctioneer's platform. Some of the more than two dozen reporters were more interested in the well-heeled socialites and occasional show-business celebrities who attended auctions for the excitement, as well as to occasionally add to their collections.

Interest was focused on the Jacopo da Pontormo portrait titled *Halberdier*, a painting of a young man holding a staff and wearing a sword. The portrait until six months before the auction had been prominently displayed in New York's Frick Collection where it had been for twenty years. It was always believed that Chauncey Devereau Stillman had placed it there on a permanent loan. The surprise decision to enter the painting at auction was a sad development for the Frick and a happy one for the Stillman Foundation.

Jacopo da Pontormo was a reclusive painter who, so evidence indicated, had studied under Leonardo Da Vinci in the early years of the sixteenth century. Pontormo's reputation, in need of a boost, had received one when the young man in the portrait was identified as Cosimo de' Medici of Florence, a speculation that roused heated controversy among art historians and let loose a flood of contradictory stories in the press. The controversy proved helpful to Christie's, which had mounted an energetic promotion to lift the pre-sale price to $20 million.

Standing room was five deep, and the air in the gallery had grown stale and hot. In what had become his accustomed position, Edwin Redpath Llewellyn sat at the end of a row at the front of the gallery, squeezed against the wall and fanning himself with a bidder's paddle . . . paddle number eighteen.

Llewellyn attended auctions with the enthusiasm of a low-handicap golfer at St. Andrews. He knew how to bid, rarely making the mistake of entering the competition when he was unfamiliar with the artist, the painting, or those he was bidding against. He was dressed in his go-to-auction uniform: gray trousers, blue-and-white striped shirt, club tie, and a pocket handkerchief tucked into the breast pocket of his elegantly frayed blue blazer. In one hand was a catalogue that detailed every item in the evening's sale, and cupped in the other was a pair of opera glasses. Llewellyn was an authentic connoisseur who understood fine art and could articulate his preferences and his prejudices. He was also rich, divorced, and a member of the Board of Trustees of the Metropolitan Museum of Art. After making several preliminary notes, he settled to watch the room fill, paying attention to the overflowing crowd as they took positions along the sides and across the back of the room. Llewellyn recognized some of the faces: Dupres, the wily one from Paris; Elton, the London barracuda; Takahawo of Tokyo.

His small but powerful binoculars slowly panned across the rows of standees and stopped at a tall woman wearing a strand of pearls and a brightly colored handkerchief placed carefully in the breast pocket of her tailored, pale gray suit. He caught her leafing through her catalogue, and then, suddenly, she raised her eyes and looked directly toward him. The binoculars had brought her so close it seemed Llewellyn could touch her. Blonde hair was combed back under a wide-brimmed hat that framed her face, and the bright lights made her pale skin seem nearly white and created soft shadows beneath her prominent cheekbones. The tip of her tongue moistened her lips, which parted into a smile, and at that moment he felt as if he had been caught peeking. He reacted with an embarrassed grin, then he extended two fingers upward and made a sort of friendly wave.

The auction began. Eighteen unimportant paintings were put up in the first twenty minutes, each one selling quickly as the auctioneer repeated the bids in a singsong chant accompanied by "do I hear more," then finally announcing the paddle number of the winning bidder. Then came the Pontormo. Llewellyn served on the museum's acquisition committee and joined the majority who opposed any effort to acquire the large portrait. His reason was arbitrary. Old Masters bored him, and the young man in the portrait looked inbred and arrogant; and besides, it didn't matter how he or his committee felt about the Pontormo. Gerald Bontannomo, Director of the Metropolitan, listened to but rarely accepted advice on major acquisitions.

The bidding opened at $20 million. Even to Llewellyn, who showed a practiced nonchalance toward money, it was a vastly unreasonable sum. Within two minutes it was more unreasonable. By twenty-eight million there were three bidders, at thirty, there were two. The Getty Museum's representative was in the room competing against an anonymous telephone bidder.

Quickly the bidding rose to thirty-five million. At $35.2 million it was over, and the Getty Museum was the new owner; *Halberdier* would remain in the United States. A dozen more unimportant works were hammered down, including an inferior painting by Pieter Brueghel that mildly interested Llewellyn as a purely speculative play. It was a game. If he could sneak by with a low bid, he would take it, wait a year and then sell it. He stopped raising his paddle when the bidding reached and stopped at a half million dollars, and he heard the auctioneer quietly call pass. It was a no-sale, the painting had been "bought-in." Obvious to Llewellyn and a few others, the reserve had not been met, and Christie's had entered and accepted its own bid. How much didn't matter, as no money would trade hands. The gallery thinned to a hard core of dealers and agents looking for a bargain.

Llewellyn remained seated while he made notes in the catalogue. This had become a ritual, and he had accumulated several dozen catalogues filled with prices paid for important works, along with his observations on the bidding strategies of the top dealers. When he got to his feet there were but a half dozen lingerers, including the blonde in the gray suit.

As he walked near her she said with a slightly accented voice, "I'm sorry you did not get the Brueghel."

Llewellyn stopped. He stood an even six feet, yet she was

about as tall as he. "I was looking for a bargain. It sold two years ago for nearly as much."

"Are you Mr. Llewellyn?" she asked.

"I am. But I don't believe I know your name." He said it in a way that suggested it was possible they had met before.

"I am Astrid Haraldsen, and I apologize if I seem to be"—she made a gesture as if searching for the right word—"if I am being forward."

Llewellyn smiled—a warm smile emphasized by brown eyes that were happy, too. He looked distinguished in his blue blazer and shock of gray hair. He was deeply tanned, the result of a week with old friends on Jupiter Island in Florida.

"Do you come to these things regularly?"

"I am beginning to. But mostly I go to the smaller auctions."

"Do you collect?" Llewellyn was enjoying the fact he had been picked from the crowd.

"It's too expensive." She looked down to the catalogue she had been rolling and unrolling. "I am a designer. Of interiors," she added quickly. "I look for special items for my clients."

"There wasn't much here today. Awful stuff, I thought." Then he said, "The Doyle Galleries would have better choices for you."

Her eyes came up to his for the first time. "I wanted to meet you."

"How nice." He smiled a little shyly. "How very nice."

For the instant when she looked directly into his eyes he felt as if she possessed an inner power, a nearly hypnotic influence. Certainly he felt sexually aroused. But her eyes strayed off and those feelings subsided.

Llewellyn guessed correctly. She was Scandinavian. Probably resolute, too. "Do you have a card?"

In fact she had several cards in her hand, ready to pass

them on if asked. "I have a presentation of my work. I would like to show it to you."

He looked at her card on which she had written the Westbury Hotel. "I like your address, we're practically neighbors."

She smiled, "I'm looking for a sublease. The hotel is very expensive."

By this time Llewellyn had made a more complete evaluation of Astrid Haraldsen. Her suit was silk, probably a Giorgio Armani; the salmon-colored blouse had expensive detailing; and her shoes were in the three-hundred-dollar range. She used makeup effectively, highlighting her cheeks and making her lips appear fuller. She hadn't fussed with eye liner and mascara, preferring only to accent the full brows that arched over the pale blue eyes he had noted when he first trained his binoculars on her. She had a good nose, which meant it wasn't a bad one, and probably in Llewellyn's mind not her best feature. Her perfume, Shalimar he thought, was one he liked.

After an awkward pause, he said, "Now that we've met, what can I do for you?"

"Help me to get an assignment. Perhaps a friend, or your own apartment." She hesitated briefly, then said quietly, "Because I am new and need references, I will not charge a fee."

She wasn't wasting any time, he thought. "I have friends at McMillan. You might find an opening there."

"I have worked with the finest designers in Norway and Denmark. And a very good one in London."

"Call me in a week," he said. "I'll see what I can do."

"I won't disappoint you." She turned her eyes to meet his. "Thank you."

It happened again. In that brief exchange, Llewellyn felt that she had exuded some sort of extraordinary energy. She turned and walked toward the door leading out from the auction room. He watched her, his smile still in place. He added great legs to the inventory he had made.

At the door Llewellyn was met by a short man blessed with a marvelous voice and bright eyes that lit up a small, round face. "Who's your friend?"

Llewellyn showed one of Astrid's cards. "New York's newest interior decorator drumming up business. Interested?"

"She's too tall. We'd never see eye to eye." The short man laughed. He was Harvey Duncan, director of Christie's Impressionist and Modern Paintings Department. "What did you think of the Pontoromo?"

"Not a great deal," Llewellyn replied. "Not worth what the Getty paid."

"Agreed," Harvey said. The brightness in his eyes suddenly faded. "I've been waiting to give you a piece of bad news we received from our Moscow agent this morning. The media's not in on it yet." He moved closer to Llewellyn. "The Cézanne self-portrait in the Hermitage was destroyed."

"Destroyed!" Llewellyn said incredulously. "How in God's name did that happen?"

"Not sure." Harvey shrugged. "We haven't received a complete report, but we think it was sprayed with some kind of acid. Whatever it was, the painting's a complete ruin."

Llewellyn stared past Harvey Duncan to the small stage, where minutes earlier a painting, to his mind of no great consequence, had sold for $35 million. "Any idea who did it?"

Harvey shook his small, round head. "No. But I suggest you tighten up security around that collection of yours. You act as if all you had were a few old copies of the *National Geographic*."

In fact, Llewellyn had inherited a collection of paintings. The star among them was a self-portrait by Cézanne. His grandfather had bought it from Cézanne's agent Ambroise

Vollard in 1903. The others were the work of run-of-the-mill artists and together were worth a fraction of the value of the Cézanne. He had acquired other paintings, each one valuable, all by Americans except one by Marc Fortin, a Canadian.

"No one gets past Fraser, and I've got triple locks everywhere," Llewellyn said triumphantly. "And then there's Clyde." Fraser was a combination handy man, cook, and family retainer, and Clyde was a Norwich terrier with a marked proclivity for barking at the slightest provocation.

Harvey replied wryly, "Yes, of course, there's Clyde." He looked up at Llewellyn, his eyes now showing deep concern. "We're friends Lew, and I don't want anything to happen to you or your painting, but remember there are crazy people out there. One of them nearly ruined Rembrandt's *Night Watch* a few weeks ago. Fast work and a layer of lacquer saved it."

Harvey gave Llewellyn a firm, yet friendly pat on the shoulder. "They're mad, some of them. And people get hurt."

Chapter 3

On Tuesday the 13th, shortly before noon in the National Gallery off London's Trafalgar Square, the miniature pagers carried by security personnel emitted an irregular beeping sound that meant an emergency condition existed and commanded all guards to report immediately to their duty stations.

In the corridor off Gallery A an attaché case had burned furiously, throwing off thick, black smoke. It had caused hysteria among the visitors, particularly the crowds in rooms where the smoke had reached. The beeping of the pagers had been joined by fire alarms sounding throughout the great old structure. Foam was needed, and a crew arrived to smother the stubborn blaze and put out a row of fans to blow away the dirty, foul-smelling air. Though nearly all of it had been reduced to black ash, the attaché case was surprisingly recognizable, its metal lock and hinges intact. Someone had scooped the remains into a plastic bag.

The entire floor had been evacuated as a team from the security department began their investigation, and the curatorial staff made a room-by-room assessment of the damage. The smoke had been cleared within an hour, and the only apparent damage had been a burned scar on the wood flooring and a fine layer of soot that settled over several nearby pictures. The incident was put down as one of those bizarre and troubling affairs and most likely an accident caused by someone too embarrassed to explain what happened.

By two o'clock the gallery had been reopened, and soon after, at 2:15 according to the records, a young Australian couple had informed the guard in Gallery A that something was wrong with one of the paintings, a small Cézanne self-portrait, one that the artist had painted of himself without a hat, looking dead-even at the viewer. The paint had begun to dissolve, and splotches of foam the size of large coins were spotted over the canvas. Tiny wisps of what seemed to be smoke escaped from the foam, and a sharp, sour odor surrounded the picture. The painting had been rushed to the conservator's laboratory where it had been bathed in mineral oil and the action of the acid halted. But all efforts to save it were too late.

There were no clues, nor had there been a warning or letter or even an irrational phone call. Bottom line: No one claimed responsibility, yet it was obvious that the smoking briefcase had been a diversion and had quite admirably served the purpose of emptying the gallery of visitors and security personnel.

The incident had been reported in the morning tabloids, and one speculative writer with the *Sunday Sport* had gratuitously given the destroyed painting a value of $29 million. Another suggested an investigation into the Gallery's security system was long overdue. The *Guardian*'s headline escalated the affair to the level of a national disgrace, and an editorial in the *Times* concluded, ". . . there is much to explain concerning the woefully inadequate, if not complete absence of, proper surveillance and security. We have lost a national treasure."

On the following morning, the director of the National Gallery, Sir Anthony Canfield, K.B.E., convened a meeting at ten o'clock. In attendance were three chief supervising security managers; the guard assigned to Gallery A, plus guards from the adjacent galleries, corridors, and all entrances to the building. A Miss Cook took verbatim notes. Also present was Elliott Heston, Commander of Operations Command Group—OCG—under which was the Arts and Antiques Squad, Metropolitan Police. The director of security, a curiously private man named Evan Tippett, was attending a conference in California. He had been reached by phone and given preliminary details of the painting's destruction. He had asked several questions, then directed that a full report be on his desk when he returned.

Elliott Heston focused on what he considered to be the most intriguing question: "Why a Cézanne self-portrait? Any thoughts on that?"

"I haven't a clue," Canfield replied, "but whoever's up to this horrible mischief has a ways to go. Lionello Venturi's catalogue of Cézanne's paintings shows that he completed twenty-five self-portraits. Not the life's work of a man lacking ego, would you say?"

Heston ignored the question. "Any other portraits in England?"

"There is one. Owned privately by some upstart collector south of London . . . uh, man named Pinkster." He handed a sheet of paper to Heston. "This inventory of the self-portraits is the best we've got, but it's incomplete and woefully out of date because at least two of the portraits have been sold, and we don't have a record of the new owners. And two more are on loan, and we're not certain where either one is at this point. There's a separate report that describes a self-portrait owned by an American named Llewellyn. It's a bit of a mystery because the public has never really seen it. We've got a black-and-white photograph and not a very good one. But its provenance is flawless. Add that to the others and there are—correction—were—twenty-six in all."

Heston stood, shook hands around the table, then eased himself out of the meeting room. He went on to his car, walking with long, deliberate strides. He was tall and angular, with the build of a distance runner, which he had been during his school years. His hair was unruly and would likely fall across his forehead. His face, like his body, was long and narrow, and it had the inquiring look of a policeman, and he wore gold-rimmed glasses selected by his wife, who insisted they gave him a scholarly air. His driver saw him taking the steps two at a time and pulled the car forward.

"The Abbey," Heston said, getting in beside the driver.

The car maneuvered around Trafalgar Square onto Whitehall, past the government buildings to Victoria Street. Heston entered Westminster Abbey by the west door where he was confronted by a half-dozen tour groups. He walked along the north aisle to the transept and stopped between the choir and the high altar. An organ played, accompanied by a brass trio. Unusual, he thought; perhaps a rehearsal for a special event. Then he turned toward the choir, where, as he suspected, seated in the first row was a man keenly involved with whatever he was writing in a notebook perched on his lap. Heston circled around a group of tourists, came up behind the man, and leaned down and said in a heavy accent, "You got a special pass to sit in there?"

Without looking up, the man replied, "That's an obscenely terrible accent, Elliott."

Heston smiled and sat next to the man, whose attention remained fixed on his notes. Heston had come to the Abbey numerous other times to find his man in the choir or, if the crowds were unusually thick, in the small and quiet Chapel of St. Faith. Heston had attended the memorial service for a popular assistant commissioner of New Scotland Yard and another time had witnessed an Easter service at the urging of his wife. Otherwise he rarely visited the great abbey and knew it mainly as a tourist attraction or as a spiritual hideaway for the Arts and Antiques Squad's Detective Chief Inspector Jack LaConte Oxby.

"They know me, but they might ask you to step down from the choir," Oxby said matter-of-factly.

"Then use your considerable influence, as I rather like the view from here. What's the music about?"

Oxby said, "It's for old King Ed the Confessor. It's his nine hundredth birthday."

"Has it been that long? It hardly seems it." Heston hoped to raise a smile from his obstinately independent companion.

Oxby turned. No denying he was a small man, though it seemed there was a largeness to him, because even as he sat, his eyes were nearly level with Heston, who stood several inches taller. When he shifted his weight or moved his arms, it was apparent that he had a coordinated and well-conditioned body. His nose was long but somehow it did not dominate his face. No, the real fascinations about Oxby were his eyes and his voice. The eyes were perfect; a blue-gray that penetrated with curiosity or warmth, humor or intense determination as the circumstance required, and his rich baritone had been trained for both singing and acting. He spoke French with the ease of a Parisian and Italian with the singsong fluency of a very proper Florentine. Oxby had also mastered the infinite ranges of accents and idiosyncratic slang of the language spoken throughout the British Isles. He could identify and mimic a solicitor from Glasgow as well as a Liverpudlian stevedore.

Heston's smile faded. "Something's come up, and you've got a new case."

Oxby widened his eyes in acknowledgment and to signify he wanted to hear more.

Heston placed a copy of the *Sun* on top of Oxby's notebook and paused while Oxby stared at the screaming headline and a photograph of the portrait taken before its destruction. "I know you're just back from the country, but don't you ever read a newspaper?"

"Certainly not that one," Oxby said disdainfully, his eyes

focused on the front page of the newspaper. "I'd rather you told me what happened."

Heston took the paper back and swacked it across his thigh. "There's not much to tell. Whoever did it created a diversion, then sprayed the painting with some kind of exotic acid or solvent, then disappeared." He filled in with the sparse details that he had picked up earlier.

Oxby turned to a clean sheet in his notebook. "What's a Cézanne self-portrait worth these days?"

Heston laughed. "A ridiculous amount, I'm sure. I don't buy them, you know. Depending on size, and which one, I suppose ten million . . . fifteen? More?"

"Much more," Oxby said firmly. "And perhaps a little more now that one has been permanently removed."

"I thought of that. An interesting speculation."

"Do we know how many self-portraits there are?"

"Canfield told me that Cézanne painted twenty-six in all. We still have one in England, owned by an Alan Pinkster who I believe you know."

"I've met him, twice perhaps. Lot of money, bit of a pain."

"One of the twenty-six is owned by a New Yorker. Also wealthy. It came into his family a few generations ago, and it's still there. We don't know much about it."

A man dressed in plain cleric's clothes came up to Oxby and touched his arm. "I'm terribly sorry, Mr. Oxby. The choir's coming along for their rehearsal any minute now." The man spoke with a rich cockney accent.

"It's all right, Teddy. We're moving on." Oxby motioned for Heston to step down from the choir. "Now there's authentic cockney," he said with admiration. "Teddy's fifth-generation East End." He led Heston through the accumulating crowd.

Heston's driver had pulled beside a row of taxis. Oxby said, "I'll walk. Officially, I'm still on holiday."

"It's important that we talk, Jack. There'll be hell to pay

if we don't nip this thing right off. There's a call in from the
director and—"

"We'll talk," Oxby said, moving away. "You know, Elliott, I'd be mad as hell if this were happening to a Manet or
a Degas." He shook his head slowly. "Cézanne isn't one of
my favorites." Then he brightened. "Cheerio . . . see you in
your office." Instantly he was absorbed by the crowds con-
verging on the great cathedral.

He crossed Victoria Street and continued to Broadway,
covering the half mile in six minutes and arriving at New
Scotland Yard ahead of Heston. He was surprised to find
two of his assistants waiting, both wearing worried expres-
sions. Detective Sergeants Ann Browley and Jimmy Murratore were young, bright, and ambitious. Ann was a bit of an
anomaly, as her family was old money with strong links to
London society, while Jimmy's Italian-born parents worked
long and diligently to make a living from their bakery shop
in Brixton.

"Something's gone wrong," Oxby guessed.

"Very wrong," Jimmy said. "We just got word that the
self-portrait in Alan Pinkster's collection was destroyed."

Oxby's eyes narrowed. "Acid, or whatever they're
using?"

"I'm afraid yes," Ann replied. "Pinkster himself called,
mad as a hornet and as much as saying it was our fault."

"And him with a security system good enough for the
queen's jewels," Jimmy said.

Heston arrived, frustration clearly showing. "Bloody
damned press will have us responsible . . . see if I'm not
right." He went into his office, the others following. "When
did it happen?"

"Probably during the night," Oxby said. "Pinkster's collection isn't open to the public except by special arrangement."

"A group from the Danish embassy was on a tour, eighteen in all," Ann said. "They were gone from the gallery be-

fore five, and apparently everything was in good order when they went off."

Heston said, "Jack, you're on this now. Tell me what you need, but get something sorted out quickly."

Oxby instructed Ann to assemble a file on Pinkster and his collection. To Heston he said, "I want Nigel Jones." Then he went to his office and collected a notebook and palm-sized tape recorder. At the precise moment he picked up his phone to order a car, it rang. A voice said, "Detective Tobias is in the lobby. Shall I send him up?"

Oxby sighed heavily and said softly to himself, "Alex old friend, you promised that you'd give me fair warning." He called Ann into his office and thrust the phone at her. "Alex Tobias is at the reception desk. Get him on the phone and tell him I've got to run off but say that I'll stop to see him on my way to the garage. And Ann, see if you can have a decent car waiting for me."

"Alex, you scoundrel," Oxby said, reaching the reception desk, "You promised to call ahead of time."

"Don't lecture me, young Jack, I've been taking orders from every member of my family since we left New York, and I don't need any more of it from you." His scowl turned to a smile and he extended his hand.

Alexander Tobias was on the comfortably portly side, with a thick, fluffy crop of gray hair and heavy-rimmed glasses set on a slightly bent nose. He wore a mustache, a nearly solid thatch of hair, and had a florid face that showed equal amounts of curiosity and compassion. Tobias had had a successful career and was considered a superb detective. But he had never mastered the nuances of police politics, which meant that while he had edged into the top ranks of the New York City police department at age fifty-five, he had been passed over for appointment to a deputy commissioner's spot. At fifty-eight, and at his request, he took the rank of sergeant detective and was reassigned to the major case squad, where he investigated art forgeries and thefts. He and Oxby had first paired up on a Rembrandt stolen from a London gallery and traced to New York. The case began a professional relationship that had grown into a deep friendship.

"We flew in from Dublin a day ahead because once our son was married there wasn't any purpose in staying around, and Helen was anxious to visit her sister, who couldn't come to the wedding because of some damned bone problem."

"So they took away all the telephones in Dublin and in the airport, and you want me to believe you couldn't call me," Oxby said, chiding his friend.

"Believe what you damned want to believe. Your sergeant said you've got to run down to Surrey, something about another Cézanne?"

"Want to come with me?" Oxby asked. "They've destroyed three of them now, and it's damned serious destruction that's going on."

"I can't, Jack. I've got to meet Helen, and we leave tomorrow. It's why I took a chance I'd catch you this morning."

"I'd like for you to come," Oxby said.

Tobias shook his head. "And I'd like to go."

Oxby was assigned a standard Ford Escort with a black exterior, gray interior, both in need of a thorough scrubbing. He drove south from London over the Vauxhall Bridge, through Kensington, then on the A23 to Surrey.

Oxby and Pinkster had met at a furniture auction, but it was doubtful the wealthy art collector would remember their brief encounter. Oxby remembered. Alan Pinkster was thirty-eight years old, tenuously married to his third wife, and the father of one daughter, now ten, who lived with her mother. Wife number one, on whom Pinkster had settled a small fortune, had recently been in the news about her own remarriage. Although Pinkster had been labeled a billionaire in New York, the financial community in London wondered how much of his assets were offset by deals and heavy borrowing. Having learned the art of arbitrage from a trio of infamous Wall Streeters with whom he had worked for three years, Pinkster knew that a small percentage of a massive amount of money was a surefire route to great wealth. An expert in junk bonds, he had made megamillion-dollar leveraged buyouts by the time he was twenty-seven. There was little doubt on either side of the Atlantic that Alan Pinkster knew how to make and spend money on a grand scale.

His home was near Bletchingly, a country town in the heart of Surrey. Over several years, aided consecutively by his three wives and twice as many interior designers, he had put an old manor house through an arduous renovation. Pinkster had also built a modest-sized gallery to house his surprisingly impressive art collection.

Waiting beside an elongated Mercedes parked next to the gallery was a clearly agitated Alan Pinkster.

"Are you from the police?" he asked abruptly.

Oxby was equally abrupt. "Yes," and offered his card.

Pinkster had an intensity about him: firm set mouth, and dark eyes that fixed on whomever he was talking with. His hair was brown and groomed, and his body was fit and covered with expensive clothes.

"I want the bloody bastard that did this to pay an awful price," Pinkster said angrily.

"What price had you in mind?" Oxby asked.

"I'm serious. I want whoever did it to be hurt. Hurt painfully, then put away for a good long time."

"That would indeed be a high price," Oxby agreed.

Pinkster led the way into the gallery. There had been a gala celebration when Alan Pinkster officially opened his gallery two years earlier. A grand affair, by all accounts, replete with tents and sculpted ice and buffet tables lined with food and fine wines. CNN televised it, and the BBC put it

on the news. It had been another attempt mounted on a mon-
umental scale for Pinkster to crash into London society.

The basement of the gallery was half display, the other
half given over to restoration and repair. On a large table
under bright lights was the self-portrait. A glance at the
painting proved to Oxby that its condition was even more
grotesque than he had imagined. The face of the artist was
discernible but as if drawn by an insane hand. An ear had
come loose from where it belonged and was about where the
nose should be. The mouth was a gaping red hole. The eyes
had slid into the blackness of Cézanne's beard. Oxby's re-
vulsion was as much over the painting's hideous distortion
as the cruel fact that a great painting had been senselessly
destroyed.

Oxby broke the silence. "When did you learn about
this?"

"First thing this morning."

"Can you be more specific?"

Oxby looked inquiringly at the small group huddled near
the door. Here was the gallery's curatorial staff, competent
by all accounts. A young man spoke up.

"Eight o'clock. I was the first to spot it. Usually Mr.
Boggs is here before eight, but he hasn't shown all day."
Boggs was Clarence Boggs, formerly the senior curator of
the Wallace Collection in London and known to be consci-
entious and loyal.

"Eight this morning is when you discovered it," Oxby
said. "But not when someone poured acid on it."

Pinkster was impatient. "It was perfectly fine late yesterday, and this morning—"

"I'd like to meet with Boggs," Oxby said.

"And so would I," Pinkster said irritably. "Where in
God's name is he?" He aimed his question at the three men
and two women who constituted the group by the door.

The same young man spoke again and said that Boggs

seemed upset over a phone call he had received the previous afternoon.

"When was that?" Oxby asked.

"Just as the Danish group was leaving."

"And what happened?"

"He went off. Put on that old hat he always wears, took his stick, and went off."

"What kind of stick?"

"Just a walking stick. Mr. Boggs is a walker. Says it helps get his mind sorted out when there's a problem." The young man added, "His daughter's had problems lately."

Oxby approached the small group. "I would like to have a brief chat with each one of you before you leave. As it is important that you tell me what you have observed in the last twenty-four hours, I'll ask that you don't talk among yourselves about the painting or speculate as to what might have happened yesterday."

They looked at each other, shrugged, and began to make a silent exit from the room. When they were gone, Oxby walked to the table and stood opposite from Pinkster, the destroyed portrait between them.

"How much insurance do you carry?" Oxby asked conversationally.

"I don't know. My collection has been assessed in astronomical numbers, but it would hardly fetch those figures, even in a good auction."

"I recall that you paid a little over three million pounds for the Cézanne landscape. You've owned it for five years, and it would probably bring seven, perhaps eight million today." Oxby's memory was to the art world what a conductor's mastery of a symphonic score was to music. He could match painting to purchaser, to price, to date of sale and, finally, to the auction house. "I also recall that you came across the self-portrait in a business transaction."

"It was one of the few unencumbered assets owned by the Weissmann brothers. We bought their brokerage company shortly after the drop in stock prices in 1987. Their business had fallen to a trickle, and they were getting old, both in their eighties. George Weissmann died in December of that year, and Louis had a stroke several years after that and has been in a wheelchair ever since."

"Did you know they owned a Cézanne self-portrait?"

"It's my business to know such things."

"How much did you pay for their company?" Oxby didn't expect an answer, and Pinkster didn't disappoint him.

"It was a private transaction," Pinkster replied stiffly. "The matter has no relevance to your investigation."

"Perhaps not, for the present, at least." Oxby gave notice that the issue was not dead.

"When do you plan to interrogate the staff?"

"Shortly," Oxby replied. "But first I have one or two questions I hope you will answer."

"Of course." Pinkster crossed his arms over his chest, the dark eyes fixed intently on Oxby.

"Where did you spend yesterday?"

"In my London office. I had a brief lunch at the Connaught. Returned to Bletchingly at seven. We had guests for dinner."

Oxby was amused that anyone could have a brief lunch at the Connaught.

"Have you received any phone calls or correspondence that have been out of the ordinary?"

Pinkster reflected for a moment, then shook his head. "Can't say I have. But all that sort of thing is screened by my secretary."

"Perhaps I'll talk with her."

Pinkster then abruptly ended the interview by turning away and walking off in the direction of his house. Oxby returned to the gallery. One by one he interviewed the staff, and once again the young man who had spoken up earlier was most anxious to share all he knew. He was slight, with blonde hair and soft features. His name was David Blaney.

As he had with the others, Oxby exchanged small talk, then informally eased into a conversation centered on the previous day.

"Had you any particular assignments to deal with yesterday?" Oxby asked.

"For some weeks now I've been preparing a brochure designed to show off Mr. Pinkster's collection, as well as the building. It's quite unique to work in a small museum that has all the challenges and problems of a large gallery. Yesterday we were photographing some of the statuary. We have a Rodin and one by Henry Moore, you know."

Oxby was impressed and said so. "A group from the Danish embassy was here. You saw them?"

"Indeed. I had the photographer take candid shots of the group. I thought I'd work one into the brochure." Then David shook his head. "But they were nearly all women."

"Something wrong with women?" Oxby asked with a bemused smile.

"Nothing at all," David replied defensively. "But I was hoping to use a picture that had both men and women in it."

"Do you have the photographs?"

"I'll have proofs in a day or two."

"Ask your photographer to safeguard the negatives. I'll want to see all of the photos he took."

"He can be the devil to get on the phone, but I'll try."

"When did you last take a close look at the portrait?"

"Two days ago we fussed over it for several hours. Cézanne often laid his paint heavily on the canvas, and on that portrait the impasto was very heavy, as if he had used a cement trowel to lay down the paint . . ." His voice trailed off.

Following the interviews, Oxby returned to his car to wait for Nigel Jones and to record his impressions of the time he had spent with Pinkster and his gallery staff. Suddenly there was loud shouting, and Oxby looked up to see Alan Pinkster running toward the gallery. Pinkster's face was flushed, and agitation showed in the way his head jerked nervously. His feet clattered over the gravel driveway, and he stopped a few feet from Oxby. His lips were moving, but there was no sound. Then came the words: "The police called." Pinkster's eyes widened into a helpless stare. "Boggs has been murdered!"

Chapter 4

It was a minute past one on Wednesday, and the main terminal of Gatwick Airport, London's number-two terminal, was choked with passengers. A man approached the newsstand off the south corridor. He was carrying an oddly shaped black bag, a small satchel shaped somewhat like an oversized sausage. He was tall, over six feet, and wore a dark blue suit, shirt with no tie, opaque sunglasses, and a summer straw hat with a broad brim. As he moved past the newsstand he swept up a copy of the *Financial Times* and the *International Herald Tribune*. He studied the front pages of the tabloids, chose one, tucked all three newspapers under his arm and paid for them, then went into the adjoining restaurant and bought coffee, which he took to a table against the wall where he was in clear sight of the restaurant's entrance. He snapped open the *Times* to the stock listings and scanned the columns, pausing occasionally as if interested in a particular company. Next he leafed through the pages of the *Tribune*. It was a bold line of type running across the bottom of the *Sun* that had caught his attention: CURATOR OF PRIVATE GALLERY SLAIN.

On page three was a photograph of the Pinkster Gallery and another of Clarence Boggs and Alan Pinkster admiring a nude statue by Rodin taken on the day it had been placed in the gallery. The article was brief and included a statement by the Reigate police implying that Boggs had been murdered but that further details would be announced pending results of an investigation being conducted by a team from the Metropolitan Police. On the chair beside him he placed the black bag and his hat, then he leaned back and sipped the coffee. It was cold.

There was a bigness to the man: broad through the shoulders; long and thick-fingered hands; a large, somewhat handsome face. His light-brown hair was streaked with sun-yellowed strands and combed back over his ears. His lips were full and set over a wide chin in which there was a deep cleft, which was slightly off center and made one side of his face seem broader than the other. He glared up to the digital clock above the cashier: 1:14. He lowered his gaze to watch a woman push her tray forward, pay the cashier, then turn to survey the room. She was simply dressed in a sweater and slacks; her dark hair framed a pretty face that showed only a blush of pink lipstick. Astrid Haraldsen had put herself together for traveling: plain and comfortable and incognito. She walked to the table next to where the tall man sat and pushed aside the empty cups and the ashtray.

"Won't you sit here?" he asked in a deep voice with the unmistakable singsong lilt that clearly suggested he was Scandinavian. "That table is very messy."

"Norsk?" She asked.

"Ja," he smiled.

She placed her tray at his table and sat. They talked amiably for several minutes, speaking in a blend of Norwegian and English. A young couple came to a nearby table. They giggled and occasionally leaned together and kissed. Astrid watched them, and she looked at the other tables and at the people waiting to pay the cashier. The smile she had brought to the table faded.

"You look tired," he said without inflection. When he continued he spoke only in Norwegian. "Your hair is showing under the wig. Fix it before the wrong person becomes curious."

He watched as she felt for the line of hair that covered the pale yellow of her own. She pulled a wave of dark hair over the top of her forehead. "You look pale," he said. "Do you feel all right?"

"Why did you do it?" she said in a thin voice, ignoring his question. "Why, Peder?"

The man she called Peder put the black bag on his lap and set his hands on top of it, one across the other. "The curator was a potential troublemaker. He followed us into the gallery after I sprayed the painting, and I was certain he had smelled the solvent."

She shook her head. "No. There was a strong odor of paint in that room. You heard someone say that the ceiling had been painted that morning." She rubbed her hands nervously. "A miracle, you said."

"A coincidence, I said. But it was no miracle that you asked questions about one of the paintings. You were not to talk with anyone."

"I asked a harmless question."

"He answered it, too. And looked at you closely, then at me. Later, he can put the two of us together. And so can that damned photographer. He took pictures of everything that moved."

"But I was wearing this," she ran her hand through the dark hair. "They'll look for a secretary named Muller from Copenhagen."

"I wasn't wearing a disguise," Peder said.

"Nothing can happen," Astrid said.

"One good photograph could create a big problem."

"How do you know if they have a good photograph?"

"Find the photographer. See what he's got."

"You can do that?"

He nodded. "I must."

Her eyes flashed, and she looked down to the newspaper. A finger moved back and forth beneath the photograph of Clarence Boggs. "You didn't have to kill him."

"He had an accident," he said impatiently.

"You said no one would be hurt. Now someone is dead."

"And a photographer took pictures. That changes everything."

He leaned toward her and spoke in a quiet, urgent tone. "You have a job to do, and I expect you to do it."

A trio of young American businessmen claimed the adjacent table. They were congratulating each other on a successful trip.

Peder eyed them, then continued, still speaking in Norwegian. "When do you see Llewellyn again?"

She smiled briefly. "I will make arrangements when I call him from the airport this evening."

"Does he live alone? A man so rich must have help."

"Another man lives there. His name is Fraser. Just that. I learned from a delivery boy about him. He may be older than Llewellyn. But the boy said he talks in a funny way and that he is strong."

"Are you saying that man guards Llewellyn's paintings?"

"Maybe he does. And there's a dog," Astrid added. "The boy said the dog is the kind that barks all the time."

Peder drummed his fingers on top of the black bag. "I want you to learn everything about the painting. Measure it if you can, see how it is framed, what sort of backing does it have, is an alarm attached to the frame, and what kind of an alarm if there is one. How difficult would it be to take the painting out of the frame and what tools would be needed? Most of Cézanne's self-portraits are small."

"If I've judged Edwin Llewellyn correctly, he's put his painting into a frame that is very large, very ornate, and very expensive."

Peder hunched forward. "Learn everything. No mistakes and no half pieces of information. Is that understood?"

"I will learn the answers to every one of your questions, and a great deal more about Llewellyn and his painting and the old man and dog." She stared at him, almost defiantly. "How much time do I have before you want me to take it?"

"The plans have been changed. There will be a special exhibition of Cézanne's paintings next January in the south of France. In Aix-en-Provence. I was told that Llewellyn has agreed to loan his portrait to the exhibition, and that he may want to deliver it personally. In that case it may be easier to take the painting from him while he is transporting it." He ran his fingers across her hand, "By that time, you and Llewellyn should be very good friends."

"I think that wherever Llewellyn goes, the dog will go." A little laugh escaped, "And the better the dog knows me, the more it will bark when it sees me. It's a silly problem, but a problem."

"Perhaps I have a solution." Aukrust unsnapped the straps on his black bag. It was made of leather and was eighteen inches long and round like a bolster pillow. It was a medicine case designed for a homeopathic physician. In it was a honeycomb of compartments that held four two-ounce glass-stoppered bottles, six three-dram, ten ten-dram, and twelve one-ounce vials. In all there were more than thirty homeopathic remedies with names like nux vomica, jatropha, and apis mellifica, known also as honeybee poison. There were pockets for powder papers, surgical knives in sterilized sleeves, sutures and needles, a stethoscope, tape, bandages, and miscellaneous medical supplies. The initials CRM were goldleafed on the side of the case. A British passport said he was Charles Metzger, a medical doctor. His card announced he was a practitioner of homeopathy and gave a London address. But she had called him Peder. A Norwegian passport in an inside pocket of his jacket identified him as Peder Aukrust. A French visa listed an address in Cannes.

"This is for you." From one of the pockets inside the medicine case he took out a lipstick and held it in front of her so she could see its soft gold color. She looked at it curiously.

"It's not an ordinary lipstick." He pulled off the cover. "Let me demonstrate. Twist to the right and you have lipstick. 'Passionately Pink' they call it," he grinned uncharacteristically. "Twist to the left and you see nothing. But press it against the thigh of Llewellyn's pet and a hypodermic needle will spring out and release 2 cc's of trianylseconal, which will silence the bark quickly . . . and forever."

Astrid stared at the lipstick case for several moments. "But, I don't want to kill it."

"It's only a dog," he said flatly. "We can't take chances."

She put the cover on the lipstick and dropped it into her purse. "I want you to come with me."

"That can't be. There are matters here to settle while you are in Boston," and for the first time he smiled as if actually enjoying himself.

"Peder," she began, her eyes unable to look into his, "when we started you said that three paintings would be destroyed. Now it's four."

He shook his head vigorously. "The world will do nicely without a few of Cézanne's portraits. Besides, each remaining one will be worth a great deal more than before."

He again reached into the black bag, took out a brown envelope and handed it to her. "Here is five thousand dollars. I'll send a bank check for more. You'll have it in a week."

She put the envelope in her purse. "I'll call you on Sunday at the same time," she said. She looked at him, closed her eyes briefly, then got up and went out into the terminal.

He watched her leave and continued staring at the spot where she disappeared among the milling passengers. By his hand was the newspaper and the photograph of Clarence Boggs. He glowered menacingly. "Fucking photographer."

A man came to the table, put down his tray and sat. Aukrust turned to him, nodded silently, then gathered his newspapers and the oddly shaped black bag and walked out to the line of taxis.

Chapter 5

The Thames River may be the most famous short river in the world. Only two hundred miles in length, it is perhaps better known for its great width: three hundred yards shore to shore at London Bridge and at its estuary to the east of London the banks are nearly six miles apart. Because of the severe bomb damage to the great docks during the London Blitz in World War II, and because of the dramatic changes in the way goods were shipped in and out of London, vast stretches of the river suffered decades of neglect and deterioration. Then came a massive rebuilding project on the Isle of Dogs after the war that brought a renaissance to the great river, an event damned by some, cheered by others, bringing financial disaster to its developers.

River traffic had changed, too. Barges, small freighters, and pleasure craft replaced the huge containerships. Beneath brightly painted Albert Bridge, at the foot of Royal Hospital Road was Cadogan Pier, home port to a hodgepodge of private and charter boats. One was a reincarnated forty-year-old harbor tug, its hull painted black, its rails and deckhouse in bright yellow and green. It flew several pennants, among which were a faded British flag and a bright new Greek flag. Carved into a piece of polished wood, painted in gold letters, was the boat's name: *Sepera*.

A woman came on deck and spoke to a stockily built man who stood at the railing. "Is it time, Nikos?"

He answered, "A new one is coming, and the new ones are always late the first time."

"His name," she said. "It is not a Japanese name." Then she shook her head, "Is it Mezzer? or how do you say it?"

"It's not a Greek name," Nikos replied. "Dr. Mets-gar, I think." He turned to her. "You have an easy time of it tonight. Only to make the big room ready and take him there."

His black eyebrows were like two wooly-bear caterpillars joined at the bridge of a strong, broad nose. Over his mouth was a bushy mustache swirled out to carefully scissored tips. He drew heavily on the stub of a cigar then flipped it into the water. "We are to go to the barriers and turn back at Greenwich. An hour's cruise, I was told. No more."

"I would prefer to cook a meal," she replied. "It is boring to do nothing." Her hair was black, and her eyes were a deep, dark blue, like the evening sky. Her skin was the color of pale olives, and her name was Sophie. Nikos was native to Pátrai on the northern coast of the Peloponnesus. Sophie's mother was Sicilian, and she was born in Italy and had lived in five Mediterranean countries while growing up. Her family was headed by a wine-loving father who could never remain employed as a boat builder.

That Nikos and Sophie were captain and first mate on a converted tug was its own story. The previous summer they were two in a crew of eleven on a yacht that reached Portofino and remained anchored there while its owner entertained business friends vacationing on the Italian Riviera. Nikos served as second mate, and Sophie worked in the galley and tended to the needs of the owner's wife. It was then that a guest offered them a boat and a salary and the chance to begin their own charter business on the Thames River in London. Neither had been to England; they spoke little English and knew nothing about the Thames and the changes taking place on the Isle of Dogs or about the landmarks along that sometimes treacherous waterway. But they were guaranteed work visas, licenses, and permits, and in the first year while learning the language and becoming acclimated to their new life, their benefactor promised to keep them busy with his own needs for the boat. He allowed them to give the boat whatever name they wished.

As the air cooled, a mist rose up from the water and spread across the Embankment. A figure appeared and stopped next to a small pagoda beside the dock. Nikos watched the tall man come past the boats tied up next to the *Sepera*, a canvas bag slung over his shoulder. He paused at each boat, as if searching for a particular one. When he reached the *Sepera*, he stopped. Then, after looking back along the route he had taken, he walked slowly toward the opening in the railing that ran along the sides of the ungainly old tug. Nikos was there to greet him.

"Dr. Mets-gar? Do I say it right?"

Peder Aukrust looked intently at Nikos, then at Sophie. He nodded and said that he was.

Sophie stepped forward and gave a weak, but welcoming smile. "Please come with me," she said and gestured toward an open door leading into the cabin. Toward the bow, steps went up to the pilot house; a small room aft contained chairs, tables, a television, and a bookcase. There was a narrow door, and she opened it. "The steps are very steep," she said attentively. They started down a sharply angled flight of stairs, paused on a metal grill landing, then continued down another flight. She waited until he joined her belowdecks in a room barely four feet square. She pushed open a door, revealing a room that was as wide as the boat, thirty feet long, with a ceiling twenty feet above the wood floor.

"This is what is called the Grand Salon"—she grinned for having pronounced the words so well—"and everything is here for your comfort." Next to the door they had entered were two cabinets built into a mahogany-paneled wall, each with bright brass hinges and latches. Sophie swung open the door on the left. Inside was a well-stocked bar, a wine cabinet, and an icemaker. Behind the other door was a miniature, fully equipped galley.

"What may I make for you?" She said the words precisely, in an oddly pleasant combination of her own accent and proper English.

He looked at the rows of bottles behind her. "Scotch whiskey and water," he said; "only a little whiskey."

Sophie prepared the drink with professional dispatch and handed it to him. Her smile had not faded, and she turned and went out through the door they had entered. The latch clicked. He was alone.

Grand Salon was an apt name for the room in which he found himself. The paneled walls were deep red mahogany and windowless. Set out from each long wall were leather couches, their color nearly the same dark red as the polished wood in the walls. The floor, made of wide planks and joined with wood dowels, was original to the boat. Neatly laid into the wood floor near the entrance to the room was a bronze plaque. It read: KING WILLIAM, MAY 12, 1909, CRAWFORD YARDS. The wall at the far end of the room was bare except for a giant-screen television. Four oversized chairs occupied the center of the room, and Aukrust wondered how they had been brought down the steep stairs. Beside each chair was a small chest, and on each was a leather folder containing a writing pad and pen. One chair was clearly meant to be more important than the others, so he thought of it as the "important" chair, larger than the others. On the painted chest next to it was a telephone and lamp.

Then came the sound of a diesel engine rumbling at low power, sending thick vibrations through the boat. He felt a rocking motion as the *Sepera* started under way, and the engine settled into a deep purr. The television screen brightened and a clear picture resolved out of the static. A camera positioned somewhere above picked out other boats on the river and automobile headlights moving along the Embankment, then four creamy yellow smokestacks at the Battersea power station. Aukrust tried opening the door, but as he had assumed when Sophie went from the room, the clicking of the latch had been the sound of a lock tumbling into place. He made a slow turn around the room, inspecting the panels and concluding that each would swing open if he could find a way to move them. The engines were in the stern, but there was no obvious way of reaching them. He sat in the important chair, drink in hand, and stared at the television screen.

A series of blasts came from the *Sepera*, three short bursts followed by three more. The last three came from speakers behind the television screen. Then silence followed by a high-pitched whistle. Silence again. Then clicking noises as if channels were being switched. Finally a faint buzzing sound that faded and was replaced by a man's voice.

"Peder, my friend, I apologize for not joining you, but I thought it might serve our mutual interests if you visited the *Sepera* alone the first time. Nikos and Sophie will tend to your needs, and after listening to the message I have recorded, you will find the door has been unlocked and you may inspect this old boat if you wish."

Peder Aukrust showed little emotion during the comments made by the voice so eerily detached from the pictures on the television. He wore, if anything, a bemused expression, perhaps one of admiration. He recognized the voice and knew its owner very well.

"Of course we have important business to go over." The unhurried, relaxed tone had suddenly changed. The pleasantly polished voice was businesslike.

"You have done well thus far, three paintings in eight days. I had doubts that could be accomplished, particularly the National Gallery. However, the unpleasantness in Surrey and your ingenious method for the disposal of Mr. Boggs may have produced too many complications . . . too many unnecessary trails for the police to follow."

Aukrust took a sip from his drink, never taking his eyes from the screen, which now showed a sailing yacht returning from what probably had been a cruise in the channel.

"I understand there is another nuisance. A photographer was in the gallery."

Aukrust reacted angrily. "Damned stupid mistake and something's got to be done about it."

The voice continued. "His name is Shelbourne, and he has handled the photographic requirements of the gallery from time to time. But to avoid the chance that one of his photographs might include you or Astrid and might get into the hands of the police, I suggest that you pay a visit to his studio and destroy both the prints and the negatives. I will see to it that Shelbourne receives an assignment that will take him away for a week. His studio is on the main business street in Reigate, and it's not likely you will have a problem with alarms, as Ian Shelbourne is distressingly careless about such things."

There was a click, then, as if recorded at a different time, the voice was brighter, less ominous. "I assume you chose to sit in the largest of the chairs in the center of the room. Next to it is a chest, and in the drawer are three envelopes. Please open the largest one."

It was a thick, manila envelope, closed with a metal clasp. In it were three smaller envelopes. The first contained English pounds, the second French francs, the third American dollars. He riffled the notes but didn't count the amounts. He smiled.

"The second envelope holds additional money to cover expenses for Astrid Haraldsen in New York and Boston. I have considerable misgivings about sending her to the Boston Museum. Understand this," the voice again more urgent, the tone a pitch higher, "if she fails or, far worse, is apprehended, our affiliation will end, and you will be cut off from further payment and protection."

Aukrust stormed out of the chair. "You're in too deep!"

he shouted at the television screen. "You can't turn your back on me."

Calmly, the voice continued, "In the third envelope is a receipt from the Grand National Bank in Luxembourg confirming the deposit of your fee to numbered account RS-1104."

Aukrust read the brief note, folded it, and put it into a zippered compartment in his shoulder bag. He did the same with the money.

"Now, finally, I will talk about the DeVilleurs portrait. Only it and the one owned by Llewellyn are owned privately and are part of a small collection. Either one will bring a huge price from a small group of wealthy collectors in Hong Kong, America, or Japan. You must impress on Astrid the importance of developing a close relationship with Llewellyn. Only with his complete trust will we have access to his painting. As for Madame DeVilleurs, she was recently widowed, and though she is an older woman, she will be receptive to the special attention I expect you to show her. The small business I asked you to set up in Cannes will serve that purpose. Just as Astrid must win Llewellyn's affection, I expect you to gain Madame DeVilleurs's devotion and trust."

Aukrust seemed amused by the challenge.

"I will join you the next time you visit my retreat on the water," the voice went on, "when we will review our progress and put new plans together." There was no farewell, only a faint hum in the speakers, then silence.

Aukrust sat. He glanced up to the television screen. The picture changed into a swirl of geometric designs that constantly created new shapes. At the center was a circle that grew larger and brightened into a hypnotic pulsation. He sat in a contemplative, slackened pose and stared. Peder Aukrust could entrance himself and did so by first excluding the sounds and visual distractions that surrounded him; then he allowed selected episodes from the past to stream across his consciousness. He would recall an incident or an action he had taken and detach himself from any personal responsibility for the consequences of whatever it was that had happened. It was a form of cleansing, of absolution. And in Aukrust's mind, it was permanent and binding. He began to draw out of his memory several incidents that his powerful denial had sanitized, events that had happened many years earlier, in Oslo.

Aukrust had received a degree in pharmacology from the University of Copenhagen, as well as a companion degree in biochemistry, in which he had proven particularly adept. After four years as a hospital pharmacist he had been recruited into the Norwegian government's department of internal security, due principally to the fact that he single-handedly shut down an organized ring of drug thieves that had penetrated the hospital's supply chain of barbiturates and mood-altering drugs. Peder had a badge and authority and soon acquired a reputation for securing confessions or tips on drug shipments and money-laundering contacts. Aukrust's methods were unpleasant but effective. His superiors looked the other way, satisfied to have results. Then a witness refused to cooperate, and Aukrust increased the severity of his persuasion. Force turned to violence, and the would-be informant, according to Aukrust, had an accident. He was found dead, his neck broken. There was a coverup, but six months later Aukrust was transferred to a tedious job with no hope of promotion or reassignment. Guilty of causing the man's death, he had never accepted so much as a shred of responsibility. Why should he? He had never been accused. The law never spoke, so he was fully convinced that nothing had actually ever happened, nothing for which he was either guilty or innocent.

Slowly, he turned his gaze from the screen. He rose and went to the door and tried the handle. As he had been promised, the door was unlocked.

Chapter 6

Before checking onto the flight in Gatwick, Astrid Haraldsen stopped in the women's lavatory long enough to transform herself to the blonde Norwegian pictured and described on her passport. Her flight was on the ground at Kennedy Airport at 2:43 in the afternoon. She cleared customs, then, pulling her suitcase behind her, went to the phones. She called the Westbury Hotel for messages that had accumulated in the last five days. She smiled when she heard Edwin Llewellyn's name.

She dialed his number. "It's Astrid. You asked me to call. You said in a week."

"I didn't want you to forget. They said you were out of the city."

"I was, but I'm back. I'm calling from the airport." There was a pause, Astrid waiting for his reaction.

"I'm free this evening. Are you?" Llewellyn asked.

"I might fall asleep on you."

"We'll make it an early evening. Come here for a drink and a light supper. We'll pamper you."

She agreed and went out to find a taxi.

Llewellyn's townhouse was on East 65th between Park and Lexington. It was prime real estate territory where townhouses sold for $2 million and some went for eight. In spite of corporate downsizing and shake-ups in the financial world, there were many in the new group of wealthy young men and women who didn't balk at seven figures for the just-right townhouse on the proper street on the East Side. Llewellyn, however, was getting by on old money and, unless he wanted to invade principal, was stuck on a fixed income that in the previous year had yielded something slightly under a million and a half. Alimony for two previous wives was the largest entry in his budget. His first wife finally had remarried halfway through the year, and wife number two's attorney responded by demanding an increase in alimony on the grounds that his client could not possibly live in her accustomed manner on a quarter of a million a year. Besides, the money that had been going to wife number one was now available, and . . .

The townhouse had been built in the 1890s, and, like the others that surrounded it, was long and narrow and five floors high. Llewellyn's father had put in a garage in 1932, a questionable investment that proved wise over time. A long corridor was next to the garage and behind it an apartment consisting of a bedroom, small living room, and kitchen that opened onto a patio—it was where Llewellyn's houseman lived.

Colin Fraser was a Scotsman and nephew to another Fraser who had served Llewellyn's mother and father for thirty years, and who had been practically an uncle to Edwin Llewellyn while the latter was growing up. Fraser was ruggedly built, though not tall. His red hair was shot with gray, and the lines that had deepened around his eyes and mouth gave his face the appearance of a life spent in the strong winds of the Scottish Highlands. He was divorced and had a grown son, now a doctor, who lived in Glasgow.

Also in the household was a friendly, though noisy, Norwich terrier named Clyde, who, when Llewellyn was away, spent most of his time in Fraser's quarters, close to the food supply and the garden patio.

Llewellyn's townhouse had the distinctive trappings of a bachelor and an art connoisseur. Against the east wall a staircase ran from the cellar to the top floor. Climbing the stairs, one passed an eclectic display of early Mexican paintings, pieces of della robbia, a ten-foot-long cabinet filled mostly with Chinese export, and an assortment of American Indian war bonnets. The largest room on the second floor overlooked 65th Street, was paneled in dark oak, and had been the scene of countless receptions and cocktail parties. The middle room was a windowless dining room; behind it was the kitchen. On the third floor were the bedrooms. The master's bedroom in front was every bit as large as the room beneath it. It was in blues and grays with a mammoth bed and a cavernous bathroom, with a combination bathtub and jacuzzi only slightly smaller than a swimming pool. Llewellyn's study was on the fourth level. It was square and overlooked the street. It was a room of surprises and comfortable richness, a space that was a joy to be in. Set out from a side wall was an intricately inlaid pier table that had value easily into six figures. The parquetry floors were covered by assorted oriental rugs. Two bay windows gave the room added depth and sunlight. Built into the high ceiling were spotlights, each trained on one of the many paintings that hung on the interior walls. Behind the table Llewellyn used as a desk was a wall section that had been given special treatment. Mounted prominently, and in a carved and gilt frame, was his Cézanne self-portrait. Engraved on a brass plate attached to the bottom of the frame was the title *Portrait of the Artist with Ocean Background*.

Fraser greeted Astrid and, at her insistence, guided her up the stairs. She wanted to get a feel of the house. Clyde yapped and wagged his tail, and Astrid swooped him up into her arms and let him lick her nose. She fussed over him, and they were solid friends by the time they reached Llewellyn's study.

Llewellyn was in his J. Press khakis, his blue Brooks Brothers blazer, and his Liberty scarf tied like an ascot. "So you ducked off to—my God, where the hell did you go? And was it business or fun?"

"Some of each. I went home." The lie was said easily and with a comfortable smile. Clyde barked and jumped onto a sofa then back to the floor.

"I hope there wasn't any problem at home?" He asked with obvious concern.

"No problem," Astrid's smile held steady. Then one little lie became two, and she said, "Just family matters."

"Good," Llewellyn said, "for those kind of trips I like the Concorde for a fast turnaround."

"Not on my budget, and it doesn't fly to Oslo."

"It is a bit pricey," Llewellyn acknowledged. "I think of it as a power flight," he laughed, "like a power lunch. I've taken it a few times, and I think the men on those planes devote an incredible amount of time and effort trying to preserve their precious time and effort." He looked at her, grinning. "If I sound envious, I'm not."

Astrid stood and turned slowly, looking carefully at Llewellyn's study. "I like what I see," she said approvingly. "I wouldn't touch a thing."

"I wouldn't let you. This is my home, my castle, my power study."

Astrid had changed into a plain, pale brown linen dress with a scooped neckline that Llewellyn noticed appreciatively. She moved gracefully, occasionally touching a picture frame or turning a porcelain bowl over in her hands. She circled the room, then stopped in front of the desk and faced the Cézanne.

"It's beautiful," she said.

"We think it's the last of his self-portraits, maybe as late as 1902. And we believe it's the best. Notice how relaxed he seems, as if he wanted you to know that he's a regular guy and doesn't have to prove something every time he picked up a brush. My father believed that if the painting could talk, he would be saying, 'Let's share some wine and our thoughts with each other.' My grandfather bought it from Cézanne's dealer, man named Vollard. That was 1903. He brought it home, hung it right there, and it's never left this house. Not even when I had it cleaned and put it in a new frame."

"I can understand why you keep it where it is safe."

"It isn't my fault it has been on that wall for more than ninety years. My grandfather's will stipulates that whoever inherits his paintings can't sell, loan, or publicly display any one of them."

Astrid moved close and stood directly in front of the painting. She said, "It's as if he just painted it. Even the water looks wet." She touched the background of blue water. "Why did artists in those days paint so many self-portraits?"

"They were always experimenting with their technique, and I suspect a little ego was involved. When they needed a model, they could always use themselves."

"Is it true that he painted more than twenty self-portraits?"

"Twenty-six, counting this one. God knows there might be another one hidden in an attic somewhere in France."

"It would be worth a fortune," Astrid said.

"I suppose. Worth more now that a few have been destroyed."

Without turning, she said, "What a dreadful thing! I read about it. Someone put paint on them?"

"Like hell they did. In fact we wish they had. They used an acid of some kind, a damned powerful acid."

"Can't the paintings be fixed over?"

"Restored? Not at all. It was potent stuff. The paints were completely melted."

"You must be careful to protect this one."

"I'll protect it with my life." He smiled. "Well, maybe I won't go that far. But I'll take good care of it when I take it back to Cézanne's hometown."

Astrid was still standing with her back to Llewellyn. "Where is that?" she asked in a hushed voice.

"Aix-en-Provence . . . in the south of France. A small museum has big plans for a Cézanne retrospective, and I'm going to help them. But it's hush-hush for now."

She turned to Llewellyn and said excitedly, "I would love to see it."

"Perhaps we can arrange something," Llewellyn felt her enthusiasm. He looked past her toward Fraser, who had come into the study.

"I promised something to eat, and Fraser is telling us he's ready. I hope it's not too warm on the roof, but there's usually a breeze."

Chapter 7

Clarence Boggs's death had shocked the tight-knit neighborhood in the town of Ockley where for seven years he had been known as an outgoing, amiable sort, and who had recently been seen doting on his precocious granddaughter. A Mrs. Jacobson could not stop effusing, "Such a love, he was. And so good to all the children." Others had expressed similar sentiments over the loss of their friend. There was disbelief that he had died in such a bizarre way, yet his elderly sedan with its crushed grille and fender stood as silent testimony. After it had been picked clean of every possible clue it had been brought back and parked in the gravel drive alongside his modest home. Several other cars were now parked beside it, and a young policeman stood by the steps leading to the front door. Inside, Jack Oxby had set up a temporary field office. Ann Browley and Nigel Jones had joined him, and they were now seated around Clarence Boggs's dining room table.

Ann was going through a period of anger, trying vainly to hide the fact that she was personally distressed by Boggs's murder and the destruction of the Cézanne paintings. But Oxby had discovered that Ann's feelings never interfered with her ability to be objective as she worked a case. He was amused by a charming dash of superiority she occasionally displayed, a trait undoubtedly inherited from her socially well-placed mother, who could not become reconciled to Ann's becoming a "police person." She made an entry in her notebook, then looked up at Oxby. "Are we here to talk about the murder of Mr. Boggs or of Mr. Cézanne?"

"We are investigating the murder of Clarence Boggs, Annie, but you have a good point. Perhaps the psychiatrists will say there's been a second murder. Are you all set, Jonesy?"

"I have to start by saying it was a fiendishly clever way to kill someone. Though it took a bit of luck."

Nigel Jones was tall and extremely thin, and everything about him seemed to come to a point. His nose was sharply pointed, as was his chin, and even his hairline had a sharply pronounced widow's peak. He spoke deliberately and precisely, and had a keen and, at times, dark sense of humor. Nigel Jones had degrees in general medicine, pharmacology, and chemistry. This breadth of formal education was topped with an insatiable curiosity. He was one of a scant few in Scotland Yard's Lambeth forensic labs who were called on to gather evidence at the scene of a crime and also work up the evidence in the laboratory.

Ann asked, "What's so awfully clever about poisoning someone?"

"It wasn't an ordinary poison. Certainly not one delivered in an ordinary way."

"Let's start at the beginning, shall we?" Oxby said and began to read from the notes he had put in front of him. "Boggs left his home at approximately 6:45 A.M. on Tuesday the nineteenth, drove to the newsdealer where he bought a copy of the *Sporting Life*, stopped nearby for a container of coffee, returned to his car where he read the racing charts, circled his bets for the day, and drank his coffee, all of which was his usual morning routine, or so we've been told. He then drove east on Reigate Road, and about a mile outside of Ockley his car slowed and veered sharply to the left where it struck a stone wall head-on. Boggs was seen getting out of the car and walking, staggering, approximately fifteen feet, then collapsing to the ground. A motorist traveling behind Boggs witnessed all this, pulled off the road, examined Boggs, and stated that he could see no signs of life. He drove on to a telephone and notified the police."

Oxby placed a single typed page on the table. "This is a copy of the local police report. It states that a Constable Wagner was first on the scene and confirmed that Boggs was dead; that an ambulance arrived at 7:27 A.M. and removed the body to All Souls Hospital in Reigate."

Oxby looked up to Jones. "We know what happened, suppose you tell us how it happened."

Nigel Jones had listened carefully, his body stiff, as if he were sitting at attention.

"Mr. Boggs got a fatal dose of what is called DFP. Its chemical name is diisopropyl fluorophosphate and is in the cyanide chemical group. It is viciously toxic and classified as a nerve gas by the military. Some variants of the chemical are formulated in low concentrations as insecticides and used primarily in agricultural applications. A derivative is also used in the treatment of certain eye disorders." He turned the page. "Mr. Boggs breathed the vapors in the confinement of his automobile—the windows were closed. Immediately upon inhalation he suffered severe visual disorientation, due to an extreme contraction of pupil known as miosis. Also severe pain and profuse sweating. At the same time his pulse slowed, his blood pressure dropped precipitously. Within the first minute he involuntarily defecated and urinated. His instincts—that's all that was functioning at this point—allowed him to open the door, then stagger from the car. He managed four or five steps perhaps, then collapsed. I estimate he was dead several steps before falling."

The forensic specialist placed a small cardboard box on the table. "DFP vapors were released from this crude but ingenious device. You'll recognize this as a common facial-tissue box. But what we found inside was anything but ordinary. On the bottom is a babyfood jar, and in the jar an ounce or two of a clear liquid. Stretched over it is a piece of ordinary plastic wrap, secured with an elastic. Next is a simply constructed wooden frame that holds a juice strainer directly over the jar. In the strainer is a plastic spoon, and you'll note that the handle's been snapped off." Jonesy took an eye dropper and squeezed a filmy liquid into the spoon. This whole affair was put beneath the driver's seat in the victim's car. Once Boggs started up and the car moved," he shook the box gently, "the liquid in the spoon spilled onto the plastic stretched over the jar beneath it just as you see it happening now."

Oxby and Ann watched the drops fall onto the plastic, forming a small puddle. The plastic dissolved, and the liquid fell directly into the solution in the babyfood jar. There was a chemical eruption, and a steamlike cloud rose up over the table. Oxby immediately turned away and Ann covered her face.

"Nothing to fear," Jones smiled, "quite harmless. But sufficient to demonstrate how Mr. Boggs was killed. It's very clear that when he stopped for his morning coffee, someone opened the door to his car and placed this under the driver's seat. It can be done in about fifteen seconds. I know, because I tried, and found the trick is placing the bowl of the spoon in the strainer, then filling it with mercuric chloride. I estimate that Boggs began to inhale the fumes ninety seconds after he had finished his coffee and got out onto Reigate Road. I've already told you what happened next."

Ann took the box, removed each element, and placed them on the table in front of her. "Everything here can be bought in a supermarket. Even I could put it together."

"You won't find diisopropyl fluorophosphate in garden supplies," Jones replied. "In fact you won't find DFP anywhere except from a very few chemical specialists."

"How difficult would it be to make the stuff?" Oxby asked.

Jones smiled, aware that Oxby was not deterred by the near impossible. "DFP isn't a benign chemical that one makes by mixing together the contents from a bottle marked A and one marked B."

"Suppose I know something about chemistry or was a chemical warfare officer in the military." Oxby gave Jones a hard glance, "Do I need a fully equipped laboratory to put it together?"

"If you knew what you were doing, no," Jones said. "You'd need a few basic lab appliances, perhaps six or eight items. I'd have to check into that."

"Do check on that," Oxby repeated, jotting another note. "Now if I don't put it together myself, where can I buy it?"

"From a distributor of chemicals or, more likely, a pharmaceutical provider. As I mentioned, a dilute solution is used for certain eye disorders. Glaucoma, especially. In full strength it is put up in vials of one gram, each one packed in a doubly sealed canister."

"How many grams were used to kill Boggs?"

"I'd guess sixty grams, about two ounces." Jones rubbed his nose contemplatively. "Expensive stuff."

"How expensive?"

"Sixty grams would cost about three thousand pounds if purchased through regular sources."

Oxby made a low whistle. "Someone buying sixty vials would cause a stir, I'd guess. What's more curious is why anyone would go to the bother. There are easier and cheaper ways to kill someone."

"Not as certain as DFP," Jones added.

"I'm told that Mr. Boggs had some rather serious gambling debts," Oxby said. "If his creditors had reached the end of their patience, they resorted to a strange form of punishment."

"Nothing surprises me anymore." Nigel Jones stood and stretched his long body. "We found nothing else in or on the car except for a few nearly indecipherable fingerprints, which we've sent on to C3 for analysis and look-up." He shoved the box and its contents to the center of the table.

"This contraption gives us a slight glimpse into the mind of the person who conceived the entire affair, but as Ann rightly observes, anyone could assemble it. Question is, why choose such a sophisticated chemical? Showing off, perhaps? The important matter to wrestle with is the diisopropyl fluorophosphate and determine how it got into the hands of the murderer. We'll put together a list of the pharmaceutical and chemical companies that sell the compound, and I assure you it will be a very short list."

Oxby nodded. "He didn't have much family. A daughter nearby. I'll look in on her." He made some final notes, then looked up. "Jonesy tells us that DFP is hard to come by, and that means there aren't many sources for it. I want you to work together on this. Annie, you concentrate on the continent and let Jonesy check into sources in the UK. But get on it quickly. We need some fast answers."

Chapter 8

Peder Aukrust banked his fee of nearly $21,000, holding on to $2,000 for new clothes and travel expenses. He rented a car in the name of Charles Metzger, and by noon on the day after he had been on board the *Sepera* he drove directly south from London to a bleak little inn named the Morningstar near the tiny village of Thursley. That night he drank heavily, ruminating about the Hermitage museum in St. Petersburg and the burning briefcase that camouflaged his artful performance in the National Gallery. He grimaced at his failure to bring himself to full climax with Astrid on the night following their visit to the Pinkster Gallery, consoling himself by blaming her, repeating over and over that she was a "cold bitch not worth a good fuck." His emotions, magnified by alcohol's mischievous way of expanding reality, replayed in his mind. He again watched as he put the box of poison beneath Boggs's car seat, then his imagination played out Clarence Boggs's final, torturous moments. It was the middle of the night when he finally fell onto his bed, mumbling incoherently about memories of his mother.

It was noon the following day before Aukrust came out of a troubled sleep. The day was cool and cloudy, and for most of the afternoon he walked the paths that curled through fields outside the little town and past a golf course. That evening he ordered a bowl of beef soup and a roll that he didn't finish, then went to his room and planned the next day.

From Thursley he drove east to Reigate and squeezed his

rented car into a spot on the High Street near the heart of the shopping district and close to a cluster of stores consisting of a florist, a dressmaker specializing in wedding gowns, and a photographer's studio with the name Shelbourne on the window. It was mid-afternoon. He walked past the florist, then the dressmaker, and paused at the photographer's shop, where he found a handwritten sign on the door explaining that Shelbourne had been unexpectedly called away and would reopen on Monday at noon. "Pinkster's done his job and got the photographer out of town," he mused to himself. There was a slot in the door for customers to drop their exposed film when the store was closed. Same-Day Film Developing, a sign read. A display window was filled with samples of Shelbourne's photographs. A few were portraits, but most were commercial assignments. Aukrust peered beyond the photographs into the shop where a film-processing machine took up a third of the space, the balance given over to cameras, lenses, film, and the usual assortment of photographic accessories. Curtains pulled to the side revealed a portrait studio.

He continued past three clothing stores to a narrow lane, which led to an alley that ran behind all the shops. A delivery van went past him, kicking up a spray of fine dust before parking behind the florist shop. Two men were unloading panels of plasterboard from a truck behind an empty shop in the process of renovation. Each shop in the alley had a rear entrance, two or three rubbish bins; behind one was a small flower garden. Aukrust continued on to the back of Shelbourne's shop and up four steps to a loading platform and a steel door. Ten feet to the right of the door was a window that had been painted black, in which was an exhaust fan, and behind which, Aukrust computed, was Shelbourne's darkroom. He tried the door. The handle turned easily, but the door was secured by a single-dead-bolt lock about twelve inches above the latch. There was no evidence of an alarm, only an innocuous sign: NO ENTRY—PLEASE USE FRONT ENTRANCE.

He returned to his car and searched the trunk for the tire changing kit. Mixed in with the jack were two fifteen-inch lengths of steel, which when fitted together served to pry off the hubcap and leverage the jack that raised up the car. He put the tools next to his medicine kit, locked the car, and went for a walk through the town. He made two stops. The first was the Royal Oak pub, where he spent forty-five minutes and had a sandwich and a pint of ale. At his second stop he bought a newspaper, which informed him that the sun would set in the London area at 6:18. He returned to the car at 5:30, and for the next hour he watched as one by one the shops emptied of customers, lights went off, doors were locked.

A sprinkling of clouds low in the western sky helped turn the air to a purple, with sprays of orange sunlight striking the windows to make it appear that little fires were burning inside. Then came the dark gray of evening, and in another thirty minutes it was nighttime in Reigate. Aukrust seemed to become part of the local scenery as he drove his car close to the other cars clustered near a restaurant a quarter of a mile away. He parked his car, then walked back along the street across from the photographer's studio. He stood in the entryway to a real estate agent's office and surveyed the row of stores across from him. His timing was good. Every shop but one at the far end of the block was closed, the traffic had thinned, and what remained was moving away from the center of town. He went quickly across the High Street and through the lane to the alley where he stopped. A bare amount of light came from the back of a gift shop and from a light still burning on a loading platform behind another shop in the opposite direction. He went on, ready with the tire iron. He reached the door, and forced the flattened end between the door and the jamb. He pulled with all his strength. The slim bolt snapped easily. Aukrust stepped in and worked his way to the room behind the black painted window. As he had been told, Shelbourne didn't believe in alarms.

Aukrust found the darkroom and a panel of switches on

the wall inside the door and flipped them on. Two red lamps burned dimly, one between a photo enlarger and a cabinet containing trays of photographic paper, the other suspended over a table on which were the developing and fixing trays. An amber-colored bulb burned from a gooseneck lamp on a desk, its light spilling onto file cabinet just inside the door.

The top drawer contained job folders for each of Shelbourne's customers; three of the fattest folders were marked Pinkster Gallery. As Aukrust looked through the folders, a figure moved away from a rubbish bin behind the adjacent shop. A small, wiry man scampered over and onto the platform, then after a brief pause went through the door.

Inside the folders were manila envelopes, each one identifying a project. Also inside were negatives inserted into clear plastic sleeves, notes, a record of expenses, and contact sheets on which were printed as many as thirty-six tiny photographs from a roll of 35mm film. He inspected each envelope until he found the ones containing photographs of Astrid and him at Pinkster's gallery.

Built into the table top was a sheet of frosted glass illuminated from below. He spread the negatives on the glass, then leaned down to inspect the small images. He chose those in which he and Astrid appeared and set them aside.

"Evenin', mister," the scruffy little man standing at the door said. The sudden intrusion stunned Aukrust.

"I saw you come in and thought I'd ask if you got any job I could do."

Aukrust smelled the gamey odor of ale and urine.

"Maybe you could help me with fifty pence?" He shook his head. "No food for two days."

"No money," Aukrust said, recovering, "and no jobs. Come back in the morning. Maybe we have something for you then."

The man's head tilted, and he looked up to Aukrust. "You talk like my friend Swede. We was on freighters a while back."

Aukrust took another step, waving the man toward the

rear door. He picked up the tire iron. "In the morning, I said. Now get going."

"Before—when you came in here, I heard you." He went on, a curious innocence to the way he spoke, "Not quiet, like you had a key."

Aukrust grabbed a bony shoulder and turned the little man around. He looked down at the bearded face, at the fleshy nose with a fresh cut on its side, into watery, lifeless eyes. "What are you saying?"

"I'm sayin' who is this big man without a key? A friend of Mr. Shelbourne?"

"A business friend."

A wide grin erupted on the grubby face. "Shelby's my friend, too," he said. "He takes pictures of me. And he pays me. Two quid he pays."

The man turned his head up, the tiniest glint of pride showing in an otherwise dull face. The tire iron swooshed through the air. Instantly, his mouth and eyes popped open, and he fell onto the floor. The little man rolled away and got to his feet. Aukrust grabbed his sleeve, but the man pulled free and ran across the platform and jumped down onto the gravel, landing awkwardly. Before he could regain his balance, Aukrust was on him.

"No . . . no!" the voice pleaded.

A single, violent blow to the head above the right ear killed the man, but Aukrust swung again. The second strike crashed on an angle across the pitiful man's face, splitting open his nose. Aukrust lifted him as if he were an oversized, dirty doll, staring at his bloodied face in the semidarkness.

A car's headlamps poked into the black air from a few hundred yards away. Aukrust ran, carrying the body to a rubbish bin, then crouched in the black shadows. The car continued slowly toward him. He heard the radio. Police on routine patrol. It paused when it was directly behind Shelbourne's shop. Aukrust tensed. He began counting to himself, as if knowing how long the police car did not move would make a difference. Slowly, it moved on.

Aukrust pressed his fingers tightly against the man's neck, not expecting to find a pulse and not finding one. His only thought was that he had been inconvenienced, that he had come to dispose of several negatives but now had a body to get rid of. He went over to the shop where, earlier, he had seen workmen unloading a truck. Close to the building was a dumpster half filled with old lath and plaster. He went back for the body, carried it to the dumpster and put it inside, then covered it over with the old plaster.

Slowly, Aukrust worked his way back to Shelbourne's darkroom and to the negatives on the light table. Finally, he could complete what he had come to do. He took a bottle from his medicine case and poured a clear solution onto the negatives. After half a minute tiny bubbles began to appear on the emulsion, then the images dissolved into a dark gray slurry. He rinsed the negatives at the sink, blotted them with a paper towel, then slipped them back into the sleeve. He obliterated the corresponding small photographs on the contact sheets in the same way, then put the negatives and photographs back into their folders before returning them to the file cabinet.

Next he rubbed a cloth over everything he had touched, checked for footprints, then, certain he would leave the darkroom precisely as he had found it, let himself out.

When he reached his car Aukrust noted it was several minutes past eight o'clock. To deal with the problem of the photographs had taken less than an hour . . . and that included the inconvenience caused by the little man who smelled of piss and asked for fifty pence. He drove north to the M25, then west to a motel near Heathrow Airport.

Chapter 9

Bletchingly Parish in the County of Surrey was chartered over a thousand years ago, and the Church of St. Mary's in the center of the village was about half as old. Jack Oxby knew of the small church with its horizontal tower and graveyard of headstones, many of which were so weather-worn as to defy even the most skillful rubbing. Now he sat in the familiar quiet of a church sanctuary where he would not be disturbed.

His thoughts centered on how Clarence Boggs had inhaled powerfully toxic fumes and had died quickly and painfully. Coming to light was the fact that Boggs's gambling debts had become considerable. Dangerously so, Oxby mused. Gambling debts were often called in with threats of physical violence, and occasionally force was used to enforce the demands. In the rare instance when the ultimate punishment was meted out, it was usually quite brutal and served to send a powerful message to others who weren't paying up. Even so, a dead man can't pay a gambling debt.

The pews in the nave were a mix of old and new. Oxby sat in an old one, on the aisle, his shoes off, his feet on a prayer cushion, an open notebook on his lap. On the back of the pew in front of him was carved the date December 25, 1715, and the word "Noel." Unexpectedly, he was greeted by the pastor, the Reverend R. Peter Zimmer, who had a large, round head and fat cheeks the color of strawberries. "St. Mary's is usually locked," he said with a mild voice, explaining that vandals and petty thieves made that necessary but that too often the security was lax.

It was not surprising that the local vicar knew that a valuable Cézanne owned by Alan Pinkster had been destroyed and that Clarence Boggs's car had crashed. He also knew that Boggs was dead. They talked agreeably for a number of minutes, the Reverend Zimmer confessing that he envied the exciting life of a Scotland Yard investigator, and Jack Oxby recounting his many visits to churches, cathedrals, and temples in and near London.

"My mother church is Westminster Abbey," Oxby said matter-of-factly, causing the Reverend Zimmer to narrow his eyes and purse his lips quizzically.

"Did you know Mr. Boggs?" Oxby asked.

Zimmer shook his head. "Only vaguely, he was not a member of our congregation, but then I'm not sure that he was a member of any church. But a decent chap, as I remember. He had lost his wife, but had a charming daughter. Gillian, I believe. And there's a granddaughter. A bright little child. I recall seeing Mr. Boggs at our church bazaar."

"When was that?"

"Hasn't been a year. We chatted briefly."

"I understand he bet heavily on the horses," Oxby said. "Had you heard of his gambling habits?"

The pastor took his hand from his pocket and put it to his mouth. "Very little, except that there was a rumor that he was gambling and losing." He sat in the pew with the date carved on the back and turned to face Oxby.

"It's quiet here," Zimmer said, his eyes slowly scanning the old windows and ancient carvings. "Too damned quiet if you want my opinion. Perhaps you can bring us a little excitement and solve a murder mystery sitting in our pew number twelve." He stood and held out his hand. "Stay as long as you wish, but do us a favor and lock up when you leave."

Oxby gripped his hand and thanked him politely, then

watched the pastor disappear behind the altar and presumably from the church. Left behind was the mild odor of alcohol mixed with the scent of peppermint that had doubtless come from the bits of candy the pastor surreptitiously pulled from his pocket. Perhaps he had come to taste the new communion wine, Oxby thought benevolently.

His attention returned to Clarence Boggs. If the curator had fallen so deeply in debt as to cause his creditors to poison him, then careful inquiry would bear that out. Oxby had arranged for Jimmy Murratore to use his extensive contacts in London's gambling community to look into whether Boggs had been made to pay the full price. Jimmy knew the bookies, the touts, the hangers-on, and the money lenders. Some lenders were respectable, others were tied to the syndicate operated by an unscrupulous element and inevitably involved in drug trafficking.

Oxby turned his gaze to the window and the soft light that oozed through the old stained glass. His thoughts were concentrated on the self-portrait and Boggs's job as curator in the Pinkster gallery. Someone had been in the gallery and sprayed the painting. Approximately sixteen hours later Boggs was dead. Did all that go together with more significance than the fact that Boggs had large gambling debts? Whoever killed Boggs knew the man's habits and either knew him personally or had observed him over a number of days. Again, Oxby was bothered by the strange use of a chemical that was not only difficult to buy but potentially lethal to whoever used it.

Oxby began to write. He filled a half dozen sheets, then carefully read aloud what he had written. He asked himself questions, and the ones he could not answer he listed again on a clean sheet.

It was like a school examination, and Oxby wanted to make a perfect score.

*   *   *

In the afternoon, Oxby found himself in a small meeting room in the banking offices of the Nationwide Anglia Trust in the town of Dorking, a half hour's drive from Bletchingly. Keith Eustace, the branch manager, was assembling a record of Boggs's banking activities covering a two-year period and began painting a picture of the curator's tragic descent into financial ruin.

"Two and a half years ago he had twenty-four thousand pounds in savings and a checking account that carried a very nice balance at the end of each month." Eustace licked the first two fingers of his right hand and flipped the pages. He had coal-black hair and white skin, which prompted Oxby to wonder if he ever dared walk in the sunshine. "In April, two years back, he took five thousand from savings. And— hmmm—let's see." He continued licking the two fingers and flipping the pages, "Except for December, January, and February, he went on withdrawing from savings without making a deposit until the funds were depleted."

"When was that?"

"This month, a bit over two weeks ago."

"How were withdrawals made?"

"Nearly all withdrawals were transferred to his checking account."

"Can you tell me if he issued any large checks subsequent to the transfers?"

Eustace looked and began shaking his head. "In most instances he wrote checks to himself and took cash, from what I see here."

"Allow me to see one month's activity," Oxby requested.

Eustace demurred briefly, then put all of the records on the table. "Blast it," he said with a sigh. "Do your job. I've got some phoning to do, and you can look through these while I'm at it."

Oxby smiled appreciatively. He sorted through the pages of checks, discovering as he knew he would that he could gain insight into the kind of man Clarence Boggs was by the

kinds of purchases he had made. Because Boggs was a widower there had been checks made out on the same date to
Highlawn Cemetery and to a florist in Reigate, payments
made in honor of his deceased wife. Checks payable to a
cleaning service appeared monthly, then were discontinued
as the balance declined. In each of three recent months,
when a transfer of funds from savings had been made, and
some were large amounts, a check in the same amount had
been drawn to himself for cash.

A number of checks were payable to Gillian MacCaffrey,
and each one prompted Oxby's curiosity. The first was for
fifty pounds, the second for twenty. Oxby had not taken special note of the checks until, in the third folder, he found
four checks made payable to the same Gillian MacCaffrey in
larger amounts: two hundred, and one hundred fifty pounds.
Oxby studied the most recent statement, which had not yet
been closed out and which held the canceled checks that
would have accompanied the statement. Sixteen in all. One
check for three hundred pounds, made payable to Gillian
MacCaffrey, had been endorsed with a signature stamp that
included an address. He copied the address onto his pad and
put all the records back on the table just as Eustace returned.

"Find what you're looking for?"

"Yes," Oxby said brightly. "I've had a peek into Mr.
Boggs's life and see a twist or two."

"That's jolly fine," Eustace said as he gathered the papers. "Anything more we can do?"

"Allow me to use the phone."

"My pleasure. I'll say goodbye." He shook hands and
was off.

Gillian MacCaffrey lived in Red Hill, one of the points of
a triangle formed with Bletchingly and Dorking. The information operator intoned a number, and Oxby dialed it. A
child answered, a little girl. Oxby asked for her mother, and
after a moment a quiet voice came on the line.

"I'm dreadfully sorry about your father," Oxby said with sincerity. He introduced himself and asked if he might meet with her for several minutes. Oxby waited for an answer, then said, "We want to be certain that if someone caused your father's death we will be able to find that person."

"He was killed, you know," she responded.

"That may be so," Oxby replied respectfully, and quickly added, "In an hour then? I'm just in Dorking and can find you in good order."

Another brief silence, then she gave him directions.

Gillian MacCaffrey lived in the old part of town, where the homes were snuggled close together, each with a patch of ground in front and one in back. End-of-the-season flowers dotted some patches; in others the vegetable plants had been turned into the soil.

Gillian answered the door. She was dressed in a dark-blue pantsuit and looked too warm in it. Oxby judged her to be in her mid-thirties and losing her youth and prettiness to unkind vicissitudes. The door was pushed open wide by a towheaded little girl whose eyes gleamed with grit and curiosity. Oxby asked if she had been the one who answered the phone when he called.

She nodded vigorously and said her name was Meghan.

"Are you going to help my mother?" she asked in the no-nonsense way of children.

"I'm going to try, Meghan."

"Come in, please," Gillian said and led the way to a small, simply furnished living room. "Be a dear, Meghan, and put some water on to boil."

Meghan smiled at Oxby and went off with a touch of importance in her stride.

"You said on the telephone that you thought your father had been murdered."

"He wasn't the kind to commit suicide. Never in a million years."

"I'm not suggesting that he did, but the times and circumstances change, and often people change, too. The ones least likely to hurt themselves are suddenly vulnerable. What kind of changes did you see in your father in the past year?"

Gillian patted her neck and the sides of her face with a handkerchief. "None that would make him take his own life," she said resolutely.

"Your father was having financial problems, and I believe that you've had your share of those problems, too." He shifted around in the chair to face her directly. "Please don't be embarrassed by my questions, but I must know if what I have just said is true."

Gillian turned her eyes away from Oxby, then down to her hands that pulled and twisted the handkerchief. "We've had terrible money problems. My father began gambling a few years ago."

"Was he wagering heavily?"

"My father had never made a bet in his entire life, but once he began he couldn't stop. He had saved a fair amount, I believe. But what he had, he lost. Every penny of it."

Oxby remained silent.

"We were doing all right, me and my husband Bob, that is. Bob and his partner bought a plastics company three years ago. The partner handled the books and the finances, and Bob ran the factory. The partner was an old friend, at least we thought he was. He had been stealing money all along, and when Bob found out it was too late. The partner skipped out, leaving Bob owing everybody and with no credit."

"Your father helped?"

"It was a loan. I kept track of every check. He wanted to send more, and it's why he kept betting, he said. He was going to win a basketful. Always a basketful." She shook her head and burst into tears. Then she wiped the tears as Meghan came back into the room and stood by her mother.

"Shall I fix the tea?" she asked very properly.

"Perhaps Mr. Oxby would prefer coffee," Gillian said.

"No, tea," Oxby said emphatically. "And I hope Meghan will make it for me. I like it strong—with sugar."

Meghan beamed and ran back to the kitchen.

Oxby smiled and watched the little girl go off. "Can you describe your relationship with your father?"

"We were very close and for a long time," Gillian said wistfully. "Even more after mother died."

"When did you see him last?"

"Tuesday evening. That was his night to have dinner with us."

"Was he in good spirits when he arrived?"

"In fact, he wasn't. One of those tours had been in the gallery that morning and was very slow. He argued with the tour director who stopped in front of every painting and gave a lecture, which my father said was just to make her sound like she knew something. He'd had run-ins with her before."

"That was the Danish group," Oxby suggested.

"He didn't say what group it was, just that the director was difficult. There was a photographer taking pictures, and then my father became upset because a man and a woman fell back from the rest of the group. That sort of thing could make him angry."

"There are always laggards," Oxby said. "They take notes and put them with all the other notes they never look at again. What else did he say about them?"

"He said that the woman carried one of those large tote bags over her shoulder and that he was afraid they might put something in it."

"And did she?" Oxby asked.

"Not this time. But father knew that people stole from each other. Fold-up umbrellas or a camera when someone was careless. He thought it strange that this woman strayed away from the group."

"What else did he say about her?" He waited a moment, then added, "Describe her, perhaps?"

"He said she was tall and pretty, and at one time she asked him about one of the paintings."

"Did he say where they were in the gallery when this happened?"

"It was near the end of the tour, but I'm guessing. He was trying to speed them along and wanted the stragglers to catch up with the others. He was always worried that someone might steal the Rodin statue. It isn't very large, but it's extremely valuable."

"So this happened where the Rodin is displayed?"

"I can't say where, but that might be what he meant."

Oxby studied his notes. "Do you mind going over everything one more time? The smallest detail can be very important, and perhaps you'll remember one or two."

Meghan came from the kitchen, proudly holding a tray on which was a cup of tea and a dish piled high with sugar cubes.

"Well now, that's handsome," Oxby said, taking the cup and stirring in four cubes of sugar. "I do like it sweet," he said pleasantly, and for that moment Meghan forgot her sadness.

Gillian closed her eyes, breathed deeply, and retold the events of the previous Tuesday when her father had come by for his weekly dinner. Oxby let her talk without interruption, sipping his tea, making an occasional note. When she concluded, Oxby asked her to sort through her memory a final time and see if she could remember any other comment her father had made. A silence of two minutes was interrupted when Gillian said softly, "He said that he wasn't gambling. That it was over."

Oxby asked one last question. "How did he seem when he left . . . depressed . . . good spirits?"

Gillian's response was immediate. "As he was leaving I felt that he was quite himself. My father was the kind who would brood and be angry, then after he got it all out, he would be fine. He wasn't one to hold things in; it's why he liked being here with his family." Then she looked up at Oxby and fresh tears appeared.

"Why did someone kill my father?"

"I can't tell you. But I promise to have an answer soon." He stood, started to leave, then stopped and looked back at Gillian. Her arm was around Meghan, holding her tightly.

"Please look over your father's papers and any mail that has been sent to him in the past few days. Call me if you find anything you feel I should know about." He handed her his card.

Before letting himself out Oxby bent down to the little girl who was still nestled against her mother. "Thank you for the tea, Meghan. It's the best I've ever had."

Chapter 10

Rain and heavy winds slowed air traffic into the Nice air-port. After an hour delay the plane landed, and Peder Aukrust made his way through a terminal clogged with weekend travelers and bought a local newspaper. After a crowded ride on a shuttle bus to an extended-time parking lot, he faced a hundred-yard run through a cold rain to reach his car, an eleven-year-old Peugeot station wagon, which refused to start immediately. When it finally did, he allowed the car to run until the engine was dry and the car was warm. As he waited he leafed through the newspaper, amused by an article in which the director of the Réunion des Musées Nationaux had issued a warning to all museums in the country to tighten security; that a dangerous, possibly deranged fiend was loose; that three of Cézanne's portraits had been viciously destroyed.

Aukrust paid for four days of parking and drove out to the A8 and west on the wide autostrade to Cannes. In spite of the storm he reached the turnoff into the city in less than twenty minutes. At the sign to the beaches and main shopping district, he turned onto Rue Faure. Three blocks further on, he stopped in front of a shop identified by a new sign over a single, large window that read: ARTISTS SUPPLIES—FRAMING.

There were two locks in the door, and he put a key in one and inserted a plastic card in the other. The door opened into the darkened shop. Three feet along the wall was a panel

with three rows of buttons. A red light glowed, signifying
the alarm system was still armed. After, he pushed the buttons in proper sequence the red light went off and a green
flashed. He pushed more buttons and ceiling lights came on.
Paintings, drawings, and artist's supplies filled display cases
and shelves. Along one wall were scenes of Provence, some
of reasonable quality, most the work of amateurs. A display of
sample frames occupied space against the wall to the left of
the entrance; contained in it were perhaps a hundred different
styles, materials, sizes, and colors.

Behind the counter was a door of unusual complexity. It
was eight feet high and four feet wide and made of two-
inch-thick wood covered by a steel plate on the inside. The
frame was made of heavy-gauge steel. There was a lock
above and one below a door handle set nearly six feet from
the floor. A third lock was at the top of the door. Aukrust unlocked all of the locks then pushed the door open. Beyond
the door was another room, nearly square and somewhat
smaller than the outer space in the shop. In the middle of the
room was a table the size of a billiard, covered with a tightly
woven carpeting material. The table was used for cutting,
then beveling the glass used in picture frames. The flat surface was also used for the repair and assembly of picture
frames. To the side of the table was a rack filled with sheets
of glass, and beside it a wooden box that contained scraps
and odd pieces of glass.

Cabinets from floor to ceiling lined one entire wall.
Aukrust opened the doors to one section and put away his
medicine case. One of the deep and wide shelves held a variety of bottles and jars in every size and shape; on two adjacent shelves were racks of test tubes, reagent bottles,
beakers, an etna, a distiller, a chemist's scale, assorted jars
and stainless steel tools, a centrifuge and a quantity of laboratory instruments. Other shelves contained the fixtures and
accoutrements of a pharmacist's shop. One of the cabinets
held several dozen homeopathic remedies.

Against the rear wall was an old vault that a previous tenant had installed. It was huge piece of steel and lead, and one marveled that it had been possible to move it at all. In spite of its size and weight, it was more useful as a fireproof storage vault than a safe for valuables. Aukrust turned the huge dial forward and back, then opened the door and took out a small, flat package. He removed the paper to reveal a painting that measured a mere seven by ten inches.

He turned it over and inspected the precise stapling of the canvas to the new wood stretchers he had made. Then he set it on the table and surrounded it with four lengths of framing stock that had been mitred and cut to size. Tomorrow he would finish remounting the painting. For now he was content to lightly touch the paint and inspect the minor details of the canvas. He had cleaned the little painting; perhaps it had been the only time in the painting's one-hundred-year-history that it had been cleaned. It was the portrait of a young girl, one with fat, full cheeks and cupid's bow lips. Behind her flowing blonde hair were white and pink carnations.

The painting was by Pierre-Auguste Renoir.

Chapter 11

Margueritte DeVilleurs had grown tired of wearing the mourning band, and as she dressed for the day she took the piece of black cloth from her dressing table and ceremoniously dropped it into the wastebasket. Not a soul was counting the days since her husband Gaston DeVilleurs failed to wake up on his seventy-fourth birthday. On this day of liberation Margueritte selected a brightly colored dress, one she had purchased in Monaco the week before. In her younger years she had been pretty, and, though her well-groomed hair was now gray and her waistline a touch heavier, she was still described as dignified and very handsome. She was seventy and moved on a tennis court or a dance floor with surprising grace.

A strong brew of coffee sent an aroma from the kitchen. Emily, companion and housekeeper, had put the day in motion. Though Emily was younger than Margueritte, time had treated her unkindly, and it showed on the working woman who had barely tolerated Gaston but was passionately devoted to Margueritte. In a home without children, Emily had become family.

The DeVilleurs home was perched on a bluff on Cap d'Antibes overlooking the Mediterranean, with a view of Nice and the Maritime Alps behind it. Gaston had loved Nice, Margueritte despised it; an irritation that had helped divide their marriage. Margueritte was born in Salon-de-Provence, midway between Aix-en-Provence and Aries. Her father traced his roots to Lucca, Italy, where his ancestors had built an olive-oil factory in 1757. Then, a hundred years later, a member of the family traveled to Lourdes with a crippled son, subsequently returned with the rest of his family, settled in the Provence, and developed new olive-tree groves and, not long after, a factory to produce great quantities of olive oil.

The company prospered over the years and by the end of World War II was a prominent worldwide marketer of fine quality olive oil. Margueritte inherited the business, and Gaston had been installed as managing director. Over the next forty years he successfully masterminded the inexorable decline of the prestigious company while simultaneously siphoning off assets to build his own net worth. Bad advice from a lawyer named Frédéric Weisbord coupled with disastrous losses in the stock market had pushed the company to the brink of bankruptcy. In spite of the downspiraling of the company's fortunes, however, Weisbord had managed to cling to the role of family adviser and legal counselor.

Margueritte continued to wear sable, not told that the DeVilleurs's wealth was disappearing until Weisbord announced the bad news at the end of July; and in mid-August the decision to sell the company was made. To everyone's surprise, a buyer stepped forward and the transaction completed early in September. Only after the papers were signed did it dawn on Margueritte that the lawyer had been planning to sell the company all along, that the buyer who had miraculously stepped forward had in fact been patiently waiting for Weisbord's call.

After the sale of the company, Margueritte discovered the true despair of her financial position. The proceeds yielded only enough money to liquidate Gaston's debts and buy a thousand shares of stock in the newly organized company that had bought her family's business. She owned the Antibes home, furs and jewelry, and several acres of land in the

country outside of Salon. It had been a wedding present
from her father, and in spite of Gaston's incessant impor-
tuning, she never transferred title. The Antibes home would
bring a handsome price, but it was heavily mortgaged, another unwanted surprise from Gaston.

Then there were the paintings. If Gaston had been inept
at all else, he had shown a deep affection for fine art. He and
Margueritte had put their incompatibility aside and over the
years bought and sold until they had assembled a small,
valuable collection. Margueritte became a shrewd trader,
and in the end the DeVilleurs collection consisted of eleven
paintings, the least valuable of which was a small yet perfectly lovely Renoir. There were two by Pissarro, one by
Mary Cassatt, a Caillebotte, an early Picasso, a Corot, two
by Sisley, and prized above all, two Cézannes. One was a
country scene, the other, and the centerpiece of the collection, a self-portrait. Margueritte was attached to the country
scene depicting a farmhouse near Salon. It reminded her of
a sweet childhood.

With the period of public grieving behind her, Margueritte looked forward to a visit from the new owner of a
small framing shop situated in Cannes. Margueritte grudgingly shopped in Cannes, and a month earlier had met a tall
Norwegian in one of the food shops. Both were inspecting a
supply of oranges shipped in from Africa, and he had helped
her put her groceries in the car. She had been charmed by his
accent and his bearlike bigness and pleased when he introduced himself and invited her to see his shop. She found him
kind and knowledgeable and, at the same time, felt that he
was sexually intimidating. And that excited her. After several more visits to his shop, she decided to entrust him with
an important assignment. She removed her precious Renoir
from its frame and gave the canvas to the owner of the shop.
She asked him to carefully clean the painting and prepare a
new frame.

A station wagon turned into the driveway. It pulled to a

stop in front of the house and out of it stepped a tall man wearing a light ran suit and peaked cap. Emily answered his ring and escorted him to the garden.

Peder Aukrust seemed taller and more handsome each time Margueritte met with him. She had judged him to be forty and was studying him more carefully than before. His face was tanned by a genuine Côte d'Azur sun and his eyes under heavy brows moved constantly, reminding her in a strange way of a mischievous little boy. His hands were as large as melons, and she feared her own hand would be crushed when she extended it in greeting. His French was workmanlike, well influenced by his guttural Scandinavian inflections.

"You have a beautiful home."

"Thank you," she replied warmly. "Everyone likes the view over the water, but I prefer the land and the changing colors."

Emily brought a tray with coffee.

"Your choice of a frame is a success," he announced, then unwrapped the package and held up the Renoir for her inspection.

Margueritte's smile matched the one in the painting. "Let's put it where it belongs."

She took the painting to a room that at one time had been the dining room. Two years earlier it had been converted to a gallery. Windows were removed and skylights installed to provide a flood of natural light, and yet there was an auxiliary light beamed at each painting. Aukrust stood in the doorway, his eyes darting from painting to painting.

"Do you like it?" Margueritte asked.

Aukrust didn't reply immediately, but moved to the center of the room where he slowly turned a full circle, studying each painting briefly. His attention was drawn to the Cézannes that were hung next to each other, his eyes fixed on the self-portrait. In a hushed voice he said, "It's a beautiful collection, you chose wisely."

Margueritte was pleased by the mild praise. She put the little portrait by Renoir in the space immediately to the left of the Cézannes.

"You like it then?" Aukrust said.

"Yes, very much. The new frame makes the others look very sad."

He smiled and gestured broadly. "Then you'll come back to my shop and choose new frames for the others."

"Only for the ones I will keep. Let the new owners choose their own frames."

"Which ones will you keep?"

She touched the Renoir, "This is my friend and will go in my bedroom. It's not one of his best, but I like it and that's what matters." A few steps took her to the pair of Pissarros, and she put her finger on a picture of a flower garden that exploded with a blaze of color. "And I will keep this one." Then she moved in front of the Corot, a mere twenty-four square inches of pure charm, "I can't part with this one, it has special meanings that are important only to me." Two more steps took her to the Cézannes. "I know this old farmhouse, it's only a ten-minute walk from my childhood home."

She stared at the painting and her eyes misted. "It's my favorite." She extended her hand until her fingers gently touched the still shining paint.

The sound of a ringing phone came from another room. Emily came to the door, and a tilt of her head gave the message. Margueritte excused herself.

Aukrust went immediately to the Cézannes and ran his hand over the frame of the self-portrait. The painting, not including the heavy six-inch frame, measured nearly twenty-six by twenty inches and was quite large for a Cézanne self-portrait. He pulled it away from the wall and found that the protective heavy, brown paper covering the back was torn in the lower right corner. He allowed the painting to come back to rest against the wall, then stepped in front of the Pissarros just as Margueritte came back into the room.

She said, "I neglected to tell you that theft alarm sensors have been put on some of the paintings."

She could not see the surprise on his face. He said, with a flat voice, "I was hoping to find that you had protected them."

"When my husband was alive we didn't think to take any special precautions, but when I realized that Gaston could not stop someone from running off with a sterling soup spoon, I knew we needed better security. Then Frédéric Weisbord became involved, and he had alarms put on the Cézannes and the Pissarros. Freddy's a perfectly dreadful man, what Gaston saw in him I'll never understand."

She came beside him. "I turned off the sound on the alarm system, but if they're tampered with, a light goes on at several places in the house." She looked up at him. "The lights were on."

"I'm afraid that's my fault . . . I was curious, but I didn't see the sensors."

"They're in the frame, very small, and very hard to find," she said proudly.

"But someone could cut the painting from the frame. Thieves don't care for frames."

"Why steal a valuable painting at all? They can't be sold, even privately. Except for an obscenely low price to some kind of strange recluse living in Antarctica." Then her eyes widened. "Freddy became so obsessed with protecting the paintings that he had fluorescent dye injected into each one. The insurance people are the only ones pleased by all our precautions." Her expression turned angry. "Since my husband's death, Freddy's taken a fanatical interest in the safety of the paintings."

"Is the alarm connected to the police?"

"Yes, and they're very angry with me. We've turned in

too many false alarms, and they've threatened to put us off their list if it happens again."

"Show me the alarms. I have a customer who might be interested in the system."

Margueritte pulled the painting away from the wall and pointed to the frame where the backing was ripped. "Here, where the wood is joined you see a circle the size of a small coin. Under that is the alarm and battery."

"How much movement before the alarm goes off?"

"You can jar the painting or straighten it and nothing will happen, but pull it away several inches or take it off the hooks and the alarm goes off."

He ran his finger over the circle of wood. "An alarm will stop the amateur, but nothing stops a professional."

"I suppose that is true," she sighed, "but I'll only have four to worry over."

"When will you sell the others?"

She shook her head. "Gaston's will requires us to sell each one at auction. While that may mean a higher price, I care more about who buys them than how much money is paid. But it matters to Freddy because he gets a commission when each painting is sold." She touched the frame of Cézanne's self-portrait. "This painting has been in a private collection for too long and should be in the Musée Granet in Aix."

"Will Weisbord allow you to sell it to them?"

"He insists on following the terms of the will." Her eyes widened and anger showed. "He wrote it, of course."

"Perhaps you can loan the painting to the museum."

She shook her head vigorously. "Freddy saw to that, too. He'd like to see every one sold, and for the highest possible price."

"Perhaps I can help."

Margueritte's eyes brightened. "What can you do?"

Aukrust lifted the portrait from its hooks, then held it at arm's length. "You can ask me to replace the torn paper, here on the back." He turned the painting around and pointed to the paper. "I could also check the canvas for mildew or mold, then replace the hanger wires." He grinned. "I could find several months' work once I began looking for it."

"Of course. Old paintings and frames always need fixing," she mused. "I promised the director at the Granet that they can display it during their Cézanne exhibition when it opens in January. You could deliver it to them." She laughed. "Freddy would be furious. He claims it will bring a record price."

"For a Cézanne, it might," Aukrust agreed.

"The Granet has raised seventy-five million francs, that's more than enough."

"In an auction in New York or London it would bring twice as much."

She folded her arms across her chest and stared at the self-portrait then toward the country scene. Her mind was racing, and she was suddenly struck by the immensity of what was before her. Neither she nor Gaston had purchased or sold a painting in nearly seven years; instead they had traded shrewdly, reducing their collection from more than thirty paintings to the eleven that were on the walls in front of her.

A new determination had come over her, and she spoke firmly. "I will speak with Freddy about the will. My family's money paid for these paintings, and I'm not going to let a selfish old fool tell me how or when or to whom I must sell them. For the present I'll leave everything as it is."

She smiled. "On to more important matters. Let me pay you for the new frame."

Chapter 12

Lancet Ventures Ltd. occupied the thirty-first floor of National Westminster Tower, the tallest building in the City of London, though no longer the highest in all of Greater London, as that distinction belonged to One Canada Square on Canary Wharf, the spectacular and speculative real estate development that had come into being in the middle of the Thames River. Lancet's offices were furnished in an understated elegance and, by the reckoning of some, expensive beyond reason. The grandest space of all was a conference room that commanded a view of the Thames to the south and St. Paul's Cathedral to the west. Beneath a wide spreading chandelier was a table made of teak inlaid with blond and brown grained woods, surrounded by two dozen high-backed chairs upholstered in a silk fabric designed with eagles and lions and purple-red roses. A painting by Jackson Pollock and one by Andrew Wyeth were given prominence on an interior wall and were flanked by two unremarkable paintings by contemporary British artists. One, a geometric exercise in shapes of red, was by Margaret O'Rourke and aptly titled *Untitled A* while the other, *Number 3–1954* by Jeremiah Tobin, was a vast canvas of blue with streaks of purple and green that had been applied by a broom swept over wet paint.

Lancet Ventures was owned equally by First Bank of New York and London/Westminster Securities. The New York offices were precise duplicates of those in London and were located on the thirty-third floor of the World Trade Center towers in lower Manhattan. Lancet's business was the infusion of capital into new enterprises, and over a three-year period Lancet had scored a few hits but too many misses; so word had come down from the executive suite to "stop the bleeding."

The senior managing partner from New York had come to London to meet with his counterpart about the ominous signs that Lancet's largest deal, a once promising investment in high-priced fine art, was about to turn sour. At stake were loans of over $100 million, and also in the jaws of jeopardy were the partners' share of profits and the nearly $3 million deposited to their escrowed "set-aside" accounts.

Harold "Bud" Samuelson was a thin-lipped, short man with alert, searching eyes, a tan from the sun room in the New York Athletic Club, and a nervous way of talking with his hands and odd shakes of his shoulders. He was forty-two, University of Missouri and Harvard Business School, and known as a shrewd negotiator.

London's senior managing partner was Terrance Sloane. Terry Sloane was forty-five and had reached his position through gutsy hard work and a brilliant record in international assignments. He was not old school, only reasonably well-connected socially, but had succeeded on the strength of a sharp business mind, old-fashioned common sense, and a penchant for working twenty-hour days.

Samuelson had spent his entire flight on the Concorde preparing himself to face the man who had been advanced a kingly sum to acquire a collection of great paintings but who had failed to generate the promised profits. In the process Samuelson had put himself on a sharp edge, and now his face was fixed in taut determination. His first words gave away his pent-up frustration. "The bastard's going to give us a weary story and demand an extension. Hear what I'm saying, Terry? He'll go for the fucking initiative and do all the demanding."

"He might have a good argument, Bud. Remember, he's had an incredible loss, made doubly so with the murder of his curator."

"I'm sorry about Barnes or whatever his name was, and about the painting, too. I didn't know he owned that kind of stuff."

"The curator's name was Boggs," Terry Sloane said, "and his 'stuff,' as you call it, is first rate."

"We were pretty damned stupid to get sucked into a deal where we can't invade his personal holdings, especially when the bastard's got God knows how much tied up in his own paintings. He's got a pair of balls the size of the Tower Bridge, for Christ's sake."

"We were stupid for not knowing more about the art market."

Samuelson was not interested in talking further about his or Terry Sloane's stupidity. "I assume the painting was insured, and pretty well spread around."

"Lloyd's, probably."

"You know damned well he's going to demand an extension."

"Wouldn't you?" Terry Sloane asked.

Samuelson flipped open a folder. "Here's six pages of all his goddamned assets—not including his painting. He's got money. Plenty of it."

"He's leveraged up to his neck."

Beverages and ice had been set out on a table beneath the large blue painting with the purple and green streaks. Samuelson poured a tall glass of soda water and returned to the table. As it was customary for the visiting senior partner to sit at the head of the table, Terry Sloane had staked out his position to Samuelson's right, and in front of the chair to Samuelson's left were pads, pens, and a telephone.

"He'll be exactly ten minutes late," Terry Sloane predicted, and added wryly, "It's part of his charm."

At that moment the door opened and an attractive woman

came into the room. "Hello, Bud," she said warmly. "You didn't stop to say hello."

Samuelson stood. "You were having a torrid affair behind closed doors." He held up his glass to her. "I didn't peek."

Her reply was to close her eyes and shake her head gently. "Do you want me to sit in or listen in?"

"I'd prefer that you listen, Marybeth," Terry Sloane said, getting to his feet and coming to her side. "Alan's apt to be on his high horse, and he's easier to deal with when he doesn't have an audience."

Marybeth Warren was a lawyer and a good one. She had been chosen as general counsel from the parent bank's fifty-lawyer legal department. She was an American married to an Englishman and the mother of two small children. Marybeth was an all-around success yet was not in the conventional mold of highly accomplished people who also exhibit strong personality quirks. There was something awesome in that.

"I feel badly about his curator, that was terrible news. If there's a chance, I'd like to say that to him." She paused momentarily. "I want you to tell him that the meeting is being recorded. I know you don't like doing that, but I do."

The men exchanged glances, then Samuleson spoke up. "We'll explain that he's being recorded—that it isn't bullshit time."

Marybeth smiled. "You still have a delicate way with words, Bud."

Terry Sloane's secretary came into the room and announced that Mr. Pinkster had arrived.

It was exactly ten past six o'clock.

Alan Pinkster and Bud Samuelson first met in Japan in the mid-eighties. Pinkster was with an aggressive New York-based brokerage house that was expanding its international department. Samuelson was second in command of his bank's Tokyo office. Terry Sloane and Pinkster knew each other through their wives; they had been schoolmates.

Pinkster's wife, after her divorce, remained a close friend of Sloane's wife and became the source of information about Pinkster's celebrated pursuit of wealth and possessions.

Pinkster came into the room, his high anxiety-level clearly showing, his air of confidence equal to a board chairman who had summoned his minions to announce plans to snap up his largest competitor. His usually crisp appearance was marred by the rash on his forehead and cheeks that he had been unable to put under control. His gruff greeting was meant to convey that he was anxious for the discussions to begin and be over quickly so he could go on to more important matters. He put his thin briefcase next to the telephone, pulled the chair away from the table and sat. Samuelson and Terry Sloane remained on their feet, waiting for Pinkster's early head of steam to subside.

"Long time no see," Samuelson said, then added, "Sorry about Boggs. That's awful stuff."

Pinkster turned his head up. "I lost two good friends."

"Boggs was a genuine tragedy. The loss of the painting was terrible, but it was a painting, and those things can be replaced."

Pinkster stared hard at Samuelson. "Not that painting. It was irreplaceable."

"It puts you in very good company, I'm afraid to say," Terry Sloane said.

Pinkster ignored the comment and, looking at Samuelson, said, "How did your Cardinals do this year?"

"You really want to know? The pitching staff had an ERA of 4.68, and the team couldn't hit shit. That's how."

"You Americans go on about baseball with numbers and statistics." Terry Sloane interjected. "Is that the fun of it?"

Samuelson said, "Alan was a Yankee fan when he was in New York. Right?"

Pinkster nodded his reply, then turned his eyes to the notepad. He took the pen and wrote the date at the top of the page. "Shall we begin?"

Terry Sloane replied, "Before we start, Alan, I want you to know that our discussion is being recorded, and you will be provided with a copy of the tape. Do you understand?"

Pinkster nodded.

Samuelson spoke up. "For the record, please acknowledge that you understand that our discussion is being recorded."

Pinkster said angrily, "I acknowledge that you've got a bloody tape recorder going."

Samuelson neatened the folders and notepads that he had set out on the table and looked directly at Pinkster.

"There's a substantial amount of money at stake in all this, and I'm sure that you want to see a fair resolution as much as we do. Eighteen months ago we put $40 million into your Pacific Bowl operation. Six months later, another twenty-five, and forty more in March of this year."

"A hundred and five million," Pinkster said with closed eyes and a flat, impatient voice. "I know the numbers."

"I think, for the record, we should go over all the numbers," Samuelson said with firm insistence. "Interest payments to date total $2.5 million. The principal has not been reduced. Total outstanding interest due on the account, as of close of business today, is $6.84 million."

"Less three million." Pinkster handed Samuelson a draft made payable by the Sumitomo Bank of Tokyo.

Terry Sloane twisted forward and ran his hand across his chin. "That's not enough, Alan. Not even a good try."

"It's bloody damned enough," Pirikkir snapped. "And under the circumstances, a goddamned good try."

Samuelson got to his feet and took several steps toward the row of windows. He turned, shoved both hands into his pockets, and began speaking softly and deliberately.

"Alan, I've watched you operate in Japan and New York, and I know you're a bright son of a bitch with a God-given talent for making money. But good as you are, you can't control events, and you can't control markets. You can just read them."

Pinkster sat motionless, all but his eyes, which shifted upward and glared at Samuelson.

"The Japanese had a financial scandal a few years ago. There were suicides and arrests. A pretty awful mess. I learned recently that you were in on that deal, that you were one of a few non-Japanese who were offered a private placement of Recruit Cosmos stock, and you made a shitpot full of money."

"Less than two hundred thousand," Pinkster said. "And that has nothing to do with Pacific Bowl."

"We think it does," Terry Sloane said.

"I'm telling you it doesn't," Pinkster said defiantly.

"The Recruit Scandal is long over with, we don't care that you made some money. What's important to us is the fact you were cut in on the deal." Terry Sloane leaned back in his chair. "We want to know why."

Pinkster rubbed ointment over his lips. "I got a phone call. Nothing remarkable about that. I knew a lot of people, and I gave them a good tip from time to time." He made several indecipherable scribbles on the notepad. "I'm the best at what I do, and in Japan you get rewarded for doing it."

"You were trading heavily with Tokyo's largest securities firms. With Nomura and Nikko and not with your own company. Why?"

"I was trading for special customers."

"You were employed by Aubrey & Weeks and were handling customer trades through other brokerage houses? Isn't that a bit odd?"

"I had opportunities on the side. They couldn't be handled in the usual way."

"You say you got a phone call on the Recruit deal. Who was that from?"

"I can't tell you."

"Oh, but you can," Samuelson said. He stood beside his

chair, an arm draped over its high back. "We're into Pacific Bowl to the tune of 105 million bucks plus interest, and every goddamned thing you do is our business."

"The call was from the chairman of Recruit. I'd helped him buy several paintings. He was returning a favor."

"They're big on that . . . you do me a favor, I do one for you."

"Private placement of a new stock issue was common practice. And legal."

"Then why did so much shit hit the fan?" Samuelson asked. "The country went crazy over the Recruit scandal."

"Because three cabinet ministers accepted stock donations from Recruit. That's different from buying the stock, even at a steep discount. They resigned, and that forced the prime minister to resign. The head of Nippon Telegraph and Telephone got mixed up, and he quit. Is that crazy enough?"

"And you came out of it clean as a goddamned whistle?"

"First off, I'm not the bloody head of the Japanese government or the world's largest corporation. And I didn't take a donation, I was given the chance to buy a thousand shares, and I bought them. All perfectly legal."

"What I'm driving at, Alan, is the fact you were on the inside track. That you were meeting all kinds of people."

"And I said there's nothing wrong in that."

Samuelson shook his head. "Nothing wrong with the right people. But you met some of the 'wrong' people."

"What do you mean by that?" Pinkster shot back.

"I mean that you had connections with organized crime figures." Samuelson sat on the arm of his chair, arms folded across his chest. "You were doing business with heavy hitters in the Yakuza."

"The Yakuza isn't the Mafia."

"Oh yes it is. They make money the old-fashioned way, they kill for it." Samuelson smiled at his little joke. "What does the name Susumu Ishii mean to you?"

"Ishii is a very wealthy man. He likes early Picasso . . . plays a good game of golf."

"He should play golf very well," Terry Sloane injected. "He owns four golf courses."

"What did you do for him?" Samuelson asked.

"A while back the Japanese began buying important art. At first it was a genuine desire to own Western paintings, but quickly they began competing among themselves for more expensive works. I saw an opportunity to buy in Europe and New York, and sell in Japan—"

"We know all that," Samuelson interrupted. "That's why you put Pacific Bowl together and came to us for money. We saw it as purely speculative but with better than average chances for returns above 50 percent. The downside risks were pegged to how well you bought in your inventory."

Pinkster turned away from Samuelson. He made another note on the pad but said nothing.

Terry Sloane broke the silence. "You have a relationship with Akio Sawata. How is that getting on?"

"Strictly business," Pinkster answered.

"Automobiles, real estate, prostitution? That kind of business?" Samuelson demanded.

"Extortion or fraud?" Terry Sloane added to the list.

"Sawata's a wealthy man, and I didn't ask for his pedigree or where he made his money." Pinkster pushed himself away from the table. "He bought art, and that's all I cared about."

"Then why do we have a problem? Sawata is one of the wealthiest men in Japan, and you don't give a shit if he's Shinto, immoral, or a fucking agnostic. But the way I read it, he's mixed up with Pacific Bowl and owes a lot of money."

Pinkster shook his head. "I don't have a contract. Sawata doesn't make contracts."

"For Christ's sake, how can you do business without a contract? Don't you have something? A letter?"

Pinkster added more ointment to his lips. "When you do business with Sawata you talk about many things, and then he will describe a painting and say that he wants it. Then he bows."

"That's it? He fucking bows?" Samuelson was back on his feet, his hands jammed back into his pockets.

Pinkster nodded. "In your American vernacular, he fucking bows."

"He told you about a painting he wanted?" Terry Sloane asked.

"Akio Sawata and I had talked about the paintings of Georges Seurat. There's not much of Seurat around, and the ones that are privately owned are in America. I knew interest was building for Seurat and so did Akio. Timing was good, or so we thought, and I said I'd keep an eye out, and as chance had it I picked up a rather nice drawing at a Sotheby's auction in New York. It was four hundred thousand dollars. I sold it to Akio for half a million. Then a dealer in Chicago wrote and described a painting that was perfect for Sawata. A large painting, done shortly before Seurat died." Pinkster turned away from both men. "I began negotiations, and immediately there was an announcement from Paris that a Seurat retrospective would open in the fall. The damned French never paid much attention to Seurat, and now they were out to make something of him. The dealer doubled the price to $8 million, and I took it before it went higher."

"What did Sawata pay for it?"

Pinkster did not answer immediately but instead scribbled another note. He looked up at Samuelson. "He hasn't paid anything. He said the price was too high and that he was going to close his galleries."

"He bowed, goddamn it," Samuelson said. "You said it was the same as a contract."

Pinkster turned on what was neither a bold nor happy smile. "You're terribly naive, Bud. Sawata bowed, and all that meant was that he would like to have a Seurat. It didn't bind him to buy anything."

"You knew that?"

"Of course. It's part of the risk. I'll get what I paid for the Seurat, but that will take time." Pinkster got to his feet and looked sternly at Samuelson and Terry Sloane. "I suggest that you listen very carefully to what I'm going to tell you."

Samuelson returned to his chair. Terry Sloane shifted to face Pinkster and said, "A reminder, Alan. Everything is being recorded. If you've got something to say off the record, I suggest you tell us later."

"What I've got to say will be very brief, and you can damned well record it." He sat on the edge of the table and looked out the window at the darkness falling across the big city.

"Let's go over a little history together. The Japanese have always had a fascination for Western art. During the eighties they began to buy Old Masters and European art. Paintings were a good investment and a sure way to add to one's prestige. In particular they liked the French Impressionists, and so the wealthy businessmen began to compete with each other, one trying to buy a more valuable painting than the other. A man named Morishita, who had once been convicted for extortion and fraud, spent $900 million on his collection. Ryoei Saiti, head of giant paper company paid $82 million for a Van Gogh and $78 million for a Renoir, then had the audacity to add a provision to his will requiring that the two paintings be burned along with his own body when he was cremated. The Itoman Trading Company bought over four hundred paintings at a cost of nearly a half billion dollars, and the Mitsubishi Corporation bought two Renoirs from a couple of Frenchmen for $30 million."

Pinkster had circled the conference table as he talked, then came back to his chair.

"Forgive my lecturing you, but it may help to refresh your memory and bring you closer to the problem. It was the

Japanese who made the art market, and it is the Japanese who are destroying it. Their economy has shifting sand under it. When you consider a stock market trading at a hundred times earnings and scandals tearing up the financial landscape every other year, it's a recipe for disaster. Do either of you know what *zaitech* means?"

"Creative accounting," Samuelson said. "Two sets of ledgers and all that good stuff."

"Nothing so ordinary," Pinkster disagreed. "They were more innovative. To them, *zaitech* is financial engineering. For our purposes it's the use of art as a substitute for currency." Pinkster returned to his chair and settled into it. "The government's put a lid on real estate. But if a property owner wants a higher price, he'll take payment of the fixed price plus a small Degas or a Picasso drawing. That's *zaitech*. I supplied three customers steadily, each bought one, sometimes two paintings every month. Then the Ministry of Finance began investigating every transaction over a hundred million yen. Art as a substitute for hard currency became less popular."

"What are you saying?" Samuelson's patience was running low.

"I'm saying that I have an inventory of twenty-one paintings that cost a bit over $98.5 million. Normally I could sell them for between $150 and $180 million. But the art market is ice cold, and I can't get $80 million for the lot."

"There are other buyers besides the Japanese," Terry Sloane said.

"Let me get this straight." Samuelson leaned forward and stretched his arms out stiffly, the palms of his hands flat on the table. "You can't get your price because the Japanese economy is fucked up, and you want us to wait it out? Is that what I'm hearing?"

"That's pretty much the way it is. I can't say how long it will take, but their economy will come back."

"Along with new and better forms of *zaitech*?" Samuelson said bitterly. "We're not in the business of waiting. We put money into a business, and we expect it to earn more money. We're not waiting."

"Extend the deadline for interest payment another thirty days. It's less than $4 million. I'm good for it."

"I don't want to wait any thirty goddamned days." Samuelson slapped the table with both hands. "You've got five days."

"I can't accept that."

"You damn well can, or we'll start action on all the other shit you own." He moved a folder out from the others in front of him. "There's our contract. Failure to pay interest in a timely manner is cause for cancellation and opens the way for one fucking big barrage of legal action."

"You knew that art was a volatile commodity when we made our arrangements two years ago. You've got to be more patient."

"You're playing with our money, and I don't like that. You haven't risked one of your own fucking pennies and now to save your ass, you're going to have to."

"I'll put a battery of lawyers against you." Pinkster reached across the table, grabbed the contract and waved it at Samuelson. "They'll tie this into a dozen knots, and you won't see any more money for years."

"You're bluffing, Alan." Terry Sloane got to his feet. "Make us an offer. Something like full payment of interest in a week, return of half the principal in a month. Give us something to work on, and we'll try to go along with you."

Pinkster glared at Terry Sloane, then at Samuelson. He got up and went to the windows that looked down to Tower Bridge and the Thames. He stood as if frozen for several minutes, then said without turning, "I'll work it out."

"What in Christ's name does that mean?" Samuelson asked.

Pinkster had gone to the door. "Precisely what I said. I'll work it out." He opened the door and slipped out.

Samuelson started after him, and Terry Sloane put up his hand. "Let him go, Bud. You gave him a deadline, and he took it. Let's see what he comes up with."

Samuelson's response was a grudging "OK." He crossed over to the painting titled *Number 3–1954*, glared up to the massive field of blue with the strange colored stripes that wandered through it in no understandable way. "Who's responsible for this fucking atrocity?"

Terry Sloane came beside him. "I take it you don't approve." He grinned. "You should know that the staff is evenly split. Half don't like it . . . the other half hate it."

Chapter 13

Sepera was anchored a hundred yards off Battersea power station and showed a pair of green lights at the opening in its railing on the starboard side and three lights in a straight vertical line (two whites and a yellow) on a pole behind the pilot house. It was nearing ten o'clock, commercial traffic had slowed to a trickle, and the river was dark.

Nikos stood, waiting. He glanced up to the pilot house where Sophie's face reflected the aqua fluorescence that glowed from a row of radar screens. Her eyes looked past Nikos at the running lights on a boat approaching fast from the stern. The boat was nearly on them when its power was cut, and it seemed to rise up, then settle on the water, heaving in its own turbulence, edging closer to where Nikos stood with a looped hawser in his hand. The boats came together, and lines were deftly attached to the stout bitts on the tug and across to the brightly chromed cleats on the cruiser.

A chattering in Japanese came from the cabin of the cruiser, then a man emerged followed by a shorter figure carrying a large, flat zippered case that could easily hold an unfolded copy of the *London Times*. When they reached the point where the two boats were lashed together, their talk ceased, and helping hands guided them across to the tug and into the care of Nikos. He led them inside *Sepera* and down to the Great Salon.

Instead of four chairs and four tables in the center of the room, there were three chairs and one table with a lamp that glowed softly, creating a round pool of yellowish light. The light did not reach to the walls, so much of the room was dark.

"Please you be comfortable," Nikos said. "I will get you a refreshment if you wish, like a good whiskey?"

"Later. After we've done our business." The reply was in English. The accent, to an Englishman's ear, was pure New York City.

Amid the steady hum from an engine making electrical power there came the faint scraping of metal, then the sound of a door sliding open, then closing, and Alan Pinkster came into the pale fight. He was holding a towel wrapped around ice, and he dabbed at his face and above his eyes, where there was an angry redness. He said, "There will be more light in a few minutes."

"Good evening, Miss Shimada." He forced a thin smile. "Please sit down."

Mari Shimada was facing the lamp. She was small. Her black hair fell across her forehead and was cut short in a pageboy style. Her features were Eurasian, nearly perfect, and her makeup was startling: a creamy white face with large slightly turned eyes outlined in black, her lips and long fingernails colored a deep crimson. She slipped out of her coat, revealing a slim figure squeezed into a black leotard. She wore a short black skirt cinched at the waist with a gold buckle. Pinkster had seen her before, and as then marveled at her compact voluptuousness.

"Welcome, Mr. Kondo," he said, then snapped a finger in the direction of Nikos. "Our guests would like a drink."

"They say no drinks. Maybe some later."

"See that Mr. Kondo's boat is anchored and the proper lights are on. Then untie and move away." He looked at his watch. "We are to return by 11:30."

Nikos touched the peak of his cap and left the salon.

"Why so late?" Kondo asked. "We can complete our business in thirty minutes."

"I have more than the Seurat to show you."

"You said you would not have the other paintings in London."

"Conditions have changed."

"You have them here, on the boat?"

"Surprised? What safer place than an unsinkable tugboat?"

"Mr. Sawata thinks your Seurat is a very excellent painting. He also said you paid too much for it."

"The price is fair," Pinkster said irritably. "That's not Sawata's business."

"Such information is my business," Kondo said. "I may agree with Mr. Sawata."

Kondo's head was large and perfectly round and seemed stuck on top of a short, thick neck that was covered by a white turtleneck sweater. His glasses had heavy black rims and rested on his nose like ocean divers' goggles. He wore a navy blazer with bright gold buttons and a bold emblem sewn onto the breast pocket. His skin was dark and seemed more so in the faint light.

Pinkster said, "The French decided in their infinite wisdom to celebrate the anniversary of Seurat's death and pay him an overdue tribute. So after years of neglect the prices have gone sky-high. You are aware of that, Mr. Kondo?"

Kondo nodded. "I must stop prices from going higher."

"But once you own a painting you want the price to start up again. Correct?"

"You know the business."

"Who is your client?"

Kondo shook his head. "That is confidential."

"Is he a collector or an investor?"

Kondo smiled. "Very successful at both."

"Is he in the securities business?"

"His business is making money," Kondo said with finality.

The main engines were turned on, followed by a slight

motion. The boat was under way. "Where is the painting?"
Kondo asked.

Pinkster pressed buttons on a slim box shaped like the remote controls for a television. A light came on high up in the
salon and focused on a large painting mounted on the wall
behind Pinkster's chair. The colors were bright, as if the sun
had bleached even the blue-green from the water, and a
young man standing in a boat was helping a girl take a long
step down to join him. Mari Shimada went to the painting
and inspected it with a magnifying glass.

"What are your thoughts, Mr. Kondo?"

Kondo adjusted his glasses. "It's good, from what I know
of Seurat. But Ms. Shimada is the expert."

Mari spoke animatedly, whether praising or finding a
minor fault. On balance she liked it and gave her generous
approval.

"How much?" Kondo asked.

"Eleven million dollars," Pinkster replied.

Kondo's large head rolled from side to side. "I offer you
eight and a half million, fair profit of a half million over
what you paid."

"It was a private sale. You don't know what I paid."

"My friend in Chicago told me it was $8 million."

"Your friend got bad information, Mr. Kondo." He
rubbed the cold towel over his cheeks and got to his feet.
"Seurat's become popular, and there are precious few for
sale. The price is eleven million."

Kondo went to the painting, inspected it carefully. "My
offer is nine."

"The price is fair—and firm." Pinkster said each word
slowly.

Kondo motioned for Mari to join him in front of the Seurat. He spoke to her in an unintelligible stream of Japanese
that was too fast for Pinkster to decipher. Perhaps it all
meant something, or more likely it was part of Kondo's ne-
gotiating strategy.

"Show us the other paintings," Kondo said. "There may be another painting that will allow us to make a fair bargain."

Pinkster pressed more buttons on the remote controls. The light on the Seurat dimmed, and simultaneously another light splashed over a Picasso. "This is *Seated Nude*, painted in 1911. Small, I grant, but properly priced. I expect $2.5 million."

The light dimmed on the Picasso, and a third bright light fell over a somber interior scene. "This is a rare Edouard Vuillard, painted in 1893 and called *The New Neighbor*. The pride is $7 million."

As the light on the Vuillard dimmed, another brightened and shone on an energetically expressive painting filled with printed messages and slogans. "This is by Jean-Michel Basquiat, a New Yorker whose career as a Neo-Expressionist flashed briefly. He died of a drug overdose at twenty-seven. This is *Fish Market*. An excellent purchase for a million-two."

Again a light dimmed, and another burned brightly. This time it was Monet's *Woman with a Blue Parasol*. Pinkster praised the sun-drenched garden, then added, "You may recall that this painting was originally quite wide, too wide for the taste of an early owner who cut away ten inches—but to some critics it was an improvement. It's an important painting, and I expect $12 million."

The next was by Marc Chagall. It was a wildly colorful circus scene, highly spirited and amusing. "I have not put a price on this painting, but will not let it go for under five million."

Pinkster stood in the circle of subdued light that illuminated the Monet, his face as red as the roses in the garden in the painting. "I have one more painting to show you. It was offered to me this past winter, and I took a chance on it. It is not to everyone's taste, but it will be of interest to someone who maintains a private collection."

Six paintings were now in subdued light, and then as he had done before, Pinkster turned on another light. This one seemed brighter than the others and was focused on a painting of three jockeys atop their mounts; behind them were crowds of horse racing enthusiasts. "This is *Before The Race* by Edgar Degas."

Kondo rushed toward the painting. "Where did you get it?"

"It came through Switzerland, and that's all I will say about it."

"Stolen from the Burroughs Collection in Boston," Kondo said excitedly.

"Quite right," Pinkster said calmly. "One of twelve paintings, and now they're all coming to the surface. All but the Vermeer. They say that one's worth sixty million."

"I know where it is," Kondo said; "not exactly, of course, but it's in Japan."

"In a normal market this painting would be worth $20 million. But as I've never traded in stolen art, I'll ask you to tell me what it's worth."

Kondo stared at the three jockeys. "It varies from buyer to buyer, painting to painting. You bought it for resale, and you must put a price on it. Whoever buys it will decide how much it's worth to own a famous painting only he can enjoy."

Pinkster manipulated the remote switcher, and all the lights glowed at full intensity. "What do you think, Mr. Kondo?"

"That you're brave or crazy to show us the Degas."

"I choose my audience very carefully," Pinkster smiled. "I believe you have one client who would like to own the Degas."

"More than one would like to own it, but only one who would dare."

"Show it to him."

"You will let me do that?"

"We'll divide everything over the two and a half million dollars I paid for it."

A lopsided smile spread across Kondo's round face. "I might get five million, an outside chance for six."

"Six will do nicely," Pinkster said, smiling authentically for the first time. "They cut the canvas from the frame when it was stolen, but a small loss. It must be remounted, of course." Pinkster took the painting from its temporary frame and placed it between sheets of clear vinyl, then handed it to Mari, who slid it into the zippered case.

It had all moved smoothly from Pinkster's perspective, even to showing the Degas. He had excited Kondo into taking it to Japan where he was certain to show it to the top brass of the Yakuza and encourage them to bid among themselves. Pinkster was amused by the thought of the heads of Japan's organized crime competing for a painting that the eventual owner could show only to those few who had bid against him. It had also gone well because Kondo's famous temper hadn't flashed even briefly. He was known to bully dealers, even private collectors. He could easily do it, as he was tall for a Japanese and thick-shouldered. Some knew of his close connection with Isorai Tumbari, acknowledged to be the senior leader of Yakuza . . . Tumbari, who had started with a collection of oriental art, which he gave to museums as a show of civic generosity . . . Tumbari, who relied on intermediaries like Kondo for advice and reciprocated by assigning a few of his men to enforce arrangements Kondo wished to make.

Pinkster knew that Tumbari was not Kondo's only patron. He also associated with a marginal element in Japan's affluent society where, as Kondo had said, "there's no taste, but an endless stream of money." Kondo had himself become a wealthy man but was highly secretive and frequently paranoiac. He always carried large amounts of money and also a snub-nosed Semmerling pistol, which he had used on two occasions. Once when he had been unable to strike a deal on his terms he fired the gun into the ceiling in sheer frustration. One day, thought Pinkster, the gun might be aimed at a lower target.

"About the Seurat?" Pinkster said. "Will you buy it?"

"We're two million apart."

"Make an offer."

Kondo returned to the row of paintings and once more walked slowly past each one. He crooked his finger at Mari, who joined him. They stopped in front of each painting, talking fast and shaking their heads vigorously. Then Kondo returned to his chair and said he wanted some cold beer. Pinkster went to the bar and returned with a glass and three bottles of beer on a tray. Kondo drained one bottle in a single gulp.

"I want the Seurat, and I want the Basquiat. But more than either one, I want a Cézanne."

"I don't have a Cézanne. My self-portrait was destroyed. You know that."

Kondo smiled. His eyes closed and seemed to disappear behind the glasses. "There are some things about the destruction of all the Cézannes that is most puzzling."

"Merely puzzling?" Pinkster pressed the cold towel against his forehead. "It's an utter obscenity. There have been terrible losses. Millions gone up in an acid spray."

"All the more reason I want a Cézanne. If his still lifes can auction for twenty million, a self-portrait will bring forty." Kondo got to his feet, loomed over Pinkster, and said, his voice rising, "I want one, and I want you to get it for me."

"After losing one, so do I!" Pinkster said angrily. "There are only two in private hands, and neither one's for sale."

Kondo patted the big zippered case. "The Degas is for sale." He grinned. "I could sell the same painting several times and take a higher commission with every sale." He shook his head gleefully. "There are a few men with great amounts of money and the same quantity of greed and ego.

They would each want to own such a painting for a year perhaps, then after they're tired of it, sell it." He glanced toward Mari for her smiling approbation. "Who owns the Cézannes?"

"A middle-aged American with a fondness for beautiful women and a recently widowed French woman who may sell her painting for half its worth to a museum in Aix-en-Provence."

"Do you know these people?"

"I have met the American, but only briefly. I know the French woman's name and know that she lives in the south of France."

Kondo rubbed his nose thoughtfully. "I repeat. I want a Cézanne self-portrait."

They could feel the boat turn, then stop. The big diesels shut down. Pinkster checked the time. It was 11:35.

"You came for the Seurat. What's your offer?"

Kondo replied without hesitation. "Eleven and a half million for the Seurat and the Basquiat, and I will take the Degas and we split the profits."

Pinkster patted his cheeks with the cold towel. "Certified bank drafts and cash."

"The same as before." Kondo took an envelope from inside his jacket. "Here are eleven drafts, each for $1 million, plus two each for $250,000." He smiled as he put several of the drafts back in the envelope. "I was prepared to pay more."

Pinkster returned a weak smile. "I was prepared to accept less." He extended his hand. "We each think it was a good deal."

They filed up the steep ladder to the main deck of the tug. Before stepping across to his boat, Kondo put himself squarely in front of Pinkster. "Someone is behind the destruction of the Cézannes, and I believe you know something about it." He took hold of Pinkster's shoulders with strong hands. "If you do know and don't bring me into your confidence—" Kondo intensified his grip on Pinkster's arms, then ever so slightly pushed him away before letting his hands fall to his side.

Pinkster replied, "That's foolish talk. Positive rubbish."

Kondo said, "Is it rubbish that you have no insurance on your Cézanne? Perhaps in the interest of research, you will permit Mari Shimada to inspect the remains of your painting. She will perform . . . an autopsy."

Before turning away, Kondo said, "Expect a phone call, and we will make arrangements."

Chapter 14

An invitation to the opening of the American Artists in New England Exhibition was a highly prized piece of paper. Perhaps it was a case of nationalistic pride or, the promise that it would be an evening more noted for who would be there than for all the art on the walls. The "who" was to include a former president and his wife, a once-upon-a-time governor attempting a political comeback, two ex-Celtic basketball players, and James Wyeth, who was the only celebrity still gainfully employed. Chauncey Eaton was the director of the Boston Museum of Fine Arts, and he had planned an exhibition that would be the first major showing of American artists who had lived and painted in a New England state. Four Winslow Homer paintings were the centerpiece; other works ranged from primitive portraits by Rufus Hathaway to the abstractions of the Dutch-born yet thoroughly Americanized Willem de Kooning.

On the day after she met Edwin Llewellyn at Christie's, Astrid Haraldsen had flown to Boston for a visit to the Boston Museum of Fine Arts, where she had presented herself as a photojournalist with ties to major Scandinavian newspapers. She had been given a press pass and a packet of information that described each artist and every one of the 116 pieces of art in the exhibition. Astrid was, in fact, an adequate photographer, having learned about cameras and lenses during the year she studied interior design at the Kunst Og Handverks Hoyskole in Oslo. She had other skills.

Peder had taught her the importance of time and place, drilling into her how essential it was for her to be familiar with distances, steps and elevators, the location of phones and lavatories, and how each was equipped and lighted. "Know where you must go and how you get there so well that you can do it in the dark," he had told her. Again she covered the distance from the large reception hall to Cézanne's self-portrait, and again checked the precise number of steps from the top of the grand staircase (forty-three) to the entrance to the French Impressionists gallery. The painting had not been moved nor had a sheet of Plexiglas been put over it, as some had speculated. It was as before, fully exposed and vulnerable.

Astrid's first visit to the museum had been on a hot August day when she and Peder had driven to Boston from New York. It was during the six-hour drive that Peder had told her of his contract to destroy self-portraits by Cézanne in St. Petersburg, London, and Boston. She remembered how he enthusiastically described the new solvent he had compounded and how the chemicals worked through the layers of lacquer into the paint. It was during that same visit when they learned of the exhibition of New England artists and that a gala reception had been scheduled for the evening before the show opened to the public. It was then that Peder conceived a plan for Astrid to follow.

Peder's own plans had changed drastically in the six weeks since their visit to the Boston Museum. Astrid felt there had been too many changes, too many dangerous changes. Her reserves of nervous energy ran low too often, and she frequently dipped into the supply of medications Peder had put together for her. She had started with a small dose of amphetamine, but within four days she had doubled the dosage and had persuaded a doctor in a walk-up office on East 14th Street to replace her Valium prescription, the one she had "carelessly left behind in Norway." More recently she was alternating the amphetamine with 10 mg tablets of Valium, and though she was aware there could be serious consequences, she was quickly drawn into a whirlpool of highs and lows, allowing the drugs to twist her mood and spirit.

Now, ten days later, she found that it was taking an extraordinary effort to prepare for the mission. She was careful to darken her makeup and eyebrows and comb the hair of the brown wig so that it looked very much to be her own. She wore pants and a jacket on which she pinned her press badge.

Her camera equipment had been rented from a dealer on Lexington Avenue and consisted of two Nikon bodies, a choice of lenses, high-speed Ektachrome, and 1000-speed black-and-white film. An accessory bag contained it all plus a flash attachment, a notepad, and, in separate compartments, a pen-sized flashlight and an aerosol can with a hairspray label.

The reception began at 6:30. There were two bars and two tables of food. There were no speeches, and word quickly spread that the former president would be unable to attend, but that his wife was on her way down from their summer home. Guests arrived and were served drinks in plastic cups, and those who wandered into the galleries wandered back to wait for the celebrities.

Astrid ordered a vodka and soda and drank it quickly. It burned the back of her throat and made her cough, but she asked for another and drank it more carefully, wanting badly to feel heat in her stomach and the feeling of calm the alcohol would give her. She wanted desperately to level out the fear that was beginning to build inside her.

The reception and special exhibition galleries were on the main floor, and the bars and food tables were in a long gallery that regularly held paintings loosely categorized as American Modern. The VIP party would enter the west wing. Astrid took a position at the bottom of the staircase that led up to the collection of European paintings. The noise generated by several hundred people became a persistent buzz that was punctuated by high-pitched laughs and occasional shouts of friends greeting friends. Then a quiet came over those nearest the west entrance, and a hush rolled over the entire assemblage.

Astrid climbed a few steps and focused her camera on the figure at the leading edge of the group entering the hall. The former First Lady wore a bright blue dress, a strand of pearls, and a flattering tan that contrasted with her white hair. She was flanked by Chauncey Eaton plus a half dozen of his associates and a single secret service agent. Astrid continued taking pictures and, after each click of the camera, moved a step higher. When the attention of the guests was squarely on the honored guest, Astrid turned and ran quickly up the remaining steps to the second floor.

She was in the William Koch gallery, a long, narrow room illuminated by small ceiling lights. They cast soft shadows and reached only dimly into the display galleries that were at each end. She stood at the entrance to the darkened gallery that contained the French Impressionists. She stepped off fifteen paces, then turned to her left and took out the flashlight from the camera bag. She stood absolutely still, hearing the music and hum from several hundred patrons of the arts rising from the floor below, listening to her own heavy breathing. Astrid flicked on the light, and it shone straight ahead onto the portrait Cézanne had painted of himself in 1898. The artist, then nearing sixty, was wearing a floppy beret, his white beard neatly trimmed. Then she took the can of hairspray from the camera bag—SofTouch was the name on the label—and took off its cover. She stepped closer to the painting.

She paused, hearing a saxophone playing music programmed for the gray-haired, deep-pocket crowd. She held up the can unsteadily and aimed the spray nozzle at the artist's forehead. Her fingers tightened.

A woman's voice called out in a frightened whisper.

"Eddy? Eddy, where are you?" Astrid dropped the flashlight then quickly retrieved it and turned it off. She knelt on the floor, frozen in place.

"Damn it, Eddy. It's dark. I'm scared."

Then a man's voice. "For Christ's sake, Shirley, what're you doing up here?"

Excited words were exchanged, then a scampering of feet, and the couple disappeared.

Astrid got back on her feet, turned on the flashlight and held the can up again. "Do it!" she said in a low, hoarse whisper. "Do it and get out of here!"

Seconds went by . . . a half a minute. She stood as if transfixed by a power flowing off the canvas. Then she cried, and her arms fell to her side. She dropped to her knees and sobbed. She cried out of fear that Peder would be furiously disappointed, and she cried with relief that she had not sprayed the devastating liquid over the painting.

She covered the spray can and slipped it into the camera bag, then went back through the tapestry gallery. Ahead was the staircase that led down to the first floor, and at the top were two men wearing the uniform of the museum's security staff. She continued past them, busy again with her camera, seeming intent on getting an unusual shot of the guests below. But her heart was pounding, and she cared only about escaping into the night air.

She ran, nearly stumbling as she went to her car and got inside. Then an awful feeling of nausea came over her, and she opened the door, turned and vomited onto the gravel. Finally she was able to stand and lean against the car and breathe in the cool air. And let the tears flow. Peder might punish her and hurt her, but the agony of the decision that had been plaguing her for so long was finally over. That had been pain enough.

She drove to Logan Airport and was on the midnight shuttle to La Guardia.

Chapter 15

Information concerning the destruction of each self-portrait had flowed into Interpol World Headquarters in Lyon, France. Details varied from the most reliable in the instance of the "smoke and burn" case in London's National Gallery, to the sketchy and obtuse reports from the police in St. Petersburg, which had been made more confusing by the heavy hand of a new police regime in Moscow. Data that related to the "Bletchingly Incident" (subtitled Pinkster Gallery) had been supplied by the Surrey Police as well as Scotland Yard, and each were vying in a territorial dispute for ultimate investigative responsibility. Usually if the Yard wanted to win such bureaucratic infighting, it would. However well or poorly the information had been gathered, all of it was eventually submitted to the appropriate National Central Bureau (NCB) in each country and sent to the receiving unit of the Secretariat General at Interpol.

From Interpol, following the processing of incoming information, an all points bulletin (APB) was generally telecommunicated worldwide by Interpol's Notices Group. The APB was short on details, promising additional information in a Stolen Art/Cultural Property Notice due to be faxed the following morning. It was, in Interpol jargon, a Blue Notice, which both gave and asked for information on a specific crime or criminal. A Red Notice urged capture and arrest, frequently followed by extradition procedures. Interpol's Notices Group also issued Green, Yellow, Orange, and

Black Notices, each designed to disseminate or request information on a range of international crimes.

Now, Tuesday morning, Ann Browley had arrived at her customarily early hour and had gone routinely to the Information Section and made copies of all incoming communications relating to the Cézanne investigation, which, on this morning, numbered two. One message was for her; the other a copy of the APB, which had been received over Scotland Yard's secure lines to Interpol and the FBI in Washington. She then looked for Jack Oxby, only to learn that he too had arrived early, had also checked into IS, and had gone off. When Ann finally reached her office, she found a note taped conspicuously to her chair. The message elicited a wry smile.

Visiting the spirits. Back at ten.

J. Oxby

Westminster Abbey had opened to the rush of tour groups, and Oxby had earlier followed a familiar route to an obscure door off the Dean's Yard, rung the bell, and was admitted into the south nave.

Jack Oxby was most likely the only person in London who knew that the ghosts of the great men memorialized in Westminster Abbey met regularly for spirited debates on the condition of man, or about the state of the arts, or about politics, or, the women in their lives. He sometimes took one of his problems to the Poets Corner where he selected one or two of the minds best suited to whatever was nagging at him. Of course, it was Oxby who played all the roles, arguing strenuously with himself at times, and all the while focusing his thoughts in such a way that he was often able to see through whatever problem he was dealing with and arrive at a solution.

As he looked up to the crypts and plaques that commemorated the great men, Oxby thought of Ruskin's high moral passion for fine art and Henry James's probing insights into the intricacies of the human character. He was alone and spoke aloud, as if the great men were sitting across from him. He posed his questions then imagined their replies. The exercise was, in fact, the working over of his own thoughts, impregnated with fresh insights. It was a serious form of meditation, and it was hard work. After an hour he went to his favorite seat in the choir, where he filled a half dozen pages with facts and speculations, and from these he began to shape a hypothesis that, while riddled with too many assumptions, became a specific and tangible approach to the investigation.

Oxby was certain that the burning of the self-portraits was meant to shock the art world, yet there might be an even greater purpose. But what could that be? And who was behind it? What kind of person could do it? His eyes were closed, his concentration on the range of possible reasons for the attack on Cézanne's self-portraits. Revenge, money, notoriety—it could be one or all or none. Or it could simply be the work of a deranged mind.

He knew from Interpol's reports that all the self-portraits had been destroyed by the same powerful solvent, but no other circumstance, fact, clue, or hint of motive was common to the three incidents. A tour group visited the Pinkster Gallery. A smoking briefcase camouflaged the act of destruction in the National Gallery, and only wild assumptions had come in from the investigators in St. Petersburg.

"Three paintings are gone," he said aloud. "The Hermitage, the National Gallery, the Pinkster. No pattern to that, or is there and I'm missing it?" He repeated the unanswerable refrain: "Why Cézanne's self-portraits?"

In the afternoon he was scheduled to receive Nigel Jones's report on the chemicals recovered from the remains of the National Gallery and Pinkster portraits. Then there would be time with Ann Browley when he would learn of her progress in the search for sources of diisopropyl fluorophosphate, though he was not expecting much hard information so early in the hunt. Jimmy Murratore's report on Clarence Boggs's gambling history was due.

Oxby stepped down from the choir, turned to the high altar, nodded respectfully, then exited through the door he had entered and set out on Victoria Street. His office in New Scotland Yard had a single window that looked out on a sliver of St. James Park four long London blocks away. There was a desk, two side chairs, a file cabinet, and a cork board, on which were pinned routine office memos, assorted notes, newspaper clippings, and photographs. He put his briefcase on his desk and began unloading an armful of books that included John Rewald's *Paul Cézanne* and Lionello Venturi's catalogue of the artist's paintings. He looked up to find Ann Browley in the doorway, a worried expression showing clearly on her pretty face.

"Nothing's come of my inquiries on the DFP question, and the big drug companies are as bloody damned bureaucratic as our own government." She came into the office. "And soon as you ask for a fast response they damned well build in another two-day delay."

Oxby smiled at Ann's attempted tough talk. "Where's Jimmy?"

"Gone for coffee, I suppose. I'll fetch him."

Oxby sat behind the wall created by his books and briefcase and stared at the notes he had made at the Abbey. Jimmy Murratore appeared, coffee in hand, and sat across from Oxby. Ann slipped into the third chair.

"What's new at the racetrack?" Oxby asked.

Jimmy shook his head. "It was easy enough to learn that Clarence Boggs was losin' a bucket of money on the horses, in fact he developed quite a reputation for losin' at the track. Until July he had booked with one agent, an old chap named Terry Black, but that changed. Black's health was growin' bad and he was lookin' to retire. So he sold his books to a syndicate, one that's got five principals. I know one on a kind of personal basis, a guy named Sylvester. I checked the others, and they're okay." Jimmy turned the page in his notepad. "Then—middle of August—they cut Boggs off. He'd gone over twenty thousand pounds."

"Surprised they let him go that far," Oxby said.

"There's more to it, because old Terry Black may have put one over on them. The syndicate hadn't sorted out all of Black's accounts, and it seems that Boggs owed a few more thousand. They might have looked the other way, but they weren't going to blink at all on the twenty thousand."

"What does the syndicate do with people who owe over twenty thousand pounds?" Oxby asked.

Murratore answered immediately. "They don't kill them—not as a rule they don't."

"What do they do?" Oxby paused. "As a rule."

"Bring in the lawyers."

Oxby showed his surprise. "I'd expect more severe measures."

Jimmy nodded. "There's a few bad apples that play dirty and hire an 'enforcer,' but if someone's in debt, makin' him dead won't do much good."

"But Boggs was circling his bets in the newspaper less than an hour before he was killed. Was he still betting?"

"He got mixed up with a two-man operation, an unlicensed bunch that gave him credit."

"Do you know them?"

"One's a jockey, least he was until he got warned off for throwin' a couple of races, and the other's an Indian who was waitin' tables a year ago. Neither one's got what it takes to put together the poison package that did old Boggs in."

The phone rang, Ann answered. "It's David Blaney at the Pinkster Gallery. He's finally got the photographs and asks if you want to see them."

Oxby looked at his watch. "Tell him we'll be there by two o'clock."

The photographs were set out on the same table where Oxby had seen the wretched remains of the self-portrait. There were more than a hundred prints, but only twelve that showed the group from the Danish embassy.

"I'm sorry it's taken so long," Blaney said, "but the photographer's been off on assignment, and it wasn't until this morning that I talked to him."

"Did he give a reason for not returning your calls?"

"No, not specifically. He gets assignments and goes off. But he told me that Mr. Pinkster had the prints."

"Why would Mr. Pinkster have them?"

"It's not unusual. Mr. Pinkster insists on seeing all the photographs before they're shown around. It's his gallery and his money," he smiled. "Besides, the photographer's a friend."

"What's his interest in seeing them?" Oxby asked.

Blaney shook his head. "Mr. Pinkster wants to see and know everything. It's his way."

Ann asked, "I'd like the photographer's name and an address where he can be reached."

"It's Shelbourne. Here, I'll write it down." Blaney wrote the information on a piece of paper and handed it to Ann.

Oxby and Ann studied the photographs, occasionally asking Blaney to identify where each one had been taken. Oxby held onto one of the photographs as he inspected the others under a magnifying glass. He took the photograph he had been holding and studied it for a full minute. "Tell me again where this was taken?"

Blaney looked at the photograph carefully. "In the reception hall."

"At the beginning of the tour?"

Blaney nodded. "Probably before the tour got under way."

"Can you have it enlarged?"

"I'll have Shelbourne send it directly to you."

Oxby took all of the photographs of the Danish group and put them in numerical order. "They begin with 74 and end with 88. The print we want enlarged is number 81. Numbers 77, 83, and 84 are missing. Could they be mixed in with the others?"

Together they sorted through all of the prints looking for the missing ones. "Not here," Blaney said. "That's odd. Unless Mr. Pinkster held them out for some reason."

Ann looked again at the photo Oxby asked to be enlarged. "What's so special about this one?"

Oxby said, "There are two people in it and one is a man. The only man who was in the group. Neither the man nor the woman appears in any of the other photographs but, of course, three of them are missing." He put the point of his pencil under the two figures. "They were with the group when the tour began and then fell behind the others. Boggs complained about stragglers, and his daughter remembers that he referred to them as a couple . . . as in one of each: a woman and a man."

Chapter 16

Edwin Llewellyn's bed was an extra-wide, extra-long, super-king-size affair that was luxuriant to sleep in, read a good book in, have breakfast in, and have long sexual encounters in. To Llewellyn's dismay, the latter had in recent days been few in number, a situation he felt obliged to do something about. Fraser had brought a breakfast tray, the newspaper, and Clyde, who ate the bacon then snuggled in about thigh-high where he lay under sections A and D of the *New York Times*.

On his calendar for Wednesday were two appointments: the first at ten with Charles Pourville, an assistant curator at the Metropolitan; the second at eleven with Astrid Haraldsen for a tour of the museum. The last time he had seen Astrid she had said something about a nuisance trip to Washington and refused his offer to take her to the airport. Now he began worrying that the nuisance had turned into genuine trouble. He dialed her number a second time. Still no answer.

While he showered he thought of his meeting with Pourville, the young Frenchman he'd taken under his wing because he was an innovative curator and because Llewellyn genuinely liked him. Pourville had been instrumental in persuading the Metropolitan to participate in the upcoming Cézanne retrospective and had been named as consulting curator to the exhibition.

At nine-thirty on the dot, Llewellyn got a London call

from Scooter Albany, an old friend who correctly labeled himself a good television journalist and a lousy drunk. CBS had tolerated Albany's irresponsible drinking beyond reasonable patience then had reluctantly given him a generous severance along with a final trip to an alcoholism rehab where he once again learned how to put the cork in the bottle. He failed miserably, however, in keeping the cork there. Scooter was one of the unfortunates who knew how to stop drinking; but didn't want to learn how to stay stopped. He had covered royalty, politicians, drug rings, natural disasters, and the art world and decided the art world was safer and gave better cocktail parties. Now he was freelancing for a cable news service.

"I just got back from Paris where they're beginning to rumble about all the Cézannes going up in clouds of acid. It put me in mind of you and that family legacy of which you are so richly undeserving. I don't usually think about you, so it's a good excuse to call." There was a noisy snicker. "How're you anyhow, you old fart?"

Scooter hadn't changed, Llewellyn thought. It was mid-afternoon in London, and his friend was well on his way to another dive into alcoholic oblivion. The wonder was that he could carry on with his job and turn in a sparkling five-minute segment for the evening news.

"This old fart's just fine," Llewellyn shot back.

They talked for several minutes during which Albany shared the few facts and pet theories he had on the paintings and said he hoped that the bizarre goings-on would be good for a half-hour television piece.

"Scotland Yard won't make a statement without a hundred strings attached to it, but surer'n hell there's been a murder mixed in with the Pinkster painting and that ought to scare a little bit of shit out of you." Albany signed off with a clear warning. "They're playing hardball, Lew; I suggest you behave yourself and put that painting of yours in the attic of a nunnery in Kansas City."

"I'll behave myself if you will," Llewellyn said. "And if you're going to follow up on the story, you might want to sit in on a security meeting that's coming up in a few weeks. If you're interested I'll see if I can get you a ticket."

"Damn right I'm interested; get me in the front row."

They rang off, and Llewellyn dialed Astrid a last time and was more angry than annoyed when there was still no answer.

When Charles Pourville returned to his office he found the chair behind his desk occupied by Llewellyn, his elbows resting on the arms of the chair, his palms together as if in prayer.

Llewellyn looked up. "I'm beginning to get good and goddamned angry about this nonsense with the self-portraits." Pourville unloaded an armful of books and began putting them in the shelves. "I've been trying to figure out why they chose Cézanne's self-portraits. Any thoughts on that? Maybe someone thinks Cézanne's paintings are undervalued, and by eliminating a few the rest become worth more. Supply and demand. Probably makes my painting worth more."

"Especially yours because there's a mystery about it. If it were mine, I would be concerned."

"Why does everyone think I'm not concerned? I damn well worry and want to get it to Aix-en-Provence safely."

"Then come to the registrar's meeting. Curt Berrien confirmed it for ten on Thursday."

"I'll be there," Llewellyn said.

Curtis Berrien was the Metropolitan's registrar, a complex and highly important job that included registration of every piece of art in the museum and the signing in and out of paintings on loan. Berrien's staff was also responsible for the packing and shipping of incredibly valuable pieces of art.

Pourville gathered up another armful of books. "I've got

a lecture in ten minutes." And he was off. Alone, Llewellyn called Astrid, relieved that finally she answered. He sounded like an angry father.

"Where the hell have you been?"

"Washington. I told you."

"Perhaps you did, but I was beginning to worry."

Silence. It held for half a minute, then she said, "I am happy that you were concerned. I stayed over an extra night. I wanted to sleep so I turned off the phone."

"Then you're all right?"

"A little tired."

"You haven't forgotten our date?"

"I'm looking forward to it."

"I've arranged for a tour by a young woman who knows the museum better than . . . well, than our beloved director."

"I'll be there at eleven," Astrid said; "by the flowers."

The tall urn Llewellyn stood next to was one of four filled with identical arrangements of late summer hydrangea, giant dahlias, and white spider mums. His eyes were fixed on the main entrance to the Great Hall, and precisely at eleven Astrid came through the door.

The little grin on his face widened as she approached him. "Good morning and welcome back to New York." He kissed her cheek and smelled the perfume that was now impressed into his memory. "Tell me when you're going to stay an extra day. I worry."

She pursed her lips thoughtfully. "I'll try."

Kim Klein, their guide, joined them. She was short, stocky, wore glasses, and was in every way different from the tall, blonde Norwegian.

"I understand you would like to see what goes on behind the scene."

"I can see the galleries on my own."

"My penance for having learned what goes on in every nook and cranny is to find myself escorting a VIP who wants to start out by standing in front of a famous painting that isn't even in the Met's collection." Her eyes darted from one to the other in a mischievous way, "I call them Very Important Bores."

"I don't want to be a bore," Astrid protested.

"You won't be."

Kim led the way. All the staff seemed to know her, and she, in turn, greeted nearly everyone by name. They went down one flight of stairs, walked through two libraries, then on to a series of very large rooms closed to the public where paintings and statuary were stored in controlled temperature and humidity. Here were the not-so-great pieces of art by great artists, the donations from well-meaning patrons, and the works of lesser artists not yet—and most likely never to be—recognized. Other rooms housed carpenters' and electricians' shops. Eventually they entered a small elevator, and Kim pressed a button marked PH.

"We have a penthouse," she said in her puckish way. "It's where we make things last a long time."

Kim put her own key in the lock of a wide, high door, then ushered her guests into a room that was ninety feet long and opened to the sky with a sloping wall of glass. The room faced north, and the glass angled back so that half of the forty-foot-high ceiling let in diffused, natural light. Kim introduced her guests to the assistant director of the conservation department, who guided the little tour group past a row of easels, where they paused to watch skilled artists at work. They were told how warped panels were being straightened, how the X-ray and the computer were employed to reveal the underdrawing in centuries-old paintings, and why natural resins were preferable to synthetics.

"We are principally concerned with preserving our collection. There is a difference between conservation and restoration," the conservator said. She was a young woman with soft, blue eyes and a name Llewellyn recognized as Dutch.

Llewellyn asked, "Can anything be done with the Cézanne portraits?"

A frown replaced the smile. "From what we know, the destruction is complete. And the paintings can't be reconstructed. Even if it were possible, they would no longer be Cézannes."

Llewellyn did not answer, but nodded and thoughtfully bit on his lower lip.

After a while they circled back to the high, wide door and gave their thanks. The tour ended in front of the employees' cafeteria, where Kim said her good-byes.

Astrid said, "Thank you, it was perfect." She did not wait for a response, but kissed Llewlleyn on his lips and said softly, "Tusen takk."

He watched her walk away, a trace of her perfume caught in the palm of his hand. He followed behind her then began walking faster and caught up to her as she turned into the Great Hall.

"I had hoped we would have a chance to talk. Let's have dinner. Something special."

Astrid laughed. "I think I would like that very much."

"Fraser is still the best chef in Manhattan, as long as it's veal chops or chicken piccata. Eight o'clock?"

"Eight-thirty," she said.

He gripped her hand tightly, then let her go.

Fraser chose the chicken for the simple reason that his butcher did not have veal chops. Just as well; he personally preferred chicken. He dispelled any illusions that he was the finest chef in Manhattan, and only a magnificent salad made his dinner a mild success. Llewellyn improved matters with a bottle of Châteauneuf-du-Pape.

Conversation during the meal began amiably, each telling the other of their early school years and of their families. Astrid had lost her parents when she was barely nine and had grown up in the home of a strict and unloving grandmother. Her mood darkened as old memories came to life.

"At first I lived with my father's mother. She was kind, and I was comfortable with her. But she was sickly, and there wasn't much money. She died when I was twelve. I cried for weeks. Then I was put with my other grandmother, who lived in Trondheim. I hated it," she said bitterly. "School was boring, and life at home was always so serious. There was money, but my grandmother wouldn't give me any. Then she said with a trace of anger, "My girlfriends had an allowance." She was now talking slowly and in a voice barely above a whisper. "So I learned to steal. I thought it was all right to steal because then I had money and I could be like my friends. I became good at it." The smile disappeared. "I was caught and punished." She stared blankly at a few white carnations Fraser had found in the patio. "Later I went to the design school, the Kunst Og Handverks."

Llewellyn poured the last drops of the wine into his glass. "I was, in the vernacular, spoiled rotten. My father gave me money and expected me to spend it wisely, but nonetheless, spend it; then he taught me how to invest and preserve it. Money was revered beyond church and the family name. It seems you had too little when you were young; I had too much."

He held up his glass. "Here's to us. Survivors."

"You have good company with Fraser and Clyde and your beautiful paintings. I can't feel sorry for the way you have survived."

"I wasn't complaining, but the painting is an example of how possessions can possess. I can't say I truly enjoy it because up to now I haven't been able to share it with more than a few friends."

Astrid smiled, "You're famous because of it. Is that so bad?"

"Very bad." He shook his head. "The price was too high. But that's enough serious chatter. I'll get some brandy."

She said softly, "I feel very comfortable." She drew him close to her, then kissed him firmly on the lips. It was more than a kiss of appreciation, it was clearly an invitation.

He held her tightly and returned the kiss. "I know a better place for us to sniff brandy. And it's the good stuff, too." He tucked a bottle of Courvoisier under his arm, put two brandy glasses in one hand and Astrid's hand in the other and led her up a flight of stairs. At one end of his bedroom was an oversized leather chair, and next to it a long, low cabinet in which was a wealthy bachelor's accumulation of electronic gadgetry. He turned on the audio system and Borodin's Orchestral Suite flowed from four speakers. They faced each other, nearly touching, faces relaxed and smiling self-consciously. She unloosened his necktie and slipped it over his head. Then she unbuttoned his shirt, kissing him each time a button came free. Without exchanging words, they went to the bed, where each helped the other in the ritual of undressing and passing quickly through the brief awkwardness of seeing each other naked for the first time. They sat cross-legged on the bed. They sipped their drinks slowly.

Nothing about her disappointed him. He ran his tongue across her mouth and chin, then slowly down her neck to the deep hollow between her breasts. For nearly an hour they kissed, exploring with fingers and tongues, discovering how to excite the other into low murmuring sounds of pleasure. He entered her, and she moved her hips and thighs, thrusting forward then away until he felt the ecstasy of his climax.

They lay in an embrace, neither speaking. The music ended, and the sounds of the city trickled through an open window.

"You were gentle," she said in an almost surprised yet very soft voice.

"Beauty wears a sign, 'fragile, handle with care.' "

Then, quite clearly, her mood changed. She stared at him, eyes unblinking, her lips slightly parted but silent. She rose up and sat on the edge of the bed. Suddenly she was on her feet.

"Are you all right?"

"It's late," she said.

"A little past eleven."

"When you're alone in this city, after eleven is late."

"I'll take you home," he said with tenderness. She dressed and put on fresh lipstick. She did it all quickly and without speaking. She brushed her hair, and he wanted her to stop and say that she would stay; he wanted her to smile, but her smile was gone. She inspected herself in the mirror and said she was ready to leave.

They taxied to her hotel, where in a single fluid motion, she gave him a motherly kiss, opened the door, and stepped out to the sidewalk. He watched her disappear into the lobby of the hotel, then ordered the driver back to 65th Street, and on the return thought about the day that had started with the phone call from Scooter Albany, his brief meeting with Pourville, the tour with Kim Klein, then finally dinner and an hour in bed with Astrid. He remembered how eagerly she had encouraged him, and how skillfully she had performed. But why, when he said that beauty must be handled carefully, had she become so detached and distant?

Astrid locked the door and went directly to the window where she stared down to the red taillights moving west along 69th street. But it was a blinking red light reflected in the window that caused cold fear to sweep over her. It was the message light on the telephone. It meant, she feared, that Peder had called, wanting to learn how well she had carried out her assignment in Boston and asking her to share her excitement with him. He would also say that he had not read about it in the newspapers. Then, when she learned what actually had happened, he would be angry, perhaps violently so. The fear of facing up to Peder had swept over her when she was with Llewellyn. She wanted at first to confide in him, but instead she ran from him. Her amphetamine supply was gone, and Valium merely smoothed her out for several hours, then left her depressed. Heroin would put her at ease, just a touch of white lady, she thought, a small amount in her left forearm where she had put a needle so many times.

She undressed and showered, first in warm, soothing water, then gradually she turned the water to an icy cold and forced herself to stay under the harsh spray until she was gasping for air. She put on a thick, white bathrobe, went back into the darkness by the window, and rubbed a towel through her hair. She stared, trancelike, at the blinking red light, her thoughts a jumble. Out of the confusion came a fresh memory of Edwin Llewellyn, of his room and the music. His bed. His warmth.

The phone rang, a jarring, unwelcome sound. It was a quarter to twelve, barely dawn in Cannes. Time was unimportant to Peder.

A trembling hand reached for the phone. She took the receiver in both hands and said, "Hello." The word was barely audible.

"Astrid, darling." It was Llewellyn, sounding jaunty and cheerful. "I've called to say I had a marvelous day, and I hope you did as well." There was a pause, then he continued. "You were a bit on edge when I dropped you off," and he rambled on as if he were not certain what he wanted to say but pleased he was saying whatever came out. "I meant to ask if you were free on Thursday. I've got a dinner party to go to, and I want to show you off. Don't misunderstand, they're perfectly lovely people, just rich and terribly social. More important, someone might give you an assignment." He laughed. "They all have deplorable taste and need you."

She smiled. "Yes, I'm free." She wanted to say more, but the words didn't come to her.

"I'll pick you up at six," he said enthusiastically. "Oh, by the way, I have your earrings."

She touched an ear, surprised she hadn't missed them. "Bring them on Thursday?"

"Of course. Sleep well, darling," he said.

She put down the receiver. A police siren wailed, and as usually happens in New York, another did the same. The sounds died away, replaced by the low whisper of the air conditioning.

When the phone rang again, her hand was still on the receiver. She picked it up, hoping Llewellyn had called again. An indistinct, metallic-sounding voice came from the receiver. "Hello . . . hello . . . Astrid?" The voice became insistent. "Astrid?"

She put the receiver to her ear, and the deep-pitched voice became clear.

"Hello," she said mechanically.

"I called earlier, did you get my message?"

"I haven't had time to call."

"You are never too busy to call me." The voice was hard. "Did everything go well on Monday?"

"I'm very tired. I was with Llewellyn today," she said with the hope of moving to another subject.

"Tell me about Monday," he insisted.

"Everything went as you planned it. No one saw me go up to the galleries, and I got to the painting. I was alone. I took out the spray can, Peder, I truly did, but I . . ." She began to cry. "I'm sorry, but I couldn't do it."

"That's not acceptable." His voice grew loud. "The plans aren't subject to your whims or being sorry. Do you understand?"

"I can't destroy something beautiful."

"It's a picture of an old man. That's not beauty. Money is beauty."

"You don't have to destroy any more."

"Yes, my Astrid. One more, one in America. The newspapers and television will make a sensation of it." Again a short silence. He went on calmly. "You must return to

Boston and do it properly. There will be more receptions and more special exhibitions and more occasions when they ask their benefactors for more money. You see, I have agreed to remove four of the paintings. It must be done."

Her head was angled to the side, both hands cradling the phone. Her eyes were closed as she listened to the man to whom she had sworn her unreserved loyalty. She suddenly felt an intense desire to please him. "I'll try," she said. "I'll try."

"You will be proud," Peder responded. "And my love for you will be eternal."

"Do you truly love me?"

During a short pause she heard the faint sound of laughter on the satellite connection, then the words, "I love you."

Tears fell on her cheeks. "Thank you, Peder."

"You are getting on with Llewellyn?"

"Yes, as you asked me to do."

"And you have become good friends?"

"We are good friends, yes."

"Good. He is important to us." She collapsed into a chair, waiting for Peder to continue. "Prepare new plans for Boston as early as possible. I'll call on Thursday, six o'clock New York time."

"I will be with Edwin—with Llewellyn—on Thursday evening."

"I understand," he said.

There was a brief silence. "Peder? Please don't be angry." There was no reply, only a click when Peder put down the phone.

She began to sob. "Please, Peder, I want you to love me."

Chapter 17

Jack Oxby guided Ann Browley to a narrow mews off Campden Hill Road where there was a small shop with a faded sign that read: THE KITCHEN. He was in and back in a minute, a bulky, strange-looking mass of cowhide clutched under his arm. "Good as new," he said, affectionately patting what could only be described as old leather stitched together to form a bag of some sort.

"Next time you must meet Thomas Kitchen. He's eighth generation, would you believe?"

Ann would believe it because she had indeed met the incumbent Kitchen and knew the history of the Oxby briefcase. She knew that it had been designed for Oxby's father and made up by Tom Kitchen's grandfather. Oh, she had heard it all before, and she knew how Oxby treasured the "bloody satchel," as some called it, and its cavernous depths that could hold enough evidence to convict half a dozen criminals. Three years earlier, Oxby's wife had secretly taken it to have the initials J.L.O. embossed in gold leaf as a birthday present; it was when Ann joined the squad, and she remembered how pleased Oxby had been. She also remembered Oxby's total desolation when three months later leukemia took his Miriam away.

"We'd best move on," Oxby said. "We've somehow got ourselves behind schedule." Ann shook her head resignedly and steered the car in the direction of the Strand and the Courtauld Institute of Art, which had moved into Somerset

House, where the work of Britain's center for the study of art history was housed, together with a modest assemblage of French Impressionists, Old Masters, and a few contemporary paintings.

Bertha Morrison was a research whiz at the Courtauld, a one-time librarian imbued with a deep love for art. She had perfected a special ability to find where art had been and was today and thus was a valuable source of information for art historians the world over.

Glasses attached to a gold chain rested on her generous bosom, and her graying hair was combed back and captured by a giant tortoiseshell clip. Ann suspected from the way she spoke that she was northern Scottish and was pleased that she had sized up the woman quite accurately on the strength of two brief phone conversations.

"No one has fussed over Cézanne's self-portraits, not until recently of course," Bertha Morrison said. "But that's true of his nude bathers and that damnable mountain he was forever painting." She looked solemnly at her guests. "We no longer have a Lionelli Venturi telling us where everything is and who owns it."

Ann turned toward Oxby and saw his sour expression.

"But I understood you had the information," Ann protested.

"My dear," Bertha said, "of course I have the information. I merely wanted Inspector Oxby to be aware that a search of this scope doesn't come easily, even to a first-class researcher, and certainly may not come at all to someone with a lazy curiosity."

"Bertie wants us to think she had an impossible task," Oxby said with a wink, "that way it makes her accomplishment appear all the more incredible."

Bertha ignored the comment and opened the folder in front of her. "I'm certain there's more data out there—there always is—but I don't think it will change what we've got here." She gave Ann and Oxby a computer printout. "Now pay attention, Jack, because I'm going to tell you more about Cézanne than you're prepared for. It might come in handy later on.

"All of Cézanne's works were catalogued in 1936 by Venturi. At that time he listed 838 oil paintings, of which 154 were portraits."

Ann's furrows were deepening. "I'm sorry to appear stupid, but who was Venturi?"

"He taught art history at the University of Rome and was the first to research all of Cézanne's paintings. In all, Venturi catalogued twenty-five self-portraits, a large number in one sense, but less than 3 percent of Cézanne's total output. Venturi never recorded the portrait owned by Mr. Llewellyn, the American. The numbers I refer to are those Venturi assigned each painting."

"So, Bertie," Oxby said, "with the destruction of three portraits, there are twenty-three to account for. Can you?"

"Eighteen are in museums, their provenance and location accurately accounted for, as you'll discover in the report I have given you. That leaves five. One is in Paris and is known as the *Self-Portrait in a Soft Hat*. It's numbered 575 and is owned by Gustave Geffroy, who descends from a wealthy aristocratic family. Geffroy has a sizable collection in his country home that no one sees except his close friends."

Oxby made a notation next to Geffroy's name.

"Number seventy, known as *Self-Portrait with Long Hair*, is in Spain," Bertha continued. "It is owned by Baron von Thyssen who moved his entire collection to Madrid."

"It's a safe bet the Baron's collection is under tight security," Oxby said.

"Then there's *Self-Portrait in a Straw Hat*, Venturi number 238. This was owned by a family named Lefebure, also in Paris, and was sold privately in the mid-eighties to a family in Hong Kong."

"I don't see a name," Oxby said, his finger tapping the report Bertha had given him.

"I don't have a name, but the painting has been positively traced to Hong Kong. It's owned by one of those anonymous people who doesn't want anyone to know they've got money and possessions. You know the type."

"I don't know that type, Bertie."

Bertha continued. "I don't have confirmation, but I was told the portrait has been put in a bank vault."

Ann dutifully put a question mark beside number 238.

"That, of course, leaves two, the DeVilleurs portrait in Antibes and the one owned by Edwin Llewellyn in New York."

"A first-rate job, Bertie."

"Thank you, Jack. Meantime you might pay attention to our fee and the expenses we've run up on this little assignment." She handed Oxby an envelope. "Always a distinct pleasure doing business with you."

On the return to New Scotland Yard, Ann asked whether or not Oxby would be surprised to learn that another portrait was destroyed.

"I don't see a clear pattern, not enough to allow me to lean one way or the other. Yet I know for a certainty that every one of the eighteen portraits that's in a museum is fair game." He sighed. "Most of those museums haven't tightened their security worth a damn. Consider this fact, Annie: Three of Cézanne's self-portraits have been destroyed, and in a few months a major show of his work opens in Aix-en-Provence. That's not a coincidence."

"How many people do you think are involved?" Ann asked.

"I'd say that it takes two to attack the paintings, and beyond that I guess another one or two are calling the shots. If I had to put money on it I'd say no more than four."

"Nationality?"

"I haven't a clue. Not yet. That's why I want to know

more about the chemicals and where they're coming from. And the photographs. Any news from David Blaney?"

"He keeps saying 'tomorrow,' and I keep saying that's not good enough."

Neither spoke again until Ann turned onto Broadway, then to a parking spot. Oxby remained in his seat, still silent until he said, "One more—they're going to get at one more portrait."

The usual complement of furrows spread across Ann's forehead. "Why, suddenly, do you say that?"

He turned to her and smiled. "Hunch, intuition, something on those lines." He looked at the clock on the dashboard. "It's a good time to call Alex Tobias. I want him to pay Mr. Llewellyn a visit."

Chapter 18

This was a day Margueritte DeVilleurs had looked forward to with no small amount of foreboding. She had invited Frédéric Weisbord to be present when she formally accepted an offer from the Musée Granet for the purchase of the Cézanne portrait. Aukrust had come early to examine more closely the paintings Margueritte said she would not sell. Since he delivered the Renoir to her, they had been together twice. Once they had spent a day in Cannes and soon after had driven beyond Monaco into Italy, where they lunched at a seaside ristorante in San Remo. In spite of the difference in age, she felt comfortable with him, reacting happily to the warm attention he paid her. He was her grand *ours,* a big bear, whom she fantasized might engulf her in his arms.

Gustave Bilodeau, Conservateur du Musée Granet, was expected at three o'clock. Margueritte knew that Freddy Weisbord would fume vociferously about the Cézanne self-portrait and threaten to force a sale in London or New York. Worse, he would demand that she turn the entire collection over to him immediately. She hoped that by bringing the stubborn lawyer together with Bilodeau, he might soften his opposition. The lawyer was seventy-six, his emphysema worsening, no thanks to his refusal to give up a two-pack-a-day habit of unfiltered Camels, his only acceptance of anything American. Weisbord seemed even older than his years, and Margueritte dared hope that he was slowly dying and that she might help in some way to speed the process. She felt no guilt in this, as she wanted an end to Freddy's meddling.

"C'est assez! Fini!" she was prepared to tell him.

It was nearly three o'clock, and Weisbord was unexpectedly late, a rarity, she thought unhappily. She was in her bedroom, in front of a large mirror, brushing her hair, and imagining she was confronting Freddy, angrily repeating the words she had rehearsed over and over. When Emily announced with contemptuous brevity that he had arrived, Margueritte calmly applied a touch of lipstick and a faint blush of color above her eyes, delaying another several minutes to allow the lawyer's impatience to put her at an advantage. Finally she went out to greet him.

Weisbord was a small man, nearly bald, with stray strands of white hair combed over his ears. He wore glasses and squinted, and his little chin and thin lips made him appear all the less imposing. Brown-stained fingers held a cigarette, and he coughed as if constantly clearing his throat.

"You're making a mistake by selling to the museum." His voice was surprisingly virile and etched by years of heavy smoking. "Several dealers have told me that the portrait will bring a minimum of twenty-five million dollars . . . and probably a great deal more."

"And how much would you get from that?"

"That's not a consideration," he coughed.

"It is to me."

"I'm paid to advise you. It's an arrangement we've had for thirty years."

"C'est assez! Fini!" The well-practiced words came out ringingly clear. "I will from this day on handle my own affairs and make my own decisions. The bank will provide advice on financial matters, and if I need legal advice I shall call on my new lawyer."

His cough worsened. "You can't do that," he protested. "It's not like . . . like changing butchers."

"Oh, but it's exactly like choosing a new butcher." She smiled, "You put it perfectly, Freddy."

"That's not as Gaston would . . . would like it," he wheezed.

"But it's all done, Freddy. All the old accounts have been canceled and a new one opened at a new bank and in my name only."

Weisbord choked and coughed, sounding like an old motorboat engine that wouldn't turn over. "You know nothing about finances," he managed, "nor do banks."

Her eyes widened. "Are you suggesting that you do? You did what two centuries and a half dozen wars couldn't do. You destroyed my family's business with your bungling and selfishness." She waved her hand. "You're an old man with old ideas. Emily and I will do just fine."

"Emily?" he laughed. "You'll make a rare duet."

Margueritte heard a man's voice in the entryway. "I have an important guest," she said, in a way that suggested Weisbord had been demoted to a level below spear-carrier.

Emily appeared at the door, followed by a man wearing a rumpled seersucker suit, checkered shirt, and narrow tie. Gustave Bilodeau was perhaps forty, with the earnest look of a well-informed scholar. He had a huge mop of brown hair that rose up from a deeply tanned forehead. His mouth was large and expressive and smiled nervously to reveal chalk-white teeth.

Madame DeVilleurs and Bilodeau greeted each other like old friends, then offhandedly she said, "This is Mr. Weisbord, he was my husband's lawyer." She emphasized the past tense.

"You're the museum director," Weisbord said accusingly and went on the attack. "You've no right to take advantage of Madame DeVilleurs. The Cézanne is worth a fortune, not the insulting amount you have offered."

"You must excuse Monsieur Weisbord. It is no longer his

business what I do with the painting, and he only pretends to know how much you have offered."

"Have you been a buyer and seller of art?" Bilodeau asked in a gentle voice.

"I have drawn the papers for every sale and purchase in the DeVilleurs collection," Weisbord answered grandly. "I have been family counselor for more than forty years. Beyond that I assisted Gaston DeVilleurs in the negotiation for both Cézannes. It was I who discovered the Renoir. A perfect jewel."

"You told him not to buy it," Margueritte interrupted.

"Not true," he coughed. "It's so small. I merely warned against paying too much."

"You haven't shown me the Renoir," Bilodeau said.

"It has a new frame," Margueritte said happily, "and I had it cleaned."

"Who did that for you?"

"A new man. In Cannes."

"What's his name?" Bilodeau asked.

"Aukrust. Peder Aukrust. A perfectly delightful man."

"Then the painting is with you?" Bilodeau asked warily.

Margueritte's smile broadened. "Of course. Peder is very responsible."

"I must meet him. It's my business to know the new people. Especially the good ones."

"You shall meet him. I have asked him to prepare a report on the condition of the self-portrait. I'm afraid there are many small problems with it."

Weisbord lit a fresh cigarette. "It is in perfect condition."

"Not so," Bilodeau said. "I studied it myself. I recommend a new canvas support, and there is mold damage in a portion of the beard. There are also scratches across the background, in the window area particularly."

"You make it sound as if the painting's in a state of terminal decay," Weisbord said, whining.

"These are small problems, but they can worsen, particularly the mold, which can be insidious. The spores multiply, and you can't see it happening without a microscope."

As if not hearing Bilodeau's reasoned explanation, Weisbord continued to complain. "You've cooked up a bad repert to justify your low price."

"Please, Monsieur Weisbord. These are not problems that would have any effect whatever on the painting's value. I merely bring our attention to several defects that must be corrected."

Unseen by Weisbord or Bilodeau, Peder Aukrust was now standing just outside the room. Margueritte saw him and smiled.

Bilodeau turned to Margueritte. "I have the agreement for the sale of the painting."

"Let me look at it." Weisbord began changing his glasses.

"You needn't bother." Margueritte pulled his hand down the way she might command a child. "I want the Musée Granet to have the painting. They do not have a self-portrait in the Cézanne collection, and I feel very strongly that they should have mine at whatever price they can afford."

Weisbord coughed painfully. "It's not your painting to do with as you please. Gaston specified that if any painting in the collection is sold, it must be entered for sale at one of the major auction houses. Gaston knew that would be in your best interest."

"It was always as much my painting as Gaston's. Now that he's gone, it is totally mine. It doesn't belong to 'the estate,' as you would like it to be. In fact your only concern is to administer the will that you wrote, arrange for the auctions, and take your big fee."

"If you give away the most valuable painting in the collection, what will you do with the others?"

"She will not give us the painting," Bilodeau protested. "We have long-standing offers from two anonymous benefactors to purchase a self-portrait."

"How much?" Weisbord demanded.

Bilodeau shrugged. "I cannot tell you. They insist the amount be kept confidential."

"What is their price, Margueritte?" He coughed, and his face turned scarlet.

She glared at Weisbord, hoping a paroxysmal attack might eliminate his meddling forever. "I am accepting their offer and will not go back on my word."

Weisbord shook his head. "You are stubborn, and foolish, too." He turned to Bilodeau. "Cézanne's self-portraits will double in value as a result of this mad destruction, and I insist that Madame DeVilleurs adhere to the terms of her husband's will. I remind you that she does not have the right to sell any painting, and further, she cannot convey clear title under the circumstances. In the art world, that is a very important document. The Code is quite clear on this. If she attempts to sell I will file papers to set aside the transfer."

Tears of anger fell on her cheeks. "Leave, Freddy; go away."

"Our offer is a fair one," Bilodeau argued. "Consider that the Musée Granet is where the portrait should hang. Cézanne was born in Aix, he lived there most of his life, the two are inseparable."

Weisbord coughed, more of a grating rasp. "Explain to your benefactors that I must know how much they will pay. You can assure them their offer will be considered."

"I will ask. But under any circumstance, the portrait must be part of our Cézanne retrospective, which opens in January."

"You're not waiting for the tourists?" Weisbord asked in a contemptuous tone.

"We have international sponsorship from Michelin and an American company. The exhibition will be the most comprehensive assembly of Cézanne's work ever shown!" Bilodeau spoke with passion.

Margueritte waited for Weisbord's reaction. A showing in the retrospective would enhance the value of the painting, and yet Bilodeau might be innocently self-inflicting a mortal wound.

"Until we resolve the eventual disposition of the painting, I must take possession of it."

"You will not touch it," Margueritte said firmly. "Furthermore, you won't file any papers, and you won't set aside the transfer of title."

Weisbord waved his arms defiantly. "You intend to sell the Cézanne self-portrait in clear violation of the terms of the will," and with that he started for the gallery. Margueritte stepped ahead of him and began calling for Peder. Weisbord showed surprising strength as he pushed past her and into the gallery and to the wall where the Cézannes were hung. Next to the painting of the farmhouse near Margueritte's childhood home in Salon-de-Provence was a large empty space.

Margueritte gasped. Peder was not in the gallery, nor was he anywhere in the house. She looked out to the driveway and saw that the station wagon was gone.

Weisbord volubly declined to accept the fact that the self-portrait was missing. He thrashed about the house, looking under beds and behind sofas in a vain search. A long, loud coughing attack forced him to stop, and when he recovered, red-faced and breathing painfully, he lapsed into an inconsolable silence. Only when he had searched every conceivable hiding place did he speak to Margueritte.

"You've tricked me somehow, but I will have the last word." To Bilodeau he said, "It's obvious that you are in on this conspiracy, and I warn you that I will take decisive action if the painting should ever appear inside the Musée Granet."

The little man stormed off, enveloped in his own angry black cloud. He turned the wheels of his car too abruptly at the end of the driveway and crossed over the edge of a flower garden, flattening what had been a clump of pink and white chrysanthemums.

Gustave Bilodeau had endured Weisbord's outburst in silence and awed surprise. Margueritte comforted him, "Freddy is a mean and stupid man, pay no attention."

"But he has said that we must never show the painting. What will he do?"

"Talk. He will talk, talk, talk. He will threaten and talk more."

"But the painting?" Bilodeau asked. "Is it safe?"

"Quite safe," she said confidently. "And you will have it, just as I agreed. We will play Weisbord's game but not by his rules."

Bilodeau looked puzzled. He had come prepared to hand a check to Madame DeVilleurs and return triumphantly to Aix with the Cézanne beside him.

"You will have the painting for your exhibition," she said, a mischievous glint showing in her bright eyes, "and nothing Frédéric Weisbord may say or do will stop that from happening."

Chapter 19

There was no mistaking who owned the richly modulated baritone that came from the other side of the well-guarded conference room door. It was a perfect voice, too perfect for Llewellyn's taste, and it belonged to the director of the Metropolitan, Gerard Bontonnamo, who fit the tall, dark, and handsome cliché, with voice to match. So trite, but so damned true, Llewellyn grudgingly conceded. He showed his ID and went into the room where Bontonnamo, all six-foot-five of him, stood at the far end of the room. The director paused while Llewellyn eased himself into a chair.

"Thank you for joining us, Mr. Llewellyn," Bontonnamo said with the reproving tone a teacher might use on a tardy student. "I believe you know we are discussing the Cézanne retrospective, and I've just made it abundantly clear that I'm not happy that we're sending our Cézannes to an unprotected little city in the south of France at a time when all this damnable destruction is going on. Frankly, Edwin, I think you'll be well advised to keep yours at home."

Llewellyn knew that Bontonnamo was not inviting him into a conversation, so he sat back comfortably and put on a benign smile.

"Saurand called me this morning," the director continued, "and yesterday I talked with Kuntz in Berlin, then Sir Alex in London, and half a dozen others who are, to be blunt, goddamned outraged." Bontonnamo was well connected to his counterparts in every important museum; all members of a special clique of super-elitists, all highly charged intellectuals who lived in a world of their own. Guy Saurand was *directeur* of the Louvre, which put him on top of the list of Conservateurs des Musées de France. Bontonnamo went on, "We don't have a self-portrait, and you know I'd damned well give a Picasso and a couple of Renoirs for one." Bontonnamo paused, then continued, "I realize this whole thing is tragic, but it's news. Big news, and the press is having a grand time pointing out that we don't have a self-portrait to protect."

Llewellyn smiled inwardly at the remark, knowing full well that even though New York's Museum of Modern Art had a Cézanne self-portrait, the media had rarely potshotted at the Met for not having one. It was, rather, vintage Bontonnamo, once again asking for a loan of Llewellyn's self-portrait. The downside of all this was that with his painting scheduled to leave the country, Llewellyn was about to lose the argument that his grandfather's will restrained him from loaning it.

There were five other people in the room, four seated at the table and one who was standing looking bored, as if he had heard the director's speech before. Curtis Berrien was chief registrar of the Metropolitan, a high-ranking position of considerable power and authority. No painting entered or left the premises without a member of the registrar's office inspecting it, recording its source, and corroborating its condition with a member of the curatorial staff. When a painting or any piece of art was put on loan, a release was given in the registrar's office, which was in turn responsible for packaging, shipping, and arranging for proper insurance while the object was in transit and while on display. In most instances a painting on loan would be covered by a blanket policy carried by the borrowing museum; however, this would not be the case with the Musée Granet—all loan contributors were responsible for their own insurance. Even the major corporate sponsors of the retrospective—names like Kodak and Michelin—had not offered to pay for the insurance. Premiums had increased substantially and might go even higher if the assault on the portraits was not resolved. Berrien had argued against participating in the retrospective a year earlier, but even he had not anticipated the tragic losses. Now his arguments were being given a second hearing.

Llewellyn and Berrien were friends, an important ingredient in their relationship. Berrien could be gruff, even insensitive at times, but it was his blunt way of speaking his mind. He could be exciting, too; daring, and adventurous, as in going off on an exploration of Tibetan art in rarely explored parts of China. His bold personality frequently was reflected in the way he dressed, which today was a blue-and-white striped shirt and brilliant red suspenders. He had a strong body, stood five-eleven, and weighed a stocky 190 pounds; he had a large head that had a bald spot on top ringed by salt-and-pepper hair cut short. The skin was deeply wrinkled on the back of his stout neck, and his nose was off line, a casualty of his determination to be on the boxing team at the Maritime Academy. After a four-year hitch in the maritime service he enrolled at Emory University, where he picked up a law degree, a wife, and traces of a Southern accent.

Bontonnamo's speech ended. His final exhortation was that extra and exhaustive precaution must be taken in the packaging and shipment of all paintings going to the Granet, all of which underscored his resolve to go ahead with the Met's participation in the big show.

Berrien waited until the door closed. "You heard the man. It might be a damned stupid decision, but for now that's the way it is." He stepped to the head of the table and gestured toward Llewellyn. "For those of you who haven't met our guest, this is Mr. Edwin Llewellyn. He's one of our elective trustees and serves on the acquisitions committee. Let me add that he's our friend, and as you heard from the director, Mr. Llewellyn owns a Cézanne, a painting that grows more famous every day. I've seen it, and in my opinion it's the best of the whole damned lot." Llewellyn was amused. Berrien was not an art scholar, but his enthusiasm was authentic.

Berrien continued, "Lew, these are some of my people. I think you know my assistant, Helen Ajanian."

A woman with heavy eyebrows turned toward Llewellyn. Helen Ajanian had been assistant to Berrien's predecessor and had been with the Metropolitan for thirty years. She smiled pleasantly at Llewellyn, an expression that belied the fact that she was known as "top cop." It was Helen Ajanian who enforced the strict rules of the registrar's office.

"Next is Harry Li."

Born in Taiwan, Li had been educated at the University of California at Berkeley. His black hair fell across the edges of large, dark-rimmed glasses. Beneath hair and glasses was a handsome, if delicate, face with Eurasian features. He nodded and grinned simultaneously.

"Over there is Jeff Kaufman."

The young man thrust his hand across the table and vigorously shook hands with Llewellyn. Kaufman said that he had heard about the Llewellyn portrait and was looking forward to getting it safely to France.

"Harry and Jeff are a team," Berrien said. "Jeff's our resident expert on transportation and insurance. Insurance is tricky and expensive. Transportation can be complicated because many of the items we ship must travel in total secrecy. When we send a painting worth $25 million to Tokyo, it doesn't go Federal Express.

"Harry's responsible for occasionally putting things in packages that don't look like a package for what's inside. He also has to make sure that nothing is damaged. We rarely lend our Etruscan pottery, but when we do, you can be sure Jeff is using some pretty exotic packaging materials."

Berrien was behind Helen Ajanian. "I rely on Helen to tie everything together. If she doesn't sign off, it doesn't ship." He motioned toward Pourville. "And, of course, you know Charlie Pourville."

Llewellyn glanced over at the young curator, then at the others. "I want the best from all of you. The painting you are going to send to France has not been out of my family's hands since it was bought in France and brought to New York a long time ago. Nearly a hundred years, now. It's not only valuable to me, but I like to think it has great meaning to the entire art community. Protect it, please."

"Count on us, Lew," Berrien said. "Our plans are pretty well under way; it was just a question of whether it's a go, or no-go." He shook his head. "Look's like it's go. But, Lew, you can still back out."

"What am I risking?" Llewellyn asked.

"I'll answer, if I may," Helen Ajanian said. "There's always a risk when we lend something from our collection, whether it's a risk of fire or breakage or poor conditions in the exhibiting museum. Six weeks in uncontrolled humidity can play havoc with an old painting on wood. It's a horribly obscene thing that's happened, and it makes absolutely no sense. But neither did the fire that destroyed two of the Albrecht Dürer woodcuts we loaned to the Vienna Museum a few years ago. There are always risks—it's just that we're dealing with some new ones this time."

"I would think security at the Musée Granet would be as tight as at Camp David," Llewellyn said.

"I'm afraid not," Pourville replied. "It's a small city with a police department that's stretched to the limit. January isn't a tourist month, but the students are there in full force. In March the crowds return, and the police will have their hands full. Besides, Gustave Bilodeau has limited personnel, and his guards are not very well trained."

Llewellyn said, "I was told they'd be sent a fully trained staff, that the Louvre and the other big French museums are supposed to help."

Pourville smiled. "Perhaps. I know that a traveling exhibition of Cézanne's paintings was in Aix in the summer of 1961.

Security was very good, or so they thought, and on the third night there was a break-in and five paintings were stolen."

"We'll damn well have to do better than that," Llewellyn said resolutely. "The insurance people and the museum directors will demand it."

Berrien nodded. "For Christ's sake, we are demanding it. That's why we've called a security meeting. Frankly, I don't give a damn what Gerard Bontonnamo says, because if the security plan isn't up to snuff after that meeting, you can bet your sweet ass—excuse me Helen—the Met won't send so much as a postcard."

The meeting continued until noon. Harry Li and Jeff Kaufman made articulate presentations, yet neither gave details of their plans for disguising the packages or their strategy for moving those packages from New York to the south of France. But they freely confided to Llewellyn that the paintings would be shipped to either Madrid or Geneva a minimum of six weeks in advance of the opening of the retrospective.

Berrien adjourned the meeting and said to Llewellyn, "I want you to meet a friend of mine, someone you'll like knowing."

Llewellyn replied, "Tell me about him."

"His name is Alexander Tobias. He's with the New York Police."

"Why does he want to meet me? Is he some kind of an art buff?"

"In a way. He had a long career in criminal investigation, developed an interest in art, and likes doing what he knows best: investigating art thefts and forgeries."

"What's his interest in my painting?"

"He's got tie-ins everywhere, including the FBI and Interpol. But his contact in Scotland Yard suggested that he pay you a visit. He asked me to set up an introduction." Berrien rubbed the back of his neck, and his expression changed to match the serious tone of his voice. "I think you should talk with him. OK?"

Llewellyn nodded. "Have him call me."

Chapter 20

The dinner party Llewellyn invited Astrid to attend was being held in Thomas A. Ridgeway's triplex on the top floors of a well-appointed apartment building on Fifth Avenue at 73rd Street. In spite of, or because of, his impeccable credentials as one of the remaining authentic New York WASPs, Tom Ridgeway was both a "good guy" and a good friend. It was Tom's wife Caroline who was considered such a pain in the ass. She greeted Astrid with the lukewarm smile she accorded persons on her long list of the ethnic "underclass." Attractive as she appeared and gracious as she acted, Caroline was five and a half feet of pure bigotry, and her prejudices were in imminent danger of embracing all of Norway.

"Meet Astrid Haraldsen," Llewellyn said, giving his hostess an obligatory peck on the cheek. "But let me warn you, Astrid, behind Caroline's pretty face is all lollipops and ice cream."

"What's that supposed to mean?" Caroline said acidly as she gave Astrid a receiving line handshake. "I'm delighted you've come," she said coolly. "Lew will show you where to find everything. He's very good at that."

Llewellyn took Astrid's hand and led her to a magnificent room with great, high windows overlooking Central Park. A late autumn sun was about to disappear, and the sky was streaked with bold colors. A man approached them. He was barely Astrid's height, a bit portly and gray-haired, and his good features were all at ease.

"You're Astrid," he said. "I'm Tom Ridgeway. Welcome."

In quick succession, three couples arrived. Ernie and Sally Simpson were the seniors in the group. Ernie was old money and old shoe, while Sally was on a constant diet, trying to become a size twelve and not succeeding.

Stephen Urquhart and his wife, Diane, were equally imbued with the trappings of Scottish traditions and possessed an unspotted bloodline. Popular in their small group of intimates, they were considered insufferable snobs by all others.

Jim and Marilyn Cox were the last to arrive. He was Wall Street, and she was inclined to keep her husband away from attractive women. Astrid qualified. Jim was also well on his way to a serious drinking problem. He gulped down a half glass of pure Dewar's during the few minutes it took to greet Astrid and Llewellyn, then ran off to find a refill.

The ritual of the cocktail hour proceeded in a predictable pattern: drinks from a well-stocked bar and finger food served by an obsequious little man. Just as the men had maneuvered to form a circle around Astrid, Caroline announced that dinner was being served.

After a clumsy toast proposed by Jim Cox, Caroline asked if Astrid had plans to redecorate Edwin Llewellyn's house. "You must admit, Astrid dear, it needs a woman's touch."

"It's been touched by too many women," Llewellyn complained good-naturedly. "I like it the way it is."

"The Scandinavians have such a different sense of design," Caroline said with a snide curve to her voice, "I'd like to hear how Astrid feels about that."

Astrid turned and saw Caroline's frozen smile. She knew everyone was watching her. She looked across to Llewellyn. He nodded, reassuringly, then turned to Caroline. "You could use a little help with your East Hampton house, Muffin. Why not give Astrid a stab at it."

"Great idea," Tom Ridgeway said.

"It's a hideous idea," Caroline said, her defenses up. "The beach house is perfectly fine the way it is." She retreated from the subject, "We'd like to hear what Lew thinks of the dreadful things that have happened to those poor Van Gogh paintings."

"You mean Cézanne," her husband corrected.

"Of course, Cézanne. I thought I said that."

"For God's sake, Lew," Jim Cox said, slurring his words and waving an empty glass. "They might come and burn up that picture of yours."

"Aren't you a little worried?" Sally asked.

"Concerned, yes. Worried? Only a little." Llewellyn shifted in his chair. "My painting is safe."

"Did you say earlier that they haven't a clue as to who destroyed those paintings?" Tom Ridgeway asked.

"I don't believe they do. But you know, I'm damned angry about losing the portrait in London's National Gallery . . . then Alan Pinkster's portrait. . . ."

"Serves the son of a bitch right," Jim Cox said. "He's a wiseass bastard who steps on everyone who gets in his way."

"Stop it," Marilyn Cox said angrily. "You have a dreadful tongue."

"Jim's right," Caroline said. "Alan Pinkster tries to buy his way into the right crowd every time he comes to New York. I think he should stay with his own kind."

Llewellyn spoke up. "I don't completely share Jim's opinion of Alan Pinkster. He's cocky and sometimes he can be a rude son of a bitch, but he's made it on his own. More than some of us can say."

Tom Ridgeway nodded but held his tongue.

Llewellyn went on. "I'm also damned angry because

Pinkster's curator was murdered. I hear that Scotland Yard believes the two crimes are tied together."

"I hadn't heard that," Steve Urquhart said.

"They've kept it pretty much under wraps. But the press is beginning to hop on the story. You'll be hearing more."

Jim Cox got unsteadily to his feet and held up his glass. "Here's to Eddie Llewellyn's painting." He ran his words together sloppily and listed badly. "I sure hope nothing happens to it." He emptied the glass and sagged back into his chair.

The dinner ended without further incident, and the group assembled in the room with the windows for coffee. Astrid peeked at her watch. It was 9:30. The Simpsons said they would have to make it an early night. Llewellyn said that he and Astrid would have to do the same, and minutes after saying their thanks and goodnights, they were in a taxi. Another five minutes and they were in front of Astrid's hotel.

"I felt a little sick for a minute," Astrid said.

"You covered it well," he said. "One of Caroline's bad shrimps?"

"No. Just tired."

"Get some sleep, darling," Llewellyn said, and kissed her gently on her lips. She ran her hand across his cheek and returned the kiss. "Call me?" she said.

She got out of the taxi and ran into the lobby.

She was inside her room at ten o'clock, locked the door, then leaned against it. Her heart was racing, and she stood, unmoving, her arms behind her back, her palms pressed flat against the door. There was a tightness and an ache that ran up her back and across her shoulders. She moved a hand to her neck and rubbed at the tenseness. She moved to the window and looked out, staring blankly at the night sights. There was no message light on the phone, a small relief. She switched on a table lamp.

"Don't be frightened." The voice came from behind her.

"Peder!"

Aukrust stepped into the light and came to her. He put his arms around her. "I've missed you," his voice flat, without feeling.

Her head was on his shoulder, and she breathed in the smells that came with him. He turned her head, his huge hands holding her tightly. Then he kissed her. A lusty kiss, but without the passion she had felt from Llewellyn. She broke away.

"Why didn't you tell me you were coming?"

"I wanted to surprise you."

"You don't like surprises."

"I made an exception this time."

She looked at him closely. He looked tired and needed a shave and change of clothes.

"When I decided to come to New York I had barely enough time to get to the terminal. Then there was a delay in getting off the ground and more delay in the air. We didn't land until seven o'clock, and by then you had gone to your . . . what was it . . . dinner party?"

"Yes, and I was here at ten o'clock." She smiled briefly. "But why are you here?"

"To do what you failed to do."

"No, Peder, there's been enough."

"We are following a plan. No exceptions."

He took out his wallet and thrust it at her. It was thick with money. He took a handful of bills and waved them excitedly. "There will be more . . . much more."

"What is so special about the painting in Boston?"

Aukrust glared contemptuously at her. "Don't you realize that the police and their forensic experts are trying to learn who sprayed the precious paintings in England and Russia?" He laughed. "They are busy in laboratories attempting to discover what kind of chemicals could do such terrible damage." His eyes flared. "They wonder if another painting will be destroyed." His head shook crazily and his voice rose.

"But there will be no more. Not until the greatest of Cézanne's paintings are put together in a small museum in a little city in the south of France."

Astrid sat on the edge of the bed. "Then what will you do?"

"That will depend on the winter auctions. Cézannes should sell at record prices."

"And if they don't?"

"Then I may have to spray my chemicals over another painting. And another, if necessary. Perhaps it will be the now-famous portrait owned by your friend Llewellyn."

Astrid was on her feet. "No, Peder! That's a beautiful painting. I've stood in front of it. I've touched it. You can't!"

"Is your concern for the painting or for Llewellyn?"

"You told me to become his friend," she said defiantly.

He stood silently, his back to the single light in the room, his face in shadow. He took off his coat and threw it onto a chair, then suddenly his arms shot out, and he pulled her against him. He kissed her, a long, smothering kiss. Then he fell onto the bed. "I'm tired," he said; "undress me."

She bent over him and did as she was told. She had humored him this way before, when he said he was tired or when his mood was depressed or when his anger was at a boil.

"Take off your clothes and get beside me," he said.

"Please, Peder. I don't want you to hurt me."

"Take off your clothes," he demanded.

Slowly she undressed, then slipped under the sheet beside him. He rubbed his hand across her stomach, then over her thighs. "You are cold," he said.

"I'm frightened."

He turned onto his back and lay motionless. There had been times when they lay close together for a very long time before Aukrust decided whether to have sex or simply to fall into a deep sleep. Their sex was occasionally tender, but at other times his passion exploded and he caused her pain and humiliation.

"Listen carefully," he said. "We must talk about tomorrow."

Chapter 21

Before falling into a deep sleep, Aukrust explained the role Astrid was to play at the Boston Museum of Fine Arts. In the morning he went over her duties with numbing repetition.

She could no longer keep her feelings bottled up. "I'm frightened . . . please, Peder, please understand."

"Nei," he said gruffly and turned from her.

The plane landed and began to taxi to its ramp. Aukrust had placed his medicine case on the floor between his feer. He had carefully gone over its contents in his shop in Cannes and had either repackaged or eliminated any item that could possibly arouse suspicion when the bag made its journey through airport security.

"There is nothing to fear," he said in a soothing voice. He took her hands and gently rubbed them. "In a few hours it will be over, and you'll be on your way back to New York." He smiled at her and whispered, "You are very precious to me." In that instant a fresh surge of confidence swept through her.

It was agreed that they would separate and not meet again until they reached the critical part of the plan Aukrust had so carefully put together. Astrid was wearing a gray suit with low-heeled shoes. Her dark wig was neatly combed. She lengthened the strap on her handbag and draped it over her shoulder then strode out to the taxis. She gave an address in Beacon Hill, a shop where she browsed before going into several other stores. Shortly after noon, she picked over a salad in a neighborhood restaurant. She looked at her watch frequently, and as she was preparing to pay her check she checked a cosmetic case inside her handbag. Her fingers felt for a hypodermic needle. Astrid knew about needles and about finding a vein. This time the syringe contained thiopental sodium. "Pentothal," Aukrust had assured her; "a short duration, garden variety anesthesia."

She visited a souvenir shop where she purchased a bright red plastic lobster and put it into a small bag to enhance the image of a tourist on her first visit to Boston.

Aukrust had also taken a taxi. He had gone to Cambridge, across the Charles River, and to the Fogg Art Museum. He made a hasty tour of the rooms, bought a thin art book at the gift shop, and was also carrying a small paper bag that suggested he was on a holiday and was enjoying the great art offered by Boston's museums. At two o'clock he hailed a taxi and a half hour later was in the Museum of Fine Arts.

He wore a tweed jacket and a tan cashmere cap and fit unobtrusively into the crowds that had come to see the American Artists in New England exhibition. He very carefully checked his medicine case and watched the attendant put it on a nearby rack.

He went first through the New England Artists exhibition, then to the second-floor galleries. As he had anticipated, there were not many visitors, as attention was focused on the exhibition on the first floor. He picked up a brochure with a floor plan of the museum, studied it for several minutes, then proceeded slowly through three rooms of early European art. He was scouting for changes that had been made since his last visit: new television cameras, ropes to hold the tourists farther away from the paintings. But he found that security in the galleries was no more stringent than during his first tour of the museum.

He entered the Impressionists gallery and made a quick

inventory, carefully measuring distances and timing every move. He confirmed that Cézanne's self-portrait was still in its center position on the main wall and that the long bench was still directly opposite the painting. A single attendant was on duty, and a solitary visitor stood in front of a painting of cornflowers by Monet.

Aukrust activated the timer on his watch then walked briskly to the staircase, down to the tapestry gallery, and past the lower rotunda to the checkroom. He looked at his watch again: fifty-one seconds. He could do it in forty-five. At several minutes before three he took the stairway down to the cafeteria, where he took a cup of coffee to a table and waited until 3:15.

Astrid had walked through Boston Common to Boylston Street, where she hailed a taxi, and arrived at the museum shortly after three. She entered the main entrance, went directly into the rotunda and past a portion of the New England Artists exhibition to the wide stairway she had climbed four days before. She leaned against the railing and closed her eyes, feeling her heart pounding and the terrible fear returning. She remembered how Peder had smiled at her, how he assured her it would be over quickly and she would be on her way back to New York. It would be all right, she thought, and continued up the stairs.

Aukrust had gone to the front of the museum and then to the Egyptian rooms on the second floor. He would approach the Impressionists gallery from the east wing. At 3:35 Astrid was in the Barbizon gallery standing in front of a painting by Millet. She stared at *The Sower* for a full minute but would be unable to remember anything about the picture because her mind was riveted on the instructions Peder had drilled into her. At 3:40 she stepped the Impressionists gallery and slowly worked her way past four paintings. Only one concerned her. The plaque next to it read:

PAUL CÉZANNE, FRENCH, 1839–1906
SELF-PORTRAIT WITH BERET
OIL ON CANVAS, 25 X 20 IN.
C. 1898–99

She backed away and sat on the bench. The guard shuffled in and out of the wide doorway. He was young and bored and passed the time restacking the folders in a rack attached to the wall. At the far end of the gallery a couple moved from painting to painting. A student sat cross-legged on the floor, a pad in her lap, copying the figures in a Gaugin painting.

Aukrust came into the gallery. He looked at his watch, and at 3:45 the brochure with the museum's floor plan fell from his hand. He picked it up. It was the signal.

Astrid opened her purse and, from a plastic pouch, took a damp wad of cotton and rubbed it vigorously over the inside of her arm and several inches above her hand. She made a fist, then expertly inserted the hypodermic needle into a vein. Quickly she returned the syringe to her purse and snapped it closed. She had started to count as soon as she had squeezed out the Pentothal. She lost count at thirteen. Her head sagged, and she slumped forward onto the floor.

The art student saw her fall and ran to her. "Help, someone. Get help!"

The guard came to Astrid's side, and the young couple rushed to her but stood by helplessly. Aukrust appeared and knelt beside her.

"I'm a doctor," he said with a heavy accent. He lowered his head and listened for her breathing. Gently, he opened her eyelids then nodded with relief. To the little group that had assembled Aukrust said, "She's breathing normally. But we must not take chances. I'll get my medicine case." To the guard he said, "We'll need water, and tell your superior we may need an ambulance." He took off his jacket and placed it over her, motioning for the student to sit where Astrid's head could rest in her lap.

He went off at a trot to claim his medicine case and returned to Astrid's side in slightly more than two minutes. The guard had returned and held two paper cups of water. "Gut, gut," Aukrust said. He selected a vial from his case and emptied the white powder it contained into one of the cups. He raised Astrid's head and let the liquid trickle into her mouth.

Two uniformed men came into the gallery and went hurriedly to the little group. Aukrust asked where they could take the young woman. "We must keep her warm."

"There's a first-aid room on the first floor."

"Please take her there. I'll follow." They gently picked her up, and a small procession formed, led by the two men carrying Astrid and followed by the others, who were curiously concerned. The gallery was empty, as were the adjoining rooms. Aukrust had gambled that he would have a precious minute to carry out his destructive assignment. He had won.

It took ten seemingly endless seconds to apply a heavy coating of solvent on the self-portrait. He then sprayed the air with a clear and odorless solution, a new chemical he had experimented with, one that produced spectacular results. Instead of masking the solvent's harsh chemical odor with another strong but recognizable scent, the new chemical acted as a malodor counteractent, a formulation that caused a temporary anosmia, a loss of the sense of smell of anyone who passed through the room. He sprayed the air once more, then returned the can to his medicine case.

When Aukrust located Astrid in the first-aid room she was sitting on the edge of a cot, sipping from a glass of water. "How is my pretty patient?" he asked in his thick accent.

"They said that you helped me."

He took her hand. "Feeling all right, are you?"

She nodded. "Yes. A little—" she touched her head.

"Like a dizziness?" he said.

Astrid smiled. "Yes, a little."

"Are you visiting friends?"

She nodded, then smiled. "I am to meet them at the hotel."

"Perhaps I can take you there."

A guard came into the room. "The ambulance is here."

Aukrust ran his hand over Astrid's forehead, then felt her neck. It was a very professional and authentic summing up of her condition.

"I don't think we'll need the ambulance." He looked at the assortment of personnel that had crowded into the small room. "It was a precaution, in case the young lady had a serious problem. But I see she is recovering, and I will be able to escort her to her friends."

A man carrying a cellular phone entered the room. A thin, metal name plate pinned above the breast pocket on his coat said he was a supervisor. He leaned down and said to Astrid, "May I have your name? Just a precaution to protect you as well as the museum."

"I will take responsibility," Aukrust said. "She is a little disoriented and frightened. You understand."

"Then, your name, sir," the man insisted.

Aukrust gave a hard stare at the supervisor and at two uniformed guards still lingering by the door. "Metzger," he replied softly, and turned away. "Dr. Metzger," he repeated in an accented mumble.

"Do you have a local address or—"

"You will have no worry about the young lady. She merely fainted and will be perfectly all right by the time I return her to her friends." He took Astrid's arm and helped her to her feet. He reassured the supervisor there would be no further problem then guided Astrid to the main entrance and a line of waiting taxis. Aukrust gave the driver instructions. "Logan Airport, international departure."

"You feel all right?" He spoke in Norwegian.

"Yes, all right," she answered, also in Norwegian. "A little thirsty."

"It does that sometimes."

She turned her eyes from him. "I went past the painting, the portrait, and I looked at it . . . at him. I wished that it didn't have to be . . ."

"It is done," he said with finality. His hand tightened around hers."The reporters will make a sensation of what happened today."

"And the police, too."

He nodded. "Yes, the police," he added zestfully. "They will have new samples of the chemicals, just like all the others. But what else will there be for them? The doctor who came to the aid of the pretty lady who fainted? The pretty lady?"

"Should you say you are Dr. Metzger?"

"At times I am Dr. Metzger. Besides, I'll be who I want to be," he said defiantly.

Astrid held his hand tightly. "Let me come with you."

"Not now. I have business in Cannes and perhaps in Aix-en-Provence."

The taxi stopped at the international building. He kissed her, a perfunctory kiss, the kind a husband gives a wife who has dutifully driven him to the airport to catch a plane that will take him to more exciting adventures. He got out of the taxi without another word or gesture.

An hour later, Astrid's shuttle to New York rose up through a ceiling of black clouds and leveled out in a purplish-blue sky. Long pink clouds were strung out like ribbons that had come untied from a magenta red sun. Astrid stared at the streaks of color reflected on the airplane's wing and felt alone and unrooted. She closed her eyes and softly cried.

Chapter 22

Frédéric Weisbord lived in the Saint Étienne district of Nice on a sloping acre of land that his wife Cécile had selected to satisfy her somewhat eccentric love of gardening. The buildings consisted of a rambling turn-of-the-century house and a structure that doubled as garage and barn. Beyond the latter were the gardens: one for vegetables, the other for flowers, where once were planted ten long rows of clairette grapes. The Weisbords had purchased their property at the same time Gaston and Margueritte DeVilleurs settled into their home in Antibes, and for twenty-one years Cécile cared for her precious flowers and vegetables. Frédéric, for his part, became so deeply involved in the olive oil business that he ultimately closed his private law practice. Early in their marriage Cécile miscarried and was never again able to bear a child, yet even the lack of a family had become an agreeable arrangement in what most people who knew the Weisbords considered to be a union between two eccentrics.

Tragedy struck when Cécile's heart, weakened in childhood by rheumatic fever, could not keep up with the arduous hours she devoted to her gardens. Less than a month into her sixty-sixth year, on a sunny June day, just after she had divided her prized begonias and had begun to replant them, her heart stopped. Weisbord had been off on one of his business trips, and when he returned home he found a long black hearse in the driveway. The housekeeper, a no-nonsense

Italian woman named Idi, described how she had discovered Cécile, too late to bring medical attention.

For six weeks, Weisbord mourned the death of his wife though not her constant nagging to stop smoking. After another few weeks, the new widower returned to his old schedules and soon was traveling more than ever.

Almost a year to the day following Cécile's death, Gaston DeVilleurs died. Weisbord actually grieved; at least he went through the motions; and went so far as to shed authentic tears at the funeral. But forty-eight hours after Gaston was laid to rest, Weisbord turned to the important task of settling the dead man's affairs and putting in motion all the terms and conditions that he had carefully integrated into Gaston's last will and testament. Weisbord had devised a few dozen ways to receive fees and commissions while Gaston was alive, and now that he was dead, the lawyer knew exactly how to extract the largest of all payoffs.

The DeVilleurs paintings were worth a fortune, and Weisbord stood to collect a 17.5 percent commission on the gross proceeds from the sale of each one. Weisbord's income from the sale of either of the two Cézannes in the DeVilleurs collection might be as much as $4 million. All of the lawyer's fees could be found on seven of the fifty-six pages required to set forth the details of the will—a masterpiece of obfuscation.

There were complications, however. Margueritte had proved to be more obstinate and independent than he had anticipated. Her threat to sell the self-portrait to the Musée Granet was troubling, but considerably more annoying was the disappearance of the painting from the DeVilleurs collection. It was obvious that the owner of the new art and framing studio in Cannes was involved so Weisbord would visit Peder Aukrust and demand the return of the painting.

On Friday, the day after the DeVilleurs portrait disappeared, Weisbord drove to Cannes and located the framing shop on Rue Faure, encountering a blind that had been pulled down on the door with a small sign attached to it, which read *Fermé*. When he inquired with neighboring merchants, he was told that the new proprietor, a Norwegian named Aukrust, kept to himself but was known to take occasional trips to Paris, where he would try his luck in the smaller auctions. On Sunday Weisbord read in the newspaper that a Cézanne self-portrait in the Boston Museum of Fine Arts had been destroyed. He scissored out the article and put the clipping in the top drawer of his desk.

Not until Monday afternoon did he receive an answer to his repeated phone calls to the framing shop. Then he learned that the shop would be open the following morning at ten.

Shortly after ten, Weisbord entered the shop. A young artist was making an impassioned presentation of his paintings to Peder Aukrust, who flatly refused to take more than one painting on consignment. "Better than a boot in the ass," the artist conceded then gathered up his assorted renderings of water scenes and brushed past Weisbord.

"I am the owner," Aukrust said, "What may I do for you?"

Weisbord fished out a cigarette and lit it.

"Please don't smoke," Aukrust said and pointed to a pot of sand inside the door. "Sometimes the oils are not completely set on the paintings." He held up the canvas left by the just departed artist. "See? The smoke will cling to the light colors."

Weisbord eyed the big man skeptically, drew heavily on the cigarette, then plunged it into the sand. He coughed, only slightly at first, then into a continuous and irritatingly loud outbreak.

Aukrust waited for the coughing to subside. "How can I help you?" he asked again.

"I am Frédéric Weisbord, associate and legal adviser to the late Gaston DeVilleurs—"

"Madame DeVilleurs has mentioned your name," Aukrust interrupted.

"You were in her home last week as was Bilodeau from the Granet in Aix. I was there to explain and enforce the terms of her husband's will, and—"

"I am very busy, Monsieur Weisbord," Aukrust broke in. "What exactly is it you want?"

"You can tell me where you've hidden the Cézanne self-portrait," Weisbord demanded with a clear, firm voice pulled miraculously from the miasma in his tobacco-tarred throat.

Aukrust held out his huge hands. "A Cézanne in my shop? You flatter me, Monsieur Weisbord."

"There, behind that door." Weisbord took several steps.

Aukrust moved faster and stood in front of the door. "There's nothing there, only my workroom and supplies."

"I want to see," Weisbord said stubbornly.

"This is my shop, or have you forgotten?" Aukrust said, a touch of irritation in his voice. "If you're looking for a Cézanne, go to Paris. There are twenty-four in the Louvre."

"Last Thursday," Weisbord sputtered. "You . . . you took that painting!" The painful wheezing returned, and he began to spit into his handkerchief. "Don't deny it!"

The wheeze became a scratching, guttural noise, then for a moment he made no sound at all for the simple reason that there was no air in his lungs with which to make any sort of noise. He gasped, desperately trying to breathe, his face white as bleached bone. Aukrust looked on, fascinated that he was witnessing the awful process of suffocation. Suddenly, Weisbord shook violently, and air magically flowed into him. He fell into a chair, his chest heaving heavily.

"A drink of water, please," he said in a thin, nearly inaudible voice.

Aukrust eyed him closely. "There's no water here."

"There must be water in that room!" Weisbord said. "I won't follow you."

Aukrust hesitated for a moment, then unlocked the door

into the back room and went into it, closing the door behind him. He returned with a glass of water. The lawyer took it and drank.

"I suffered from tuberculosis when I was young and occasionally have these spells. A nuisance, nothing more."

He stood and as if there had been no interruption said with a voice now fully restored, "I am here to recover Madame DeVilleurs's painting. If you refuse to give it to me, I shall take other measures. Hear what I say, Monsieur Aukrust; the full force of the law is on my side, and I will use it if I must."

Aukrust ignored the threat and took Weisbord's arm and led him to the door. "Smoking is very dangerous," he said, pretending to care. He turned the handle. "But if you threaten me, you'll find you are flirting with a force more dangerous than cigarettes. Even more deadly."

Aukrust gently pushed the lawyer through the door, closed it, then pulled down the blind. The sign that read *Fermé* swung slowly like a pendulum.

Chapter 23

ГОСУДАРСТВЕННЫЙ ЭРМИТАЖ
Ilena Petrov

M. K. Malinkousky
Member of the Presidium
Russian Academy of Arts
Kropotkinskaya ul. 21
119034 Moscow

Dear Mr. Malinkousky:

Aleksei Druzhinin, of the University of Moscow, suggested that I write to you, and to send along his personal best wishes. Professor Druzhinin was my favorite teacher when I attended the university, and he is deeply concerned over the loss of our Cézanne self-portrait. He believes you may know of ways to put the information in this letter into the hands of people who will find the guilty ones.

During the weeks since the incident, I have asked the St. Petersburg police to take a more active role in the investigation, but they have shown little interest. I was interviewed briefly, but could only repeat how I had discovered the painting the morning after it was destroyed. Two museum guards were also interviewed, but they had been assigned to the auditorium the previous day and had not been near gallery 318 where the Cézanne was displayed. There have been no other inquiries, and I cannot explain the indifference. Perhaps it is because there is so much art in the Hermitage that the police feel the loss of a Cézanne is but one drop in a vast lake of so many paintings.

I have made inquiries on my own and have talked with every worker who might remember seeing a person or group of people who acted in any unusual way. One person, a floor supervisor who has been a museum employee for many years, did recall talking briefly to a man who had a lung illness because the tubes in his nose were attached to a cylinder of oxygen that he carried on a strap slung over his shoulder. The man was bent over and had been in the galleries next to 318 and, quite certainly, in 318 also. When the supervisor was asked if this man acted strangely in any way, he said he did not think so at the time, but when he thought about the man, he remembered that he wasn't old at all and had a strong voice, not an old man's voice.

There were two more pages of amateurish speculation and Oxby had read it all several times, but on his final reading he stopped after reaching the description of the visitor with the cylinder of oxygen. Did he really have emphysema? Did he have any authentic breathing disorder? Oxby's copy of the letter had come from Investigator Sam Turner, Police Division, Interpol, who had received it from the Moscow office of Russia's National Central Bureau, which had been sent the letter by agent Yuri Murashkin in the National Russian Intelligence Office, who had in turn been given the letter by M. K. Malinkousky in the Russian Academy of Arts.

Oxby sent Sam Turner a fax:

Sam: In re the Ilena Petrov letter: Can you arrange for an interrogation of the supervisor who saw and talked with the man carrying an oxygen cylinder? I'm curious to know in what language they spoke, how old the man was, and if he remembers any other physical characteristics; where precisely was the man when first seen, and where precisely when last seen. Run as complete an interrogation as you can under the circumstances. I know you're good at this sort of thing.

J. Oxby

Chapter 24

Margueritte DeVilleurs guided Peder Aukrust over the back roads to the Chateau du Domaine St. Martin, a small luxury hotel eight miles from Nice, tucked away in the hills above Vence. They lunched by the pool where the sun was warm and the air was cooled by October breezes coming from the Montagne de Cheiron to the north. Margueritte was at her happiest when she described Frédéric Weisbord's wild frustration over the disappearance of the painting. "He was like a child searching for his favorite toy, and when he couldn't find it, he was undone by it all. Such a fool." Her smile faded and her head shook. "His lungs are so weak, he'll kill himself, and I'll have no regrets or feel even the smallest sorrow."

"He paid me a visit," Aukrust said casually.

"In your shop?" There was surprise in her voice. "He knows you have the painting?"

"He suspects it. He threatened to call the police."

"What did you tell him?"

"That he should go to Paris if he is looking for Cézannes."

"You haven't heard the last of Freddy. He has political connections and isn't above giving a bribe when he needs help."

Aukrust nodded his understanding, then said, "What have you done about the will?"

She shook her head sadly. "Freddy has been making

changes to Gaston's will for the last two years, I now realize. Occasionally he would give me a paper to sign—I'd signed dozens over the years. But I didn't know that I had agreed to have the paintings put up for auction, with the money going into a trust. And I certainly didn't know that Freddy would be entitled to commissions from each sale."

Aukrust said, "He won't have anything to say about the portrait because he'll never touch it again."

Margueritte shook her head, "Don't be put off by his frail health."

They went about the afternoon as if they were old friends, with Margueritte occasionally nannying the big Norwegian with her good-natured warmth. "You have made this a happy day for this old lady," she said as their day together finally ended.

He looked at her somewhat quizzically. "Why are you being kind to me?"

Margueritte showed surprise. "What a silly question, Peder. Because I like you."

"You are only saying that because you want me to do something for you. A favor—"

"How can you, if you don't know me?"

"No, Peder. I'm saying it because I mean it."

"Perhaps if I knew you better, I wouldn't like you, but I hope that isn't how it would ever be." She had spoken directly to him, but he had turned away from her and was staring numbly at the darkening sky.

She put her hand on his arm. "I'll say it again, Peder. Please be careful."

It was after eleven when Aukrust turned onto Rue Faure and drove past his shop. He parked, turned off the engine and the lights, and waited for a lone walker to pass his car and vanish in the shadows. The street was dark except for the night lights in display windows and a solitary streetlamp nearly fifty yards away. He walked slowly toward his shop, paused to look in the window of a bookseller, then went ahead to the door of his shop and unlocked it. He slipped inside and felt along the wall for a panel of switches, and at the instant his fingers touched the light switch a fist crashed into his stomach and another fell solidly on his jaw. He lashed back, landing a glancing, undamaging blow, then was struck a third time on the top of his shoulder with a hard object that also scraped against the side of his head and tore his ear.

The pain was intense. He stumbled backward, separating himself a valuable few feet from the ambush. He was certain there were two men, armed no doubt, but he had no idea with what. His only advantage was in knowing how his shop was laid out—the location of counters, doors, and light switches. To his right, in the darkness, he heard heavy breathing then a voice that spoke in a slangy French he couldn't understand. Another voice replied, and he heard a faint shuffling. He edged along the counter until he was in front of the locked door that led to the back of his shop. The bare amount of light in the shop came through three small diamond-shaped glass panels in the entrance door. Two figures were vaguely silhouetted in the dim light.

Aukrust opened a drawer under the counter and took out two spools of picture wire. He rolled one of the spools across the floor, and as soon as it clattered against the wall, he rolled the other.

"What is that?" one voice asked.

"The flashlight! Put it on!" the other replied.

In that brief moment of confusion, Aukrust rushed at the nearest figure, crashing furiously into a small body, his right hand grabbing a handful of hair, his left smashing powerfully against a mouth, snapping off teeth and causing blood to fall over cut lips.

"*Arrête! Arrête!*" a frightened voice yelled out.

Aukrust responded with a backhanded swipe to the face, but was at that instant hit low in the back by whatever had crashed into his shoulder a half minute earlier. As he turned away he caught what turned out to be a four-foot length of pipe. He held onto it tightly with both hands, then yanked and twisted it, throwing his attacker off balance. He grabbed a shirt and began pummeling a head and a chest. Aukrust's shoulder and the side of his head and ear were bleeding, and the pain he felt became his license to inflict pain. One of the attackers bolted for door and was gone before Aukrust could react.

He locked the entrance and turned on the light. The remaining assailant was sitting on the floor, his back against a display case, his arms, like a doll's, flopped out beside him. There was both fear and anger in the face that stared up at Aukrust. Aukrust returned the stare, sizing up a twenty-year old with black, matted hair and a scruffy mustache that failed to make him look any older. Blood oozed from the corner of his mouth.

"Who sent you?"

The eyes on the young man hardened, and he did not answer.

"Weisbord? Was it Weisbord?" He spied a piece of paper in the young man's shirt pocket and snatched it away before a hand reached up feebly to prevent him.

At the top of a brief note was printed the name André, followed by the address of Aukrust's shop, and below that a phone number. Aukrust went to the phone behind the counter and dialed the number. It was late, the phone would not be answered immediately. He counted the rings . . . six . . . seven, then a woman's voice.

"Allo? . . . allo oui?"

"Monsieur Weisbord?" Aukrust said in a loud whisper.

"Who is calling?" the voice asked warily.

"Tell him"—Aukrust paused—"that it is Doctor Turgot."

"He is asleep, I—"

Aukrust put down the receiver.

He came back to the young man who was using his shirt
to wipe the blood from his face. Aukrust waved the paper.

"Are you André, or was that your cowardly friend who
ran away?"

The young man spit at Aukrust, a feeble spray of blood
and saliva that fell short on the floor.

"Get on your feet," he commanded.

André, if indeed that was his name, stared blankly at
Aukrust.

Aukrust snarled the command again. "On your feet, I
said."

"Take a shit," André muttered.

Aukrust aimed a vicious kick at André's shoulder, and as
he did, André turned aside, rolled over and came up into a
crouch, his right hand holding a double-edged, six-inch
knife. Aukrust froze for an instant, sizing up the unexpected
reversal. He took a step toward the length of pipe that lay
between the two but nearer to André's feet. André knew how
to handle a knife and with the agility of a fencer stepped to
his right and in the same motion sliced the knife across
Aukrust's arm. The blade cut through his shirt then across
his arm. It happened so quickly Aukrust thought the knife
had missed, then he felt a sting where the razor-sharp edge
had cut his skin.

"Damn you!" Aukrust roared, and lunged forward. André
tried stepping aside but too late, as one of Aukrust's powerful hands hit him high in the chest and spun him a half turn.
Aukrust grabbed the wrist of the hand holding the knife and
twisted it until there was a cracking sound, and André
shouted in horrible pain.

"I'll break your other hand and both feet, you little bastard!"

Aukrust struck him on the side of the face, then hit him
again causing André to moan and collapse to the floor,
where he writhed in the pain that Aukrust had inflicted so
skillfully.

"It would be my pleasure to continue," Aukrust said, "but I have another purpose for you." He picked up the knife, folded it, and slid it into his pocket. Then he unlocked the door into his workroom and went to his pharmacy, where he cleaned and bandaged the cut on his arm and applied a salve to the abrasions on the back of his head and on the painful split in his ear.

"It was foolish of Weisbord to send you here. How much did he pay?"

The young tough squeezed the hand with the broken finger in a vain attempt to stop the sharp pain that had traveled up his arm into his shoulder. André's defiance gave way to fearful respect. "My finger," he said pitifully; "can you help?"

"I'll break another," Aukrust said, as if he meant to do just that. "Answer my question, André, what did Weisbord pay you?"

"I'm not André, I am Pioli." Uncontrollably, he began to cry.

Aukrust leaned down and carefully examined Pioli's arm, then the hand. The phalange bone in the middle finger was torn clean and had pierced the skin. Aukrust stared at it with a certain fascination, holding on to Pioli's shaking hand with what seemed to be genuine concern.

"Tell me how much Weisbord paid you."

The youth sniffed back his tears but said nothing.

Aukrust's grip tightened, and with no more effort than he would exert to remove a piece of lint from his sweater, he flicked a finger against the exposed bone. The pain was excruciating, and as Pioli tried to pull free, Aukrust's hand tightened around his arm like giant pincers.

"Tell me!"

"A thousand francs," Pioli gasped.

"Each?"

"For both."

Aukrust let the arm go free. "You risk an arrest, maybe

your life, for five hundred francs? You are very stupid, Pioli, or very desperate."

Pioli pointed to the bandages Aukrust had put on the counter. He held up his hand.

"Get up," Aukrust commanded.

Pioli had difficulty standing. He steadied himself against the display case and looked at Aukrust. "Please?"

Aukrust glowered and nodded toward the door. "Out!"

Pioli reached the door then turned back. "I know something you want to know."

"Then tell me . . . and quickly."

Pioli held up his hand again. "You'll help me?"

Aukrust stared at Pioli, now looking very young and vulnerable. "If what you tell me is important."

Pioli stepped toward him. "When you go to your home tonight there will be someone waiting for you. He is called LeToque, and he will do anything when he is paid enough money. Even kill."

Chapter 25

Aukrust knew precisely where to insert the needle. He injected thirty mg of chloroprocaine, and when Pioli's pain subsided, he sterilized the wound then deftly extended the finger, repositioning the bones in their original alignment, then splinted the broken finger and the adjacent index finger together. Aukrust gave Pioli a bottle of peroxide and a towel to rub over his cuts, where the blood was beginning to turn dark and harden. When he was reassembled into a more reasonable and less painful condition, Pioli said, with growing respect, "*Merci.*"

"I don't want your thanks," Aukrust said, "but you'll stay with me until we find what kind of surprise LeToque has planned." He instructed Pioli to remain on the floor while he inventoried his medicine case, removing some items and adding others from his pharmacy. One of the items he picked out was an aerosol can that was an inch in diameter and fit into the palm of his hand. After testing the spray, he replaced the cap and put the can in his shirt pocket. He also filled two small plastic bottles with a milky fluid and put them into the pockets of his sweater. He handed the medicine case to Pioli, relocked the door into his workroom, and secured the front of his shop. It was fifteen minutes past midnight when the station wagon pulled away from the curb and headed toward the suburban apartment Aukrust had rented in the town of Vallauris, a suburb to the east of Cannes. Vallauris was an ordinary community, where he would be unnoticed and where neighbors would be likely to confine their questions to the weather and the latest soccer scores. He had located an old building which had opened a hundred years earlier as a school, was made into a ceramics factory, then, in its final metamorphosis, it was gutted and rebuilt into cheap apartments.

Apparently Weisbord had gone to extraordinary lengths to find him, or as Margueritte predicted, the old lawyer had called in a few chips he was owed by the local police. Aukrust was now angry that he had signed a month-to-month lease under his own name instead of the name Metzger that had served him so well.

The buildings along the street were a mix of small houses, factories, and an old structure in the process of being converted into still more apartments. They walked close to these buildings, avoiding the small pool of light created by a single streetlamp and an occasional spotlight shining on the gates in the chainlink fences surrounding the factories. The local residents parked their Peugeots and Toyotas on the street or in the one small parking area, which adjoined a warehouse. He inspected each car, searching for an unfamiliar one that didn't belong in the neighborhood. Then he spotted a silver Porsche 911.

Aukrust pointed at the car and whispered to Pioli, "Is that LeToque's car?"

Apparently the anesthetic was wearing off, because Pioli's concentration was on rubbing his sore hand. He nodded, "I think so."

"I don't want an opinion. Is that LeToque's car?"

Pioli sized it up more carefully and said that it was.

"Go see if anyone's in it, but do it carefully."

Pioli crossed the street and worked his way to the rear of the Porsche. When he disappeared in the darkness, a distressing thought swept over Aukrust: The little bastard's run off to warn LeToque. Seconds later and from behind him came Pioli's voice. "For sure that's his car; his girlfriend's behind the wheel listening to the radio."

He was relieved that Pioli had returned, but LeToque's girlfriend was a problem because she had a clear view of the apartment's front entrance. He went back to his car and took a flat box from his medicine case, and as he gave instructions to Pioli, he took a hypodermic from the case, plunged the needle into a vial, and loaded the syringe, then pointed the needle straight up and squeezed a few drops from its tip. They approached the low-slung car from the rear. When Aukrust signaled, Pioli tapped a coin lightly on the rear window, then Aukrust rapped loudly against the driver's door.

"Police," he said firmly.

The window opened several inches.

"What have I done?" said a high-pitched, worried voice.

"Identification," Aukrust demanded.

"I'm waiting for a friend. Is that illegal?"

"Get out of the car," he said harshly.

After a few seconds the car door slowly opened and long slim legs in black stockings swung out, followed by the rest of a girl who was perhaps twenty, tall, and with large eyes surrounded by too much blue and purple makeup.

Aukrust took hold of her bare arm and expertly inserted the needle into the flesh near her shoulder. Her eyes widened instantly and stared helplessly as the needle was withdrawn. Her mouth opened as if to speak, and she collapsed. Aukrust caught her and pushed her sagging body into the car, pulled the seat belt around her, and turned off the radio. It all happened in less than a minute.

Pioli looked at the girl then at Aukrust, and said with fright in his voice, "Is she dead?"

Aukrust shook his head. "It was past her bedtime, she's asleep."

There were six small apartments in the building where Aukrust lived, two on each floor, with no elevator and a single front entrance; fire-escape ladders were suspended from a window in each apartment in the rear. Aukrust's apartment was on the first floor, to the left upon entering, and consisted of a bedroom, a combination living room/kitchen, and a bathroom. Several steps led up to a small porchlike slab of concrete and to the front entrance, which was a steel door painted brown to look like wood. Inside the entrance was a long, narrow hall with stairs to the upper floors at the back of the hall. The doors into the first-floor apartments were immediately inside the entrance, and under the staircase was another door that opened into a tiny room inside Aukrust's apartment that at one time had been intended as a kitchen but now served as a bedroom closet. It had occurred to Aukrust that the door connecting the closet with the hall might some day be a necessary way to leave the apartment, but he had never considered it as a means by which he might enter it.

They took off their shoes, then Aukrust quietly unlocked the front door and guided Pioli to a cramped recess under the stairs in the back of the hall. Aukrust wished the quarrelsome couple who lived above him would come home at that moment, arguing as always after an evening of drinking, causing a perfect diversion. Speaking softly and slowly, Aukrust told Pioli what he wanted him to do, repeated the instructions, and put five hundred francs into his good hand.

"Do exactly as I told you," he whispered, "and when you have finished, go immediately to the bus terminal and back to Nice. You will call me at my shop next week." He put a hand over the sore bruises on Pioli's neck, not to show compassion but to convey a clear message. "And tell no one about tonight. No one."

Pioli went to the front door and let himself out with no more noise than the flapping of a sparrow's wings. He put on his shoes and began to half-hum and half-sing a tuneless song as if he were coming home from a long, liquid evening with friends. He returned to the front door, rapped against it as he opened it, and when inside, closed the door firmly, and to be certain it was securely shut, opened and closed it again. He climbed the stairs, still singing, dropping his feet heavily on the wooden treads until he reached the top floor, where he pulled off his shoes and, with the same silence as before, retreated down the stairs and out into the night.

While Pioli was performing, Aukrust had worked his way into the closet, then into the bedroom, and when Pioli's outrageous singing stopped, he stood at the door connecting the bedroom to the room in front where he imagined LeToque was waiting. Ten feet in front of him was a bed and a night table on which were a lamp, a telephone, and a clock radio with luminous green numbers. He took the receiver off the hook and placed it so the earpiece faced the door, the faint steady hum of a dial tone coming now from some place in the dark. In a minute, possibly half again that much time, the dial tone would change to another signal announcing that the phone was not set properly in its cradle. He took the aerosol can from his pocket and removed the cap.

The noise from the phone grew louder, now an annoying sound, purposely so, and perfectly pitched to penetrate into the next room.

"What's that?" a voice said in a hoarse whisper.

Aukrust positioned himself just inside the door; a small amount of light from the faraway streetlamp found its way through the window. The only other light came from the green numerals that said the time was 1:04.

The pulsing noise from the telephone grew louder.

"*Merde!*" LeToque shouted. He was now in the doorway.

Aukrust guessed that if LeToque identified the noise as coming from the phone he would blame himself for not putting the receiver back properly. But it was just as likely that LeToque would wonder how the two parts of the phone had become separated, since he had not used the phone.

Based solely on Pioli's inadequate description of LeToque as being thin, tough, and not very tall, it was not possible for Aukrust to assess his adversary. For certain, he was armed. But how? Weisbord had sent the young toughs to rough him up, and now he pondered if LeToque had been sent to search the apartment for the portrait and, if he didn't find it, to deliver an even stronger message to Aukrust.

LeToque moved cautiously into the bedroom. "Damned telephone!" he muttered and searched for the source of the troubling sound, swearing in frustration. When he located the receiver he slammed it onto the base.

"Who did this?" LeToque demanded. "Who?"

Aukrust knew that LeToque was standing next to the bed, two or three feet from the green numerals in the clock. He aimed the nozzle of the aerosol can at that spot, and to assure that LeToque faced him, he made a soft, scratching sound, like a small animal. Then he pressed his thumb against a metal slide, releasing a whoosh of air. A wide spray shot out, enveloping LeToque in a yellow mist that made his eyes burn with the pain of a live fire. LeToque raised his gun and squeezed off two rounds before he dropped his arm and began frantically to rub his eyes. One of the bullets tore across the top of Aukrust's left shoulder, and he fell to the floor before another shot might hit a more vulnerable spot. The shots had been muffled by a silencer, the sound like the clapping of hands.

The burning mist seeped into LeToque's mouth and nose, and the agony increased as he thrashed on the bed, then rolled onto the floor, clutching at his throat and shouting for water. He got to his knees, then doubled over, groaning as the fire went into his chest. Aukrust put on a light and examined his own wound before finishing the job of putting LeToque under his control. The bullet had grazed a bone on the top of his shoulder, seven inches from the middle of his throat; the wound was more painful than serious.

Aukrust pulled LeToque to his feet and forced him onto the bed. "Quiet!" he commanded. When LeToque tried to wrench himself free, Aukrust forced him back onto the bed. The powerful acids had reached LeToque's stomach, causing him to gag, then vomit. His body stiffened, and his breath came in short, painful bursts. "Water," he pleaded in a barely audible whisper.

Aukrust took a small plastic bottle from his pocket and soaked the end of a towel he took from the bathroom. He patted LeToque's face with it and squeezed drops onto his eyes.

Eagerly, LeToque tore the bottle from Aukrust's hands and drank the contents.

"You will be surprised to learn that you were sprayed with nothing more than the oils extracted from plants and vegetables. Some very rare, of course, but others you will know as mustard. Also piperine, one of the exotic pepper plants." Aukrust spoke dispassionately, in the tone of a scientist pleased by the results of a successful experiment. He found the gun under the bed, a small-caliber revolver that could have done nasty damage from short range. He emptied it and slipped it into the drawer of his night table. Then he went into the bathroom to clean and bandage his own wound. When he returned, LeToque was still lying on the bed, moaning feebly and swearing viciously.

Aukrust said, "I was careless. But you were stupid."

LeToque tried to reply, but could manage no more than an incoherent wheeze as his throat was all but paralyzed. The sound reminded Aukrust of Frédéric Weisbord after a severe coughing attack.

"The antidote will clear up your lungs and stomach." He put another bottle containing the soothing milky fluid on the bed beside LeToque.

Aukrust put on his shirt. The clock now read 1:20. It had been a mere thirty minutes since he had put LeToque's girlfriend to sleep. She would be awake but drowsy, and she and LeToque together would not add up to an intimidating partnership. But helping each other, they could manage to drive away in the silver Porsche.

Chapter 26

"It's a goddamned good thing the Paley collection went to the Modern," Curt Berrien said, looking up from a generous splash of Wild Turkey he had just poured into a bucket-sized old-fashioned glass. "Otherwise we'd be wet-nursing a portrait of Paul Cézanne at a cost of about ten grand a week."

It was nearing 5:30. The late afternoon sunlight was orange and warm and angled through the windows of Llewellyn's third-floor study and spilled over a thick red and gold Persian rug. As the sun moved, Clyde uncurled, stretched, and moved with it.

"I talked with my old friend Chauncey Eaton at the Fine Arts in Boston," Llewellyn said. "The poor guy needs some heavy consolation. It's as if he's lost his own brother."

"Chauncey's a sentimentalist, but I agree," Berrien said. "There's a crazy mentality out there that says it only happens to the other guy, but guess what? Sooner or later you're the other guy!" Berrien waggled a finger at the portrait. "Lew, you can't protect that painting with a dog, Fraser, and whatever goddamned kind of alarm system you've installed. The crazy SOBs that are burning up the portraits are too clever, and someone, namely, you, could get hurt pretty badly."

Fraser tapped on the door, opened it, ushered Alexander Tobias into the room, put a fresh ice bucket on the bar, and disappeared. Berrien greeted Tobias. "Good to see you,

Alex; meet Edwin Llewellyn, an old friend and a trustee of the Met. Also a man who serves civilized bourbon and owns that painting you're staring at." Berrien turned to Llewellyn. "Lew, this is Detective Sergeant Alex Tobias, Major Case Squad, N.Y.P.D."

They shook hands. "Thanks for joining us, Mr. Tobias, or is it Sergeant Tobias?"

"Alex," Tobias said simply and with a comfortable smile.

Llewellyn said, "Curt felt it was a good idea for you to see my house and that infamous painting; in fact he was just lecturing me on my dereliction and predicting that within a few days, the painting would be destroyed, or, failing that, Fraser, Clyde over there, and I would all be in the emergency room in St. Luke's Hospital."

If Llewellyn expected Tobias to share his little joke, he was disappointed.

"Very unpleasant places, emergency rooms." Tobias had an authentic New York accent: basic Manhattan with Bronx overtones. The portrait attracted him, and as he stepped in front of it, he took a small magnifying glass from his coat pocket. "Do you mind?"

"Please, by all means," Llewellyn said.

Tobias inspected the painting carefully. "It's one of the last portraits he did of himself, at least from the look of it. Have you photographed it in black and white?"

"I'm embarrassed to say I've been putting it off," Llewellyn replied. "I keep meaning to bring a photographer over from the museum."

"You'll discover a dozen new details that don't pop out the way you normally see it."

Llewellyn looked at Berrien, who gave a knowing wink and nodded.

"Are you a student of Cézanne?" Llewellyn asked.

The answer did not come immediately. Then Tobias said, "Somewhat, I suppose, but I try to separate what Cézanne painted from what his paintings meant to the artists who came after him. I like the way he handled people. And his landscapes, particularly the country scenes. But not all those views of Sainte-Victoire." His eyes twinkled.

"Spoken like a teacher, not a mere student." Llewellyn's pleasure was punctuated by an approving smile. "A drink, Alex?"

"Scotch and a squeeze of soda, please."

Llewellyn had just put the drink together as Astrid came into the study. He said, "Marvelous surprise, darling; I wasn't expecting to see you."

"Am I interrupting?"

"Not at all; come along and meet my friends."

As usual she was perfectly dressed, this time in an Adolfo that cost someone a lot of money, and he wondered for a moment who the someone was. He led his guests to the windows, where they sank into oversized, overstuffed chairs.

"Alex, what do you make of all this horror with the paintings?"

"That I'd like to wring the neck of the son of a bitch that's doing it." A nod toward Astrid was his expiation. Tobias ran fingers through his thick hair. "We've got a psychiatrist and a behavioral psychologist on staff, and for the first time in memory they actually agree with each other. They believe it's the work of a well-educated male, unmarried, in his early forties, and a bona fide psychopath."

"Left-handed?" Berrien asked with a straight face.

Tobias smiled. "They'll figure that out, given enough time. Since the Boston episode, we've gone in high gear assembling reports from Europe and running our own chemical analyses. Now there's speculation that a man and woman working together may have destroyed the portrait in Boston, but there's not much to go on except conflicting witness identification and a few scraps of evidence that were sent to the forensic labs in Boston."

"That doesn't sound very encouraging," Llewellyn said.

"There's a lot of hand-wringing, but truth is, fine art is an elitist preoccupation, and as long as no one was hurt, the public wants the police to concentrate on rape, drugs, and homicides. It's different in Europe. Fact is I've been asked by an old friend in Scotland Yard to learn if you might give a hand in his investigation."

"What can I do for Scotland Yard?"

"I don't have specifics, but Jack Oxby—he's with the Yard—wants to know if there's a chance you can visit him in London next week. Oxby realizes it's short notice, and he had hoped that he could get to New York. But he can't, so I'm his surrogate in a way. Could you possibly meet with him?"

Llewellyn laughed good-naturedly. "I hadn't planned on going to London so soon. Can you tell me more?"

"Only that Jack knows about you and about your painting. As for what he's got in mind, I just don't know. Nothing dangerous, but it would be a different experience for you. Even a little exciting, if Oxby's got anything to do with it."

"So far I haven't done a damned thing." He turned to Astrid. "You said you were behind in your antiquing, darling. How about London next week?"

"I'd like that."

"How do I get in touch with Oxby?"

Tobias handed Llewellyn an envelope. "It's all there. Phone and fax numbers. By the way, have any Cézannes been sold in the last few months?"

"One of his landscapes will be in the Geneva auction in December," Llewellyn said. "That might tell us something."

Berrien called over from the bar. "A Cézanne? . . . in Geneva? Are you sure of that?"

"The preview announcement came this morning." He waved a finger toward Astrid. "Be a love, and find that brochure on my desk." Astrid picked out a glossy brochure and handed it to Berrien, who unfolded it into a full-color sheet the size of a newspaper page.

"I wonder how Collyers landed a Cézanne to sell. Must be a second-rate painting."

"Not at all," Llewellyn said. "It's from Ganay's Paris collection."

"Did you read this?" Berrien asked, waving the brochure.

"I skimmed it."

"You better read it because there might be another Cézanne in that sale." He handed the brochure to Llewellyn, his finger pointing to the bottom of the page.

Llewellyn read aloud, "It is possible that in addition to Cézanne's *Orchard on a Farm in Normandy*, a self-portrait by the artist may also be offered. Should this be the case, complete information and documentation of the painting will be included in the catalogue, which will be available in advance of the sale."

"Jesus H. Christ," Berrien said, "that'll cause a stir at the security meeting."

Astrid sat on the arm of Llewellyn's chair and put a hand on his shoulder then slowly lowered it until her fingers slipped into his.

"We can fly over from London and see how they're putting their plans together. You'll like the location."

Astrid squeezed his hand. "Where?"

"It's all very hush-hush," he smiled. "I'll let that be a surprise."

Chapter 27

It was late morning when LeToque parked his silver Porsche behind Weisbord's house and told the long-legged girl sitting next to him to go into the garage "and see if the old bastard's car is there." Metallic-green sunglasses covered a swollen-shut right eye and a left eye ringed with a yellowish crust. Long-legs reported that there was no car in the garage, and the two went around to the front of the house where LeToque banged repeatedly with a brass knocker in the shape of a snarling lion's head until the door was opened by Weisbord's housekeeper. LeToque pushed past her, commanding the girlfriend he called Gaby to follow him.

He inspected the rooms on the first floor before going to the pantry for a bottle of wine and glasses then making a final stop in Frédéric Weisbord's office. The room had once been a sun parlor, then a study, now, in its final conversion, Weisbord's office. It had a row of cabinets against one wall and shelves along another; by the window overlooking the porch and rear property was a desk piled with stacks of mail, files, and thick folders tied with brown ribbon. Between the desk and the window was a cluttered credenza and a gargantuan swivel chair much too large for Weisbord and in which LeToque now sat, snapping out orders to the housekeeper and Gaby for more ice. There was about the room a strange orderliness, as if Weisbord could put his fingers on a file or letter in an instant, and there was also a heavy mustiness accented by tobacco smoke clinging to faded draperies and a soiled carpet.

On the floor behind the big chair stood a metal cylinder with valves on top and a length of clear plastic tubing with straps and a nose clip attached to the end. The three-foot-tall cylinder of oxygen was new, to judge from its glistening green paint.

The housekeeper put a bucket of ice on the desk and stood back, eyeing LeToque warily, seemingly pleased in a perverse way that his face was swollen and had the color of a severe sunburn—hot and painful. LeToque wrapped ice in a towel and pressed the soothing compress to his face. He twisted about in the huge chair, not able to fill it any better than its owner.

LeToque said, "When will Weisbord be home?"

She waved her hands. "Non lo so, presto?"

"Speak in French, you Italian bitch. What time?" he shouted at her.

"My name is Idi," she said indignantly. "I don't know because he don't say when he comes home to eat."

LeToque would wait. He handed the cold towel to Gaby and told her to wring the water out of it, then pat his face, around his eyes especially, but gently. Gaby complained that she was tired, that she had not been able to sleep once she awakened from whatever had been in the needle that the tall bastard had stuck into her.

"You got a needle and went to sleep, that makes you goddamned lucky. I couldn't breathe after what he did to me, and now I want to pull my fucking eyes out. I'm bleeding inside, I feel it, here!" and put a hand against his throat.

When the wine was gone, he shouted to Idi for another bottle, but she wanted no more of him and instead rattled pots on the stove and went noisily about preparing a meal for Weisbord, the air soon filling with the pungency of garlic and black olives simmering in oil. The aroma fired

Gaby's appetite, but was repulsive to LeToque, who complained that Idi had not brought his wine.

Gaby said, "If your throat is sore, stop drinking the wine. Spill wine on a cut and it hurts."

"And stops the bleeding," LeToque replied testily.

But he took her advice and scooped his glass into the melted ice and sipped the cool liquid, then sat back in the chair, resigned to wait until Weisbord returned, resigned to let time heal the pain, resigned at the moment, too, to rest the cold towel against his lips and stare with his one barely good eye out to Cécile Weisbord's idled gardens. LeToque was an impetuous young man with a troubled history. He was born Georges Dumauer, the youngest of six children in a poor family in Marseille, a precocious, reckless child who very early was dubbed LeToque, the crazy one. School was a sometime thing, replaced with whatever odd jobs the quick-witted youngster could come by. At thirteen he discovered that delivering drugs paid more than kitchen work in the hotel. At eighteen he was arrested for dealing in cocaine, and for the next eight years he was in and out of prison on other drug or assault charges. At twenty-six, he went to London to reform, but returned to Marseille after a year to become even more deeply entrenched in drug trafficking.

His own drug dependency turned him into an uncontrollable risk-taker and eventually a liability that was too much for the cautious drug leaders. It was then that he was introduced to Frédéric Weisbord, who could both protect him and find uses for his seamy talents. LeToque had been paid six thousand francs to deal with Aukrust, much below the proper rate for his unexpected pain and suffering.

Into LeToque's blurred vision came Weisbord's car, then the old lawyer struggling up the rear steps to the back porch, into the kitchen, and then to his study. Coughing and gasping for air, he approached his desk to discover LeToque sitting in his chair.

"What are you doing here?" Weisbord demanded.

"Waiting for you to give me more money."

"You were paid."

"You sent little boys and they were chewed up, in fact one ran away, and your Pioli"—he thrust up his middle finger from a closed fist—"Pioli is made of piss! Pioli told him I was waiting in his apartment." LeToque bolted out of the chair and grabbed Weisbord's collar. "Look at my face . . . at my eyes! He sprayed gas on me! I promise one thing, old man. I'll kill the bastard if I get the chance."

Weisbord struggled free then tried with unpracticed hands to attach the fittings from the oxygen tank into his nose and open the valve. When Weisbord had finally managed it all and slumped into his chair, LeToque turned off the valve and said, "You didn't hear? I want more money."

"All right, more money." Weisbord's eyes pleaded. "Turn the valve on."

"I have a figure in mind. Let's see if it's the same one you're thinking about."

Weisbord pulled himself to his feet and reached for the the oxygen tank, but before he could couch the valve, LeToque pushed him back into his chair. Gaby circled around the desk to Weisbord's side. "You'll kill him," she said to LeToque and turned on the valve.

LeToque reacted with a hard slap to Gaby's face, sending her to the floor. "Mind your fucking business. I've got money coming and I'll get it my way." Gaby looked up, hurt and surprised. "Get the wine," LeToque said, pulling her to her feet and pushing her toward the door.

"Sit down," Weisbord said, his voice nearly at full strength. LeToque pivoted around to find that Weisbord was holding a gun, and no ordinary revolver at that. It was an old French military weapon issued to Weisbord fifty years earlier, unusually long-barreled, well-cared-for, clean and lightly oiled. He waved LeToque into the chair beside his desk. "We'll leave the oxygen on and discuss the money you say I owe you, and we'll also talk about something I believe we both want very much to accomplish."

"You don't need that," LeToque said, pointing at the gun that rested in Weisbord's lap, the barrel aimed approximately at LeToque's spleen. "I wasn't going to let you die."

Weisbord smiled weakly. "That wouldn't be to your advantage, not when you want me to give you more money. And there will be more, but not for your first unfortunate encounter with Aukrust." He opened a fresh package of cigarettes. "When you accept one of my assignments, the risks are yours. I make no guarantees of any kind."

"More money for what?"

"For the painting neither you nor Pioli could find." He flicked a lighter and put the flame to a cigarette, dangerous beyond his understanding in the presence of pure oxygen.

But LeToque knew. "Put that damned thing away before we both die."

"Mind your damned business." Weisbord waved the gun and drew heavily on the cigarette then and almost regretfully doused it in the glass of water. He breathed the pure oxygen, his eyes never straying from LeToque.

"I must have the painting in Geneva no later than the nineteenth—in six days."

"And you expect me to take it?"

"Not alone," Weisbord said. "An employee of the magistrate's office is deeply in my debt, and he, along with a man in police uniform, will visit Aukrust on Tuesday morning. They will have a warrant to search his shop. During my own brief visit, I was able to see into the back room where Aukrust claims to frame pictures. It is likely the painting will be found in that room, in a high, old vault standing against the wall."

LeToque's agitation had subsided. "What do you want me to do?"

"Find someone who can open the vault in the likely event Aukrust won't do it. No matter what it takes, you must come away with the painting and bring it here. For that I will pay you 25,000 francs."

"That is barely enough for me, and I will have two others to pay. The price is 50,000."

A crack formed in Weisbord's composure. He coughed. A throat-clearing followed by loud, painful spasms. He gasped out, "That's ten thousand . . . dollars."

LeToque nodded. "Exactly right. Ten thousand American dollars."

Chapter 28

A nn Browley knew better than anyone where to find Oxby in Westminster Abbey, no matter into what obscure recess or cloister he might wander. She too had access to the Abbey's off-limits areas through the considerable influence of her great-uncle Sir Anthony George Browley, Knight in the Order of the Bath, whose armorial bearings and banners hung above the carved-oak stall in the Henry VII Chapel. Jack Oxby had a profound affection for the old gent, now past ninety. Early in the morning, Oxby went to an out-of-the-way table in the Chapter Library, where he spread out the notes that would be winnowed into a case progress report, a narrative he periodically added to, and occasionally subtracted from when speculations turned sour. From his satchel he took a thermos and poured a cup of strong coffee. He wrote: "The violent destruction of the paintings, the puzzling murder of Clarence Boggs, and the absence of any communication suggests that we are dealing with an intricately crafted plot that may take many twists before an explanation, and ultimately a solution, is possible. The perpetrator, whom I choose to call Vulcan, is a complicated person and most probably a sociopath. The destruction of the paintings is essentially designed to reduce the number of self- portraits and thus drive up the value of those that remain, including, incidentally, all other works by Cézanne. I am now of the opinion that two people are involved—there may be a third, and in the extreme, a fourth serving a less sensitive function. Someone plans, someone finances—Vulcan executes."

Ann slipped into the library and waited at the opposite end of the table for the inspector's concentration to wane, but it did not, not for three or four minutes. Finally he glanced toward her and said, "Good morning, Annie, care for coffee?"

She shook her head. "It's quite improper to bring coffee into the Chapel Library, and illegal, I'm sure."

"That bad?" he said, continuing with his work. "Next time I'll bring tea."

"You detest tea."

"Have you ever seen a chemical analysis of the stuff? Ask Jonesy for one. It'll scare you to death."

"You're incorrigible."

He looked up. "Got something for me?"

"A few things," Ann said, trying unsuccessfully to stifle her excitement.

"Start with what you know about the photographs. I'm very impatient about the delay, and I don't understand why David Blaney can't get hold of a few photographs after all this time."

"It's not David's fault. I drove down as you asked and discovered the problem is Alan Pinkster. David said the photographer, name of Shelbourne, was under instructions to send all photographs to Pinkster. I tried to make an appointment with Shelbourne, but he's off on an assignment."

"When's he due back?"

The tiny lines across Ann's forehead grew into dark furrows. "I can't answer that. David thinks Pinkster sends him on assignments."

"Oh?" Oxby's interest was piqued by that bit of news. "Find out if Pinkster sent him off this time." He made another note. "What else have you got?"

"Bertie Morrison phoned to say there was a rumor that

portrait number 238 might be sold, but she learned it wasn't true. In fact it was moved into a new hiding place."

"Good. One less painting to worry about." He sat back in the chair. "I know you've got more, so spit it out."

Ann heaved up her shoulder bag onto the table. "Jonesy said you won't find diisopropyl fluorophosphate in garden supplies, and he couldn't have been more right." She pronounced the name of the exotic chemical as if it were as common as table salt. "Two Swiss companies make it. A variation called Floropryl is made in America by Merck & Company, but Jonesy doesn't think Floropryl would work the same way as the chemical that killed Boggs, because it's a compound used in the treatment of glaucoma."

Oxby sat back in his chair, his arms folded across his chest, his eyes closed.

"Are you interested in what I'm saying?" Ann asked, annoyed by Oxby's nonchalance.

"Of course I'm interested, and I'm also concentrating. Please go on."

"There are two sources in the entire United Kingdom where one can buy DFP, one in London, the other in Edinburgh. There have been thirty-four reported purchases of the chemical in the past twelve months; however, all purchases were made by reputable buyers who were—" she read from a pad—"Cambridge University, Stearns, Fowler Pharmacologicals, and the London Eye Institute."

"Thirty-four separate purchases?" Oxby asked.

"Correct."

"Do you have copies of the orders, including signatures of the person authorizing each purchase?"

"Yes, Inspector, it's all there." She pronounced "Inspector" as if it were a communicable disease. "You would think I didn't know proper procedure," Ann said irritably.

"Go on," Oxby said, not looking up.

"In Holland and Belgium, DFP is classified as a nerve

gas and is under strict government control. It's available only to physicians and medical researchers."

"It must trade in the gray markets," Oxby said.

Ann smiled victoriously. "A few sources, not many, and we've identified them all. None traded in the quantities Jonesy said were used."

Oxby opened his eyes long enough to locate his coffee cup. He took a sip. "Next?"

"The Scandinavian countries, plus Spain, Portugal, and Luxembourg, require a license for the purchase of DFP. I got a lecture on why it's restricted to the pharmaceutical industry for medical research."

"Or someone planning a murder," Oxby added.

"I'd nearly forgotten about military uses for DFP, then I recalled that before the Iraqis could make their own nerve gas, they bought exotic chemicals from France." The files she had in front of her were thicker than the others. "There are five French companies that will sell you all the DFP you want. Every one has a sales office in Paris, and three have an office in either Lyon, Marseille, Strasbourg, Nantes, or Toulouse. There aren't hard and fast restrictions on buying the material, but every purchase is recorded, and eventually that information ends up in some obscure section in the Ministry of Health. Because the chemical is easily available, there's no gray market."

Oxby leaned forward and fanned through the pages of one of the files. He glanced up. "You're dying to tell me something."

Ann fished out another packet of papers from her shoulder bag. "Those printouts show every DFP sale for the past year. We combined the transactions from each company and programmed the sales by location, date, amount, and name of purchaser. Most of the sales were in Paris and were made to some sort of research or medical institution. In fact, 94 percent of all sales were to that kind of organization, with orders placed on a repeating, regular basis. Sales to individuals were also concentrated in Paris, and generally each buyer made one purchase for minimum amounts. There were three exceptions.

"The individual purchasers were named Metzger, Thompson, and Zeremany. Thompson's first order was in early June, the second in July, and the amount of DFP purchased totaled twenty-eight grams.

"Zeremany bought in June, July, and September. But the total amount he ordered came to less than twenty-four grams.

"Metzger bought twenty-five grams on August 29, twenty-five grams on September 4, and twenty grams on September 7."

"Where did they buy?" Oxby's interest had shot up.

"Zeremany and Thompson in Paris. Metzger in Toulouse and Marseille."

"What do we know about Metzger?"

"Not much. The signatures are cramped, and there is an extreme variation between them. Jonesy's got them in for analysis. We think his first name is Jacob or Janus, and he claims to be a doctor."

Chapter 29

Gaby pulled the sheet over her bare shoulders. Despite the cool air that came from the opened window, she felt warm in the bed next to LeToque, or Georges as she called him, though it angered him at times to be called by his given name. A sliver of sunlight fell across his cheek and moved slowly toward his sore eyes. "Are you awake?" she whispered, and he turned his head into the pillow.

A clock radio in the next room came on. A minute of news was followed by the weather followed by the time, 7:02. Music came next, or a facsimile thereof, made by a combination of guitars, drums, and shrieking voices. Then a breeze parted the curtains and the sunlight burst over both of them, rousing LeToque from his half-sleep. When he turned to her, Gaby nestled close, rubbing his back. Then her searching hands massaged him slowly at first, then faster in time with the music. When she had brought him to full erection, she guided him into her and began grinding her pelvis ever faster until he made a final thrust into her, shuddered, and lay still. It was over too quickly for Gaby, and she continued to twist and turn, but he pulled away and slapped her buttocks. She kneeled beside him, thrusting her small, firm breasts at him. "You fuck too fast," she pouted.

"You fuck too much," he replied, and rolled off the bed and went into the bathroom. "Fix something to eat," he called out to her.

Gaby's culinary talents were limited to instant coffee and

a heated roll, but LeToque's attention was on other matters. The redness around both eyes had improved, though the yellow crust remained in his right eye, and it now alternated between an itch and irritation. Five days had elapsed since his encounter with Aukrust; on this day he would have the chance to even the score.

A car stopped in front of LeToque's small house. The driver was a man of perhaps fifty, of average height and build. He was wearing black-framed glasses and was dressed in shirt, tie, and zippered leather jacket. The other man was not yet thirty. Swarthy, with reddish hair that lay slack over his ears, he had the build of a weightlifter: a perfect V-shape— thick chest and neck, narrow waist, and heavy upper arms.

Gaby made instant coffee, and the men sat at a round table in the tiny kitchen. LeToque had drawn a crude map of the streets surrounding Aukrust's shop, and he also sketched the inside of the shop based on Weisbord's single visit and brief glimpse into Aukrust's workroom. "In the back, here against the rear wall, is a big vault," LeToque said to the older man, whose name was Maurice. "Weisbord thinks it's old, maybe something used to store papers and records."

"Older the better," Maurice said, with a slight stutter.

"Aukrust is strong and has tricks besides." LeToque had heard about Pioli's painful encounter with the Norwegian. He turned to the muscular young man, who was much too large for the chair he was in. This was Cat, recruited by Maurice: a fighter, judging from the fresh cuts on both forearms and indications that stitches had been recently removed from a cut that ran across his face from right ear to left ear. LeToque said to Cat, "Do what you have to do, but no dead people."

"More money," Cat said in a strangely thin voice.

"That's not with LeToque," Maurice interrupted. "I pay you, and you agreed to five thousand francs."

"Not enough."

"What's enough?" LeToque asked.

"Seven thousand."

LeToque looked at Maurice and nodded. He understood that fees were negotiable.

"You'll get six thousand if it goes right," Maurice said; "no more."

Cat nodded. "It's a job, Maurice. If everyone does their job right, then it goes right. Someone fucks up . . . then it goes wrong. Either way, I get six thousand."

LeToque nodded agreement with Cat's basic, yet accurate philosophy. "We meet with Weisbord at one o'clock," he said.

The meeting was in a noisy restaurant near the rail terminal in Cannes. Weisbord, the first to arrive, claimed the private room he had reserved and almost immediately welcomed his contact from the magistrate's office, an unpresupposing man in a business suit with the look of a civil employee waiting to qualify for a pension. LeToque appeared with his group, and Weisbord assigned each one a seat, LeToque on the lawyer's left. The last to arrive, a young man in sandals and sweater, took the remaining chair. Gaby was dressed uncharacteristically in jeans and a loose-fitting sweater. She sat beside LeToque and held tightly onto his arm.

Everyone's assignment had been planned to eliminate complications and signals that could go wrong or be missed. Weisbord spelled out his plan then repeated it exactly as he told it the first time. The man from the magistrate's office was named Foultz; the young man wearing sandals was an occasionally employed actor named Claude who would accompany Foultz, wearing a police uniform. Foultz would present Aukrust with a search warrant that in point of law was not enforceable, because Weisbord had not made a formal claim and the warrant was unregistered. It was assumed that Aukrust would permit a search but only to a point; it was further assumed that Aukrust would not open the vault because he could not or because the lock was broken.

Weisbord continued, "When Aukrust opens the door to the back room, Claude will go to the front door to the shop and step outside momentarily. That will be the signal for the rest of you to move in."

LeToque's sketches were passed to Foultz and Claude, questions asked and answered, then came food and wine. When they had finished, Weisbord raised his glass. "*Bonne chance!*"

Forty-five minutes later, Foultz parked a blue Renault two blocks from Aukrust's shop. Claude fussed with his uniform and adjusted his cap to the proper angle. The street was uncrowded, a convenience that could only be hoped for. At 3:20 they went to Aukrust's shop.

"I'm closing," Aukrust said, showing surprise at the unlikely pair who stood before him. "What can I do for you?"

Foultz held out a large envelope and intoned in an officious manner, "I represent the magistrate's office of the city of Cannes and serve upon you this warrant for legal search of these premises for a painting by Paul Cézanne, specifically, a portrait of the artist, which was recently taken from the premises of its owner, Madame Gaston DeVilleurs, during the time when you were known to be on those premises. Further details are contained in the warrant. You may telephone your lawyer; however, I assure you that this warrant is enforceable and cannot be rescinded by appeal or claim."

Aukrust took the envelope and opened it. The papers inside consisted of official-looking letterheads on which were raised seals with signatures and stamps.

"As you can see, there is no painting by Cézanne here," Aukrust said, waving the papers at a display of beach and country watercolors. "I would be insane to put such a valuable painting here—even if I were so fortunate to have one."

Foultz was obviously unconnected to the art world, and

the comment meant nothing to him. He was concerned only with getting beyond the locked door.

"In the room beyond that door," he said firmly. "That is also part of these premises."

"There is nothing but a supply of frames, my tools, and a large table on which I do my work." Aukrust leaned nonchalantly against the counter.

"Open the door, Monsieur Aukrust. We are prepared to use whatever means is necessary to inspect every part of this property."

Claude stepped from behind Foultz and made a little show of moving his hand onto the stock of his holstered gun. He did it expertly, as if he might actually know how to use the weapon if provoked.

"Go slowly," LeToque said. Maurice obeyed, and as they drove past the shop, LeToque stared through the window. "Good! Pull over," he ordered. Maurice pulled to the curb. Weisbord had supplied a BMW, not a large car but, if needed, a fast one. As soon as Claude appeared, LeToque was out of the car and running, Maurice and Cat immediately behind him. Gaby was last and stood inside the door, instructed to tell stray customers that the shop was closed.

Aukrust spoke calmly, addressing his words directly to Foultz. "It's an old vault, and the lock is broken; in fact, I've arranged to have a new one installed."

Claude rummaged among the unframed canvases that were stacked against the wall then through each of the cabinets. "Nothing here, not unless you want to open a pharmacy. It must be there in the vault."

"There's nothing in the vault," Aukrust protested.

"We'll find out for ourselves," Foultz replied.

"Tomorrow," Aukrust said irritably. Behind him now stood LeToque and Cat. They were joined by Maurice.

Foultz and Claude backed away then hightailed it from the room.

"The door," LeToque said, and Cat closed it. LeToque was in charge and wanted Aukrust to have no mistake that this was so. Revenge was in the air. Aukrust looked from one to the other, alarm slowly beginning to show in eyes that were focused on the cabinets containing his chemicals and other unorthodox means of defense. He moved a step, and LeToque barked out, "Open the lock on the safe, and do it now."

Aukrust's response was to move closer to the cabinets.

"I said open the fucking lock!" LeToque made a quick jerk of his head, and Cat moved in front of Aukrust. Now they formed a triangle: Aukrust halfway between the safe and the cabinets, Cat positioned four feet ahead of him, LeToque the same distance away, but on his left.

"Checkmate, you bastard," LeToque said.

"It's an old safe and an old lock," Aukrust seemed to say wearily. Then he flung the search warrant at Cat's face and leaped past him and got his hand on the cabinet door, but Cat reacted instantly and sent a fist into the side of Aukrust's jaw, followed by his other hand in a fierce blow into the lower ribs on his left side. Either punch would have sent a smaller man to the floor but only turned Aukrust around, and he swung wildly at Cat, catching him with only a glancing blow, pulling himself off balance and making him an easy target for another series of punches to his side and stomach that Cat delivered with brutal precision. Aukrust tried to recover and half lunged, half staggered toward LeToque, who with his hands together like a tennis player about to return a backhand volley sent both clenched fists in an uppercut, catching Aukrust across his chin, knocking him heavily onto the floor, where he lay with half his body under the big framing table. Next to him was a wooden box filled with scraps from the materials he used to frame pictures, odd lengths of frame made of wood or plastic, discarded mats, wire, hardware, and glass. Glass!

He remained still, curled in the fetal position as if he were unconscious, his cheek flat against the floor. Suddenly the sharp toe of a shoe slammed against his shoulder blade, and he was kicked again in the lower back. He grunted then made a sound that was more nearly a soft moan and gripped the table leg so tightly that it caused a terrible new pain that shot from his hand up into his shoulder. Cat's shoe poked again as if he were testing to be sure a dead dog was actually dead. Aukrust opened the eye that was an inch off the floor, allowing him to see the legs of LeToque and the man named Maurice, both standing in front of the vault. He slowly raised up so he could see into the wooden box. A piece of glass lay atop other odd scraps, and he took it out and put it under his chest then lay on top of it. He estimated it was four inches wide and nearly twelve inches long.

Maurice assessed the lock, talking in a quiet jumble, speaking slowly, pausing at certain words. It was a Boulgner combination lock: sixty years old, no longer made; a good lock, but not the best. The dial was large, requiring him to stretch his fingers to the fullest to grip and turn it. There was a grating sound that meant it might be a broken lock, that Aukrust had not lied.

Aukrust moaned softly and moved a leg a few inches, testing Cat's reactions. He steeled himself, waiting for another kick. Nothing.

Maurice rested his hand for several seconds. He turned and heard a click, not an ordinary sound but it caused him to smile. "*C'est bon*," he said more to himself than the others. He dialed in the other direction until a tumbler dropped. Once more, and Maurice said, "That's three. Two more."

Aukrust heard the quietly spoken words. Maurice was obviously capable of opening the vault, his job made easier because someone long ago had set the combination to a series of easily remembered numbers, and anyone proficient with locks could anticipate that the final two numbers might relate to the first three. The first three numbers had been: ten, twenty, thirty. The next two might be forty then fifty. Maurice tried that combination but the lock did not open.

The number combination might be: ten . . . twenty . . . thirty . . . twenty . . . ten. If Maurice tried that combination the lock would open.

Aukrust pulled the glass toward him. He would have to break it to create a weapon, and it might crack into a dozen useless pieces. If only he could reach the glasscutter on top of the table.

"I think it will come now," Maurice exclaimed. "The combination was made for someone with a poor memory."

Time had run out. Aukrust struck the glass against the side of the box. It broke into three pieces. One was like a miniature stalactite, tapered to a needle-sharp point. When he gripped it the jagged edges cut his hands. He jumped to his feet and lunged at Cat, intent on taking out his most dangerous opponent. Cat reacted by instinct, putting up his hands, setting himself to wrestle Aukrust down or hit him as he had before, like a boxer. He didn't see the glass until it pierced the palm of his left hand. He pulled away but Aukrust's weight bore ahead, and the glass knife snapped. Blood spurted from Cat's hand, and the big man stared at it, curiously, strangely confused.

Aukrust swung the hand holding what was left of the dagger and a split instant before he landed the blow, he opened his fist and crashed the jagged glass into the right side of Cat's face. Cat screamed, a terrible and frightening sound. Aukrust had continued in motion toward the cabinets. LeToque tried to pull him away, but a driving fist caught LeToque on the side of his head and spun him onto his knees. Aukrust opened the cabinet and wrapped a bloody hand around a tall aerosol can.

There was a terribly loud crack. A bullet zapped into the space where the aerosol can had just been.

"Please put that down, Monsieur." Maurice was standing by the vault, a 9mm SIG-Sauer in his hand.

Aukrust was defiant and held up the can threateningly. Maurice fired again, the bullet even closer to Aukrust than the first one. "If I must, I will put the next bullet in your shoulder, I would say about here." Maurice placed his free hand on the left side of his chest. He had spoken deliberately, stuttering only on the word "bullet."

LeToque took the can from Aukrust. "Sit there on the floor," he said, pointing at a stretch of bare wall.

Maurice opened the vault. On a shelf was a painting of a bald-headed man with a full beard. Sad eyes looked out from under a black cap with a wide brim. LeToque put the portrait on the framing table. "*Voilà*," he said with a self-satisfied smile, then helped himself to a length of brown wrapping paper and put it around the painting.

"Maurice fixed your fucking lock," he said harshly, then added, "*pour rien*."

He put the painting under his arm and followed Cat and Maurice into the shop and out to their car.

Aukrust sat on the floor with his back against the wall. He seemed frozen there, staring at the hand that was crisscrossed with cuts, each bleeding, making it appear that he had put his hand into a can of red paint. He got to his feet and went behind a partition where there was a basin and toilet. He ran the water and flushed the blood away. As he bent over, his back muscles stretched painfully where he had been kicked. Shards of glass, large and small were imbedded in the palm of his right hand, and they glinted in the white fluorescent light. Painfully he picked out the larger pieces and tried washing away the others. The same ear that had been cut by Pioli only days earlier was throbbing, and he could do little more than bathe it and put an astringent on the wound until it stopped bleeding. He was less prepared for basic emergencies than for the complications and trauma his collection of exotic drugs and chemicals could cause or cure, but there were bottles of sterilized water and others containing alcohol. His medicine case yielded a pair of tweezers with which he slowly removed the tiniest of the pieces of glass. For the other pains in his ribs and the back of his head, he injected himself with 20 mg of Pantopan. Pain was replaced with euphoria. He had injected a drug that acted essentially in the same manner as opium.

All the while his thoughts were on the swift moving minutes that had just passed, on LeToque, on the one called Cat, and on the man who looked like a watchmaker and could handle a gun. He put all of them out of his mind and replaced them with a single image: Frédéric Weisbord.

He pulled down the shade and locked the door. He forced himself to ignore the pain and concentrate on his next steps. The painting was gone because Weisbord had out-maneuvered him. But the painting belonged to Margueritte DeVilleurs, who said that she cared about him and who actually meant something to him. Then a totally new thought struck him: When he got the painting back, he would not deliver it to Alan Pinkster.

Use of his right hand was restricted, and the deeper cuts were still bleeding. After changing the bandages, he found a white cotton glove. Next, he restocked his medicine bag, locked the shop, and went to his car.

He edged through the thick commuter traffic and headed north to connect with the super-autoroute to Nice. He knew the section of the city where Weisbord lived and had put the address on a piece of paper that was above the sunshade. He followed a huge truck carrying flowers to the perfumeries, an ironic counterpoint to the violence that surrounded him. He turned off at the first exit into Nice and followed signs to Saint Étienne, stopping once for directions to Weisbord's street. He drove past and saw the silver Porsche parked behind the house.

He parked a safe distance away, where he could see the front of the house and the driveway. A woman went to the garage, opened the wide doors, and went inside. There was no car in the garage. The woman reappeared carrying a large trash basket, which she was apparently going to put at the end of the driveway. He moved the car forward and pulled alongside just as she reached the curb.

"Is Monsieur Weisbord at home?"

The woman looked curiously at Aukrust. "No," was her terse reply.

"Will he be coming home soon?"

She shook her head blankly and shrugged her shoulders. He wondered whether she was telling him that Weisbord was not coming home soon or that she didn't know.

"I'm a business friend, but I've come to Nice for a brief vacation and want to pay Monsieur Weisbord a surprise visit. Will he be home this evening?"

The woman crossed her arms over her chest and when it seemed she was about to turn and walk back to the house, she replied, "I am the housekeeper. Monsieur Weisbord will be away for two days. I will tell him you were here."

"I want to surprise him. Where has he gone?"

She once more seemed to be evaluating whether to answer or not. She shook her head slowly. "To Paris, maybe. Or Geneva." Then she skittered off into the house.

Chapter 30

Christie's auction rooms were at 8 Place de la Taconnerie, Sotheby's at 13 Quai du Mont Blanc. Precisely half-way between its rivals, on Rue Rousseau, was Collyers/Geneva. The location wasn't accidental. At every turn, Collyers's aggressive new management in London was out-maneuvering and out-promoting the double doyens of the rarefied art auction world. Old-timers at Collyers referred to Christie's and Sotheby's as "the Cow and the Sow," lumping them together in frequent attitudes of disdain, in an attempt to make up for decades of being the brunt of bad jokes. Collyers had been looked upon as an upstart, barely more than 150 years old, not yet dry behind the ears. But that simply wasn't so. Collyers, founded in 1837 by Thomas Collyers and John Constable—who had had the terrible misfortune to die in that same year—was a competitive force, upsetting the old conventions and setting new ones.

In Geneva, auctions at Christie's or Sotheby's had for decades featured jewelry and precious gemstones, with the smaller houses blindly following their lead. But tradition was about to be broken. Collyers's brazen announcement that it would auction a first-quality Cézanne was beginning to yield the expected results. Dealers and collectors were showing interest, proof that many would be willing to fly to Geneva for the auction then go on to their holidays in the Alps or escape to the Mediterranean and the sun. The extent to which buyers would be inconvenienced when submitting their bids was to have to dial new country and area codes.

The resident director was flamboyant, called an auction brilliantly, and was perfectly suited to Collyers's new image. Roberto Oliveira traced his bloodline to well-connected families in the north of Italy and in Austria and was a handsome man with fair skin and gleaming blue eyes. Oliveira was a man blessed with a splendid education: Eton and Yale; and an internship as an auctioneer at Christie's in London, where he rose to the position of Director, Impressionist and Modern Paintings. Now at thirty-eight, he was the father of a teenage daughter, divorced, and having affairs in three capital cities. It was the "affair" in London who had tipped him off to the lawyer in Nice who was making inquiries into costs and commission arrangements for the possible sale of a Cézanne self-portrait. Oliveira promised heavy promotion and an elaborate catalogue, but it had been his offer to undercut the sales commission by three percentage points and the decision by management to guarantee a $27.5 million reserve that had clinched the deal with Frédéric Weisbord.

The unending stream of news stories and the outpouring of speculation on who was destroying the paintings and why meant that if Oliveira were able to bring the DeVilleurs portrait into the December auction, Collyers/Geneva would break the old record set by Sotheby's when a 101-carat D-Flawless diamond had sold for nearly $13 million, with the entire lot going for $31 million. More important it would add to Oliveira's visibility and position him for the executive director's position that was to be filled in January. The anatomy of success often included such accomplishments.

Christie's was outraged that the painting was to be auctioned in Geneva and at Collyers's no less. Their legal counsel had written an outraged letter implying that Frédéric Weisbord had been physically coerced into the decision, and if he had not been intimidated, he had been showered with unreasonable and illegal inducements. The letter covered both extremes. "Kill or kiss," Oliveira had characterized their argument. The fact was, Frédéric Weisbord wanted to sell the painting quickly, conveniently, and on the best terms.

It was 9:15 in the morning when Oliveira learned that Frédéric Weisbord was in the basement garage and that he would not leave his car until he was escorted to Oliveira's office by two armed guards. Oliveira removed his jacket and slipped on a shoulder holster that held his 22LR Llama automatic pistol. Weekly practice at the police range kept his proficiency with the small gun at a high level. He phoned for the guard to meet him in the garage.

Weisbord lowered his window a crack and demanded that Oliveira show identification. "I asked for two guards," Weisbord said irritably, coughing in obvious discomfort. Oliveira grinned. "But there *are* two of us," and he took the pistol from its holster in a swift, fluid motion. "I know how to use it," he said convincingly and handed his business card to Weisbord.

"I am Roberto Oliveira, at your service."

Weisbord was in the passenger seat, LeToque was behind the wheel, and Gaby, her eyes wide with curiosity, leaned forward from the back seat. The painting was next to Weisbord, wrapped in a blanket. Weisbord got out of the car clutching the painting, giving LeToque instructions to bring his briefcase and the portable oxygen supply. An elevator took them to the second floor, Oliveira then leading them to a room filled with unframed paintings, stacked in open shelves, and frames that were under repair or in the process of being regilded. In the corner was a camera stand flanked with lights in silver reflectors. Next to it was a man wearing a lab coat.

"The Cézanne?" the man asked.

Weisbord eyed him warily, holding the painting tightly with his thin, trembling hands.

"Who else knows I have brought the painting?" Weisbord asked gruffly.

"I confess it's not an airtight secret, Monsieur Weisbord," Oliveira replied. "My staff, the printer who is waiting for the photograph we are about to take, and my associates in London." In truth, Oliveira had let the word go out for the simple reason that the more who knew, the larger the attendance, the higher the bidding.

"No one else can know about this," Weisbord said. "There is always a danger that someone might try to steal it."

"Our vault is in a concrete bunker, and our bank has an impregnable safe. You choose which you want."

Weisbord shook his head defiantly. "I will take it with me."

"First things first," Oliveira said reassuringly. "The printer must have a photograph before noon if the catalogues are to be printed on Friday."

Oliveira took the painting from Weisbord and unwrapped the blanket. He had seen a black-and-white photograph of the self-portrait, but none in color. "From the looks of his beard, I'd say it's from his middle period, 1875 to 1878. Am I right?"

"Something like that," Weisbord said absently. "I have complete records."

"I am anxious to see how they compare with the history of the painting we have prepared. What you have brought will add considerable new detail." He gave the painting to the photographer, who went about his business with dispatch. After ten or so exposures, he disappeared into an adjoining darkroom.

"Phillipe is very good," Oliveira said reassuringly. "He will tell us if he needs to take any more exposures, but I suspect that won't be necessary." Weisbord looked suspiciously at the door to the darkroom then sat on the edge of a chair. A cigarette magically appeared, and he lit it.

Several minutes later, Phillipe came out of the darkroom and pronounced that he had two excellent negatives. "As I suspected," Oliveira said, then motioned to Weisbord. "Please follow me." Weisbord wrapped the precious painting in the blanket and held on to it even more tightly than before. They filed out to the elevator, which took them to the third floor, and then to Oliveira's office, a gracious, large room with many paintings and a magnificent display of glazed pottery from Pakistan and Iran. The windows faced Lake Geneva, and several hundred feet away the water rushed from the lake, forming a wide stream that ran swiftly past the view. The stream was the Rhône River, continuing its five-hundred-mile course south to Lyon, to Provence, and to the Mediterranean. Gaby thought it was a wondrous sight and said so in her simple way.

"Here are the printer's proofs of our catalogue," Oliveira said, pointing to untrimmed sheets that were spread across a table by the window. "It will include the new photograph and details about the self-portrait. As I promised, I have also arranged to print a separate brochure that will feature a brief sketch of Cézanne's life and, of course, your self-portrait. Beautiful, don't you think?"

The old lawyer turned the pages and grudgingly said that it might be a "handsome brochure," then added that it would be expensive as well. He lit another cigarette.

Oliveira said, "We will pay all of the catalogue expenses. The photograph that Phillipe took will go here," he pointed to a sketch of the painting on the front cover and turned the page. "There's no reason not to discuss the recent wave of terror, and we have included small photographs of the self-portraits that have been destroyed. It will add to the excitement of the auction."

Weisbord blew a stream of smoke and nodded.

"You have some papers for me," Oliveira said. "Important papers that I must see before the catalogue is mailed and the publicity begins."

Weisbord opened his briefcase. Inside were a dozen tabbed file folders. "Here is a complete record of each person who has owned the painting, starting with the artist friend Cézanne gave the painting to a year after he painted it." He handed two typed pages to Oliveira, "I believe it was Pisante."

"Pissarro, perhaps?" Oliveira asked.

Weisbord glanced up. "Yes, you are quite right."

Oliveira said, his smile intact, "The painting has an excellent provenance. That is not a concern."

Weisbord took an envelope from the folder. "This contains two canceled checks signed by Gaston DeVilleurs, a signed receipt for the deposit, and a statement for the balance due, marked paid in full. There is also a registration certificate filed in Paris and dated the day following the final payment. You will agree this is evidence of clear, unencumbered title to the painting."

Weisbord put more papers in front of Oliveira. "This is a copy of Gaston DeVilleurs's will, as entered in court on 29 June, this year. The appropriate section of the will has been marked and specifies that no painting can be removed from the collection unless it is placed in auction under the personal direction of the executor, and, as you know, that is my role." Weisbord smiled weakly. "It was obvious that Gaston DeVilleurs was looking after Madame DeVilleurs's interests."

"I assume all of the paintings in the DeVilleurs collection were jointly owned," Oliveira said.

"They were," Weisbord replied, and coughed, slightly at first, then with a painful wheeze. LeToque moved the oxygen beside him, but Weisbord waved him off. When the coughing siege finally subsided, he handed Oliveira another sheet of paper.

"This is a copy of Madame DeVilleurs's power of attorney. It allows me to act on her behalf." The single page contained three typed paragraphs, below which was a beautifully written, but indecipherable signature. Beneath the name was typed: Margueritte Louise DeVilleurs.

Weisbord sputtered. "A precaution only, there must not be any possibility of a misunderstanding." Again Weisbord went into a fit of coughing then after it had run its course, wiped his face with a handkerchief, gathered up his papers, and slid them back into the folder. He handed copies of the documents to Oliveira.

"These are for your files. You'll also find instructions for depositing the proceeds from the sale. Are there any questions?"

Oliveira read the instruction then nodded. "I see no problem. We are frequently asked to deposit the net proceeds into one of our banks in Geneva."

Weisbord got to his feet and extended his hand to a beaming Oliveira. The meeting was over.

Chapter 31

Edwin Llewellyn regularly booked himself into the Stafford for the reasons that it was one of London's exceptionally well-mannered hotels, was tucked away on a convenient cul-de-sac on St. James Place, and because its obscenely high rates had a purifying effect on the clientele. Llewellyn was given his usual corner-suite on the fourth floor and in accordance with propriety, put Astrid in her own nearby room. Astrid, for her part, would be busily engaged searching for English antique furniture for an anonymous couple she described as young, wealthy, and the new owners of a twelve-room condominium on Central Park South. They arrived mid-morning on Wednesday, lazed through the afternoon, then ended the day with an early dinner.

"Sleep well, darling," he said, unlocking the door to her room. "I'll meet you at breakfast." He kissed her on the lips. "Eight o'clock."

She stifled a yawn. "God natt," she said softly.

He was up early, ordered newspapers and coffee, and watched the morning television news. When he arrived in the dining room at ten before eight, Astrid was waiting, her coffee just then being served.

"You look beautiful—as usual," he said, and squeezed her hand affectionately. "Are you sure you won't need any help?"

"I have a list of shops. I'll be fine."

An assistant concierge came to the table and said very confidentially, "Inspector Oxby has arrived, sir."

Llewellyn smiled. "Ask the inspector to join us."

Astrid frowned. "You didn't tell me you were meeting him here."

"It's a perfectly civilized place to meet someone, and I like the informality."

She gave a hesitant smile. "It's just that I won't be able to stay long."

"For a short while, to get acquainted."

Both turned to watch Oxby come toward them, and by the time he reached the table, Llewellyn was on his feet, hand extended, surprised by the deep voice that greeted him.

"Mr. Llewellyn, delighted you've come."

"I'm happy to be here, Inspector Oxby. This is Miss Haraldsen, a friend who has come to buy some of your very best antiques."

Oxby gave Llewellyn a firm handshake, then turned to Astrid. "Antiques?" He sat between them. "What sort of antiques? Furniture, silver, paintings?"

"Furniture, mostly. I'm doing a New York apartment, and my clients love everything English."

"Nothing in New York?" Oxby asked and ordered a pot of coffee from a waiter who stared at him with a look of familiarity. "You Americans have 50 percent of everything we ever made right there on Third Avenue."

"You know about Third Avenue?" Llewellyn asked.

Oxby nodded. "Counterfeit antiques are all over, including your Third Avenue. I've been there and seen it, a year ago, in fact." His coffee arrived, and he said to Astrid, "Tell me more about what you're looking for. What period of English furniture, for example."

A blankness came over Astrid's face, and she glanced toward Llewellyn. "Period?" she repeated with an uncertain awkwardness. "I don't think that's too important . . . I'll see what's available."

"Choose late Victorian. A reliable dealer won't put you off, and it will be authentic goods. But if you're prepared to write a large check, find a couple of Sheraton chairs; they mix well with any period. In fact, I saw a pair advertised recently." He slipped a half dozen cubes of sugar into his coffee and began stirring. He eyed her carefully. "What do you think of Sheraton?"

She gave another weak smile. "Sheraton chairs. That would be nice, thank you." She turned, as if to get up. "I must go, my first appointment is at Van Haeften."

"What takes you to Johnny Van Haeften's?" Oxby asked.

The answer came slowly. "A desk. I traced a desk to that shop. It's in light colors."

Oxby tested his coffee and approved. "Did you attend design school?"

"Yes, in Oslo," she answered somewhat cautiously, "at the Kunst og Handverks Hoyskole."

"Will you be going directly back to New York?"

Astrid shifted her eyes to Llewellyn. "My plans are not firm. It depends on how soon I find the furniture." She got to her feet. "I really must go. Excuse me, please."

Oxby stood. "Good luck with your shopping, Miss Haraldsen. If you need help, please let me know. Antiques are our business, and we know the troublemakers."

Llewellyn accompanied Astrid to the lobby. "You seemed a bit nervous. Is everything all right?"

"I didn't think the inspector would be so interested in my shopping trip, and I couldn't answer all his questions."

"He's probably very knowledgeable and merely wanted to help." He took her hand and patted it. "Plan to meet me at Brown's Hotel at four, and we'll have tea."

"Will he be with you?"

"Inspector Oxby? I hope so. I plan to invite him."

She sighed, turned, and walked out to St. James Place. Llewellyn watched her disappear before returning to the dining room.

"A beautiful friend," Oxby said. "I hope that she doesn't buy a counterfeit the first time around. It's like entering enemy territory going into some of the shops."

"Yes, I've been there," Llewellyn said, agreeing.

"On the whole, London dealers are an honest lot, but we've got our quota of bad apples who deal in every deceit imaginable. They're very nearly as venal as those in the art world."

The two men asked and answered questions in an easy conversation, getting a grasp of each other. "What's your schedule today?" Oxby asked.

"I've set the day aside," Llewellyn answered. "Alex Tobias said you wanted to talk, and I have nothing more important to do than help find the son of a bitch who's burning up Cézannes and who killed Alan Pinkster's curator."

"Good. Do you like to walk?"

"Not especially," Llewellyn replied. "Why?"

"It might do you some good," Oxby said, daring to sound like an old friend. "We can say what we want, no one to eavesdrop. Besides, the English are great walkers, and that's a good reason, right?"

"By all means, let's go for a walk." As they went out to the lobby, Llewellyn said, "I've asked Astrid to meet me at Brown's for tea. Will you join us?"

Oxby smiled. "I have an un-English aversion to tea, but a huge fondness for Brown's. I'd like that."

They crossed St. James Place to a walkway that twisted through a garden of roses and boxwoods to a network of paths that spread throughout Green Park.

"When this thing started, I wasn't keen on Cézanne," Oxby said. "Frankly, I hadn't studied the man and didn't know all that much about what he had painted, and what I did know was restricted to his nude bathers and a few landscapes. But I became interested in a hurry when four of the portraits were burned up in twenty-four days."

"Have you got any idea who's behind it?"

"Not an inkling at this point, but the fact there's been so much destruction without any threats, or warning, or messages, seems, strange to say, quite important."

Llewellyn stopped and turned to Oxby. "Explain."

"If one painting had been burned without any communication, I would say it was a crank or a crazy person, and that would have been the end of it. If two paintings had been ruined and again there were no messages, I might argue that it was a wooly-headed crank who sprayed the first painting and that another person, totally unrelated, sprayed the second one. We've seen this sort of thing. It happened a year ago. A painting in a church in Paddington was badly carved up with a knife. A week later the same thing happened in Swindon, without an explanation. In my view, those were separate but related incidents and were not carried out by the same person."

They began walking again. Oxby said, "But four paintings in three countries, one murder, and still no message?" He looked solemnly at Llewellyn. "That's an authentic mystery."

They reached the Mall, crossed the wide avenue, and continued into St. James Park. Oxby quickened the pace, recounting the few significant details that were known about each incident, then enumerating the unanswered questions that surrounded the Pinkster painting and the peculiar way in which Clarence Boggs had been murdered. "Then Boston," Oxby said, catching on to Llewellyn's arm. "That sent a different message."

"What was that?" Llewellyn asked.

"All along I'd been trying to put together a picture of who this person is and what motivations are in play. Why Boston?" He gave a wry smile and turned onto a path that wound around the lake in the middle of the park.

"He must have known there were four self-portraits in America, three of which are in museums. He chose the one in Boston, probably because it was less risky than the Modern in New York or the Phillips in Washington. But it's not why Boston so much as why burn one up in America at all? The press pounced on it. Particularly the *New York Times*."

"The media is feasting on it," Llewellyn said.

"But come back to the other question, why Cézanne, and why his self-portraits? Was it because Cézanne wore a beard, or was bald, or was financially well off?" Oxby paused. "Or was it some kind of a sexual abberation: Each time he sprayed a painting he experienced the sensation of killing."

"Killing Alan Pinkster's curator wasn't a sexual abberation," Llewellyn said. "And I'm sure it was pretty tough on Alan."

"You know Pinkster?"

"Not well, but Alan's been on the social scene in New York, and I've been with him on several occasions."

"Boggs was killed approximately twelve hours after Pinkster's painting was destroyed, and I don't consider that a coincidence. He was killed with a rare poison, which suggests that someone with a knowledge of chemistry was involved. In fact the spray used on the paintings is a unique formulation, not available through the usual sources. Further, on the day the portrait was sprayed, a professional photographer was in the Pinkster Gallery and took pictures of a group of employees from the Danish embassy, including two shots that show a man and a woman we haven't been able to identify. Because the man's back is to the camera, all we know about him is that he's tall—over six feet."

"The woman?"

"The camera got her head on, but her face is a blur. We believe there were other photographs, and we're attempting to get hold of them."

They left St. James Park, crossed Birdcage Walk to Queen Anne's Gate. "I'm not a psychiatrist, but we've got a couple of men who are, and they're first rate at it. They've confirmed that we're dealing with a psychopath, not surprising, perhaps." Oxby stopped and looked at Llewellyn, his eyes bright. "I don't like using the word perpetrator because it reminds me of a purse snatcher, so I've given our suspect a name. It gives all of us on the case a point of reference, as if each of us knows a bit more about who it is we're trying to find."

"Sounds like espionage. What name did you give him?"

"Vulcan. The world's aware that every painting was sprayed with a chemical and that each one looks as if it were pulled from a fire, and I know because I've seen two of them. Vulcan seemed to fit."

"Vulcan," Llewellyn repeated the name. "God of fire."

They had angled through the park and taken Dartmouth Street to Broadway. Before reaching the intersection with Victoria Street, Llewellyn looked up at a quite ordinary building, one that was cold and impersonal, and one that might have been another undistinguished government building except for a large sign in a triangle of grass: New Scotland Yard.

"Are you taking me in for questioning?" Llewlleyn asked with mock seriousness.

Oxby shook his head amiably. "It will be you asking the questions, and as I have a serious proposition to put before you, we'll want privacy. And good coffee."

Llewellyn checked through security, pinned a visitor's badge to his lapel, and followed Oxby into an elevator. They got off on the fifteenth floor and walked through an open area crammed with desks and files and clicking fax machines and operators at consoles in front of display monitors—all enveloped by a modern cacophony consisting of the bleeping of electronic signals from telephones and shortwave or cellular radio hookups. Oxby continued into a windowless room and closed the door, shutting out the nervous noises they had just walked through. The room was square. Along one wall was a battery of television monitors and on a table set apart from the large center table were several dozen telephones, their wires strewn over the floor like black-and-red ribbons unraveled from their spools. A large blackboard on coasters was pushed against another wall. "This is primarily a conference room and when we're concentrating on a difficult case, it becomes what we call an Incident Room."

On the table was a thermos and cups. "I promised coffee," Oxby said, motioning with his hand in a help-yourself gesture. Four chairs had been pulled up to the table, two on each side. Oxby took one and asked Llewellyn to sit across from him, then he said, "The madness outside that door is a small part of the Specialist Operations Department, to which we are attached. We used to be called the Arts and Antiques, but we're carrying on under different colors. Squad SO1 deals with international and organized crime and is commanded by Elliott Heston, who, unless he's spirited off by the commissioner, will join us at 11:30. I've also asked Detective Sergeant Browley to meet with us, but first I want to introduce you to Nigel Jones. Jonesy is one of our top forensic investigators and has something quite exciting to show us."

Llewellyn poured himself a mug of coffee. He looked curiously at Oxby, and an embarrassed smile broke clear. "I never imagined I'd be inside Scotland Yard."

"It's really just a big-city police department that every now and then stretches its wings out over the whole country. I suppose you Americans think of Scotland Yard in the same way the English regard your FBI: in the way of a romanticized motion picture."

"How long have you known Alex Tobias?" Llewellyn asked.

"We go back ten years or more. And we've become especially well acquainted during the past two years, since Alex became involved in the same sort of thing we do in my department. He said you and I would hit it off."

"Do you think we have?"

Oxby nodded. "I think so."

"Tell me more about Vulcan."

"If we're right and if Vulcan shows consistent psychopathic behavior, then I believe we can entice him to reveal himself."

"How do you do that?"

"Vulcan's taste for fine art is very narrow; nothing else of Cézanne's seems to interest him, except the self-portraits. It makes me wonder if someone else is actually calling the shots or, put another way, does Vulcan have a boss? I was determined to learn if there was something in that, and so I asked our brain crackers to work up a psychiatric profile on Vulcan based on every shred of information we've got that included the chemical formulation of the solvent he has used in his attacks, the cities and museums he selected, the burned-up briefcase from London's National Gallery, the photograph taken of the Danish tour group in the Pinkster Gallery, the description of a man seen with an oxygen tank in the Hermitage museum, the man with a European accent who attended a woman who fainted in the Boston Museum of Fine Arts, the poison used in the murder of Clarence Boggs and the way it was administered, and, finally the dates and times of every burning."

"Sounds like you've got a great deal of information," Llewellyn said.

"You put it precisely. It 'sounds' like a great deal; but it's actually a short list, and it doesn't tell us if Vulcan is on his own or taking orders." Oxby pushed his chair back from the table and got to his feet. "When the list of things we know is short, we're forced to make a long list of the things we don't know."

"Want to explain that?"

"It's easy enough to put too much on the list of things we don't know, and so the secret is to be selective. In the end, we put down twelve unanswered questions."

"What kind of questions?"

"His nationality . . . are others involved? . . . if so, how many? . . . what is the motivation? That sort of thing."

"From that you build a profile of Vulcan, then go out and find him?"

"It's not that easy. On the one hand we have a few unrelated facts, and on the other are a dozen unanswered, but highly focused questions. And so we put together what we know with what we are striving to learn. The psychiatrists have made their contribution, and as we find the answers to those twelve questions and new facts are uncovered, the profile becomes more accurate. Eventually we'll know exactly who Vulcan is. But there are limits to how long we can wait before more paintings are destroyed or another person dies."

"What can you do?"

"Try to make things happen on our terms. That's where you can help us."

Llewellyn laughed good-naturedly. "What in God's name can I do?"

"You can be a lightning rod."

Llewellyn frowned. "Explain what you mean."

Oxby smiled. "Vulcan may be a psychopath and murderer along with a few other heinous personality quirks, but the destruction of the portraits was designed to draw attention to Paul Cézanne the artist and drive up the value of all of his paintings. Especially the self-portraits."

"Vulcan doesn't have a portrait; they're all accounted for. If he should steal one, who would buy it?"

"You're aware that one of Cézanne's self-portraits has never been seen by the public, has never been displayed in a gallery, has never been photographed, and has been owned by the same family for nearly a hundred years. Sound familiar?"

"My grandfather had peculiar notions about his possessions," Llewellyn said defensively.

"My point exactly. There are people who would secretly

spend a fortune for an important painting then never share it with another soul."

"Are you suggesting that if I attract Vulcan, he'll attempt to steal my painting?"

"I'm suggesting that given that opportunity, Vulcan will attempt to take your painting because, quite simply, it is immensely valuable. This assumes, of course, that Vulcan and whoever he's in cahoots with have been planning to steal a portrait to sell to a buyer who has agreed in advance to a very high price."

Llewellyn twisted uncomfortably in his chair. "I'm not sure I like this." He stood and went to the blackboard, picked up a piece of chalk and wrote "lightning rod" on the board. He turned and faced Oxby. "Tell me more."

Oxby smiled reassuringly. "You've listened very patiently, and for that I thank you. Perhaps you don't want to become deeply involved in unraveling our mystery, and if that's so, I would understand. But I suspect you recognize the immense importance of finding Vulcan before more lives are lost and more paintings destroyed. Is that a fair assumption?"

Llewellyn nodded.

"Good." Oxby tapped out several numbers on a phone and said into it, "We're ready." Then he rolled the blackboard away from the wall and stood beside it, looking for the moment like a schoolteacher. "I want you to announce through the public information office of the Metropolitan Museum that you will personally assume responsibility for the delivery of your painting to the Musée Granet in Aix-en-Provence."

"Why would I want to do that?" Llewellyn asked.

"Because under usual circumstances, your painting would be packed and shipped by the Metropolitan staff, would disappear for several weeks, and then, on schedule, appear at the Musée Granet. During that time neither you nor Vulcan would know where the painting was. But for you to be a lightning rod, you and your painting must travel together."

Oxby flipped over the blackboard to reveal a map of France. "I suggest that you fly to Paris, stay overnight at the Hôtel Meurice and on the next afternoon appear as featured speaker at a symposium sponsored by the Societé des Artistes in the Musée d'Orsay. You will speak, of course, on Paul Cézanne and his impact on the Post-Impressionists. As scholarly a talk as you wish. Most important, you will present your portrait, its first public showing at an occasion that will attract worldwide attention. On the morning of the third day you will travel by high-speed train to Lyon, and that evening you will present your painting at a special exhibition in St. Peter's Fine Arts Museum."

Oxby put a pointer on Lyon and traced autoroute A7 south. The highway crisscrossed the Rhône River for 136 miles until Avignon, where the river and road divided. Oxby tapped the pointer on the orange circle that surrounded Avignon. "On the fourth day you will travel to Avignon and stay at the Hôtel l'Europe for three days. I have made tentative arrangements for you to participate in a local arts festival on Monday the fifteenth." Oxby sat on the edge of the table, his arms folded across his chest "You will have become a celebrity in a very short period of time, and the person most interested in your trip south from Paris will be Vulcan. He will be watching you closely and I suspect will be in the audience when you make your presentations. He will be there not to hear your comments on Cézanne but to see how well protected you are and who's doing the protecting."

"I'd like an answer to that one now."

"In Paris you will be well protected by police, the security force in the Musée d'Orsay, by two from my staff, and by me."

Llewellyn nodded and leaned forward, his elbows on the table. "After Paris?"

"In Lyon, I will arrange for the local police to accompany

you in public, and I will have a private force in place in the hotel at all other times."

"In Avignon?"

"The same. It's a small city, there won't be large crowds of tourists this time of year. It's unlikely that Vulcan will try anything in Paris or Lyon. He will assume that you are well guarded, but after several days we'll let our guard down— so to speak. If he conceives a plan to take the painting, he will do it in Avignon, and in my judgment, he'll try to do it on Tuesday, January 16, the day following your last presentation."

"Would you call that his 'window of opportunity'?" Llewellyn asked dryly.

Oxby nodded. "I shall take responsibility for your safety, and you'll be guarded extremely well, but understand that it's a balancing act we've got to work out, and the trick is not to allow any of the security to be obvious."

Oxby faced Llewellyn squarely. "There will be a risk."

"How much?"

"That will depend on Vulcan. I can't honestly answer."

There was a rap on the door. Nigel Jones came into the room carrying a large, flat carton, which he placed on the floor against the wall.

"Good show, Jonesy, just in time," Oxby said, then introduced the two men. "I promise that Jonesy will clear up some of the mystery I've just created."

Llewellyn clasped Jones's hand firmly and said good-naturedly, "I have an old-fashioned fear of being struck by lightning, and I'm dead set against showing off my painting as if it were a charcoal sketch whipped up by a sidewalk artist in Montmartre."

Oxby said, "Show Mr. Llewellyn what you brought with you."

What Jones had brought was a painting, which he placed on an easel and pulled in front of Llewellyn. "Do you recognize it?"

Llewellyn stared in amazement at the painting of a woman bent forward, her strong, peasant's hands curled around a string of beads. "Cézanne's *Old Woman with a Rosary* from your National Gallery. What are you doing with it?"

"I'll explain," Jones replied, "but first I want you to tell me if you notice anything unusual about the painting."

Llewellyn looked intently at the painting for a full minute. "It's very powerful. Her eyes stare down to her hands, yet I feel that she is looking out at me ... that she will speak after she has said her final amen."

"Examine it more closely,"

Llewellyn edged forward in his chair. "The shadowed areas have an eerie denseness, a greater depth than I remember."

"Closer," Jones urged. "Touch it if you wish."

"I don't approve of touching a canvas."

"Quite correct, but you may touch this one."

Llewellyn timidly ran his fingers over the old woman's hands. "What is it?"

"A photograph," Jones replied. "One made by a process incorporating conventional and Polaroid films. A painting this size can be reproduced with cameras and enlargers fitted with fine lenses, and larger paintings are reproduced with a camera so big that two men work inside the camera's bellows. Colors are matched to the original by means of a computer with an accuracy exceeding 99 percent. Then finally the texture of the paint is applied. It's a very proprietary and secret process," Jones said.

"I'll be rolling south like a Hollywood advance man with a photograph?"

Oxby nodded. "Making news, attracting attention. Particularly Vulcan's."

"Suppose we succeed, but Vulcan gets past your security ring and we have a face-to-face?"

"In the unlikely event that happens, you'll be able to signal us, and you'll have a gun if you wish. Have you ever used one?"

"I hunted occasionally, but I haven't held a revolver in ten years."

"Are you afraid of handling one?" Oxby asked.

Llewellyn shook his head. "I could use some practice."

"We'll do better than that. You can choose your own gun then spend a day with one of our instructors."

"You sound as if I'm going along with your scheme."

Oxby gave a confident smile. "You're asking all the right questions."

"I have more. What happens to my painting, the real one?"

"With your permission, Alex Tobias will deliver it to Aix-en-Provence. His wife will travel with him, but even she won't know that Alex has the painting with him."

"Who makes the copy, or is that another secret?"

"I'll coordinate that job," Jones answered. "I'll take the original photographs, but the final product will be in the hands of technicians in Cambridge, Massachusetts."

"Jonesy will deliver the copy to your home and help install it in the frame that now holds the original," Oxby said.

"When do you plan to take the photograph?" Llewellyn asked.

"As soon as you return to New York," Jones said.

"Stay with me if you like," Llewellyn said. "I'll be in Paris this weekend, and on Sunday I drive to Fontainebleau for a meeting of the museum security managers. I leave for New York next Wednesday."

Oxby said, "I hoped you were going. I plan to attend."

"Aren't the Fontainebleau forests off your beat?"

"Not in our business."

Jones said, "That means I can shoot on Friday."

Llewellyn gave Jones one of his cards. "Call me from the airport, I'll have you picked up."

Oxby looked over at Jones. "You owe me a final lab report."

"I'll have it for you day after tomorrow. Won't be much new in it, we're still fine-tuning the formula for the solvent."

Oxby reacted somberly. "Keep at it, Jonesy. We're due for a little luck."

Chapter 32

Peder Aukrust's station wagon was a hundred yards from Frédéric Weisbord's house in a spot carefully chosen to provide a clear view of the property, including LeToque's silver Porsche parked immediately behind the house. Not quite a week had passed since he had been overwhelmed by LeToque and his gang. His right hand was still stiff, the cuts in the palm not completely healed. Worse was the infection that had developed on the right side of his face and ear. It was, in fact, so serious that on Thursday morning he had gone to the hospital clinic in Vallauris, where a young doctor meticulously cleaned his wounds and closed the cuts with twenty-eight multiple fine sutures. He was into the third day of his vigil and had not yet found a way to break through the protective shield and retrieve the painting.

Aukrust was never certain who was in the house—Weisbord, LeToque, the girlfriend, or the housekeeper. He had actually seen Weisbord go off for three hours the previous Friday afternoon, or the housekeeper had popped in and out doing her chores or as happened on Sunday had walked in the direction of neighborhood church bells. But the others? Had LeToque recruited someone like Cat to shore up the defenses?

It was also on that Sunday afternoon that Aukrust had moved the car to a spot beneath the wide spread of a huge beech tree. The weather had changed, from clear and warm to clouds and a cold wind that made waiting seem endlessly uncomfortable. He had replayed over and over the telephone conversation he had had with Astrid, amused to learn that the police called him Vulcan. Had they known, they might have called him Heimdall, the Norse god of fire. From Astrid he had also learned that an Inspector Oxby was on the case, that he was a short man who asked many questions, and that he and Llewellyn would attend a meeting near Fontainebleau whose purpose was to approve a security plan for the special exhibition of Cézanne's paintings. Once, Aukrust dozed off and imagined that Margueritte DeVilleurs was walking toward him and had stopped at his car. She smiled at him, but when he opened the door for her, she disappeared.

On this Monday afternoon, ten minutes past five o'clock, the Porsche moved slowly down the driveway. Aukrust aimed his binoculars at the driver. It was the girl, alone. She turned right onto the street, and he followed her for a mile to a neighborhood shopping plaza. Aukrust trailed, then parked two spaces away from the Porsche and watched the girl go skittering into one of the markets, then reappear several minutes later carrying a plastic grocery sack and a newspaper, hurrying still. As she bent to put the key in the lock, Aukrust appeared beside her.

"Let me help," he said.

"*Non, monsieur,*" she said abruptly. "*Non, merci!*"

Aukrust's gloved hand grasped her wrist, and his other hand took the keys away. It happened in an instant.

"Don't be frightened," he said calmly. "Let me open the door." He turned so that she could see his face.

"You can't—"

She stopped in mid-sentence, staring at the long-bladed knife he held a few inches from her throat. "Say nothing." He growled the words, then ordered her to slide across to the passenger seat. He got in behind the wheel.

She began to cry. "Put the knife away. Please." The words were barely audible.

He placed it on top of the dashboard in front of him. "I'll put it here. Where we both can see it."

"What do you want?" she asked.

"I want you to make a phone call to LeToque."

She was silent, the color drained from her face.

"Did you go with LeToque and Weisbord to Geneva?"

Again she was silent.

"Did you?" he asked with more urgency.

More silence, then she nodded.

"And did Monsieur Weisbord have a painting with him?"

She nodded again.

"Did he bring the painting back to his house?"

She seemed about to answer but turned her eyes away.

"Did he bring the painting back?" Aukrust wanted an answer, an accurate answer, but realized that his threats were frightening her. Then as if he truly cared he asked, "What is your name?"

She brought her gaze back to him. "Gaby, short for Gaboriao," she answered.

"Does your family live in Nice?"

"My mother."

"You live with LeToque?"

"Is that your business?"

"LeToque is my business. Monsieur Weisbord paid him to do this." He held up his hand and pointed to the bandages that covered his ear. "Now Weisbord is paying him for protection, but he's not paying enough."

"Five thousand francs a day," Gaby said defiantly.

"The painting he is protecting is worth a hundred million francs."

"It's a stupid little picture of a man with a black beard."

"You've seen it?"

"I fell asleep against it in the car."

"Then Weisbord did return it to his home?"

"He put it on the wall over his bed." She looked at him. "I think he puts it in his bed at night."

Aukrust familiarized himself with the cockpit of LeToque's Porsche, then started the engine, backed out of the parking space, and turned in the direction of Saint Éti-enne and a small residential hotel they had passed on the way to the shopping plaza. There was a phone booth off the lobby. He located Frédéric Weisbord in the directory, wrote down the number, then gave Gaby precise instructions for her conversation with LeToque. Gaby dialed the number and when Idi answered, she asked for LeToque.

"I'm with Monsieur Aukrust . . . he has called the po-lice . . . because Weisbord lied to you . . . it's true he has lied! . . . he can't sell the painting . . . the police will be there very soon . . . meet me at the Hôtel Gounod . . . Mon-sieur Aukrust said you must come there . . . you must tell Weisbord I've had an accident with the car . . . that you must drive his car . . . you will be away for only a short time . . . I will meet you at the hotel. . . ."

Her last words to LeToque were spoken as if she were reading a script and reading it badly. She replaced the re-ceiver. "I don't know if he will go to the hotel," she said.

Aukrust stared down at her. "He will go."

She shook her head. "He wanted to know why. You didn't tell me, and I couldn't tell him."

Gaby was trapped in the small booth. The air was hot and heavy with their perspiration and her cheap perfume. He pocketed the knife, then took her arm and backed out of the booth. In the lobby he told her to wait while he talked to a woman behind the desk then returned and said, "A taxi will be here shortly. It will take you to the Hôtel Gounod." He put money into her hand.

"But you said I could drive to the hotel."

"I've changed my mind." He moved toward the door.

"But LeToque's car—what will I tell him?"

"You just told him you had an accident."

"The Hôtel Gounod," he reminded her. He drove the

Porsche back to the shopping plaza, parked it in an unlighted area, then went to his own car.

It was nearing 7:45 and dark. There were lights in every room in Weisbord's house, including bright lights on either side of the front door. The garage was open but Weisbord's car was not in it. LeToque would be nearing the center of Nice. Aukrust parked his car at the foot of the driveway.

Voices came from somewhere along the street, a car door slammed closed, and the car was driven away. At the back of the house was a flight of wooden steps that went up to an open porch that ran the full width of the house. There were eight steps, and he went up half of them until he could see the windows in each of the three rooms along the rear of the house: the kitchen to his right, in the middle a dining room, to the left Weisbord's study. Aukrust's view into the latter room was partially blocked by curtains.

The housekeeper carried a tray of dishes into the kitchen and turned up the volume on an old black-and-white television. Flickering bluish images reflected off shining kitchen surfaces and her implacable face. He climbed the remaining steps onto the porch then went across the porch to the single large window in the study. The lawyer was at his desk, papers spread in front of him, lights shining from table and floor lamps. From where Aukrust stood, he could clearly see that Weisbord was underscoring the test of a letter or a contract. Smoke rose up from an ever-present cigarette teetering on the edge of a huge ashtray.

Suddenly Weisbord swiveled his chair and got to his feet. "Idi!" he shouted. "Idi, damnit, come here!" His shouting gave way to a fit of coughing, and he managed to shout the name once more before he fell back into his chair.

Idi came to the doorway of his office, where she stood patiently, wiping her hands on a blue-and-white striped apron. "Oui?" she said simply, waiting for the wracking cough to subside.

"Has LeToque come back?"

"*Non, monsieur.*"

"Have you turned on all the lights?"

"Like you told me," Idi replied.

"I told him not to go off, he'll pay for it, the bastard. Bring me a pitcher of water," he commanded.

Weisbord went out of view for several seconds and returned to his desk holding a length of plastic tubing. He inserted the fittings into his nose, holding them in place by a strip of black elastic he slipped around his head.

Idi returned with a pitcher of fresh water, put it on his desk, and took an empty pitcher away.

Aukrust went quietly and quickly down the steps and out to his car where he took his medicine case and long, black raincoat from the back seat. He walked boldly to Weisbord's front door. By all outward appearances he might be an old acquaintance carrying a strange-looking little suitcase. Time was important; it was a few minutes before eight.

LeToque went through the revolving doors into the Hôtel Gounod and stopped in front of the concierge's desk beneath an ancient, ornate clock. He described Gaby to the second-shift concierge and received a "haven't-seen-her" shrug with upraised hands; then he went into the restaurant and was about to barge into the ladies room when Gaby rushed up and threw her arms around him.

"Where's Aukrust?"

"I don't know," she continued to hug him. "I was frightened. It's his eyes and the way he talks and the knife," she rambled on, rubbing at her tears and smudging blue eye-shadow over her cheeks. "He said that Weisbord told lies to the man at the art gallery in Geneva."

"Aukrust's the liar," LeToque said angrily.

"He took your car."

"He called the police? You heard him?"

"No," Gaby said in her frightened little voice.

*   *   *

Aukrust rapped with the lion's head knocker again. The door opened eight inches, all that the thick chain would allow. He stood in the light and greeted the housekeeper with his most disarming smile.

"Hello again. I've come back to pay respects to my old friend. Is Monsieur Weisbord home?"

Idi looked up at the big man, who stared back pleasantly at her. He wanted her to smile, to be unafraid. "You remember I was here—when was it? Last Tuesday, of course; you were taking the baskets out to the curb."

There was a pause before she nodded. "I remember."

"I'm leaving tomorrow, and this evening was free, so I've come again to surprise Freddy."

The chain was strong, and the door was heavy. He could crash against it once, perhaps twice, but there was no certainty he could break the lock. He patted his leather case. "I have a bottle of his favorite wine."

Idi looked at the medicine case, then her eyes moved slowly up to his face and stopped to inspect the bandages on his ear. He turned his head, his smile frozen.

LeToque pushed Gaby ahead of him into the hotel's revolving doors and when they were on the street, he began to run. "Hurry," he shouted, "he's after the painting."

The faintest glimmer of a smile showed on Idi's placid face. She closed the door, slid the chain away, then let the door swing open. Aukrust tilted his head in a bow of silent appreciation, then walked past Idi into the front hallway. A stairway to the right circled its way to the second floor. Behind the stairs, the hall extended to the dining room with a door on the left, which, he was certain, led to the kitchen, and a door to the right, which would lead to Weisbord's study.

He put two fingers on his lips, inviting the housekeeper

to share in the surprise, then whispered, "Show me where I can find him. I promise not to frighten him."

Idi gestured to follow her. "He is in there." She pointed to a door that was off a short jog in the hall.

Aukrust said, "And the kitchen is there?" He pointed to it, and she nodded. "That's where you'll be?" She nodded again. "I'll come for glasses if he wants to taste the wine."

He stopped outside the study and waited for Idi to go into the kitchen—go back to your damned television, he thought—smiling at her, waiting until she backed away. He remained by the door until he heard music and voices coming from the television then went back to the front hall and up to the second floor.

During all the hours he had kept the house under observation, Aukrust imagined the size and purpose of each room. He had guessed correctly that Weisbord's bedroom was the center room in the front of the house. He felt along the wall for a light switch. A single bulb in a ceiling fixture illuminated a collection of heavy ftimiture, including a wide bed flanked by two night tables and, as Gaby had described, the portrait on the wall over the bed, suspended from the same nail that had most likely held a crucifix while Cécile was alive. He placed the painting face down on the bed, peeled back the heavy protective paper, and removed four screws that held the stretcher and canvas to the frame. He folded his raincoat around the painting, pushed the frame under the bed, turned off the light and returned to the hallway on the first floor. Everything was as he left it seven minutes before, except that the television blared even louder.

Slowly he turned the handle on the study door, then leaned against it until the door was open several inches. Sounds in the room were a gentle rustling of papers and an occasional small eruption of Weisbord's wheeze. He opened the door wider, enough to see Weisbord in profile, still bent over his work. He let himself into the room and closed the door. His back was against a row of bookshelves, and he crouched and moved toward the old lawyer. Now he could hear the gentle hiss of the oxygen as it passed through the valve on top of the cylinder.

Several more feet and he could touch the oxygen flow regulator. He put on a pair of cotton gloves, then knelt next to the cylinder. The gauge in the flow regulator was set at two in a calibration from one to eight, and he turned the regulator to eight. Weisbord was now receiving a maximum flow of oxygen, a seemingly acceptable condition; however, Aukrust knew that too much oxygen would cause a decrease in respiration and an increase in the retention of carbon dioxide. Because Weisbord had not reached a critical point with his emphysema, the rich oxygen infusion he was receiving would induce a momentary euphoria, followed by drowsiness.

Aukrust pulled his medicine case next to him and took out a green cylinder the size of a portable oxygen supply. But instead of oxygen, the unmarked cylinder contained nitrogen.

LeToque flashed his lights, then pressed hard on the accelerator, veered left, and sideswiped the oncoming car. Glass and chrome sprinkled over the street like sparkling confetti. LeToque braked and jumped from the car to find there was a hole where the left headlight had been but apparently no puncture in the radiator. The other driver stormed over to register an angry complaint, but LeToque pushed him aside, got into the car and drove away. It was 8:21.

Weisbord had slumped back in his chair, struggling to stay awake, noticing dimly that the tubes had come loose. Clumsily, he put the cannula back into his nose and looked with lazy puzzlement at the tubing that snaked across his stomach and over his legs. Then his head sagged, enough to signal that he had fallen asleep. Aukrust separated the plastic tubing from the oxygen supply and inserted it into the fitting on top of the cylinder of nitrogen.

He turned the valve, sending nitrogen into Weisbord's badly weakened lungs. Ninety seconds of pure nitrogen, and the buildup of carbon dioxide would reach the danger level. Continued intake of the nitrogen would create cyanosis: His skin would turn blue, and he would die.

LeToque broke clear of the clogged city traffic. Weisbord's conservative sedan lacked the power of LeToque's Porsche, and he swore at the unexpected traffic that slowed his progress. He turned onto the Boulevard Gambetta, south of the Saint Étienne district.

"How much longer?" Gaby asked.

"Five minutes, without these fucking cars."

Weisbord was dead. Put plainly, he had suffocated. Aukrust picked him up as if he were no more than a child's body and placed him in the oversize-chair, where it seemed that Frédéric Weisbord had been reduced to a final insignificance. Then Aukrust reattached the tubing to the oxygen cylinder.

He picked up the phone and asked for the police.

"I am calling from Monsieur Frédéric Weisbord's home. He's had a severe attack of his lung illness, and I can't find a pulse, but I'm not a doctor. Can you send an ambulance?" He gave the address, then in answer to a question said, "A friend." Then he put down the receiver, took off his gloves, and slipped them into a pocket.

Aukrust followed the sound of the television into the kitchen, where, showing great agitation, he called Idi into the study.

"I have called the police. . . . It was so terrible. We were talking, he was happy to see me. Then the coughing, and he had a terrible seizure. I'm surprised you didn't hear."

"No, the television. But he always coughed." Idi spoke as

if it didn't matter what she said or what the stranger who had come to surprise Monsieur Weisbord said or even that Monsieur Weisbord had suffered a fatal seizure. She pressed two fingers against the side of his neck and leaned down to listen for any sound of breathing. Then she straightened. "He's dead," she said with utter simplicity.

Aukrust gestured helplessly. "I was about to open the wine. I told you it was his favorite." He wiped the bottle with his handkerchief as if to make it a more presentable gift. "It's yours." He placed it on the desk.

Aukrust picked up his raincoat and medicine case, looked carefully about the study, then walked past the housekeeper and let himself out the front door. He ran to his car; when he reached it the time was 8:41.

A siren sounded in the distance. Then another, the two-note heehaw of a police siren. The sounds became louder. Lights came on in houses up and down the street. Then came flashing lights, and an ambulance pulled into the driveway, a police car immediately behind it.

Another car approached slowly. Aukrust recognized Weisbord's car. The car went by then accelerated and sped away.

Chapter 33

It had been speculated that the meeting of security directors would be held in Blois, in the Loire valley near Amboise, but with adroit secrecy, the venue was changed to a location in the Fontainebleau area, thirty-seven miles southwest of Paris. Oxby's reaction was mixed, for it meant returning to scenes with memories both sweet and sad. On Sunday he drove from Orly airport to the little town of Nemours on the Loing River. He checked into the same hotel where he and his wife Miriam had spent a torturously unhappy weekend after she was diagnosed with acute lymphoid leukemia.

In a room that overlooked red roofs to the river, he relived those first few minutes when he and Miriam were finally alone. She had said that she was not good at bravery. But no one Oxby ever knew showed such courage. And she showed it every day for nearly six months, until one afternoon her eyes closed for the last time. Alone in a room of memories, he felt an inner peace come back to him, a comfort made whole by his love for Miriam, and by her love for him.

On Tuesday afternoon he drove to Bois-le-Roi, a small, unremarkable town on the edge of the Fontainebleau forest, then five miles beyond to the Inn Napoléon located on the edge of the fifty-thousand-acre forest. It was late afternoon when Oxby turned onto a cinder-covered driveway and stopped beside the original inn, an old half-timbered affair of several stories pockmarked with patches of broken stucco.

Next to it was a low building with a row of doors and windows that repeated in the style of an old motel. Beyond was a square structure with an onion-shaped dome and a long porch, on which were stacked metal lawn chairs. A crudely lettered sign read: SALLE À CONFERENCE. Whoever had selected the meeting site had done superbly well, because the Inn Napoléon was sadly uninviting, yet magnificently obscure.

Oxby had parked his car alongside several others and taken his fat satchel from the back seat, when a man came out of the inn and walked toward him. Oxby knew Félix Lemieux, though not well. They had attended other conferences and over the years had talked on the phone or corresponded. The security director of the Louvre was small, even shorter than Oxby.

"Inspector Oxby, it is good to see you," the little man said.

Oxby nodded, held out his hand and said in flawless French, *"Comment-allez vous, Monsieur Lemieux?"*

"Very well, thank you," Lemieux replied in English, a rare courtesy. The diminutive man who would supervise security arrangements for the Cézanne retrospective continued to speak in English, a small smile on his face. "Madame LeBorgne arrived early. Have you met her?"

"We're old friends," Oxby said, and put down his satchel. A year earlier Mirella LeBorgne had been appointed directeur of the Réunion des Musée Nationaux. Oxby had been surprised by the appointment and thought she was better suited as a teacher of art history than as head administrator of an agency known for occasional internal bickering. "I expected she would send someone from her staff."

Lemieux replied, "She's insisted on coming so that she can be convinced the security will be skintight. If not, the exhibition won't open."

"I can't blame her," Oxby said.

"And I can't promise that security will be impenetrable the way she expects. It could never be," Lemieux said.

"With luck, whoever's doing all the damage might slip and be captured before the exhibition opens."

"You think that's possible?"

"Yes. And you can help by convincing Mirella LeBorgne that you've come up with one hell of a security plan then giving the press enough of the details so they'll write stories that will make the Granet out to be a bloody fortress."

Lemieux looked puzzled. "I'm not sure I understand."

Oxby leaned down to pick up his satchel. "You'll hear all about it, and I promise to confer privately with you."

A young, bearded man wearing a striped apron came out of the inn. He nodded politely and plucked the satchel out of Oxby's hands. "I am Paul Rougeron," the man said. "I welcome you in the name of my family, who own the inn. You are—"

"Monsieur Oxby," Lemieux said helpfully. "The Rougeron hope to restore the inn to its old ways as a hunting lodge."

Rougeron said ruefully, "A slow process." He pointed to the motel-like building, "Your room is there, the first room to the left, if you wish."

Oxby nodded. "That will be fine," then turned to Lemieux. "I'm anxious to know who will be here."

"There will be eleven of us." He handed Oxby an envelope.

Oxby took out a printed list and scanned the names. Evan Tippett from London's National Gallery was not included. "No Tippett, I see," said Oxby.

Lemieux's eyes turned heavenward. "Please, Inspector, I mean no offense, but there's not enough time to listen to Tippett lecture on his most recent fetish." Abruptly, he spun around and started for the inn. "We'll have a drink."

Oxby's room was simply furnished and illuminated by a single bulb that hung from the ceiling. The bed sagged in the middle, and the small bureau was missing its bottom drawer.

Mercifully, the bathroom had one each of the necessary fixtures, and all seemed to be in working order.

"It's quite simple, and I apologize," Rougeron said, "but come back in a year, when it will be very grand." He grinned and handed Oxby a bottle of mineral water before going off in the direction of the kitchen.

Oxby unpacked his clothes and file folders. There was one chair in the room, a frail, wooden armchair with an unraveling cane seat. He placed it near the window, where there was better light and where he could prop his feet on the bed. He put the list of security council members on his lap and began the process of locking each name and title into his memory.

SECURITY COUNCIL MEETING
Participants:

Musée du Louvre, Paris
    Félix Lemieux, Director of Security
        and Coordinating Director of Security

Réunion des Musées Nationaux, Paris
    Mirella LeBorgne, Executive Director
    André Lachaud, Assistant Executive Director

Direction Centrale de la Police Judiciare, Paris
    Henri Trarna, Commissaire Divisionnaire

Metropolitan Museum of Art, New York City
    Curtis Berrien, Chief Registrar
    Charles Pourville, Associate Curator
    Edwin Llewellyn, Trustee

Musée Granet, Aix-en-Provence
    Gustave Bilodeau, Managing Director
    Marc Daguin, Associate Curator and Security Director

Metropolitan Police, New Scotland Yard, London
    John L. Oxby, Detective Chief Inspector

Interpol, World Headquarters, Lyon
 Samuel Turner, Investigator, Police Division,
  General Crime

He sat motionless, eyes closed in deep concentration. Suddenly the quiet was interrupted by the noise of an automobile that pulled into the courtyard outside his window. The source of the racket was caused by the broken muffler on a dust-covered golden Oldsmobile of indeterminate vintage. Seated beside the driver was a blonde-haired woman Oxby immediately recognized as Astrid Haraldsen. Edwin Llewellyn climbed out of the back seat and stretched his legs and arms. Astrid got out of the car, as did the driver, a lean man in blue jeans and sweater who eyed the Inn Napoléon with the skeptical eye of a Guide Michelin investigator. Paul Rougeron came out to help with luggage and room assignments.

Two more cars came in rapid succession. First were Gustave Bilodeau and Marc Daguin, so Oxby deduced—their five-year-old Renault bore a Provence license plate. In the second car was Curtis Berrien, whom Oxby knew slightly. By 6:30 Oxby had put a red check next to each name on the security council roster. He had recorded Astrid Haraldsen's name and would learn who owned the golden Oldsmobile.

Though there were eleven names on Lemieux's list, it seemed that everyone had brought an aide or friend or, in the case of Llewellyn, one of each. Oxby counted thirty attendees and also discovered that the driver of what turned out to be a 1978 Oldsmobile was Scooter Albany, who had been invited—thanks to Llewellyn—to gather videotape coverage for a behind-the-scenes TV special of the Cézanne retrospective. Scooter immediately found the bar and began demonstrating his wizardry at keeping several conversations moving smoothly while writing notes with one hand and holding a perpetually fresh drink with the other.

Dinner on the first night was served from a buffet, with

everyone mingling informally. Oxby moved among the council members, introducing himself to those he did not know, pausing for longer chats with the ones he did, saving the Llewellyn group for last, where he found Sam Turner trying to persuade Astrid that until she had experienced a Calgary rodeo she wouldn't really understand the true spirit of North America. Sam was into the third year of his second hitch with Interpol and was anxious to return to the Royal Canadian Police before he would be too old to get back on track with a career assignment. Llewellyn asked how many Interpol agents had been assigned to the case.

Turner shook his head. "I'm afraid you're a victim of badly researched detective novels, Mr. Llewellyn. We're mistaken for some sort of supranational police force—that we chase the crooks. We don't do that. We collect information on drug trafficking or terrorism or the destruction of Cézanne's portraits but only when it's a crime that crosses international borders. We process the data and feed it back to the police authorities in countries that are dues-paying members of Interpol."

"But how is it that you're here—and a member of the security council?" Llewellyn asked.

"Because Félix Lemieux asked the general secretary to assign someone, and I got the nod. I wouldn't mind playing policeman just long enough to put Vulcan away, but—" he inclined his head toward Oxby, "that's the inspector's job. Come around on Thursday afternoon. You'll hear a good bit on how Interpol operates."

"I can't," Llewellyn said with genuine disappointment "I've got to be in New York."

Oxby turned to Astrid. "Will you also be returning to New York?"

Astrid avoided answering for several seconds then with a thin smile said, "I'm afraid my clients have asked me to stop in Paris and look into a few shops." She seemed genuinely upset, as if an expense-paid shopping trip in Paris was an inconvenience.

On Tuesday, presentations were made by André Lachaud and Curtis Berrien, with the greater amount of time spent in group discussions of the expenses and logistics of a major exhibition and of the complications related to securing adequate insurance to cover fire, damage in handling and hanging the expensive art, and massive liability coverage.

Early on Wednesday Scooter Albany took Llewellyn to Charles de Gaulle airport then drove into the center of Paris to drop Astrid at the Hôtel Vieux Marais on Rue Plâtre. A gray sedan followed the Oldsmobile out of the airport and into the city and parked a prudent distance from the hotel while Scooter carried Astrid's suitcase into the lobby, returned to his golden Olds, and began his drive back to Fontainebleau. A bearded, dark-skinned young man wearing jeans and a green jacket got out of the car, walked to the hotel, and went inside, where he spoke with the desk clerk then returned to his car.

Scooter returned to the Inn Napoléon shortly after eleven and tape-recorded an interview with Henri Trama, division commissioner in the Central Police Judiciary. The commissioner was a dark-haired man in his early fifties with deep blue eyes under thick brows and an exquisite aquiline nose that guaranteed his French heritage. Trama headed a special contingent of special investigators within the French interior ministry and had responsibility for the recapture of stolen art and antiquity and the prosecution of thieves, forgers, counterfeiters, and, occasionally, murderers. In spite of an outstanding worldwide reputation, Trama could be uncommunicative and a genuinely offensive boor.

During lunch, Gustave Bilodeau gave a brief presentation in which he praised "the gracious cooperation we have received from museums and private collectors who have agreed to loan their valuable Cézannes for the retrospective. January 19 will not come soon enough for all of my staff, who continue with great diligence to make this a memorable birthday celebration in honor of a great artist.

"There will be an auction in Geneva in December," Bilodeau went on; "the DeVilleurs self-portrait will be entered for sale. Madame DeVilleurs accepted our offer to purchase the painting; however, her late husband placed unreasonable requirements in his will regarding the sale of paintings in the collection. But as I speak, the will is being vigorously contested, and we have hopes that the self-portrait will be sold to our museum. It is our dream to have the portrait in a place of honor when the retrospective gets under way."

The first to speak in the final afternoon session was Sam Turner. His presentation was brief, and parts of it put a chill over the group, particularly his vivid descriptions, accompanied by before-and-after photographs, of the demise, as he put it, of the paintings. "Every piece of information we've received about these paintings has been entered into our computers. From this data we hope to find similarities between what occurred in St. Petersburg, London, Surrey, and Boston. Whatever we come up with will be sent out to you in what are called Modus Operandi Sheets, samples of which are being distributed to each of you. We've had success tracking down terrorists, but I'm afraid terrorists leave better trails than Vulcan. They usually send warnings, and most are identified with a cause or a group we've got hard information on. That's why I ask all of you to send me any detail that comes your way, no matter how insignificant it might seem."

At two o'clock, Félix Lemieux presented the security plan developed by his staff in the Louvre, with an assist from old friends in the French Secret Service. Details were contained on sixteen printed pages and bound into a black folder. Each council member received a numbered copy and signed a statement acknowledging that the information was privileged and to be kept secret. Lemieux stood beside an easel, on which he placed drawings and photographs: a detailed street map of Aix-en-Provence; layouts of the two display floors in the Granet; exterior and interior photographs of the thirteenth-century church of St.-Jean-de-Malte, which abuts the Granet, showing how it could be a haven for anyone preparing an assault on the museum. "We will place a special surveillance team inside the church, dressed in priests' robes, trained in rudimentary clerical duties, and equipped with cellular phones." Included in Lemieux's presentation were diagrams of a closed-circuit television system that had been installed in the Granet a year earlier and additional slides to show the planned enhancements of the system. "Unfortunately we have not been guaranteed installation of these changes until February 1, and we will therefore employ additional guards until the new system is fully operational."

Lemieux concluded by saying that a small army might, with force and firepower, penetrate the rings of protection that were envisioned, but it will be impossible for one or two persons to pass through undetected. The consensus around the table was that Lemieux's strategy was an imaginative combination of manpower and technology.

Lemieux's presentation set the stage for Mirella LeBorgne. LeBorgne, as Oxby knew so well, was a combination of scholar, teacher, and lecturer. She was a handsome, not quite pretty, woman of fifty-three, tall, spare, but with a wide, open face that radiated an immediately likable charm.

"Oh, my!" were her first words, said with a smile and undisguised consternation. "You know that I'm rarely at a loss for words, but at this precise moment I don't know what to say. You see, I—we have a terribly important decision to make, and while some of you have already made yours and feel that the retrospective should open on schedule, I haven't arrived at that decision, not yet at least. If the exhibit opens, and any one of the paintings is destroyed or damaged in the slightest way, I would never forgive myself, nor would millions of people forgive me or any of you. The question I am struggling to answer is this: Will Vulcan get by all of Félix Lemieux's security arrangements and do the unthinkable yet again? I am here to listen, and I invite you to speak up."

Oxby asked to be recognized. "I know you face a difficult decision; however, I strongly urge that you say yes. May I explain why?"

Mirella LeBorgne smiled. "Please, by all means."

Oxby said, "The motivation for destroying the portraits has been to send prices up on all paintings by Cézanne. Now comes the retrospective, tailor-made to send interest in Cézanne's works into the stratosphere and flush out an entirely new group of collectors, each one hoping to catch a Cézanne before prices go completely out of sight. The one concern I have about Vulcan and his pals is whether or not they have their inventory of Cézanne or if they're planning to pick up one or two between now and January 19. They won't attempt to break into the Granet; they know that this group will put an impenetrable curtain around the museum, and they will have confirmation of that fact when Félix's program is given full press coverage. In fact, they would agree that the safest place for a painting by Cézanne will be on the wall in the Granet come next January. However, between now and then, every Cézanne is at risk, and the ones most vulnerable are the self-portraits."

"We know where every one of them is," Lemieux replied. "They should be taken off the walls and put into hiding."

"If we do that, we don't catch Vulcan."

"What's your strategy?" Sam Turner asked.

"To flush out Vulcan before January 19. And we might do that by creating a situation so tempting, he'll show his hand." Oxby paused, "Edwin Llewellyn, who was with us earlier, has consented to travel from Paris to Aix-en-Provence with his now-famous Cézanne self-portrait, showing the painting to the public as a demonstration of his deep concern for the success of the retrospective. I have told Mr. Llewellyn that he will become a lightning rod, an idea which has not particularly endeared me to my new friend." The comment brought laughter, though not from Henri Trama, who got to his feet and directed a cold stare at Oxby.

"Who protects Monsieur Llewellyn, Inspector?"

"I have personally made secure arrangements, Henri," Oxby said respectfully, "and I hope to solicit additional help from your office."

"That's not a matter I can approve." He said the words quickly, perhaps angrily.

Oxby went on. "Officially, I will be on leave from the Yard during Mr. Llewellyn's trip and will keep him under close observation at all times."

Madame LeBorgne asked, "How certain can you be that Vulcan will turn into lightning and try to strike your Mr. Llewellyn?"

"Betting odds open at even money," Oxby replied.

Scooter Albany was slouched in a chair outside the meeting room, an arm drooped to his side, a hand clasped around an empty glass. As the council members filed our, he got to his feet and hovered behind Oxby while the detective had list-minute words with Mirella LeBorgne and Félix Lemieux.

"How'd it go?" Scooter asked when they were alone.

"About as I expected," Oxby replied. "Can I buy you a drink?"

Scooter grinned.

They sat by the window in the bar, "Is the show on or off?" Scooter asked cryptically.

"Very much on," Oxby said with enthusiasm. "Félix put a strong plan together, and you can help make it stronger."

"Me?" he laughed. "I don't know the first thing about security, except skirting around it to get at a story."

"But you're good at writing stories and getting them on television. Now I have a different story. Suppose you had the chance to travel with Edwin Llewellyn from Paris to Aix, and suppose he were to take his Cézanne painting along, and suppose further that you could record the trip and send nightly reports to your television contacts. Would that interest you?"

"Bet your sweet ass it would." Scooter put away half of a double vodka martini, then asked, "Why me?"

"You two are friends, and he likes your golden Olds."

Scooter tossed down the second half of his drink and got to his feet. "I need a refill." He turned to go to the bar as Sam Turner came to the table.

"Mind if I steal a few minutes?"

Oxby waved Sam into the chair. "What did you think of the meeting?"

Sam said, "It was okay. Lemieux did a good job, and Mirella LeBorgne is a sweetheart, but your little bombshell was a surprise. If you set up Llewellyn the way you described, he might end up very dead. Trama damned well didn't go for it."

Oxby shook his head. "I hoped he might show some enthusiasm; instead he froze the air. Obviously he wants to catch Vulcan, and he doesn't want to help anyone else do it."

"So who protects Llewellyn?"

"I can get help in Paris, even without Trama. And in Lyon. I don't have contacts in Avignon, but I'll have my own people."

"You're Scotland Yard, Jack, not some goddamned branch of the French Judiciare."

"Sam, I don't want to throw away this opportunity." He looked squarely at Turner. "I may need your help."

"You aren't supposed to carry a gun, and I'm not supposed to chase people—other than that, we'll make a hell of a team." He nodded. "I'll do what I can."

Scooter came back with another double, though half consumed. "Anyone want a drink? I'm buying."

Turner said, "I'll take a rain check, and don't forget it." To Oxby he said, "And don't you forget you're coming to Lyon in exactly ten days."

Chapter 34

Paris was unseasonably warm, and sidewalk tables at the cafe near the Hôtel Vieux Marais were filled. Astrid stood by an open window and watched the traffic along Rue Plâtre. It was noon. The phone rang. It was Peder.

"Yes," she answered.

"What do you see?"

"At a table outside the cafe I see the same one who followed me into the hotel yesterday."

"Are you sure?"

"It's the black man with a beard. He's wearing a sweater and a green jacket with something on the back that I can't make out."

"Alone?"

"I think so."

"Go to the cafe and order a glass of wine and something to eat. Call me from the phone inside the cafe and tell me if he's alone."

"Peder, why are they following me?" Her voice dimmed.

"They want to know why you're in Paris. They are guessing that you are meeting someone."

"Who is guessing?"

"Oxby. He's very thorough. The good ones are." He gave her his phone number and asked her to repeat it. That was it.

There were no empty tables, so Astrid sat at one with a stout, pleasant woman who was deeply engrossed in writing postcards to her friends in Waterloo, Iowa. She was also anxious to tell anyone who would listen that this was her first trip to Paris. "It's everything I had ever dreamed it would be," she gushed.

Astrid nodded politely, pretending not to understand.

The woman seemed embarrassed and went back to her correspondence.

Astrid used the little French that she knew and asked for a glass of red wine and pointed to the sandwich she wanted on the menu. The man in the green jacket sat three tables away. He had put a magazine on the table next to his coffee and occasionally looked at his watch as if he were impatiently waiting for a tardy friend.

She took a bite from her sandwich then got to her feet and said to the woman that she would come back, saying it awkwardly in French. The woman tilted her head and smiled as if she had understood perfectly.

Astrid found the phone. "Tell me again," she held the phone tight to her ear and listened intently. She returned to the table and remained there nibbling on the sandwich, sipping the wine. After exactly ten minutes she paid for the meal and went out to the sidewalk. The cafe was at the intersection of Rue du Temple and Rue Plâtre as Peder had said. She turned right and walked for two blocks. Ahead and to her left was a globe marking the entrance to the Métro. She crossed the street and stopped by a window filled with artificial flowers. She looked back along Rue du Temple. The green jacket had also stopped.

She walked faster. At the entrance to the Métro there was a news kiosk beyond the steps going down, and she went to it and glanced at a row of magazines. Then she went back to the steps, saw the green jacket walking toward her, hurried down to the trains, paid for a ticket, and followed signs to Mairie des Lilacs. She walked to the end of the platform.

The platform was well lighted, and she searched each of the faces of the people waiting for the next train. A woman holding a baby sat on one of the benches; at the end of the same bench sat an old man bent over a large shopping bag. A train was approaching, pushing the air in front of it, causing pieces of paper to float up off the track and onto the platform.

On the back of the green jacket were the words "Detroit Tigers." She searched the faces around her. "Peder?" she said in a frightened whisper that only she could hear. "I can't see you!"

Then came a crescendoing noise that seemed to explode over the platform as the train entered the station. There was a scream, louder even than the whoosh of air and the brakes on the train. The man in the green jacket bounced off the side of the first car, his body thrown down onto the platform with enough force to roll him over several times before he came to a rest against the legs of a bench. What Astrid would remember was a single frozen image as if taken from a horror film: terror in the man's face, his arms splayed out in a wild attempt to save himself

The old man with the shopping bag took Astrid's arm and rushed her past the crowds getting off the train and gathering around the man, who lay flat and unmoving. They went up the street, where Peder threw the bag into a refuse container and jammed the beret he had been wearing into his pocket.

Chapter 35

Two banks of lights flooded over Llewellyn's self-portrait. The painting had been taken from its frame then fastened to an easel, but not haphazardly; Nigel Jones had put a level against it to be certain the painted surface was perfectly perpendicular. Beneath the painting he taped a narrow strip of colors that ranged through yellow, red, blue, and black, "target colors," Jones said without explanation. The camera was a Sinar 8 X 10 viewcamera. The film was Ektachrome 64T, a professional quality positive-transparency film, loaded into sheet-film holders. Twenty of them. The four lights were 3200K tungsten lamps in aluminum reflectors. The camera was mounted on a thick-legged tripod, adjusted so the center of the 650mm Schneider lens was aimed precisely at the center of the painting, a half inch below the tip of Cézanne's nose. Jones had squared the film plane with the level, making certain it was also perpendicular. These precautions, he was told, would avoid a condition of parallax, an avoidance essential to taking a photograph without distortion. Then he disappeared under a black shroud and studied the image projected onto the ground glass, choosing Cézanne's eyes and the hair in his beard as points of focus.

Jones's expertise with a camera had been, until this assignment, about equal to that of the average owner of a 35mm camera who took family pictures on the weekend. A crash course in studio photography had been provided by

Gabriel Levine, one of London's top portrait photographers.

"I'm as ready as I'll ever be," Jones said. "Wish me luck." He slid film into the back of the camera, set the shutter speed and lens opening, then squeezed the cable release and made the first exposure. Levine had prepared a chart indicating twenty combinations of lens openings and shutter speeds, and if Jones were to duplicate what he had learned from Levine, he was guaranteed to produce six out of the twenty photographs within a balanced exposure range.

"There must be something I can do," Llewellyn said.

"Indeed there is. I'll need a taxi to the airport in about thirty minutes."

Llewellyn signaled Willkie on the intercom. "Mr. Jones will be leaving for La Guardia at 2:45, and we'll drive him over."

Jones rechecked the focus before each exposure. At 2:20 the job was completed. "I'll ring you if I have to reshoot." Jones said as he put the film into a canvas shoulder bag. "I trust I can leave the lights and all?"

"Of course," Llewellyn said. "Any chance you'll have to reshoot?"

"A slight one, but I'll know for certain this evening. I'll phone before ten o'clock either way. One last favor: I'd like to ring the laboratory and confirm that I'm on my way."

"Of course." Llewellyn motioned toward the phone.

Jones called and talked with a person named Garrity, then said he was all set. The drive to La Guardia might go quickly for a Friday afternoon, Willkie predicting that they were exactly twenty minutes in front of the weekend traffic.

"Who's Garrity?" Llewellyn asked.

"Lee Garrity was with your Treasury Department; be now freelances in counterfeit investigations. Knows every copy process there ever was, and with today's imaging technology, that's a full-time occupation."

"What happens next?" Llewellyn asked.,

"I'll try to explain what I've learned since we talked about it in London. The shots I took this afternoon are like the color slides you take with a 35mm camera, only much larger. The best one of the lot will be placed on a light table and scanned with a laser and divided into twenty thousand color units called pixels. Each pixel is evaluated with reference to the color target I put below the painting, the band of color you noticed. Each pixel is then converted into an electronic signal and stored on a disk, very much like a digital recording. That means, in computer language, that your portrait will be converted into thousands of zeros and ones.

"The computer evaluates this information and adjusts for the color peculiarities of Polacolor film, then a second generation transparency is created. That transparency will be projected onto a sheet of Polacolor film to the precise size of your painting. With all color variations accounted for and adjusted, we should then have a finished photograph that matches exactly with the original."

Llewellyn digested all that Jones told him, looking thoughtful though a bit confused, and asked, "But a Polaroid photograph has a smooth surface, no matter how scientifically it's made. How do you give it texture and the swirl of brushstrokes like *The Old Woman with a Rosary* that you showed me at Scotland Yard?"

"It's done by applying a clear, thick gel over the photograph," Jones went on. "Before it hardens, one of Garrity's artists will use a brush and a palette knife to re-create the texture and brush strokes of the original. That will take place in your home, where the artist can use the actual painting as his guide. Finally they'll put on a coat of UV-absorbent lacquer to add a soft patina and prevent color fading."

Llewellyn said, "What a hell of a way to make a photograph, or is it a painting?" Then he looked out just as Willkie turned off the Grand Central Parkway and said quietly to himself, "It better be damned good—it's got to fool a lot of people."

"I beg your pardon, Mr. Llewellyn?"

Llewellyn turned back and smiled. "Nothing, Jonesy. I was just preparing myself to become a lightning rod."

Chapter 36

At Oxby's urging and in response to Elliott Heston's persistent petitions, the assistant commissioner, Scotland Yard's number-two officer, authorized Operations Command Group (OCG) to upgrade the search for Vulcan to priority status. With that new emphasis and while Oxby attended the security council meeting, the Arts and Antiques Squad's conference room had been officially transformed into a command center, or Incident Room, in the parlance of the Yard. Oxby had flown into Heathrow Friday evening, gone to his flat where he sorted out his notes from the security council, and settled personal matters that had piled up during his absence. By midnight he was in bed with a book to put his mind in neutral but was asleep in minutes, the unopened book by his side.

Saturday morning at eight o'clock he had no sooner stepped from the lift on the fifteenth floor when Ann Browley took his arm and ushered him hurriedly to room 1518 where Jimmy Murratore stood waiting.

Three desks were clustered at the far end of the room, two side by side facing a third. Oxby's desk, complete to the last paper clip, had been brought in from his office. There were five phones, two on direct outside lines, one on a dedicated fax line. The computer was linked to the Forensic Science Laboratory, Criminal Intelligence Unit. It also interfaced with the Crime Support Unit, which had a round-the-clock secure satellite-connection to Interpol. The Incident Room was open for business.

Along the wall to the right on entering was a row of cork
panels, each one four feet wide and nearly twice as high.
There were five in all, and at the top of each panel was a
subject heading in bold letters.

VULCAN
DEAD PAINTINGS
CHEMICALS & POISONS
SPECULATIONS & CURIOSITIES
DEAD PEOPLE

Taped or pinned to the cork were notes, phone numbers,
assignment notices, photographs, news clippings, reports
from other police authorities, and, in the center of each
panel, a daily summary and commentary on progress or lack
of it, with reasons stated.

Oxby said, "What's 'dead people' about? One dead person's enough."

"There's been a murder in Reigate," Ann said. "The body
was found in the road that runs behind Shelbourne's studio.
Here's the police report." She pushed the two-page report
across the table.

Oxby read it quickly and looked up.

"We learned about it Friday," Ann said, "while you were
still in France. David Blaney called to say that when Shelbourne returned he discovered that his darkroom had been
broken into and that negatives and prints had been ruined.
That same day we learned the body had been found."

Oxby said, "The report is vague about the victim. What
do we know about him?"

"Not much. He was a local drifter—a homeless type the
shopowners called Sailor. We don't have hard evidence to
link his death with the break-in, but I know they go together."

"You have an accounting of all this?" Oxby asked.

"It's on your desk," Ann said, having anticipated the
question.

"Negatives destroyed, so there are no photographs," Oxby said quietly and with obvious irritation. "They were important, all right—important enough for murder."

Oxby went to the panel marked Dead Paintings. "I don't have anything to add to this, and I hope neither of you does, either. My rational brain says Vulcan has stopped at four, but my irrational brain tells me Vulcan doesn't behave rationally. The Museum of Modern Art in New York put their new portrait twenty feet from the down escalator, and I worry about that kind of carelessness. I'm also concerned about the De-Villeurs portrait." He stopped roving and leaned against the table. "That leaves the Llewellyn painting. Mr. Llewellyn has accepted the pied piper role with understandable reluctance, but I also think he's excited by it. Unfortunately, he likes to travel with companions we need to know more about. On this trip he's agreed to take only his man Fraser, his dog, and a reporter friend who might put out television stories each day."

Oxby stepped to the panel headed Chemicals & Poisons. "Anything new in this area?"

Ann said, "I wanted Jonesy with us, but he's not back from Massachusetts. I requested that he inspect the negatives at Shelbourne's because apparently they were destroyed by an acid. I'm disappointed that I have no more to report on the person who bought so much DFP in Marseille."

"Metzger?" Oxby said.

Ann nodded. "Dr. J-something-or-other Metzger. We don't know any more about him than we did two weeks ago, and I'm not optimistic we ever will."

"But worth keeping after," Oxby said. "Find Dr. Metzger, and you've probably found Vulcan."

He turned back to the panel headed Speculations & Curiosities. "What have we got here?"

Ann said, "I'm still curious to know why Clarence Boggs was murdered and equally curious to know why the killer used such a rare poison and went to such lengths to place it the car in that strange homemade affair. It's curious that

Metzger bought so much of the poison in Marseille." She paused and put on her own quizzical expression, "And isn't it terribly curious that Mr. Pinkster removed his self-portrait from his insurance policy this past June? Then the photographs, the photographs we'll never see, because, curiously and coincidentally, the negatives were destroyed. Who knew about the negatives? Conceivably Mr. Pinkster knew, and David Blaney. Perhaps even Clarence Boggs. But he was killed. Vulcan knew a photographer was in the gallery that day, but did he know who the photographer was?" She nodded. "I think so. And poor Sailor. What did he know?" The furrows deepened, "Like Alice said, it grows curiouser and curiouser."

"Good show, Annie. What about you, Jimmy. Any curiosities?"

"I'll start out sayin' I don't have space in my brain for all the curious things Sergeant Browley's got crammed into hers. I've laid to rest any lingerin' doubts I had about Mr. Boggs's gamblin' activities, so I've got no more curiosity about any of the agents doin' him in. But I do have a first-class curiosity that's been takin' me places I've never seen. Seems when we put Mr. Pinkster's name in for a background check, one of the reports we got was from the Port of London sayin' the guy's a licensed waterman. It's a provisional license because he hasn't taken any tests and keeps askin' for extensions and pays all the fees on time. Some pals in the Thames Division helped me track the boat to Cadogan Pier. Would you believe we found a bloody tugboat? Crew's a Greek couple. Tug's even got a Greek name—*Sepera*—and a Greek flag flying off the stern."

Oxby wrote *Sepera* on the board and stared at the word for half a minute. "It could be a lark," he said finally, "or some kind of investment. A boat for hire?" He turned to Jimmy. "Get yourself back on a police launch with your chums and see what Pinkster's doing with a tugboat. If you have a problem I'll work it out with Chief Inspector

Wycroft; he was just made number two in the Thames Division. What else have you got?"

Jimmy shook his head.

"Annie," Oxby said, "Make sure Jonesy gets into Shelbourne's darkroom, then I want you to speed up your investigation of Astrid Haraldsen. She's somewhat of an enigma, beautiful and dull, or pretty and damned smart, I'm not sure which. Be sure that Intelligence checks her record at the design school in Oslo—name of it's in her file." Oxby was now standing by the panel headed Vulcan. "Regrettably, I can't add to our profile of Vulcan—any thoughts I've got belong under curiosities, and we've got enough of those."

Oxby reviewed the assignments he'd given his assistants then sent them away with the admonition that there would not be much relaxation until the investigation had moved further along. Before going off, he walked slowly past the five panels, pausing for several minutes in front of each. He secured room 1518 and started for the lift. Before reaching it he was met by a staff officer from Heston's office who handed him an envelope. "I tried your office, but half the furniture was missing. Is everything all right?"

"Quite all right, thank you." The envelope was marked urgent, and inside was a decoded message from Henri Trama that had been transmitted by the Direction Centrale de la Police Judiciare, Paris:

Surveillance of Astrid Haraldsen terminated . . .
Our agent critically injured while following
subject . . . incident occurred Rambuteau Métro
station 3 November 1310 hours . . . danger and
consequences of your request not fully
described . . . complaint filed . . . search for
Vulcan in France not your responsibility.

Chapter 37

Heavy weekend traffic and the remnants of a brief shower slowed the traffic through the London streets and made the drive to Bletchingly a bore. Oxby's decision to pay Alan Pinkster a surprise visit had been initially prompted by a presentation made by Félix Lemieux, which dealt with the escalating cost of insurance and how difficult it had been to obtain coverage for those paintings in the retrospective that were not insured by the loaner. Mixed in with the files he had taken to France was a report on the insurance status of the Pinkster collection, information which had been compiled by the Fraud Squad and which, if accurate, could discredit statements made by Pinkster. News that a drifter named Sailor had been murdered was another reason for Oxby's surprise visit. He would interrogate Pinkster without another officer present, a violation of procedure. But he did it all the time, and he knew that Heston would raise hell.

Alan Pinkster's manor house had originally been named Valley View. It had been built in 1848 and faced out on a once-pristine valley that was now encroached upon by the Godstone Hills golf course and a stretch of the M23 motorway. A Mrs. Padgett, squarely built and mannish, answered the door and gave her name and rank (property manager). She seemed unimpressed by Oxby's credentials and was slow to reveal that Mrs. Pinkster and her daughter were in Maidstone, Kent, for the weekend and that Mr. Pinkster was expected "sometime later in the day."

Oxby discovered the art gallery was locked shut, and there were no cars to indicate that any of the staff had come to work on this Saturday. He had hoped to find David Blaney, but was instead confronted by a guard on patrol accompanied by an intimidating Doberman. He returned to his car. Thirty minutes later a familiar black Mercedes appeared.

"What on earth brings you here?" Pinkster asked with undisguised irritation.

"Questions," Oxby answered with a mischievous smile. "My business is questions, and if I don't ask any I may I find myself in genuine difficulty."

"Look here, Inspector, I'm not pleased with surprise visits from the police, and just now I've got a terribly busy schedule."

"Ten minutes tops," Oxby said encouragingly. "I really need your help."

Pinkster frowned, shook his head nervously, and gingerly patted the red skin above his lips. "Damn it all, let's get on with it." He pointed toward a terrace at the side of his house. They sat on fat lemon-yellow cushions in white rattan chairs. Oxby dropped his cap onto the slate and took out his notepad and tape recorder. "If you have no objection, I'll turn this on." He flipped on the recorder and placed it on the table between them.

"Mr. Pinkster, is your painting still in the gallery?"

"Why do you want to know?" Pinkster asked imputatively.

"We have no photographic record of it, before or after. It's important we have those for our records."

"Photographs of a jellied mess? What possible use can that be?"

"As I said, for the records, and so our forensic experts can make comparisons to the other paintings. I respect that it is your property, but your cooperation will be very much appreciated."

"I can have it photographed. Tell me what you need."

"Then what's left of the painting is in your gallery?"

"You seem surprised," Pinkster said.

"It's possible the insurance people might have taken it."

"They're not interested."

"Why is that, do you suppose?"

"I don't know," Pinkster said flatly.

"I made some inquiries into how the insurance companies were handling these huge losses. We assumed there was
no insurance—at least as we know it—in the case of the
painting in the Hermitage. The painting in our National
Gallery is covered under an Arts Council cooperative program, and thus far we haven't received a report on the
Boston Museum's loss. Yours is the only one that was privately owned, and it seemed reasonable to assume that you
would have theft or damage insurance through Lloyd's, or at
least involve them indirectly through a reinsuring arrangement." Oxby leaned forward. "But Lloyd's reported that all
of your paintings were covered under a floater policy in
which they were a participant, and that the Cézanne self-
portrait had been taken off the policy in June. Is that so?"

"The premiums were outlandish. I was trying to negoti-
ate more favorable costs."

"With Lloyd's?"

"I—don't recall. Besides, I have someone in my firm follow up on those things."

"You allowed such a valuable painting to go uninsured?"

"I object to your inference, Inspector," Pinkster said indignantly. "That was not my intention, and I bloody well
didn't think it would be destroyed."

"But Mr. Pinkster, you knew there was a danger—"

"Which is precisely why the premiums became so high."
Pinkster looked across at Oxby for the first time. "I had
planned to take the painting off the wall and, in fact, had instructed Clarence Boggs to make arrangements." The redness around his mouth seemed to intensify. "That didn't
happen as you know."

"Would you intend to use the same photographer who was in the gallery the day the painting was destroyed?"

Pinkster turned away. "I don't contract for photographers, David Blaney handles that sort of thing."

"I see." Oxby flipped a page in his notebook. "By chance did you see the photographs that were taken on that fateful day?"

Pinkster shook his head slowly. "I received a report from Blaney about them, but photographers are frequently in the gallery for one reason or another."

"I believe Blaney said that you had insisted on seeing the photographs before they were shown to anyone." Oxby turned a page, "Here it is. I have a note to that effect."

Pinkster sighed deeply. "I was terribly upset at the time and I—" His legs and arms were moving nervously. "I recall now that I did know which photographer had the assignment, and I instructed him to send the photographs to me before they were circulated."

"You forgot that you had seen the photographs, yet in fact you had called the photographer. A bit unusual, perhaps?"

"I bloody forgot!" Pinkster snapped angrily. "I was bloody upset then, just as I'm bloody upset right now."

"Now that you remember seeing the photographs, will you tell me if you had any particular reason for wanting to see them?"

"I hoped I'd find something that might tell me who destroyed my painting."

"But you didn't see anything?"

"No," he waved his hand feebly, "just a bunch of women. But if I had seen something you would have known. It's a silly question."

"I ask so many questions," Oxby said dryly. "I'm bound to ask a silly one now and then. A bunch of women, you say. But there was a man in one photograph."

"Perhaps there was, I don't recall." Pinkster moved back

in his chair and sat stiffly. "Why all these questions about photographs?"

"Apparently there are several photographs we haven't yet seen. Blaney tried to order another set of prints from the photographer. His name escapes me, but I believe it's one you know—"

"Ian Shelbourne."

"Yes, of course, Shelbourne. He didn't respond to any of our phone calls, apparently because he had been called away on assignment." Oxby checked the tape recorder then put it back between them, continuing to talk in a chatty, conversational manner. "And another thing. A homeless old fellow known as Sailor was found dead in the alley behind Shelbourne's shop. Had you heard about that?"

Pinkster tensed, only slightly, but Oxby saw it, "I don't keep up with the homeless," Pinkster said, attempting black humor unsuccessfully.

"I don't suppose you do. But someone broke into Shelbourne's darkroom and destroyed everything to do with the photographs that were taken on that particular day in your gallery. "They used an acid. Maybe—just a guess—they used the same solution that was used on the paintings. What do you think?"

"What are you suggesting?" Pinkster flushed.

"It's not a suggestion, really, merely following a notion that because you know Shelbourne, it's possible you knew about Sailor and the break-in."

Pinkster sighed noisily, as if to say he was answering the last question. "Shelbourne came to me before we began construction of the gallery and asked if he could photograph the building as it went up, said he planned on doing a photo journal or some sort of thing. I told him to go ahead, and he's been one of our photographers ever since. I don't meddle in his business and don't know about the Sailor person or break-ins."

Pinkster abruptly got to his feet, pointed to his watch and said, "Your ten minutes are up, Inspector."

Chapter 38

Pinkster waited until Oxby's car made the turn at the foot of the driveway then went to his office in the gallery and dialed a long series of numbers. He clamped the receiver against his ear, heard a faint hum, then the sound of a phone ringing.

"Oui." A single word answer, but no doubt that Aukrust said it.

"They're asking questions about an old man. What happened?"

"A mistake. He came into the darkroom, and that was wrong. He ran away, but I caught him and—"

Pinkster waited for the rest of the explanation. "Go on, what in bloody hell happened?"

"I shook him, and he fell."

"You pushed him. You bastard, you killed him."

"I said it was a mistake."

"You make too many mistakes. You don't think, and you were bloody damned stupid."

"Don't talk that way to me."

"I'll talk however I damned please. Why didn't you take the files away and burn them? Why leave more evidence?"

"What's left of the solvent is oxidized. It will take months to duplicate my formulation," he said with pride in his voice, "perhaps forever! You are wrong. I didn't leave evidence."

"More stupidity. You honestly believe you can outwit the

most sophisticated forensic laboratory in the world? You're an insufferable egotist."

"I said there is no evidence."

"A dead body is evidence. Forced entry into Shelbourne's darkroom leaves evidence. Negatives destroyed with your damned special chemicals are evidence."

Aukrust did not answer. Finally Pinkster said, "I want you in London on Thursday. Go on board the *Sepera* at six o'clock and have the DeVilleurs painting with you."

Afternoon ended and evening began in a seamless change of light, from sun to neons and incandescents, some blinking a fiery Christmas greeting. Astrid's room was dark and small, and from the foot of the bed where she sat, she could touch the faded draperies that flanked a single, narrow window. Below, at the corner, was the café, bustling with young office workers spending relaxed minutes with friends. That morning she had walked toward the cafe, expecting to pass the young woman with dark hair who had replaced the agent with the Detroit Lions jacket. The woman was gone, as was the dark sedan she usually sat in. Astrid went to a neighborhood market and bought cheese and croissants then returned to the hotel by circling the block but saw no one that qualified as a replacement "follower." Somehow, however, she was not convinced she had been abandoned.

At nine o'clock she would meet Peder, and they would have dinner. She had been given explicit instructions: a taxi across the Seine, then another one back to Gare de Lyon, where she was to walk through the station to Rue de Chalon and on to the windows of a children's clothing store. Peder would join her, and they would walk to a small neighborhood restaurant near the St. Antoine hospital.

Astrid's words came in a rush, but barely louder than the hushed conversation of a young couple at a nearby table. "There's no one, Peder, not the woman, and both cars are gone. But I still imagine I'm being followed, that someone's watching all the time."

"I'm leaving tomorrow." He put a finger under her chin and tilted her head back. "You must stay until Llewellyn comes to Paris."

"No, Peder, I don't want to stay here alone."

His hand moved quickly, and he pinched her chin with the vice formed by his thumb and fingers. "You will do as I say."

"Please? Can't I go with you?" He tightened the vice so that she could barely speak. "You're . . . hurting . . ."

"Stop telling me what you will and won't do. They can only watch you. So let them watch while you go back to your business of shopping for antiques, exactly as you told Llewellyn and Oxby in Fontainebleau. Understand?"

She nodded, and he released his grip. Immediately she rubbed at the soreness then timidly asked, "How long will I be alone?"

"A few days, a week."

"Why are you in Paris?" she asked.

Immediately forgotten to him was the pain he had inflicted on her moments before. He took her hand and rubbed it gently, and he did it without awareness of her fear that he would clamp his huge hands over hers and hurt her again. His anger had simply expired, and he said, "Because I want to be with you, to have you kiss every part of me." He whispered, "To make love."

Chapter 39

"Park there, Emily." Margueritte DeVilleurs strained forward, pointing to the driveway that ran beside Frédéric Weisbord's home. "I haven't been here since Cécile was alive," she said wistfully. "Such a marvelous person. She had to be—married to Freddy was purgatory on earth. But she had her gardens." She pointed again. "Park here." They climbed the stairs to the porch and rapped on the front door. The chain was withdrawn and the door opened.

"I am Margueritte DeVilleurs and have come with my companion. I phoned to say I would be here today."

Idi stood to the side, her head cocked and her face screwed into a perplexed expression. "You are Madame DeVilleurs?"

"I am, of course," Margueritte replied with obvious certainty. "Does that surprise you?"

Idi studied Margueritte and said, "Only that Monsieur Weisbord said you were an old woman, he said—"

"He said many things that were not true." Margueritte responded with the usual intolerance she attached to all references to Frédéric Weisbord. "I knew him all too well, and it's why I haven't set foot in this house since his wife passed away." Margueritte took quick inventory of the rooms connected to the hall, then said to Idi, "I've come for a painting Monsieur Weisbord took from me."

Emily moved abreast of Idi, and now she and Margueritte flanked the housekeeper. Margueritte said, "The painting is a portrait of a man,"—she held her hands apart—"so big, and in a frame. Have you seen it?"

Idi's hand shot up, pointing to the floor above. "He put it over his bed, a man with a dark beard." Idi nodded. "But it's not there. It's gone."

Margueritte reacted sharply. "How do you mean, it's gone?"

"It's not there any more," and her hands waved again. "I didn't go to his bedroom until—I think it was Monday, and he died Friday evening in his office just over there." She waved in the direction of the office. "They asked me to find his best suit to bury him in—that's when I saw that the painting was gone."

"Have you looked for it?" Margueritte asked anxiously.

Idi shook her head. "I didn't like it enough to care if it was on the wall or not."

"Perhaps he put it in his office. Take me there."

Idi guided Margueritte and Emily into the room that had been unused for a week, the air redolent with stale tobacco smoke. They looked everywhere the painting might have been concealed, but in minutes it became obvious the hunt was futile. "Could it still be in the bedroom?" Margueritte asked.

They paraded up the stairs to Weisbord's bedroom, and all three looked through closets and in a high, wide armoire; then they hunted in the other bedrooms, then back to Weisbord's bedroom. Idi pointed to a picture hook on the wall above the bed. "That's where he put it."

Margueritte's eyes darted from closets to bureau then down to the bed, which had been neatly made with a thick spread pulled tightly over a mound of pillows. She sat on the bed and ran her hand over the spread as if it were possible the painting was beneath the covers. "Look under the bed, Emily. We haven't tried there."

Emily got on her knees and probed under the bed. "I've got something," she said, and pulled out the frame.

Margueritte knelt beside Emily, the empty frame in front of her on the floor. "That's the one." She glanced at Emily then up at Idi, her eyes sad. "Why would he take the painting out of the frame?"

"There was a man," Idi began, "who said he was a friend. He came that night to surprise Monsieur Weisbord. He had a bottle of wine. A present, he said."

"What did he look like?" Margueritte asked.

"Tall, I remember," Idi said, her eyes closed, testing her memory. "He had brown hair and a bandage on one ear, and he carried a strange kind of bag under his arm; it was long and round."

"Was he French?"

Idi shook her head. "He spoke French, but with an accent I don't know."

"Scandinavian?" Margueritte asked, then spoke several heavily accented sentences. "Like that?" she asked Idi.

Idi thought for a moment. "Maybe that way."

"It was Peder," Margueritte said to Emily. "I want to go to the office again."

Emily carried the frame, and they returned to Weisbord's office where they were assaulted with a new odor, a sweet, artificial smell of flowers, the kind made strong and bottled into cheap cologne. Seated in Weisbord's oversized chair was LeToque, his black hair combed slickly across the edges of his forehead and over the tips of his high cheekbones. One eye was still red and moist, yet on the rest of his thin face was a supercilious, smug expression. Standing beside him was Gaby, wearing a short skirt and black stockings and emitting the *grande-odeur.*

"Why are you here?" Idi demanded.

"To have the Italian *putain* cook for us."

Idi grasped a glass paperweight from the desk and raised it over her head, "You bastard, call me a whore—I curse your family, everyone!"

"I hope you do." He mixed the words with a high-pitched

giggle, then jumped up and grabbed the paperweight from Idi's hand. "They are shit, and you can put a curse on them all, my father first." He looked insolently at Margueritte. "Do you have business here?"

"Of course I have business," Margueritte said. "Monsieur Weisbord was my lawyer, his wife a dear friend. I have been here many times." She sized up the young man as brash and potentially dangerous.

"I have business, too. Money. I got sixty thousand francs coming."

"A good deal of money," Margueritte said. "How did you earn so much?"

"That was between me and the old man," LeToque said.

"But Weisbord is dead, and there will be no money unless you file a claim against his estate. You'll need proof he owed you money."

He shook his head. "What fucking business do you have with Weisbord?"

Margueritte bristled, then revised her assessment of LeToque, seeing him now as insecure and unable to understand why he was unlikely to collect any money owed him by Weisbord. "My business is to recover a painting Weisbord took from me."

"He had a painting that he was going to sell in Geneva." LeToque pushed away from the table. "I drove him to the gallery and was with him when he made arrangements. They said it would sell for 250 million francs."

"Where did you last see it?"

"In Weisbord's bedroom. He hung it over his bed like a goddamned crucifix."

"It's gone. We found the frame under the bed."

"The bastard Aukrust—he took it. He was here the night Weisbord died."

"He said he'd kill me," Gaby chimed in excitedly. "He pointed a knife at me." She put a finger on her throat.

"No, no," Margueritte protested, "that isn't his way. I know him. He's gentle and—"

"He's gentle like a wild-ass bull. Look here at my eyes, still red from what he sprayed over me. And he put a piece of glass through a pal's hand. He killed Weisbord is what I think."

Margueritte sat in the chair next to the desk. "Could you find him?"

"I'm here to get what Weisbord owed me. There's silver and china and other paintings I can sell."

"You won't take a spoon from this house," Idi glowered.

Margueritte said, "Find the painting, and I'll pay you ten thousand francs."

"Ten? I'm owed sixty."

Margueritte shook her head. "I knew that old lawyer all too well. You won't collect one franc."

LeToque's eyes darted from Gaby to Margueritte. "And what do I get if I can't find it?"

"Prove that you tried, and I'll pay you five thousand francs."

Chapter 40

Oxby's penchant for operating independently was shaken a bit when Elliott Heston sent his inspector a memorandum in which the service's stricture on investigation procedure was cited; specifically, that a second officer is required during an official interrogation. It was a mild reprimand, accompanied by a note something to the effect that it was unlikely another warning would be necessary. Heston had also asked Oxby to kindly inform him of any unilateral action he had taken in the Vulcan case but that he had "inadvertently" failed to report. Heston's notes were brief, the scoldings never personal. Oxby did what he always did with these memorandums. He crumpled this one into a small ball and lobbed it into a wastebasket.

The loss of the photographs preyed on Oxby's mind. It was more than what the photographs might have shown; it was the fact that whoever spilled acid over the negatives was also responsible for destroying the paintings—or so it was becoming apparent to Oxby. A workable hypothesis, he thought. There was also the strong suggestion that Pinkster knew much more than he had admitted. And what of Sailor, whose autopsy showed he had had a ravaged liver and an ulcerated stomach but had died from a fractured skull? Perhaps it was just as well that Heston had reminded him of protocol and that Sergeant Browley was accompanying him on his visit with Ian Shelbourne. Perhaps he would be able to concentrate on what he wanted to learn.

Ian Paul Shelbourne was a man of forty, a bit paunchy, with prematurely gray hair, pale blue eyes, white skin, and was dressed in faded jeans and sweater. He spoke in a soft monotone and suggested that the interview be conducted in his portrait studio, where they settled on an odd pair of chairs, with Shelbourne perched on a piano bench in front of the powder-blue scrim where his subjects sat for their portraits. With clothes, hair, and eyes nearly the same color as the background, it seemed that Shelbourne might actually disappear. Too many hours in the darkroom, Oxby thought.

Oxby began the questioning. "How long have you known Alan Pinkster?"

"Five years, I suppose. Or six. About that."

"How did you get to know him?"

"We were introduced shortly after he bought the house in Bletchingly. We rarely saw each other for a year or so, but then we're not exactly in the same socioeconomic sphere. Several years later I got an assignment from *Country Life* to cover the party he gave after his house had been redecorated. That's when he announced his plans to build his art gallery and when I got the idea to make a photodocumentary of the construction, from groundbreaking to dedication. He thought it was a good idea and gave me a contract."

"Did that help overcome the fact you were not in the same socioeconomic sphere?"

"Not exactly, though we became more friendly."

"Are you the official photographer of the Pinkster gallery?"

"I suppose, but only informally."

"Was it unusual for Mr. Pinkster to ask to see your photographs before they were shown to Clarence Boggs or David Blaney?"

Shelbourne thought briefly about the questions. "He would occasionally ask to see my photographs before I submitted them to Blaney."

"Do you have a personal relationship with Mr. Pinkster?"

"I'm not sure what you mean by 'personal.'"

"Do you see him socially?"

"I said we are not in the same—"

"Sphere, I think you said. Even so, did you see him socially at all? Twice a month—twice a year?"

"Something in between, I would say."

"Would you say that you are personal friends?"

"After six years, we are friends of a sort. But what's that got to do with the negatives."

"You're perfectly right, Mr. Shelbourne. It may have absolutely nothing to do with the negatives. It seems I get going on questions sometimes and . . . well, forgive me."

"I understand," Shelbourne said.

"About the negatives. Miss Browley asked David Blaney to order a complete set of photographs, and I understand he called to give you that order. But you were away on an assignment. Can you tell me the nature of that assignment?"

"Photographs of new manufacturing facilities at the Oxford Fabrics Company."

"Where is that located?"

"In Ashton. Outside of Manchester."

"That's not far away. Was it a difficult assignment?"

"The assignment was straightforward, it was the weather that was difficult."

"How is that?"

"We were washed out by rain for nearly a week."

"Do you recall the dates?"

"Sometime in the middle of the month."

"You were gone for quite a while. Two weeks, or was it longer?"

"I also had a personal matter pending at that time."

"Exactly when did you discover that your shop had been broken into?"

"As you can see, I'm not terribly good about dates, except that it all happened on a Saturday, and Christmas wasn't too far off. I don't offhand know what date that would be."

Ann supplied the answer. "The fifteenth."

"Yes, I remember now, that was the date. But it was the seventeenth, Monday, when I learned from Blaney that he wanted another set of prints. That's when I discovered someone had broken into my darkroom."

"When did you tell David Blaney about it?"

"I think on the next day, Tuesday."

"Weren't you alarmed to discover the negatives had been ruined?"

"Yes, of course."

"Did you notify the police?"

"Not right away."

"Why was that?"

"Looking back on it, I don't know why. Foolish that I didn't."

"Who did you tell?"

"Blaney. And I told Alan Pinkster."

"Was he upset?"

"He was sorry that someone had broken into my shop, but when I told him the only damage was to negatives of the tour group he didn't seem terribly upset." Shelbourne returned to the bench and sat.

"Did Pinkster seem surprised that someone went to a considerable effort to destroy only those negatives?"

"He didn't say anything to that effect."

"Why do you suppose someone would want to destroy pictures of a group of Danes?"

"I haven't any idea, Inspector. I'm so relieved that nothing else was damaged that I haven't given it much thought."

"Did Pinkster know that we had requested a duplicate set of the photographs?"

"I don't believe I ever told him. Blaney might have said something."

Oxby said, "I want you to recall the group that went

through the gallery. There were about twenty-five, and all were from the Danish embassy in London. Do you remember anything about them?"

"Frankly, I don't. I see so many different groups during the year and usually have no reason to know one from another. We were taking photographs for a new brochure, and David asked if I would use up a roll on group even though he felt it wasn't a typical crowd."

"What did he mean by that?"

"That they were mostly women."

"A typical group would be men and women?"

"Yes."

"But there was at least one man. Did you notice that?"

Shelbourne paused and stared down at his hands, which he was vigorously rubbing against each other. "I can't remember precisely. Perhaps I vaguely recall seeing a man in the group."

"Can you describe him?"

Shelbourne closed his eyes and winced as if trying to bring up a mental picture, then he shook his head, "Honestly, I can't remember anything except that he was taller than everyone else, but most men are taller than women, so that's no help. You must understand that I use a motorized camera with extremely fast film to catch candids of a group passing through as that one was. When I can fire off in rapid order I'm bound to get a few exceptional shots, perhaps even some unusual lighting that might give an extra quality to a photograph. That keeps my attention on the equipment, making sure the film's advancing and the settings are correct. I have a good eye for composition, but it's not trained on who's in the picture. Not group shots, certainly. I knew we would make contact sheets and eventually I would see every photograph that I took. Even the one I don't remember taking."

"Contact sheets?"

"I lay five or six negative strips directly on photographic

paper in a sandwich of clear glass, pop on some light, then develop in the regular way. I like to get thirty-six exposures on one sheet."

"How many contact sheets do you make?"

"One for each roll of film."

"Where did you put it?"

"In the file along with the negatives."

"Where is the contact sheet of the Danish tour group?"

The photographer made a futile gesture with both his hands. "It was ruined along with the negatives."

"How carefully did you look at the contact sheet before it was destroyed?"

Shelbourne smiled indulgently. "Please realize, Inspector, that the photographs are the same size as the negatives, not much larger than a postage stamp, and I don't inspect them for content. I run a crayon through the shots I feel are out of focus or badly exposed."

"Do the enlargements carry any identification?"

"I put a code on the back of each photograph. Perhaps there's a sample on that table." Shelbourne sifted through a stack of photographs and came away with two. He gave one to Oxby and one to Ann. "You'll see there are numbers and letters. They identify the customer, the project, date, and film-roll number. With that information I can locate the negative in very short order and make a print in half an hour."

"Mr. Shelbourne, you are a professional photographer and an expert on film and photographs. If you wished to destroy some negatives, how would you go about it?"

"Burn them, I suppose. They make a lovely fire."

"Indeed," Oxby said simply. "We're about out of questions; however, I do want to ask you about the man named Sailor. The Reigate police reported that his body was found behind your shop. Did you know him?"

Shelbourne nodded. "First off, he wasn't found behind my shop, it was two shops along the way. Yes, I did know him, all of the shopowners knew him."

"What can you tell me about him?"

"He was out of Dickens, one might say. A drifter, what are called homeless now. Sober, he was a good worker, but he was too fond of the bottle. He had grown old for his age, wizened up along with a twisted nose and a few scars that gave him a marvelous face. I paid him to pose, and he came to like it because it made him feel important for a little while. A few of my best shots are in the front of the shop."

"We saw them," Ann said.

Oxby said, "Was he well liked?"

"I think so, but I can't speak for the others."

"Was he the sort to make enemies?"

"I can't imagine it."

Oxby thanked Shelbourne and preceded Ann to the showroom. The Christmas wreath seemed out of place, he thought, though the holiday had come and gone less than a week earlier. When they were on the pavement in front of the shop, he said to Ann. "I want to see where they found Sailor's body."

"It's been several weeks," Ann said. "The Reigate police report was very thorough, and you said—"

"And I have always said, Sergeant, that no report substitutes for the real thing." He started walking.

"I was afraid that's what you would say," she said, following him to the service road behind the shops. Just then, Shelbourne appeared on the receiving platform.

"You have a call, Inspector. Sergeant Murratore . . ."

Chapter 41

Peder Aukrust put his passport on the counter and peered down at a beefy, bespectacled agent who at that precise moment stifled a yawn. The agent compared the photograph to the man standing in front of him, pawed through several pages in a thick notebook, then ran his finger down rows of numbers, closed the book, glanced up, and asked routinely, "Where did your flight originate?"

"Paris," Aukrust answered. The agent made a notation, stamped an empty page with a loud slap, and said mechanically, "Enjoy the new year."

"*Tusen takk.*" Aukrust nodded with forced pleasantness. He had forgotten that it was a new year, the third day, in fact. He went through customs without incident, found a taxi, and an hour later was at the King's Arms Pub on Cheyne Walk near the Albert Bridge, several hundred yards from Cadogan Pier. It was 4:30 when he arrived at the pub and took a position at a table by a window from where he could see the pier and *Sepera* moored just beyond the blue-painted pier-manager's shed. At five o'clock the locals began crowding around the bar, and an hour later two red lights atop the sternpost on the *Sepera* blinked off and on. Aukrust hoisted up his travel bag and went out to the street, crossed through the commuter traffic to steps that led over the stone wall of the embankment, then walked down the gangway to the pier.

"You saw the signal?" Nikos asked from the top of the gangway.

"Of course. I came immediately. Where is Pinkster?" Aukrust demanded.

"We will meet him at the Tower Pier," Nikos said. "He will not arrive there until 7:30."

"Go now," Aukrust said emphatically.

"Mr. Pinkster is very precise," Nikos said. "We will be early."

"Then we'll be early." Aukrust glared at Nikos. "We go now."

Sophie stood in the doorway and greeted Aukrust by calling him Dr. Metzger, remembering his first visit to the *Sepera* and asking what he would drink, or whether he wanted coffee.

An eighth of a mile behind the *Sepera* a police launch attached to the Thames Division of the Metropolitan Police followed quietly. Three men were on the black-hulled boat with black-and-white checkered markings on the white cabin. All were police officers, career members of the division, each having served two years with Scotland Yard, and each with prior service in either the Royal Navy or the Merchant Navy. Sergeant Jeff Jennings was the ranking officer, Constables O'Brian and Nestor handled communications and observation.

Sepera passed Tower Pier at 6:48, continued on course for five minutes, then circled back to an open mooring near a sightseeing boat tied up for the night.

When *Sepera* came about, Jennings cut his engines and made a hard turn toward the middle of the river. "Tell *Ben Jolly* to take over at Tower Pier," Jennings called out to O'Brian. He then turned back to his original course and passed the *Sepera* just as it settled against the dock.

Aukrust saw the other boat, but not until it cruised past did he realize it was a police launch. He watched it continue under Tower Bridge, then he returned to the deckhouse just as Alan Pinkster came aboard. It was 7:30.

"A police boat just went by," Aukrust said.

"I saw it," Pinkster replied. "Patrol boat. Some days the bloody river is filled with them."

Ben Jolly was a utilitarian-looking motorboat masquerading as a slug on water. It was actually an unmarked police boat capable of chasing down any floating object between Darford Creek and Staines Bridge, the fifty-four mile stretch patrolled by the Thames Division. It was a small, cramped cruiser that consisted of a hull, a powerful motor, and radios. A fixed cowling covered the two-man crew headed by Sergeant Tompkins. The second man, on special assignment and dressed in a heavy black jacket and wool cap, was Detective Sergeant Jimmy Murratore.

The *Ben Jolly* was difficult to spot, as it was painted in shades of dark green and gray and sat low in the water. It lurked less than a hundred yards behind the police launch and was now directly off Tower Pier, where it waited for *Sepera*.

"To our success." Alan Pinkster poured champagne into long-stemmed glasses, handed one to Peder, raised his own, and took a sip. "And to Paul Cézanne and all the pictures he painted of himself." He drank again. "Join me, Peder. Drink to the recovery of the DeVilleurs portrait. Splendid work."

Aukrust returned a cold, penetrating stare that made every inch of his tall body a mass of intimidation. He went to the circle of chairs and sat in the one obviously meant for Pinkster, the one by the table. He put his glass down next to the telephone and said, "If you're in a mood to celebrate, we should talk about money again."

"I've paid you bloody well," Pinkster said, then touched the soreness around his mouth with his fingertips. "We agreed on your fee for the delivery of the DeVilleurs portrait."

Aukrust replied, his head nodding slightly, "You remember that the painting had been scheduled for auction and would set a new record price. Fifty million dollars, some were saying."

Pinkster smiled and sipped the champagne. "And I'll sell it for a record price."

"You get more, I get more," Aukrust replied. "Besides, I didn't plan on the little bastard who surprised me while I was in Shelbourne's darkroom. You owe me for that."

"I don't pay for mistakes. That was your problem."

An intercom phone rang. Pinkster spoke briefly into it then put it down. "There will be more money. After the sale."

The *Sepera* began to move. "Where are we going?" Aukrust asked.

"I'm meeting with my Far Eastern dealer, the one I've described as rather special, the one whose clientele collect art on a grand scale."

"Why do you want me to meet him?"

Pinkster refilled his glass. "You won't actually meet him, but you will be able to watch him and listen to him. I want you to hear what he thinks about the DeVilleurs portrait and how much his client will pay for it." Pinkster settled into the chair beside Aukrust, his grin now grown to an expectant smile. "I'm anxious to see the portrait." He nudged his shoe against Aukrust's travel bag.

Aukrust was slow to reply. "I don't have the painting."

Pinkster's smile collapsed. "You didn't bring it with you? Is that what you mean?"

Aukrust nodded, "I said I didn't bring it with me." The voice was ice.

"What have you done with it?"

"I put it in a storage locker in the railroad station in Aix-en-Provence."

Pinkster exploded. "That can't be true . . . you wouldn't be so stupid as to put a painting worth a goddamned fortune in an ordinary locker—"

Aukrust rose up and let fly with a clenched fist against Pinkster's hand, propelling the champagne glass against the wall, "Don't talk to me that way."

Pinkster put up his hands as if to ward off Aukrust's next blow. "I . . . I can't believe you would do such a thing without permission."

"Permission to do what? I was nearly killed when they took the painting from me. The old man paid for that. He paid, all right." He made an expression that was as much a grimace as a grin. "Hear what I'm saying? He's dead."

Pinkster was breathing in short, nervous bursts. "I hear you."

Aukrust went on. "Before they open the exhibition I will give Madame DeVilleurs her painting."

"Will you sit down?" Pinkster asked respectfully, the lower part of his face now painfully splotched. "You didn't tell me that you like Madame DeVilleurs. I understand that, she's been good to you. Is that right?"

"Yes," was Aukrust's simple reply.

"And I can understand that you want to do something for her, something important . . . to make her happy."

"When she learns the painting is being returned to her, she will be happy."

"But there may be something else, something better you can do. She must need money—that's it, her husband is dead, and she has no income."

"She has property and other paintings worth millions."

"Then she doesn't need the portrait. Don't you see, Peder? The painting is more important to us. I promised it to Kondo." The words, thin and soft, barely escaped from Pinkster's mouth. "He can sell it for nearly as much as it would bring at the auction. There will be a great deal of money to share. You understand that, don't you?"

Aukrust remained silent. Pinkster was on his feet, his arms extended out as if pleading for help, "Say you understand," he said, "Say that you do, Peder. Say anything, for Christ's sake!"

Lights shone from a dozen new buildings on Canary Wharf, highlighted by One Canada Square, which soared up like a giant beacon. *Sepera* was in mid-river, three hundred yards from the new complex. *Ben Jolly* backed away into the darkness along the west shore of the Thames. Jimmy Murratore trained night-vision binoculars on the tugboat.

At 7:45 a small boat pulled alongside the tug. Two figures could be seen stepping onto the deck of the *Sepera*.

There was another room on the *Sepera*, reached through a sliding panel in the wall beneath the television screen mounted high up on the forward bulkhead of the Grand Salon. It was a stateroom of elegant proportions, lavishly furnished and equipped with electronic gadgets that included closed-circuit television linked to cameras in the deckhouse and two others concealed in the salon. In this comfort Aukrust would be able to observe the meeting between Pinkster and Kondo. Pinkster had rehearsed his presentation of the DeVilleurs portrait, even to the stubborn position he would take on the price he would demand from Kondo. But now he was recovering from the shock of not having the portrait and faced with dealing with a personality as unpredictable and dangerous as Peder Aukrust.

Kondo and Mari Shimada came aboard the *Sepera* at 7:50. Pinkster immediately focused on Degas's *Before the Race*. "What have you been offered?"

"Isorai Tumbari will pay six and a half million dollars," Kondo asserted. "We're assured of that much, though I have told him I want seven."

"You should have taken the six and a half; we agreed that was a good price."

"Why, when he'll go higher? To increase his appetite I let him hold the painting."

"Why did you do that?"

Kondo grinned reassuringly. "The Degas is safe, Alan. Besides, we have other paintings to discuss with Mr. Tumbari, and to show our mutual trust is very good business." Kondo, paused, then lowered his voice. "Trust in this business is very important. Without it, there is no business. But enough about morality," Kondo said. "Show me the Cézanne."

Aukrust moved closer to the monitor where he could watch Pinkster, who had retreated into his chair as if hoping he might be swallowed up by it.

"Something very unexpected has happened. There was no chance to call you. The DeVilleurs portrait was not delivered to me, a mistake, of course. I didn't authorize—"

Kondo reacted slowly, as if what he had heard was a complete mistake. "Is this a bad joke? I haven't come all this distance to learn of stupid incompetence. Let me tell you that I deal with broken promises in very special ways."

"I had no control over it, I swear," Pinkster insisted. "Do you think there have not been difficulties in taking a painting of such value?"

Kondo's grin returned, but there was no humor in it. "Then I'll take your portrait, the one you say was destroyed like the others."

"It *was* destroyed," Pinkster said defiantly. "You know that perfectly well."

"No, Alan, I don't know that perfectly well. You have not allowed Miss Shimada to examine what's left of your painting." Kondo shook his large head vigorously. "No more excuses, no more delays."

Pinkster turned to the small, exotic woman, who had remained in the shadows outside the circle of chairs. "I'll make arrangements."

"When?" Kondo demanded, "Next week?"

"No. The week after."

"Not acceptable, Alan," Kondo said with utter finality. "Miss Shimada will be in your gallery next Tuesday." He looked at his watch, "January 8. In the morning. Ten o'clock."

Pinkster daubed at the redness around his mouth. "There will be another Cézanne portrait in France next week."

"Yes, the American comes over," Kondo said. "What about it?"

"They are saying it is the best of all the self-portraits. Perhaps I can arrange . . ."

"Don't make another promise you can't keep, Alan. I prefer that we sell your portrait."

"But you asked for a self-portrait, and I have every intention of obtaining one for you."

"If Miss Shimada confirms that your painting was destroyed, then I will be happy with the one owned by Mr. Llewellyn."

The *Ben Jolly* was two hundred yards astern of the *Sepera*, its bow facing the oncoming tide, its engines at a speed to let it hold position. The small boat that had earlier delivered two passengers came alongside and tied up as the same passengers returned from their visit. Jimmy radioed Sergeant Jennings. "Do a friend a favor and call in one of the other lads to follow the boat and find out who chartered it."

When Pinkster returned to the salon, Aukrust was waiting for him. "How are you going to convince Kondo that your portrait was burned up?"

"Let Shimada look at it; she'll discover shreds of a very old canvas and a syrup of paint that's traceable to the south of France."

"It's possible she can prove it wasn't a painting by Cézanne."

"I don't think she can. In the extreme it would take sophisticated technology."

"She could take samples to Amsterdam where there are specialty chemists who make paint analyses for museum curators from all over the world. Then what do you do?"

Pinkster shrugged. "Then I would be forced to bring Kondo into my confidence."

Pinkster stared blankly at the darkness beyond the circle of light. "How much do you want for the DeVilleurs painting?"

"It's not for sale," Aukrust said without hesitation.

"Kondo wants a self-portrait, and if he doesn't get one he'll cause trouble."

"Are you suggesting that Kondo have an accident?"

"He isn't worth anything dead." Pinkster eyed Aukrust carefully. "That leaves the Llewellyn. Can you get it?"

"For a price."

Pinkster said, "Half a million pounds."

Aukrust shook his head. "Half of what Kondo pays."

At Tower Pier, Alan Pinkster jumped down to the pier and went hurriedly to the gate and a waiting taxi. Jimmy Murratore lowered the binoculars and looked at his watch: 9:10. The tugboat started up again and lumbered its way west under London Bridge. Sergeant Tompkins radioed his counterpart and requested that the police launch lie off Battersea Power Station and wait until *Sepera* returned to Cadogan Pier. Thirty minutes later, when the tug had been maneuvered against the pier, the *Ben Jolly* came around from a point below Albert Bridge and was made secure less than a hundred yards away. Jimmy watched a figure, the captain he assumed, throw hawsers onto the pier, tie up, then scramble aboard and disappear into the pilothouse. Signal and running lights were shut down, except for a light in the pilothouse and another at the railing to illuminate the steps across to the pier. The captain was joined by a woman, and they walked off the boat and continued past the pier manager's shed then up and over the Embankment.

"That's the whole bloody crew," Jimmy said. "Gone off for a pint before last call." He turned excitedly toward Sergeant Tompkins. "Take me over there, by the petrol pumps. I want to see what's on that old tug."

"Be careful doing that without authorization. It's getting late, and if they went for a pint before closing they could be back in under an hour."

"Stall them and ask questions—who owns the tug, how old is it, that kind of thing. You're in uniform and they don't want trouble."

"Same goes with me," Tompkins said. "Don't pull me into something where I don't belong."

"You do belong, Tommy, the owner of that tugboat wasn't meetin' with a few casual friends in the middle of the Thames River to talk about his bloody golf handicap. I'm lookin' to find a murderer, and I need your help."

Jimmy slipped a flashlight into his jacket then jumped across to the pier and went quietly to the *Sepera*. The door to the pilothouse was locked, but a window had been left ajar, enough so that he could slide it open then reach in and turn the lock. He walked through the pilothouse and the cabin immediately aft and into an adjoining cabin, in which were crammed two small beds and a tiny bathroom. He opened another door and flashed his light on the steps angling sharply down to a deck twenty feet below him. He descended to the small vestibule. Toward the stern was a door that apparently led into the engine room. He tried the other door. It opened into a black space his flashlight pierced, revealing a room of considerable size. He entered the salon, his light aimed directly at the cluster of chairs in the center of the room.

He turned back toward the door through which he had entered, noting the cabinets built into the wood paneling. Then he went to the circle of chairs, and chose to sit in the one next to the table. When he panned his flashlight across the wood panels, the light revealed there was a change in the

wood grain design at approximately five feet intervals. He
shone the flashlight directly into one of the seams, and the
light reflected off metal—concealed hinges, he was certain.
The panels opened, but how? He pressed and probed,
searching unsuccessfully for a way to open the panels. He
went back to the chair and studied the table and everything
on and under it. In a small drawer in the table he found
notepads, pens, a calendar, and a telephone instruction manual.

The telephone keypad was unusual in that there were two
rows of buttons below the three rows of alpha-numeric buttons. There were six buttons in each of the two rows; the
buttons in the top row were numbered, the buttons in the
other row were lettered. He lifted the receiver and heard a
familiar dial tone, but when he pressed a numbered button it
had no effect on the tone. He tried other buttons with the
same result. He leafed through the manual. A sliver of paper
fell from a page marked "Program Activation." On it was a
diagram of the keypad, along with instructions to press six
of the regular telephone keys in a specific sequence.

Jimmy touched the keys, and a tiny green light at the top
of the keypad glowed. He pressed the button marked "One"
and instantly a soft noise came from his left. He shone the
flashlight onto the wall and saw the first panel begin to turn.
When he pressed button "Three" the panel in front of him
slowly turned. When the button directly below the one
marked "Three" was pressed, spotlights suspended above
him shone down onto the reverse side of the panel, which
was now turned out to the room. Jimmy got to his feet and
went to the painting that hung against a blue muslin background. It was Chagall's *Circus Scene*.

His flashlight spilled onto the next panel. "Good God,
what's this doin' here?" Jimmy whispered aloud. He had not
put a light on over the panel but played his flashlight over
the small picture that hung on the interior of the panel. He
stared, disbelieving, for a second or two, then from behind

him a hand crashed down on the flashlight, and strong arms wrapped around his chest and came up under his arms then clasped tightly behind his neck. Powerful arms and hands were holding him in a full nelson. It had happened in an instant. Jimmy forced himself down to his knees and pitched forward, twisting as he fell, reacting instinctively to his academy training. But Aukrust, heavier and stronger, had tightened his hands against the back of Jimmy's head, forcing his chin down onto his chest.

"You bloody bastard," Jimmy managed to say. "I'm with the police and—"

"You can be the Prime Minister for all I care," Aukrust said. "It's time you go away, and I've got the right medicine to take you there."

Jimmy felt one hand slip away, but pressure from the remaining hand was tight against his neck. Then there was an odor in the air, a pungent, antiseptic smell. In the dim light made by the flashlight ten feet away he saw the source of the odor; the hand that had slipped away now held a piece of cloth, and it was rising toward his face. Jimmy screamed with all the force and anger he could gather, a piercing, frightening scream that was meant to surprise as well as excite him to exert his strength in one profound effort to break free. He thrust both elbows backward and turned his legs to bring their long muscles into play, then he screamed again and slipped free. He rolled across to the door and opened it. He began to climb before Aukrust could reach the steps. Jimmy had the advantage now, being smaller and more agile. He scampered up and onto the deck, jumped to the pier, and raced away into the darkness.

Chapter 42

Roberto Oliveira was not a man glued to predictable habits, yet he regularly lunched in the Grill Room at the Hôtel Beau Rivage on Quai du Mont-Blanc whenever he was not otherwise obligated. He enjoyed being fussed over and taken to the same table where familiar waiters and busboys greeted and served him with special attention. It all made a deep impression on visiting colleagues or potential customers. On the occasions when he was alone, it afforded him an opportunity to compose his proposals for potential sellers or relax over so simple a pleasure as a newspaper. On this early January day, however, Oliveira was not particularly relaxed, and the newspaper did not provide him with either diversion or pleasure. An enterprising reporter had written a postscript to Collyers's pre-Christmas auction, speculating that the auction would have been incredibly successful if Cézanne's self-portrait had been in the sale, as the gallery's high-powered publicity had promised. "No credit for breaking new ground," he said aloud, "no mention that we did sell the Cézanne landscape for eleven million. . . ." He folded the paper and slammed it on the table and was surprised to find that he was no longer alone. The occupant of the seat across from him looked vaguely familiar. He was a thin, young man with black, strangely combed hair and a longish nose. Oliveira stared at the face for a moment.

"You were with Monsieur Weisbord when he brought the Cézanne self-portrait."

"Weisbord is dead. The painting was stolen," LeToque said flatly.

"Do you think I have it?" Oliveira said, laughing, as if it were all a bad joke. "I wanted Weisbord to leave it with us, but he would trust no one. Then I learned that he died, and that was the end to that."

LeToque shook his head, "I know who has it."

"Who?"

"The one who killed Weisbord."

Oliveira shook his head incredulously. "There was nothing about murder in the newspapers. Are you sure?"

LeToque nodded. "I know the filthy bastard. If you hear about him or see him in Geneva, call me." He wrote a phone number on a matchbook cover and pushed it in front of Oliveira. "He is a big man, a Norwegian who goes by different names. The one I know is Aukrust. Peder Aukrust."

Chapter 43

Both paintings caught the clear, shadowless light that came through the bay windows in Edwin Llewellyn's study. Both were unframed and perched on an easel. On the left was the painting Llewellyn's grandfather had purchased from Ambroise Vollard in 1904, and on the right was a photographic copy so precisely like the original that only by close examination could one be distinguished from the other. The incredible gap in their respective value was $40 million, and that was rock bottom. Recent estimates for Llewellyn's painting were stratospheric, but a tally of every penny of costs for the copy came to $2,468.14, including Nigel Jones's Maine lobster dinner at Anthony's Pier Four.

Alex Tobias lifted the genuine portrait with appropriate reverence and laid it inside a flat, traylike affair, which he then slid into an open-ended case. The two parts were made from tough vinyl and painted a dull black. In all, it measured only slightly more than the painting, 19 x 16 inches, and less than an inch thick. He looked up, as if uncertain what emotion he saw in Llewellyn's face. "Having second thoughts?" he asked.

"Of course I am," Llewellyn said. "Yet I can't think of anything more important than putting a spike into Vulcan's ass."

Tobias laughed. "I hadn't thought of it quite that way; in fact I was thinking that a week in Provence was incentive enough. But that's nothing if I can't help catch the bastard."

Llewellyn picked up the plastic case. "How are you going to carry it? You can't just tuck it under your arm."

"In that old one-suiter over there." He pointed at an undistinguished piece of luggage that would have qualified as luggage for a charter member in America's oldest frequent flyer club. "It's twenty years old and looks a hundred." He smiled. "But there are two bottoms in the damned thing." He unpacked a week's clothing then lifted a bottom flap, laid the case on the bottom of the suitcase, lowered the flap and snapped it securely, then put the clothing back, closed the suitcase, and turned the dial on a combination lock. "If necessary, I use this." He fitted a leather-covered chain through the handle and looped an end around his wrist.

"Does your wife know what you're up to?"

Tobias shook his head. "Nope, and I won't tell her until we're in Narbonne. That's over the border in France, about a three-hour drive from Barcelona." He smiled, and lines crinkled around his eyes. "We'll look like a retired New York City couple on vacation. Not bad, right?"

"Not that part of it," Llewellyn replied. "Yet I feel a little woozy knowing the painting's in the bottom of an old suitcase."

"But not any old suitcase," Tobias said, "and not being carried by some careless old fart. Come over to the window, I'll show you something. In that gray sedan down there are two men, both career cops, each with their favorite piece and the experience to use it, and both are old and good friends. One will be with me until I'm in my seat on the plane."

"They know?"

Tobias shook his head. "They don't ask, I don't tell. I'll be met in Barcelona the instant we're off the plane." Tobias gave Llewellyn a reassuring smile. "Not to worry, I don't do things half-assed."

"I leave for Paris next Tuesday, the sixth, and I'll have

with me what everyone believes is the genuine Cézanne. No
escorts, no friends from the department with a gun. Just
Fraser and Clyde—" He smiled. "Hell, Clyde won't even be
with me, he'll be in the belly of the plane."

"It's not too late," Tobias said. "You're allowed to change
your mind."

Llewellyn studied the burly detective, then sighed. "I
trust you, Alex." He put out his hand and each gave the other
a firm handshake. Fraser escorted Tobias down the stairs.

Llewellyn watched Tobias get into the gray car and drive
off. "There it goes," he said aloud. "Either I've just broken
the record for involuntary philanthropy, or I've made the fattest blunder of my life."

Fraser had returned and heard Llewellyn's gentle self-
imprecation. "You've done the right thing, sir. You'll see." It
was Fraser's way to look on the bright side.

Chapter 44

Jimmy Murratore closed the door to Oxby's office then slid into the chair directly across from the detective chief inspector.

"Like I said I'd do, I made some plans to see what Pinkster was doin' with his waterman's license and a tugboat that he' had fixed up for tourists and day-trippers. Seems, though, the old tug's not been rented out—not so far as anyone I talked to could decipher 'out.'"

Oxby couldn't stop the trace of a smile that crept along the edges of his mouth. Jimmy had a way with words that ranged from dazzling to malapropian. "Enough of the preliminaries," Oxby said. "Tell me what you've been up to."

Jimmy began at the beginning, describing to Oxby how he had received cooperation from the Thames Division and followed Pinkster's *Sepera* from its home berth to a point off Canary Wharf, where it had received the two visitors.

"Next it—"

"Do we know who the visitors were?" Oxby interrupted.

"No and yes," Jimmy answered. "I had them followed, and I expect answers in a day or two. Then after the meetin', the *Sepera* pulled in to Tower Pier and Pinkster got off and took a taxi. I wanted to have him followed, but I couldn't get it lined up in time."

"We know he has two homes," Oxby said, "one on land, one that floats. Just might be he's got another, and we should know about it."

Jimmy continued describing how the tug returned to Cadogan Pier and the skipper and his wife went off to a pub. "I worked my way into the tug and down to what I figure was Pinkster's headquarters."

"What did you find?"

"A big room, but it was pitch black, mind. I had a small torch, and with that and some luck I opened a couple of the panels that lined the walls clear around the room. Inside one, panel was a paintin' by the Russian artist . . . the fanciful, bright stuff, it was by . . ."

"Chagall?" Oxby said.

"A circus paintin', lively colors and that. I can't believe what I saw next, and maybe I didn't even see it. It was a portrait, skipper, I swear, though I didn't get much of a look at it—maybe two seconds. If I saw it again I'd know it."

"Cézanne?" Oxby said softly.

"I want to say it was. Be a damned coincidence if it was some other artist. It was just then that I got smashed by some big lout who came up behind me."

Jimmy described how he broke away. "He let a hand go, and I knew what to do."

"Then what?"

"I got the hell off the boat, ran off the pier, then managed to get picked up by my chum Tompkins. We circled back and bobbed on the water until we saw the skipper and a woman go back aboard the tug. That was it. Whoever grabbed me must have gone off the boat while I was waitin' for Tompkins."

Oxby scribbled a few notes. "Did you have a search warrant with you?"

"No, Skip—"

"Did you report the incident to the duty inspector?"

"I didn't—"

"And did you attempt to contact me about this little experience immediately after it happened?"

"Inspector Oxby, I—"

"Good. Let's just keep this to ourselves, and if you receive any additional information or recall any other detail about your episode on board the *Sepera*, I expect that you will pass it on to me in person. No written reports."

Chapter 45

Kondo stopped at the gate, gave his name, and indicated that he and Miss Shimada were visiting the gallery at the request of Mr. Pinkster. One guard called in the information while another aimed a videocamera at the car and its passengers. Kondo was waved through. David Blaney was waiting and showed the way to the gallery's conservation room in the basement.

"There it is," he said sadly. "I'm not sure why you've taken a bother to come and see it, but help yourself."

Mari Shimada bowed graciously, put down a canvas bag that bristled with compartments, and immediately began withdrawing what appeared to be surgical instruments. She took out a number of small bottles containing liquids of various colors and an assorted variety of empty vials. She probed the congealed paint with tweezers and knives and collected a half dozen samples, putting drops of a colored fluid in each. Then, carefully, she poked about in the canvas and cut away several pieces, some with paint; one of them, an inch square taken from the edge of the painting, had been neither painted and varnished nor sprayed with the solvent.

She worked quickly and professionally. After forty minutes, she began gathering up her tools and vials and returning them neatly to the bag.

She bowed to Blaney, thanked him for his cooperation, then nodded to Kondo. They got into their car and drove off.

Chapter 46

Fraser and Clyde had taken an overnight Air France flight on Monday; by midday on Tuesday, luggage, dog, and family retainer were ensconced in a top-floor suite at the Hôtel Meurice on Rue de Rivoli. That evening Fraser taxied to the airport to meet Llewellyn's inbound Concorde due on the ground at 10:45. Also on hand was a contingent from the Réunion des Musées Nationaux, headed by Mirella LeBorgne. She extended a warm welcome and introduced her colleagues. "You had a good flight?" she asked.

"Smooth as glass, and on time, too," Llewellyn said.

Without warning, bright lights flooded over the group and a loud voice came from behind a camera.

"Bienvenue! Monsieur Llewellyn!" Unmistakably it was Scooter Albany.

André Lachaud, LeBorgne's assistant and as quiet as a penitent at the security council meeting, fawned and fussed over Llewellyn. "Can you ever realize how famous your painting has become?"

"We'll take you to your hotel," LeBorgne said pleasantly, as if there were no alternative.

Fraser sat next to Lachaud, who was behind the wheel of a low-slung Citroën; Llewellyn and LeBorgne were in the back. "You should know that while you are in Paris you will have the best possible protection," Mirella LeBorgne said. "Just now there is a car following, and another is ahead of us. At the hotel and during all of tomorrow, there will be

God-knows-how-many police and other agents watching every move you make."

"Too much," Llewellyn replied, almost apologetically. "All that isn't necessary."

LeBorgne shook her head and looked distressed. "I'm afraid Henri Trama agrees. He's clearly not pleased that you are taking such a risk. In fact, he wishes, and I agree, that you should go directly to Aix. Have you thought about doing that?"

"Yes," Llewellyn said, nodding, "but I'm sticking with my plans. I'll be safe." He saw her disbelief. "I truly will."

Mirella said, "I'm afraid that I must tell you that Trama may file a complaint through the National Security office."

"Complaint? About what?" Llewellyn asked.

"I can't be sure, something to do with procedure and diplomatic courtesy from Scotland Yard."

The telephone rang less than a minute after Llewellyn walked into his hotel room. It was Jack Oxby. "Trama has refused to arrange for security after Lyon. Your days as a lightning rod may be over before they begin. Disappointed?"

"Of course I am. I worked myself up for this gig, and I want to go through with it."

"I can't guarantee your safety."

"Who've you got?"

"There are two of us."

"Armed?"

"Unofficially."

"There are five of us. I'll take those odds."

"Five?"

"Fraser and I make four . . . Scooter counts for a half. Clyde's another half."

Llewellyn's presentation was scheduled for 8:00 P.M. on Wednesday, January 9. He planned to give a brief account of

Cézanne's career then unveil the portrait. It would take place in the Musée d'Orsay, a hundred-year-old railroad station that had been converted at a cost of 1.3 billion francs for the purpose of housing and displaying art from the period 1848 to 1914. Better there, thought Llewellyn, than in the Musée National d'Art Moderne in the Centre Georges Pompidou, a garishly painted building with structural steel and utility pipes crisscrossing its outside like the entrails of a mechanical dinosaur.

The throng of the six hundred who came to see the painting and listen to Edwin Llewellyn overflowed the largest gallery; not by coincidence was it the gallery that contained works by Cézanne and his contemporaries. A raised platform was at the closed end of the gallery; on it was a lectern and behind that a brightly lighted backdrop on which was the Llewellyn portrait, covered with a maroon-colored cloth.

Llewellyn had personally mounted his painting, tactfully refusing assistance and careful not to draw attention to the fact that he allowed no one to as much as lay a finger on even the frame.

He was unaware that Henri Trama had come onto the platform and was standing behind him; when he turned he did not immediately recognize him. At the security meeting Trama had dressed informally. Now he was in a black dress uniform a size too small, with strings of gold braid on the lapels and cuffs and a row of ribbons on the front.

Trama quickly dispensed with pleasantries. "I cannot guarantee your safety once you leave Lyon." He looked at Llewellyn steadily. "In fact, I cannot guarantee your safety even before that time and would be very pleased if you would go directly to Aix and forget this game that Inspector Oxby has invented for you."

Llewellyn pondered for a moment. Trama's English was thickly accented, and that, too, differed from his earlier impression. There was anger in the police commissaire's voice. Llewellyn said, "I'll be safe. I have an alert traveling companion, and a superb watchdog." He smiled a little wickedly. "Norwich terriers become particularly testy when they're away from home."

They were joined on the platform by Mirella LeBorgne and Gustave Bilodeau. Bilodeau had been allotted three minutes and would have the honor of extending a formal invitation to visit the Cézanne retrospective in his beloved Musée Granet.

Scooter Albany aimed his camera at the quartet then scrambled onto the platform and put a microphone between himself and Llewellyn. As if he had never seen a drop of alcohol, Scooter conducted a fast-moving interview and wrapped up a prime-time segment the networks would happily put on the air.

The interview continued, and Albany was joined by a team from French television. A reporter interviewed Mirella LeBorgne and Gustave Bilodeau and was about to put Llewellyn on camera when Henri Trama shooed them from the platform.

Mirella LeBorgne announced to the audience that she had been summoned at the eleventh hour to substitute for the ailing managing director of the Musée d'Orsay then read off the names of the curatorial staff who were in the audience. Gustave Bilodeau spoke briefly and nervously, as perspiration glistened on his cheeks. He was awed by the spectacle and just as awed that his dream of honoring Paul Cézanne was so close at hand.

"Come to the retrospective early, if you can," he said, extending the first formal invitation. "Opening day is January 19, the birthdate of Cézanne."

It was Llewellyn's turn. His presentation was delivered in his nearly forgotten Deerfield Academy French, but he consoled himself with the certainty that the audience had come to see his painting, not to criticize his accent. "The world owes Conservateur Bilodeau its gratitude," he said. Then, climaxing his presentation, he pulled away the cloth from his painting. A scattering of applause built to a rousing ovation.

"I regret that you will not be able to have a close look at the painting tonight," he said. "But in Aix you can spend as much time as you wish. There you will see other paintings by the genius who set in motion one of the most important art movements of this century."

Watching from the rear of the gallery was a tall man with a broad face and light brown hair. Peder Aukrust applauded, and as he did his attention was drawn to ten people in the audience. Four were in uniform. Three wore dark gray suits and white shirts and blue neckties, obviously members of some sort of police agency who might as well have been wearing badges marked Police Security. He spotted two attractive women and was amused by the way they acted like tourists, clapping and smiling and constantly shifting their shoulder bags from one shoulder to the other, as if a heavy weight were inside—perhaps a compact Smith & Wesson Bodyguard .38 pistol. Then there was a man Aukrust felt instinctively that he knew, and he tried to attach a circumstance or name to whoever it was. But he could not.

Chapter 47

Chez Blanc had become a dirty gray structure, a bed-and-bath on Rue Sedaine in a commercial section of the eleventh arrondissement, sandwiched between an empty loft building and a furniture refinisher, from which the heavy odor of paint remover and lacquer fumes rose to cast its pall over the neighborhood. Peder Aukrust had instructed Astrid to go to the address, and she had waited for him to return from the d'Orsay and Llewellyn's presentation.

"Llewellyn's got his face in the newspapers more than the president of France, and he's got as many police around him, too," Peder said, and tossed a copy of *Le Figaro* into Astrid's lap. "Look at him, grinning like he'd inherited another ten million dollars."

"The man with him, that's Fraser," Astrid said.

"The painting is not as big as you described."

"In that frame, it's very large."

He stared at Astrid, an unblinking stare that penetrated through her to the torn wallpaper behind the chair she sat in. He had been drinking—not drunk, but it showed. "I want that painting, and I want it before he reaches Aix."

"What will you do with it?"

"Pinkster can be very stupid, but he knows too much, and he has money. I made a bargain with him for your friend's portrait."

"You can't destroy it."

"Are you concerned about the painting or Llewellyn?"

"He's a good person. You won't hurt him?"

"That depends . . . on you. I want you to call and tell him you need his help."

"Help for what?"

Aukrust was at the window, his arms crossed over his chest, his back to Astrid. "You'll tell him you haven't any money and your airplane tickets were stolen."

"I can't do that."

He ignored her protest, "You will call him from the railway station in Lyon, and you will say that when you came back to your hotel room in Paris, someone was in the room, waiting. Yes, that will work."

"I said no, Peder."

"Imagine this is your hotel room, and a man was here, inside the door waiting." Aukrust stood against the wall so that he was behind the door, when it was opened. "You came into the room, your arms full of the catalogues from the antique shops, and you went to the table over there and put them down. Then you turned to close the door, but it was closed; he had closed it quietly and locked it." Peder grinned, a small, slightly crooked grin. "He told you not to shout, that if you made a noise he would hurt you—hurt you badly."

"Please, Peder, you make it sound too real. I don't want to—"

"Then he said you were very pretty, and he came to you like this and put his arms around you." Peder took her into his arms and hugged her tightly, without affection. "He kissed you then made you sit on the bed while he took your money and the airplane tickets. Then you shouted at him and ran to the door—do it! Go to the door!"

"You're scaring me, Peder, don't—"

"Do as I tell you!"

She went cautiously to the door.

"Shout at me, do it, Astrid."

"Stop it! I'm frightened, can't you see? Stop it, Peder!" And she did shout, out of real, not playmaking, fear.

He lunged for her, grabbed her arms, and ripped off her blouse, then pulled her skirt away and threw her on the bed. He hit her arm, twice, with his fist. She began to cry. "Why? Don't hurt me Peder—" Then he tore at her stockings and took off her panties, breathing heavily, covering her mouth with a huge hand. "This is what he did. Remember and tell Llewellyn."

Now she was too frightened to shout and helplessly watched as he took off all his clothes. He got astride her, glowering down at her. She raised a hand in protest, but he punched it away. He struck her cheek and hit her one last time with the back of his hand, a blow across her mouth that cut her lip. Then his glower became a thin smile, and he showed her, proudly, that he was aroused.

"And tell Llewellyn that he raped you."

Then he did.

Chapter 48

Elliott Heston closed the door to his office and went to the conference area by a corner window where Jack Oxby was bent over the table reading a letter. It consisted of three short paragraphs, barely covering half the page. Oxby read it carefully, his pencil moving line by line down to the signature. He looked up. "When did this come in?"

"Less than an hour ago. It was sent during the night from the Sûreté Nationale to their embassy and delivered by courier this morning."

"What are you going to do about it?"

"Start by explaining to the commissioner how the Yard got itself mixed up with what the French are calling Le Cirque Llewellyn. They're pissed that they had to put a special security detachment in the d'Orsay last evening, and they're opposed to giving Llewellyn any more protection when forty thousand farmers are threatening to shut down every major autoroute in France."

Oxby flushed with a touch of anger. "You'd think they knew nothing about the Cézannes being ravaged, not to mention a couple of murders. They've been asleep, Elliott, hoping Vulcan goes away before the show opens. Now that it's going to open in less than two weeks, they've come awake, and Trama is playing catch-up and wants to become a hero."

Heston took back the letter and read aloud: "We deeply regret that security for Monsieur Llewellyn cannot be arranged in Avignon . . . etcetera . . . etcetera . . . and suggest that Llewellyn go directly to Aix from Lyon." He looked sternly at Oxby. "This same message has gone to the American embassy in Paris."

Oxby got to his feet. "We can't lose an opportunity in Avignon, Elliott; that's where Vulcan will believe he has the best opportunity to try something. Llewellyn understands there won't be police protection, but he insists on going ahead. I gave my word we'd protect him, and he accepts that."

"Jack, you're up to your old tricks, playing by rules you make up as you go along. You've barely kept me posted. I damned well don't want any more surprises, and neither do the French." Heston pushed away from the table and got to his feet. "While I'm at it, you might answer three questions that are bothering the hell out of me," and he rambled on as if reciting from the catechism. "First, upon what holy tablet is it written that you can turn your sergeants into bodyguards and send them to France? Second, who approved the release of classified information on Vulcan? Third, where is your authorization to spend a day at Interpol?"

Heston's sudden rush of questions put Oxby off guard momentarily.

"Very well," Oxby began. "I'll answer in reverse order."

Heston's face tightened, and he nodded.

"As to Interpol, I have here authorization to attend the museum security manager's meeting on December 4–7. Appended to that is my request to spend one day with Police Specialist Samuel Turner at Interpol." He slid the paper in front of Heston. "I believe those are your initials at the bottom of the page."

Heston grasped the paper and lowered his glasses. "I don't recall every request that crosses my desk."

Oxby continued. "We seem to be at odds on releasing information on Vulcan, and it's critical that we see eye-to-eye on this one. I take responsibility for injecting the image of

Vulcan into the case and remind you that we are dealing with a sociopathic personality." Oxby leaned forward. "Unquestionably he is a very bright person who knows perfectly well that we're breaking our asses to find him, but I want him to be confident that we've had a serious setback because we have no authority in France and the French are too busy with other matters. If he thinks Llewellyn's dangling out there without protection, he'll try to take advantage of it."

Heston squeezed the bridge of his nose between his thumb and forefinger. "You're predicating your entire strategy on the premise that Vulcan wants Llewellyn's painting. What makes you so positive?"

Oxby closed his eyes, took a deep breath, then, choosing his words carefully, said, "Because, Elliott, I'm deeply involved with every bit of fact and well-supported supposition we have on Vulcan and whomever he's allied with. All of which feeds my instinct to tell me that he will try something between now and January 19." Oxby opened his eyes and leveled them with Heston's. "That's as clearly and honestly as I can state my case. I'll frankly admit that I'm not positive Vulcan wants the painting or that he wants to destroy it. But I feel strongly that he'll show his hand."

"Guaranteed?" Heston asked.

"Of course not; if it were, you wouldn't be putting me through this bloody inquisition."

"Speaking of which, you owe me one more answer."

Oxby said, "As for sending Sergeants Murratore and Browley to France, I took a chance that I could put them over there for a couple of days. I didn't think it would cause a firestorm."

Heston stared at Oxby, then slowly ran his finger down the side of his slender nose. "Well, it has, and it's a breach of regulations. How do you respond to that?"

"They volunteered because they're as involved as I am and they want Vulcan stopped. They're taking leave time."

"Jack, no member of our department can go into a foreign country, on leave time or not, and represent the Metropolitan Police unless, A) that foreign country has made a formal request, and, B) the commissioner issues formal instructions. Neither condition pertains."

"I'm going ahead. That way you'll have plenty of time to consider my reprimand."

"It's meddling, Jack. You'll be on French turf and calling your own shots."

"Sam Turner said he'd lend a hand. He's itching to get away from his computer."

Oxby turned away and studied his hands, keeping them folded together, not revealing any of the concern he harbored with respect to the information Jimmy Murratore had uncovered during his unauthorized and unreported boarding of Alan Pinkster's *Sepera*. Should he bring Heston into his confidence? What would be the consequences if he didn't?

Heston's phone rang. The Commander glared at the instrument, willing it to stop ringing as if he knew who was on the line. "Heston here," he said formally. Oxby stood at the window, trying not to hear Heston's side of the conversation, which he guessed was between Heston and his wife, Gretchen, who had become adept at getting past the protective ring of assistants. Oxby stared across the city at the tallest skyscraper in London's financial district.

Chapter 49

Bud Samuelson stared angrily across the wide, polished boardroom table at Alan Pinkster. His fist was curled so tightly around a bunch of pencils that his knuckles were bone-white and his arm shook uncontrollably. Terry Sloane stood beside him, perspiring uncomfortably and shifting restlessly from foot to foot.

Samuelson spoke in a thin, angry voice, "You are a shit-head, Alan Pinkster, a lying, deceiving, sonofabitching first-class bastard."

"You've made your point, Bud," Terry Sloane said. "Let him speak."

"Last time he was in this room and we let him speak he bullshitted his way right out that door and laughed at us for the next six weeks. No more of that." He glared at Pinkster. "What do you know about a man named Saburo Kondo?"

Pinkster's flushed, red face drained to a ghostly white. Perhaps he had prepared for Samuelson's scatological on-slaught but not a confrontation over Kondo. "I know he's a Japanese art dealer. Many people know that."

Samuelson had expected a noncommittal reply and got one. "Let's try another one. What do you know about the painting titled *Before The Race*?" He studied Pinkster's reaction. "In case you're having an attack of *amnesia oppor-tunus*, it was painted by Degas and was stolen from the Burroughs collection."

Pinkster looked away from Samuelson to Terry Sloane. "I don't know anything about it."

Terry Sloane shook his head. "We have information to the contrary, Alan. You've been dealing with Kondo, and according to our sources, he received the Degas painting from you and sold it in Japan for more than six million dollars."

"You got bad information," Pinkster said.

Samuelson pounced. "And you're in deep shit. I don't know how much of the six million you kept, but you'd better wrap it up nice and neat and give it to Terry." He got to his feet. "I've dealt with some fucking slimeballs before, but that was because I didn't know better. We're out of your goddamned Pacific Bowl as of now, except for one remaining detail that sounds like $106 million. We want every penny. If we don't get it, your ass goes on the block, and from where I sit, that's about twenty long, fuckless years on a prison farm."

Chapter 50

Instructions had been issued to the Police Judiciaire in Lyon, something to the effect that the American who was showing his painting by Paul Cézanne was to be provided with VIP security treatment similar to that which would be given to a middling, government official from a country with the importance of, perhaps, Belize. A newly minted lieutenant had been dispatched to the Grand Hôtel Concorde to officially advise Llewellyn that one policeman would be stationed outside the hotel room and another next to the elevators in the lobby. "Plans to assure your safety this evening are being put together as we speak." He saluted and strutted off.

Scooter Albany said, "Shouldn't you tell Oxby that on a scale of one to ten, your security risk is somewhere under zero?"

Llewellyn smiled gamely. "Oxby knows." He went into the bedroom and took from his suitcase a thin leather shoulder holster and slid out a Beretta 950-BS pistol. He held the weapon in his hand as if it were a vibrating piece of polished black metal, too heavy for its size. He slipped on the holster, put the gun into it, then checked himself in the mirror, patting the perceptible bulge below his left shoulder. At 6:00 P.M. a police sergeant arrived and announced that the lieutenant was waiting in a police car in front of the hotel. Led by a single, unmuffled motorcycle with blue lights blinking, they drove along the crowded Rue de la République to the Musée des Beaux-Arts catercorner from the Hôtel de Ville.

Local dignitaries had been assembled for a catered banquet in the main hall, and speeches of praise and appreciation were delivered by an assortment of art scholars recruited from the university and the slim curatorial staff of the museum. At eight o'clock, the tables were taken away, chairs were set up, and the public and press began filling the hall. As in Paris, and with a less uncertain accent, Llewellyn made his little speech. He drew the maroon cloth away and spoke affectionately of the painting and its meaning to France. "But come to Aix," he said, "where you will be fascinated by nearly two hundred of Paul Cézanne's paintings and drawings."

Scooter Albany shot twenty minutes' worth of videotape, and the local press took photographs and interviewed Llewellyn.

Peder Aukrust stood at the back of the room. His gaze was rarely on the platform or Llewellyn or the painting. Instead, he searched the audience for the familiar-looking person he had seen at the Musée d'Orsay in Paris. Another look at the man might tell him if his memory was playing tricks or dislodge from his memory who he was. He counted three, non-intimidating museum guards and two police. There were more, he was certain, but he could not find them. He paid particular attention to the black-haired man standing alone near the platform. His stare was met by Sam Turner, for it was he, himself studying the faces in the crowd.

"You have been generous with your hospitality," Llewellyn said, winding up his talk. "In a few days we will be in Avignon." The audience was attentive, appreciative that the American was speaking in French and doing an acceptable job of it. "Before leaving, I want to remind you that an evil and cruel person has destroyed four of Paul Cézanne's self-portraits, and the danger continues that more paintings will be burned. It is our responsibility—yours and mine—to see that this does not happen. Join me in Aix next week! Come celebrate the greatness of Paul Cézanne!" Llewellyn waved enthusiastically and shouted, "À bientôt!"

There was a low murmuring in the crowd, then applause broke out and voices were raised in shouts of "Vive le Cézanne! Vive Llewellyn!"

The motorcycle was missing from the return trip. It had been explained that there had been a serious accident on the autoroute north of the city, and the motorcycle officer had been sent to direct traffic. Shortly after eleven, Llewellyn was on the phone listening to Jack Oxby's calm reassurance that he had been under constant surveillance for the entire evening. "I'm down to one sleepy guard in the corridor," Llewellyn said without his usual jauntiness.

"We've covered you like doting mothers," Oxby said.

"I saw only Sam Turner."

"It was quite a show," Oxby said. "Turn on your television. Scooter's got you on the late news."

Llewellyn flipped on the set in his bedroom. There was a close-up of the painting, then the picture widened to show Llewellyn making his final remarks. Clyde heard a familiar voice come from the television and jumped onto the bed and barked. The phone rang, and Fraser answered.

"How good to hear from you," he said in his friendly, husky voice. "Where are you?"

"It's a . . . a surprise," she said. "May I speak to Mr. Llewellyn?"

Fraser waved the phone at Llewellyn. "You won't believe it, sir, but it's Astrid."

Llewellyn grabbed the phone. "Where in the dickens are you?" he asked like a worried father.

"I'm . . . I'm in Lyon. Are you surprised?"

"Of course I'm surprised. You didn't say anything about coming to Lyon."

"I hadn't planned on it, but something terrible happened

in Paris and I need help. I saw in the newspaper that you were coming here. Are you angry?"

"Of course not, but what happened?"

"Someone broke into my hotel room, and he . . . he attacked me."

"For God's sake, are you hurt?"

"A little, but I was more frightened. He took my money and airplane tickets."

"Where are you calling from?"

"The railway station, the one near your hotel."

There was a brief pause before Llewellyn said, "There might be a problem. Give me your number, and I'll call you right back."

He wrote out the number and dialed Oxby. "You remember Astrid Haraldsen? She apparently had a bad scare in Paris when someone broke into her room and took her money and plane tickets. She's just called me from the railway station looking for help. What should I do about it?"

"I'll be damned," Oxby said simply, and hesitated for several seconds. He then said, "Would you like to see her?"

"I . . . yes, I suppose I would like that," Llewellyn said, stumbling. "But I can't. Or can I?"

"Tell her you'll send Fraser to pick her up."

"You said I wasn't to travel with anyone, only Fraser."

"We added Scooter to the party. I don't think we should ignore a damsel in distress."

Chapter 51

What had started as a cool afternoon breeze had blustered into a strong, cold wind by the time Scooter Albany's golden Olds pulled in front of the Hôtel d'Europe in Avignon. Weather stations from Grenoble south officially proclaimed *le mistral* had swept over Provence. It was nearing nine o'clock when Llewellyn's entourage finally settled into their rooms. The quality of food was not a priority, and they ate simply and quickly. Scooter allowed as to how he felt "lucky": his way of saying he would check to see if good company with long blonde hair was sitting on a bar stool in the hotel lounge.

After dinner, Llewellyn prepared for bed, indicating that it might be a good idea if Astrid did the same.

"I won't be able to sleep," she said.

"Can't get that bastard out of your mind?"

She nodded. "It'll go away."

A bruise on her cheek had spread, though the awful color had faded. Still, her lips were swollen. She had not let Llewellyn see the other bruise marks on her shoulder and arms.

"Do you feel safe?" she asked.

"Yes, perfectly. Do you?"

"When I'm with you. But I worry about the painting. Will someone try to take it? If they did, you could be hurt."

"I don't think that will happen."

"Because there are people watching you?"

He frowned. "What people?"

"I don't know. But if the painting is so valuable, shouldn't there be someone watching?"

"Stop this silly talk about protection and people watching."

"Then no one is guarding you?"

"I said, 'enough,' Astrid, and I mean it." There was a touch of frustration in his voice, perhaps anger. He turned down the covers on the bed. "Are you coming?"

"In a while. I'm going to take Clyde for a walk."

"It's hell out there. You'll freeze."

"I won't be long."

She snapped the leash onto Clyde's collar, and they were soon on the street in front of the hotel. Clyde pulled on the leash as if he had specific designs on the low shrubbery in a tiny park-like triangle a hundred yards from the hotel. The wind was still up and cold, the sky black. Peder Aukrust was waiting.

"You're late, and it's cold." He snapped the words out angrily.

"I came as soon as I could get away."

"Have you seen the painting?"

"No, he keeps it wrapped and locked in a closet."

"Get the key."

"I've tried, but he . . ."

"Keep trying. I see two men with him, the reporter and his companion. Are there any others?"

"I've asked him, but he won't talk about it. I only know of the two men."

"He's been told to say nothing, even to you. There are others, but we can't see them." He shook his head. "Damn it, he's not being guarded by ghosts. Ask him again if he's being protected. Tell him you want to know because you are worried about him. Make him know that you care. Tell me everything when we are in Aix."

He mumbled some kind of farewell, turned, and was gone.

A hazy sun shone the next morning and throughout the day, but *le mistral* continued to blow its cold northerly winds over Avignon, relentlessly churning the air with dust and debris. Mercifully it ended the next day. Llewellyn and Fraser had previously experienced the phenomenon and were happy to remain in the comfort of the hotel. Astrid had experienced the winter storms of Norway, but *le mistral*, she discovered, could be more than an incessant cold wind: It could be deeply depressing. The day passed slowly and un-eventfully.

The Palace of the Popes carried a three-star endorsement in the Michelin Guide, and whether or not it was worth a special trip, it was arguably Avignon's most famous monument. The fourteenth-century structure had long ago been plundered of its furnishings and tapestries, but the great stone corridors and huge empty halls still reverberated with the kind of historical significance matched by only a handful of buildings in France. Signs directed traffic to the Great Audience Hall, a room nearly two hundred feet long and as wide as the length of a tennis court. It was an apt setting for the presentation of a rare painting by a French Impressionist, and somehow it lent even more importance to the portrait of an artist who had lived most of his life a short distance away.

A temporary speaker-system sent out scratchy sounds that echoed and ricocheted off the stone walls and ceiling. It was hoped that there would be a large audience to provide an absorbent buffer, a hope fulfilled as crowds began arriving early from as far off as Valence and Saint-Rémy. There was again a platform and the high-standing backdrop on which Llewellyn had mounted his painting.

Peder Aukrust took his position along the inside wall, choosing a spot beside two men nearly as tall as he. He leaned down to become less obvious than those near him then searched the audience. He was impressed by the fact that everyone was eagerly watching and listening to the six people on the raised platform at the end of the hall. He was certain that among the several hundred persons there were security agents or police in plainclothes, or if there weren't police in the old hall, then Llewellyn had arranged for his own security force. If he had, they were perfectly disguised.

In the third row sat Jack Oxby, dressed in a double-breasted blazer, a paisley-print ascot fluffed out at the neck, and a beret that was cocked at an angle over his forehead. It nearly touched the top of his thick, black-rimmed glasses. He seemed to be listening with rapt attention, even when he twisted around in his seat to look surreptitiously behind him then nonchalantly added another note in his notepad.

Shortly after eleven o'clock Llewellyn and Fraser returned to the hotel. Astrid lay in Llewellyn's bed, half-asleep, a blanket pulled over her shoulders. Llewellyn looked down at her bruised face, then lightly stroked her cheeks.

"Awake?" he whispered.

"Yes," she answered, "I think I am. Is it late?"

"A little after eleven."

She turned onto her back and looked up at him. "Was there a big crowd?"

He nodded. "I'm afraid half of them couldn't see much. An awfully big place to show such a little painting." He smiled. "But they applauded."

She fluffed the pillow then patted it. "Come to bed and tell me about it."

Following the presentation in the palace, Aukrust walked to his hotel, the Danieli, and prepared for an early start the next morning. He was keenly aware of the day and the date: Saturday, January 10. Hopes that he would have found a clear opportunity to take Llewellyn's painting in Avignon had not materialized. It would have been better to see who was guarding Llewellyn rather than to be confronted by an invisible ring, never knowing if there were gaps or where they might be.

Wind gusts continued, but by noon, when Peder reached Aix-en-Provence, *le mistral* had finally spent itself out. Aukrust parked near the railroad station. His anxiety built as he approached a row of storage lockers. At number 104 he slid in the key and turned it. He opened the door. A thick mailing-tube twenty inches long was right where he had left it.

Chapter 52

Before the plane stopped at the gangway, Alexander Tobias stepped into the aisle and opened the overhead compartment to retrieve his wife's carry-on luggage and his sport coat, all the while managing to maintain a firm hold on his one-suiter. His wife watched, amused but resigned to wait patiently to be told what incredibly important cargo was inside the old suitcase, though it didn't stop her from saying with familial forebearance, "You're more attached to that damned piece of luggage than you are to me and all your grandchildren put together."

"I don't want anything to happen to it," Tobias replied in the apologetic manner of a husband not wishing to have a minor bone of contention grow into a full-fledged argument. They passed customs with VIP treatment that materialized in the form of an official-looking young woman wearing an official-looking badge, who took their baggage claim tickets and led them on a circuitous route to the front of the terminal. A Mercedes 290 was at the curb, a plainclothes policeman standing next to it.

From the time Helen Tobias had settled into her first-class seat on the Iberia jet until they were clear of the airport grounds, she had been given one reason after another to suspect that her husband was on a mission of great importance, and his attachment to his homely piece of luggage bore that out. Helen Tobias had not been blessed with good looks, but the years had treated her kindly: Now her hair was pure white, and her eyes and mouth animated a face that was round and full and pleasantly untroubled. Thirty-five years of marriage to a policeman had taught her patience and had also honed her intuitive skills, which on more than one occasion had proved more accurate than her husband's.

"You haven't told me everything." She stared at him for a moment, then added, "When will you?"

"I promised not to say anything to anyone. Not until we've crossed the border into France."

She glanced at the clock on the dashboard and set her own watch to local time. "When will that happen?"

"An hour and half to the border, another hour to Perpignan." He pointed to the map on the seat between them, "We'll stay there tonight and get a leisurely start in the morning. We've got four days to poke around. I said we'd arrive on the sixteenth—Friday." He gave her a warm smile. "It's a great part of France, you'll love it."

"Alexander," she began, her deliberate pronunciation of his name a clear indication she wanted no-nonsense answers to questions she was about to unleash on him. "You have told me only that we are going to a town named Aix-en-Provence in the south of France, but we flew to Barcelona and are now driving, so you tell me, to France. I've been very patient about flying first class and about the way you've held on to that disgusting suitcase, even when you went to the lavatory so many times I became convinced you had a prostate problem. I have not asked why we were whisked through customs then put into this expensive car, which even I could see was under guard. Now I insist you tell me what you're up to."

"Obviously I've got something in the suitcase. It belongs to a man named Edwin Llewellyn, who asked if I would deliver it for him. He was adamant that you come with me and that we travel first class."

"Can't you tell me what it is?"

He turned to her, smiled, and said, "Yes, when we get to Perpignan."

Chapter 53

Marguerite DeVilleurs made a final sweep through the house, activated the alarm, then went out to the car. Emily was behind the wheel, waiting for Margueritte to settle beside her. At the end of the driveway a car suddenly appeared and came to an abrupt halt, blocking their way. Both recognized the car, stunned to realize it was Peder Aukrust's station wagon. Margueritte clambered out of the car with a teenager's agility.

"Peder," she cried out, "where have you been?"

He went toward her, arms outstretched, but stopped and waited tentatively, unsure of the reception Margueritte would give him. "I apologize," he said with a smile broader than he had ever shown. "I had personal matters to deal with . . . I am sorry."

"And I am disappointed," Margueritte said resolutely. "I worried about you. You disappeared and never called."

He looked away from her, head bowed as if being scolded. "It was my family," he said. "I had to go to Oslo. It was a bad time for me."

"And for me," she said sternly. "Freddy Weisbord died."

He remained silent, head down.

"You've been accused of killing him."

"You believe such a lie?" he said angrily. "Who said it?"

"That scoundrel LeToque. He said you were with Freddy the night he died. He said you had a reason to kill him."

"Kill Weisbord?" Aukrust's laugh was humorless. "He

was a sick old man who was going to die without any help from me." He slowly dropped his arms to his side, Margueritte watching. She was aware that his eyes were still turned away from hers.

"Did you kill him, Peder?"

"No." Then, to reinforce his denial, he stared forcefully into her eyes and held the gaze for many seconds. But he was the first to break eye contact and said, "The portrait. I have it."

She pointed at his car. "You have it with you?"

"Yes, but the frame is missing."

"You can make a new one. It's the painting I want to see."

He took the tube from the car, carefully twisted out the rolled canvas and unfurled it.

"Look, Emily! Monsieur Cézanne has come home."

Chapter 54

University students gathered in small groups around little round tables set outside the cafes that lined the north side of the principal avenue in what had been the capital of old Provence. Cours Mirabeau was an incomparably beautiful boulevard, particularly so when the four rows of giant plane trees created a summertime canopy of soft green through which thousands of needle-fine shafts of sunlight came down to touch the ground. Simply called Aix, a word pronounced with infinite variety, it was a city of surprising sophistication, where even in mid-winter on a cloudless and wind-free day, a coffee taken al fresco was a delight.

Near one of the three ancient and still flowing thermal fountains a grime-and-dust covered silver Porsche was backed into a parking slot. From the passenger side emerged a long-legged girl with long hair and a tired expression, and from behind the wheel came the driver, who pointed to the empty tables in a cafe near the Grand Hôtel Nègre-Coste.

LeToque pulled a chair away from a table and sat. He looked up at Gaby, who was rubbing the chill from her body. He said irritably, "Are you just going to stand there?"

"I'm cold, and I have to go to the bathroom," Gaby said.

"Then go, for Christ's sake. In there." He pointed to the inside of the cafe.

She went off, passing a waiter, who put a menu in front of LeToque.

"Two coffees," LeToque ordered. "And how do I get to the Musée?"

"Which one?" the waiter asked with a touch of disdain.

"The Granet, the one on all the damned signs. Like that one." He pointed to a banner announcing the Cézanne Retrospective, suspended across Cours Mirabeau near the Fontaine de la Rotonde at the head of the boulevard.

"Go to the clock tower then right on Rue d'Italie," the waiter said, indicating the direction opposite from the landmark fountain. "It's in Place St.-Jean-de-Malte, next to the church."

Chapter 55

By noon on Thursday, Llewellyn and his party were settled into a top-floor suite in the Hôtel Pullman Roi
René. The first to visit was Scooter Albany, who asked
Llewellyn to preview a video segment that he was about to
release to French television. When Llewellyn entered
Scooter's room, it was Oxby who stepped forward to greet
him.

"Gotta go," Scooter said to Llewellyn and went off down
the hall.

"I thought you had been called back to London,"
Llewellyn said. "I'm afraid I wasn't a very good lightning
rod. Sorry."

"I suspect Vulcan had a plan cooked up for one of the
nights you were in Avignon," Oxby replied. "But it might
have looked too easy. He wanted to see what he was up
against, and the ring around you was invisible. At least that's
my hunch," he grinned. "But my average hunch is like
three-day-old milk: sometimes sweet, the other times sour."

"Have you heard from Tobias?"

"Everything is fine," Oxby assured him. "Alex and his
wife arrive in Aix this afternoon."

"The painting—"

"As safe as when you last held it," Oxby said. "How's
Astrid?"

"Still nursing her bruises. She's genuinely concerned
about my safety and doesn't want anything to happen to the

painting. In fact she thought a couple of guards outside my room would be a good idea."

"What did you say to that?"

"That posting sentries at doors is for presidents."

"Did she ask if anyone was protecting you and your painting?"

"She got on to something like that in Avignon."

Oxby fanned the pages of his notepad. "I want you to tell Gustave Bilodeau that he can't hang your portrait until the morning the exhibition opens. Not before."

"He won't like that."

"Blame it on your lawyer."

Oxby found Jimmy Murratore in his room. The inspector had compiled a list showing where every person worth knowing about was staying. "They're pretty well scattered around, with Sam Turner staying in, of all places, the Hôtel Paul Cézanne. Ann arrives tomorrow morning. I've got her in the Cardinale, where I'm staying."

"Where did you put Tobias?"

"The Tobiases will be in the Hôtel Nègre-Coste. I don't know where the French are staying, but I do know that Henri Trama has gone incommunicado. You can be sure that he's crowing to all his cronies that our scheme didn't work. I hope he is and that his complaints get a good airing in the papers."

"Skipper, as I see it, you've got a ragtag team of three Scotland Yarders who are here without authority and who will probably be sacked as soon as we set foot on British soil. Then there's a Canadian who's come down on a lark from his post at Interpol and a retired New York cop. We're all lookin' for a phantom with a code name that means fire god."

Oxby stared solemnly at his young sergeant. "You put it well, Jimmy, except that only two from the Yard are staying on. I want you back in London as soon as you can arrange a flight. Locate Alan Pinkster and stay as close to him as if you were another layer of skin. Whatever it takes, don't lose sight of him."

Inside the Musée Granet was pandemonium: a strange, orderly turbulence that reached into every cranny of the old building erected in 1671 as the Priory of the Knights of Malta. It was as if the confusion was part of a master plan in which every component of the retrospective would explode into uncountable pieces, then magically tumble back together in a perfect harmony. With fewer than ninety-six hours until opening day the painters were still brushing a warm yellow-lime paint onto the walls in the stairwells, over old plaster in the long vestibule, and on the walls in a square-shaped reception hall. Carpenters sawed and hammered, and electricians fine-tuned the lights in the four galleries on the second floor where sixty-two oils, fifty-six watercolors, and twenty-nine drawings would be on display.

Gustave Bilodeau, his assistant Marc Daguin, and Charles Pourville from New York's Metropolitan had collaborated on the master plan for the installation of the paintings and drawings. In the central gallery on the second floor, the director had set aside important space for eighteen portraits of Cézanne's family and friends. A freestanding, two-sided display was prominently placed in front of one of two portrait walls; on a panel facing the entrance Bilodeau planned to place the Llewellyn portrait. The portrait that would go on the other side would be the subject of a surprise announcement Bilodeau would make during the reception on the eve of the grand opening.

Mirella LeBorgne appeared with her assistant and met Bilodeau in the portrait gallery. She was concerned not about which painting went on which wall, but whether there would be an exhibition at all.

"It doesn't matter if some crazy person is still out there," Bilodeau pleaded. "We're completely protected inside.

Every possible way into the museum, each door and every window, all are protected by a high-frequency-sound sensor. If someone were to get inside, every open space—galleries, stairwells, halls, offices, lavatories—has infrared alarms." He showed her a pencil-thin, inch-long cylinder. "Every picture will have one of these magnetic alarms inserted in its frame."

LeBorgne said, "You forget that four of Cézanne's self-portraits were destroyed while the museums were open. Perhaps Vulcan is too clever for your sensors and alarms."

"There will be twenty-seven guards on duty at all times, at least four guards for each gallery. Every one is experienced and has been given fresh training in our newly installed security and communications systems."

"But the security system hasn't been completed, Gustave. Not until February 1, nearly two weeks."

"The system in the portrait gallery is fully installed and tested. With extra guards. I promise, no museum in Europe is safer than the Musée Granet."

Behind the reception hall was a garden surrounded by low storage buildings and what had once been a twenty-horse stable. Four vans were lined along Rue Alpheran, the street behind the museum. They belonged to the caterer, who had chosen the stable as the site for his portable kitchen. In charge was an unshaven young man with a stout midsection that made him look old for his years. A young man was waiting for him, a broad smile on his long, narrow face.

"Need kitchen help?" LeToque inquired.

The crew chief eyed the slim, black-haired man. "Show me your hands," he said brusquely.

LeToque had prepared for the examination and held out his hands, first palms down, then palms up.

"I can use you for six hours tomorrow, five to eleven. It pays 235 francs."

LeToque's smile never wavered. "I'll be here."

Chapter 56

Astrid went warily to the desk by the window and picked up the phone. It had been ringing for half a minute, and Fraser hadn't answered.

"Hello," she ventured softly.

"I'm calling Mr. Llewellyn." It was a male's husky voice, one she vaguely recognized.

"Who is calling?"

"Alex Tobias. He's expecting my call."

"This is Astrid, we met in New York."

"You're dead right. Nice to hear you," Tobias said.

"Where are you calling from?"

"Maybe about four blocks away."

"Then I might see you. That would be nice. Wait, please, I'll find Mr. Llewellyn."

She rapped on the door to Llewellyn's, opened it, and had taken two steps into the room when Llewellyn came from the bathroom, toweling off. He stood in front of her, stark naked save for a towel tied around his waist.

"It's Mr. Tobias," she said, pointing at the phone.

Llewellyn sat on the bed. "Alex, good to hear from you." He gave Astrid an "it's okay" wave, and she backed out of the room and closed the door.

"How was your trip?"

"Couldn't have been better, except for a little rain on the second day. Helen said it was my fault, but I blamed you, said you'd picked the date."

"I'm sure my friend is all right, but I have to ask."

"He's in perfect shape, but I'll feel a damn sight better when I don't have to baby-sit him anymore."

"One more day, Alex. Just be sure he doesn't get picked up accidentally. Someone might take a fancy to that damned old suitcase of yours."

Tobias laughed, "Don't worry, it looks more disreputable than ever."

"I want you to hold on to him. We're not showing him off until opening day. And is there any way you and Helen can join us at the reception tomorrow evening?"

"Afraid not. Helen's got us going to Marseille for the day. But have a drink for me, will you?"

They talked for several minutes, said their good-byes, then each hung up. After a pause, Astrid did the same.

Chapter 57

The underground ride seemed interminable, particularly to someone with a patience factor of something less than half a millisecond. At Hampstead station, in north London, Bud Samuelson followed the crowds to street level where he referred to the instructions that took him through the village to Church Row. The popular and artsy little district could be considered as out-of-the-way only because it was three miles from central London, but the streets were thick with tourists. It was all a bunch of charming shit, Samuelson thought, as he passed the two-hundred-year-old houses and manicured gardens that lined Church Row. Ahead of him now was St. John's Church, small, old, and white-painted, with wrought-iron fences surrounding its yard and cemetery. It was twenty past four, ten minutes until the doors would be closed to visitors.

Inside there was not much except the starkness of clean walls and old wood pews; near the lectern was a bust of Keats. By a window, ahead of him as he entered, was a female wearing a long black coat that nearly touched the floor. Her head turned. The face was pure white, the features exotic, the lips a deep red. Samuelson and the young woman were alone.

"Mr. Samuelson?" she asked

"Mari Shimada?" he replied.

Chapter 58

The N7 ran west and north from Aix-en-Provence through rolling farm county. Bent over the wheel, Peder Aukrust drove slowly, his mind on how the security arrangements in the Musée Granet had been so expertly designed and how essential it was that he take Llewellyn's portrait before it was hung in the safety of the portrait gallery. It was also an urgent reminder of how little time remained. In two days the retrospective would open. He refused to admit that his task would be even more difficult than the opportunities he had passed over as the wealthy New Yorker made his journey south from Paris.

Success depended on perfect timing, and it was important that any errors in his strategy be eliminated. A night alone would help him decide how well he had planned and refresh him for what he must accomplish in the next forty-eight hours.

A gloriously colored sky was forming, with slender fingers of stratus clouds sometimes covering the sun, which was an hour from disappearing. He had eaten nothing during the day, except for a dry croissant in his cheap pension and a pear he took from a dish of fruit in the portrait gallery, when he made a thorough examination of lights, alarms, exits, windows, and sensors inserted into the back of each painting. In the pockets of his jacket were lightweight professional tools that he would use to remove the canvas from the frame.

The canvas would fit into the pocket he had tediously made by sewing half of one T-shirt to the back of another. The portrait would fit flat and tight against his broad back without being detected. It would remain there until he was with Alan Pinkster. Then he would exchange it for the largest amount of money he would ever see.

He turned onto route D543, followed its S-turning road through the Trevaresse mountains to the village of Rognes. He referred to the advertisement in the travel magazine that had inspired him to drive into the country for the night.

At a crossroads a sign to the Auberge Rois et Reines pointed to a narrow, gravel road. He turned onto it. The road twisted into a wilderness of trees and low hills interspersed with pastures and sheep. Then came another swooping turn and a final swing back to the west, heading directly into the sun, which was just then slipping behind a nearby rise. Set against the dark shadow cast by the hill was the inn.

He entered a long, dimly lighted hall with a flight of stairs at the far end and, across from it, against the wall, a small reception desk. To the right, midway along the hall, were double doors leading into a dining room, across from which was a room filled with small tables, softly lighted by rosy light coming from lamps with deep pink lampshades. Aukrust smelled a sweet fragrance and saw two men sitting at a table in the far corner of the room. He went to the desk and waited.

"May I help you?" The light and pleasant voice came from a slightly built young man of perhaps twenty-five, who appeared from a door under the staircase.

"I want to eat and spend the night. Do you have a room?"

"You're alone?"

Aukrust nodded, then noticed the earrings and the slight blush of red on the young man's lips. "Yes, I'll be alone."

"Dinner is at nine o'clock, and your room," he pointed, "is number four, just at the top of the stairs. The complete cost for dinner and your room, not including whatever you may order from the bar, is 925 francs, which we ask our guests to pay in advance."

Aukrust now saw that in addition to the lipstick the eyes were delicately made up and the face was more that of a pretty girl than a young man.

"I'm going for a walk while there is still light."

"We have a walking path that begins just behind us and is a mile through the woods, bringing you back to the front of the inn. Later, when you are ready for company, please tell me or one of the other staff members. My name is Laurent," he said, smiling.

"I choose my own company," Aukrust said firmly. The auberge was aptly named, he thought: Inn of Kings and Queens.

A wide path curved through a thick stand of trees. Aukrust began walking, slowly at first, then faster as darkness settled over the forest. He found as Laurent had described that the path circled around to the front of the auberge.

His room was all but totally dark; thin draperies on the single window were open, allowing the last of the fading daylight into the room. He switched on the nighttable lamp. He inventoried the room: a low bureau beside the window, two chairs and a frail floor lamp with a tattered shade next to one of them; and on the inside wall a curtain drawn partly across a sink, toilet, and a shower stall. Fiery red roses the size of large cabbages dotted the wallpaper behind the massive high bed; the only suggestion of comfort in the room. Obviously in this auberge, the bed was important. He locked the door then went to the window and watched the final sprays of light disappear over the little forest where he had taken his walk. He drew the curtains together, turned, and looked directly into the muzzle of a snub-nosed held by LeToque.

"You chose a queer place to spend the night," LeToque said.

"How did you . . . the door was locked."

"Laurent gave me this—" He held up a key. "I told him I was a special friend, that you were expecting me. He understood."

"What do you want?" Aukrust said, his eyes shifting quickly between LeToque's face and the gun.

"The last time there was a bed between us, you had the advantage. Not this time."

"Put that damned thing away," Aukrust demanded.

LeToque laughed. "Business first. Weisbord owed me money, and you killed him."

"He killed himself. He was a sick man."

"Suicide? Not Weisbord."

Aukrust slapped his hands against his chest. "His lungs stopped working. I saw it."

"Of course you saw it," LeToque wiggled the pistol. "You killed him."

"I went to his house to take back Madame DeVilleurs's painting. I gave it to her."

LeToque looked surprised. "She's paying me to find it."

"She has it, LeToque. I gave it to her two days ago."

LeToque cocked his head and stared disbelieving. "Weisbord owed me, but you killed him. Now you have to pay."

"How much did he owe you?"

"Sixty thousand francs."

"A lot of money." Aukrust rubbed his hands together as if working out a decision. "I'll pay it," he said, his eyes riveted on LeToque.

LeToque, surprised, relaxed his grip on the gun imperceptibly. "When?"

"I can give you five thousand now, it's all I have with me. I'll have the rest tomorrow."

LeToque was looking at a thin, beguiling smile and listening to a reassuring voice. "Give me the five thousand. Put it there, on the bed."

Aukrust took out his wallet, opened it, then began dropping five-hundred-franc bills on the bed, one at a time. They floated down haphazardly, and LeToque began to gather them. For an instant, he took his eyes off Aukrust, an instant too long. Aukrust lunged across the bed and wrestled LeToque to the floor. There were two explosions. One bullet shattered a red rose in the wallpaper, the other blew off the tassled old lampshade. Aukrust slammed a fist on LeToque's arm, knocking the gun from his hand. Aukrust swung again at LeToque, but the smaller man twisted free and spun onto his feet before Aukrust could rise to one knee. Loud voices came from the hall outside the bedroom.

"Open the door! Are you hurt?" was followed by a rat-a-tat of fists against the door, which gave way against the feeble lock.

"Stop fighting!" a man shouted. He was tall, fortyish, with long hair combed into a pony tail and tied with a black ribbon. Beside him was Laurent, with others standing in the doorway.

"I am Jean-Pierre, the owner," he said. "We don't like quarrels to get out of hand. People get hurt, and we get a bad reputation."

Aukrust got up slowly. He glared first at LeToque, then at Jean-Pierre. Laurent said, pointing to Le Toque. "He came to apologize and said he wanted to be forgiven. He said there might be trouble, and he was right."

"He wouldn't listen," LeToque said. He moved a step to his right, bent down and picked up the gun. He pointed it at Aukrust, then scooped up the bills from the bed. "You owe me big, filthy bastard. Sixty thousand, less what's here. Pay me, or I use this." He waved the gun and bolted from the room.

Chapter 59

Aukrust's station wagon was parked inside the entrance to Parc Joseph Jourdan near the city university, less than a mile from the Hôtel Pullman Roi René. He had returned to Aix in the predawn darkness and had been waiting impatiently for more than an hour. During the return drive to Aix he had excised memories of the previous evening and put LeToque in a deep recess of his mind as something to be dealt with at another time. At eight o'clock the passenger door opened and Clyde jumped onto the seat, making a sound between a bark and a growl, followed by Astrid. She slumped deep into the seat and pulled the dog to her, wrapping an arm around its head. "Be a good boy, quiet down."

"Are you sure you weren't followed?" Peder asked.

"Of course," she answered bitterly. "Would I have come into the car if I knew someone was watching?"

Makeup covered the bruise under her eye, but no makeup could conceal the sullen look spread over her face. Her eyes strayed off, and her head shook nervously.

"Describe again where you're staying: how many rooms, who is in each one."

She began, her voice a monotone. She complained that she had told all of it before, that there was nothing new to add. Peder probed for details: Where were the windows and what kind? Had she paced off the distances to the elevator and to the service elevator, and exactly where were they?

The phones—where was each placed? Describe the bathroom. Were there doors connecting to other rooms?

He bore on. "Were any police there, in uniform, out of uniform?"

"No, I didn't see any, no one like that."

"Have you seen the painting?"

"I said before, he keeps it in the wooden box. In the closet in his bedroom. Locked."

"When is he taking it to the museum?"

Astrid shook her head. "He hasn't said."

"Has he talked any more about security at the museum, shown any concern, said he was happy about it . . . or said he was unhappy about it?"

Again her head shook, her eyes closed. "Before the reception tomorrow Llewellyn will go on a tour of the museum. He invited me to go with him."

Aukrust nodded, as if putting the information to the side momentarily. "What does his man do? Fraser."

She sighed. "The same as always, food, errands, the dog."

"And does the damned dog always bark?"

Astrid tightened her grip on Clyde and said nothing.

Aukrust said, "Albany is frequently with him. He drinks but seems to do his job. Where is his room?"

"It must be very near."

Aukrust stared directly ahead, oblivious to the stream of students that walked or rode past on bicycles.

"Has there been any mail, any phone calls that seemed unusual?"

Astrid shook her head. She turned to face Aukrust but could not look directly at him. When she tried to speak, she found herself trembling with fear. Finally, the words gushed out. "Peder, you must tell me you love me. I try so hard to do what you ask."

He didn't answer. He waited until the little sounds caught

in her throat subsided. "Everything is the same with us. You hear that?"

She nodded, but her head barely moved.

"Tell me if there have been any unusual phone calls."

"Of course, he's been on the phone, ordering food, or a newspaper—"

"Something unusual," he said impatiently.

"No, only—"

"Only what?"

"There was a call from the man I met in New York. Tobias."

Aukrust stiffened. "What did he want?"

"He's here, in Aix."

"When did he arrive?"

"He called yesterday."

"You listened to the conversation?"

"I answered the phone. I listened, but nothing made sense."

"What did they talk about?"

"Tobias talked about a 'friend' he brought with him. And about a suitcase. But Americans sometimes use words I don't understand, and they only talked for a minute."

"Tell me exactly what you remember," Aukrust demanded.

Astrid tried but could only think of what she had already said, except, "Someone said 'baby-sit.' I don't know who said it."

"Did Llewellyn talk to you about his conversation with Tobias?"

Her mouth opened, then closed. Nothing came out.

"Did he?"

Clyde growled softly, and Astrid began stroking his head. Aukrust took her purse, searched through it, and took out the lipstick he had given her in Gatwick Airport. He pulled off the cap and twisted up the lipstick. "Passionately Pink—

your color." Then he twisted the lipstick in the opposite direction and a hypodermic needle appeared.

"I think that you and Llewellyn had a long talk last night, and that you haven't told me everything. Tell me what he said, or you'll go back to Llewellyn with a dead dog in your arms."

"Don't, Peder!"

He took Clyde from her and put the frightened animal on his lap. He spread the dog's hind legs and aimed the needle at the fleshy inside of the thighs. "What did Llewellyn tell you?"

"He told me that the painting he brought with him is a copy, that Tobias brought the real painting."

Chapter 60

Elliott Heston stood inside the door to his office and greeted Bud Samuelson with a quick handshake and a wave toward the table in the corner of his office.

"I won't take long," Samuelson said, "but this way I know the information I've got will get into the right hands, especially Oxby's. I can't locate him. Where the hell is he?"

"I'm afraid I don't know—for the moment," Heston said with a touch of resignation.

Samuelson placed two neatly handwritten pages in front of Heston. "This was prepared by a woman named Shimada, recently employed by a Japanese art dealer named Kondo. Know them?"

"I'm familiar with both names," Heston said.

It says that the residue from what is purportedly the Pinkster self-portrait is a piece of old art that was produced sometime around 1920. The canvas was identified as coming from either Belgium or Holland." Samuelson read, "The source of the white pigment, or titanium dioxide, identified in the sample by spectrographic analysis, is found only on the west coast of Norway, in the titanated iron ore called ilmenite. Titanium dioxide was first used to produce the whitest of all pigments in 1918 or 1919."

Samuelson said, "I needn't remind you that Paul Cézanne could not have used it. He died in 1906."

Chapter 61

Rue du Quatre Septembre ran south from Cours Mirabeau; where it intersected with Rue Cardinale was the Place du Dauphine, center of a quiet residential neighborhood that offered a great deal of old-world charm but precious few places to park a car. A red Fiat appeared and cruised around the square then abruptly turned onto the sidewalk where it came to rest half on and half off the street, its bumper against a fountain known as the Quatre Dauphins. The driver bolted out and sprinted along the narrow street to the Hôtel Cardinal.

Ann Browley came to a halt in the tiny lobby and, breathing heavily, inquired as to the whereabouts of Monsieur Oxby. She was given an envelope on which was written, in the inspector's inimitable scrawl, "Ann's Eyes Only." A note instructed her to continue on Rue Cardinale to where the street widened to create Place St.-Jean-de-Malte, where, on her right, would be the Musée Granet and, directly ahead, the church of St.-Jean-de-Malte. "I will be on the left side in the tenth row."

Vigil lights flickered on tables set against the walls along each side aisle in the nave in the old church. When Oxby had arrived earlier, he had put twenty francs in a box, taken a candle, and put its wick into an already burning one, then had placed it in a fluted metal tube. Oxby was not Catholic so his silent message to Miriam was a personal communication that if God and the saints wished would be speeded along to that other place, where he knew she was.

The inside of the old church was dark brown, and a deep patina of sienna covered the big ecclesiastical paintings by Mignard and Finsonius placed high up on the wall. Hourly chimes were not produced automatically, and none struck when ten o'clock came. At fifteen past ten he looked up to see Ann Browley walking briskly toward him.

Oxby greeted her. "Good show, Annie. Everything peaceful at home?"

She sighed with an exaggerated gush of air that indicated that she understood the irony of Oxby's question. "I thought Elliott would pop a carotid artery when I told him I was taking some leave days."

Oxby replied, "He's under a great deal of pressure and not at all eased that we're here. But I've sent Jimmy back, which should lower his blood pressure by twenty points."

Ann unzipped her briefcase and pulled out several pages crammed with single-spaced typing. "Once our International gang learned where to look, they got a super rundown on Llewellyn's girlfriend."

"Surely you've got the report memorized," Oxby said, "so spare all but the highlights."

"If you don't mind, Inspector, I'll give my report the way I had planned." She punctuated each word as if driving tiny rivets into each one. "All right?"

He glanced quickly at his watch then gave a chastened nod.

Ann began, "Astrid Haraldsen was orphaned when she was nine and was raised by her paternal grandmother until she was fourteen, when her grandmother died. She then was sent to her maternal grandmother, who lived in Trondheim. She was rebellious and had minor skirmishes with the police when she was a teenager, incidents involving petty thefts and shoplifting. Her school record was a splotchy one, some good years, some bad. When she was eighteen she was enrolled in the Statens Kunst og Handverks Hoyskole in Oslo to study interior design. But she was poorly prepared academically and lacked ability to sketch or draw. She switched to courses in photography in which she showed aptitude but was dropped from school after the first year."

Oxby was staring at the altar, then his eyes closed. "Go on," he said.

Ann's glower softened, and for the next few minutes she sketched in additional details of Astrid's teenage years. "When she was twenty and living in Copenhagen, she was arrested for soliciting, a charge that was subsequently dropped."

"Did that happen more than once?"

"A second time, with the same result."

"Soliciting," Oxby said thoughtfully; "not prostitution? There's a difference you know."

"Would it matter?" Ann asked.

"I wouldn't think so." Oxby leaned forward. "You describe an unhappy, undisciplined young person."

"And things got worse for her," Ann went on. "She became involved with drugs about this time. Several arrests but again no convictions. Not until three years ago, when she was twenty-four. She was found guilty of dealing in cocaine, barbiturates, and amphetamines."

"Incarcerated?"

"She served three months of a two-year sentence then was released on condition that she work with undercover operatives investigating a drug syndicate that had infiltrated the country's hospital system. She was assigned to a former hospital pharmacist who had exposed members of the syndicate and who had been recruited into the drug enforcement agency of the Norwegian national police. That person is referred to in the report as "the Operator."

His eyes opened. "Interesting name. Go on."

"A strange thing happened at this point," Ann continued.

"The official records on the Operator were sealed, which means, the final portion of the report on Haraldsen was not supported by official records and in fact is filled with words like 'uncorroborated' or 'unverified.' The Operator apparently killed a suspect, perhaps accidentally while attempting to secure a confession, and the whole affair was pushed under the rug and the Operator was never identified. None of this has been admitted by official sources, but the information is considered accurate. The balance of Haraldsen's sentence was commuted, and she left Norway two years ago."

Oxby slid past Ann and stood in the aisle for a moment. He took several steps toward the choir, turned, and came back. Ann watched him, puzzled.

She whispered, "You look worried."

"A little. I let Astrid travel with Llewellyn, but she was no lady in distress."

"Meaning?"

"There's a little conspiracy going on, and I don't want anyone getting hurt."

"What will you do?"

"Keep my promise and make certain nothing happens to Llewellyn."

Oxby sat next to Ann. "You were telling me about The Operator. Were we able to get more on him?"

Ann withdrew a second report from her briefcase and handed it to Oxby. "Our people stitched this material together from unofficial sources, but they claim that every word is exactly as it happened."

Oxby read the report, a scant two pages: "The government did not want to expose the cover-up; instead the Operator was given new identification and fifty thousand dollars to leave the country. A new passport and visa said his name was Charles Metzger—" Oxby looked up. "Is that your Dr. Metzger?"

Ann nodded. "It will be a colossal coincidence if he isn't. The report also gives his actual name."

"I see that." He pronounced the names several times to himself. "Can it be, Annie, that Vulcan is Charles Metzger, and Dr. Metzger is Peder Aukrust?"

Chapter 62

Layers of strong aromas persisted in the Musée Granet: high-spirited alkyds, glues, and harsh cleaners. It was an amalgam of such power that when the air was deeply inhaled it induced a euphoric light-headedness. Then as the afternoon wore on, the fresh scents from huge bouquets and tubs of flowers, and plants plus food aromas from the kitchens sweetened the chemically stained air.

Shortly after three o'clock, an oil titled *Road on the Plain* was put in place, a mercury-level sensor inserted in the back of its frame, and a spotlight adjusted to spread an even light over the blue-green mountain scene. Charles Pourville affixed an engraved brass plaque to the bottom of the frame. He gave one of the plaques to Gustave Bilodeau. "This is for Monsieur Llewellyn's portrait. He'll be pleased."

"He'll be damned," Bilodeau said with uncharacteristic bitterness. "He won't allow us to hang his portrait until tomorrow, and there's no promise we'll have it then." Then a fresh smile returned to the museum director's face. "But there are two featured panels in our portrait allery, and tonight I will have good news about one of them."

That a year's planning was about to come to a successful conclusion was a tribute to Gustave Bilodeau's gutsy determination, though it might have been in vain if Mirella LeBorgne had not been influenced by a consortium of insurance companies, which had made an extensive analysis of the security arrangements and vetted the entire staff.

The security staff now reported to a former security director in the Sûreté Nationale. An intimate of Félix Lemieux, he went by the single name Fauchet, was in his mid-fifties, and covered his inquiring eyes with a pair of green-tinted glasses.

Bilodeau had boasted that the reception would be the grandest of all grand-opening parties. That might not prove true of opening parties worldwide, but in Aix there was every possibility of it being the most lavish in the city's long history.

Scooter Albany handed a glass to Astrid and, with experienced adroitness, popped open a champagne bottle.

"Have some of the bubbly." He grinned, filled both their glasses, aiming his at hers, and caused a mid-air collision punctuated by a loud, splashy clank.

"Clumsy, clumsy," he scolded himself and fumbled in his pockets for a handkerchief.

Astrid gave an obligatory smile and went to the buffet for a napkin, then kept walking to the end of the table. She looked back at the swelling crowd, the food, and the flowers. More people came, all talking at once, making a familiar buzzing noise that likely reminded Astrid of that night in the Boston Museum of Fine Arts. The music began, coming from a quintet of musicians seated alongside the gray stone staircase that went up to the gallery floor.

In clusters were formally dressed men and women, the guests and patrons who had written large checks to help insure that the obscure Musée Granet would have its moment of fame and glory. Gathered, too, were the organizers and curators responsible for selecting the billion dollars' worth of paintings from twenty-one countries. Llewellyn put a white carnation in the lapel of his tuxedo, then took Astrid's hand. "Come join the party," he said.

A fanfare began as a tall, gray-haired woman was escorted to a microphone by Bilodeau. He asked for silence, then said, "We are honored this evening by the presence of a dear friend of the Granet. It is my honor to introduce Madame Margueritte DeVilleurs." When the applause died away he continued. "Now for the good news. Madame De-Villeurs has given me the privilege of announcing that she has donated her Cézanne self-portrait to the Musée."

The announcement came as a surprise to many, but everyone roared their approval. When the cheering subsided, Margueritte took the microphone. "I wish you could see the painting this very minute. But as some of you know, I lost my Cézanne for a while, and when he came back I decided he needed a good cleaning and a new frame. You will see my friend in a week. I promise."

Bilodeau raised both hands high over his head and pointed to the floor above. "The galleries are now open. Please go enjoy the exhibition."

Llewellyn introduced himself to Margueritte and congratulated her on her grand gesture. Instantly they were on a first-name basis, and Llewellyn floated the idea that he might give his portrait to the Metropolitan in New York. Scooter taped it all. Margueritte turned full circle, her eyes searching among the guests.

"I'm looking for someone I want you to meet, but he seems to have disappeared."

Peder Aukrust peeled away from Margueritte DeVilleurs with the first notes of the fanfare. She had insisted that he accompany her to the reception but at his first opportunity, he inquired if an Alexander Tobias was on the guest list. He was not. Earlier in the day, using a list of hotels obtained from the city's tourist office, Aukrust learned that an Alexander Tobias and his wife were registered at the Hôtel Nègre-Coste. Policy prohibited giving a guest's room number.

Aukrust left the Musée Granet by the back entrance and walked hurriedly past a bustling catering crew taking food and beverages to the buffet tables. LeToque had been toting trays in and out of the museum when he spotted Aukrust earlier. He tossed away his tray and threw his busboy uniform at the feet of the enraged caterer.

"Crazy bastard . . . fill your tray with more glasses," the flustered manager yelled, "or no pay."

"Fuck your glasses," LeToque said, and went off in pursuit of Aukrust. He headed for Rue d'Italie, a busy street behind the Musée Granet, one that was lined with restaurants and food markets. He saw Aukrust silhouetted against the lights in a pharmacy window a half block away. LeToque began running but lost sight of the big man when he went into a street that angled sharply away from Rue d'Italie. LeToque followed cautiously into the dark, narrow street. Streetlamps cast pale yellow light over the pavement. He continued past a row of darkened shops and past a jewelry store, its single window filled with cheap wristwatches, most of which said it was 9:48.

He came to a kiosk with signs announcing upcoming events at the Palais de Congress, a building directly ahead of him which at that instant came alive, as its doors opened and a stream of people flowed out onto to the sidewalk. LeToque struggled past them and climbed up several steps so that he could look back over the route he had just walked. He saw him, sixty yards away. Aukrust had doubled back to Rue d'Italie and just at the moment LeToque caught sight of him, he turned in the direction of the Cours. LeToque ran after him.

Aukrust went to the cafe next to the Hôtel Nègre-Coste, where a hundred francs quickly persuaded the night manager to part with a bottle of brandy. He slipped into the pay phone and dialed the Hôtel Nègre-Coste.

"Alexander Tobias, please."

"*Un moment, Monsieur,*" a voice said. Then a familiar tone sounded three times.

"Hello," a husky male voice said.

Aukrust silently replaced the phone.

In late afternoon he had parked his car in a cramped alley behind the hotel, near a souvenir shop and a pizza parlor. He started toward his car, stopping twice to take a deep swig from the bottle, mumbling that LeToque was a problem that required a permanent solution. Inside the car he tipped the bottle once more, then jammed the cork into it. He pulled his medicine case next to him and searched inside it for familiar shapes—the ones he would need on the professional call he was about to make. From the back seat he retrieved a bulky package wrapped in green tissue paper.

Amenities in the Nègre-Coste were minimal: no dining room or bar, only a reception desk inside the front entrance and in the rear a room that doubled for breakfast in the morning and television in the evening. In between was a staircase to the upper five floors and an elevator into which three persons might squeeze.

At the reception desk was a young student from the university, his head bent over a textbook. Seated nearby, also reading and looking acutely bored, was a rail-thin girl of perhaps nineteen, her hair hanging straight over a painfully unattractive face.

Aukrust placed his package on the counter and stared past the receptionist to a row of boxes, a number on every one and a key in half of them. "I've been asked to come and see Madame Tobias. I am a doctor and by a fortunate coincidence, we were friends when I lived in New York. I've brought flowers to cheer her up."

The young man looked up, somewhat surprised, "Is she sick? I didn't know."

"Nothing serious, but she doesn't travel well, and for the first day or two, she has a painful stomach problem. They are in room 37?"

"No, there's no heat on the upper floors this time of

year." He looked in the register. "Madame Tobias and Monsieur are in room 28, in the front."

Aukrust leaned on the counter hnd inclined his head toward the young girl. "Is this your girlfriend? She's very pretty."

The young man smiled uncomfortably and looked at the girl. "Just a friend."

Aukrust forced an indulgent smile. "You're a lucky young man," then added, "I'll see what I can do for Madame Tobias." He started off but stopped and turned back to the young students, "You needn't call; they are expecting me."

Oxby picked his way through the crowd to where Llewellyn was standing. "I see you have a new friend."

Llewellyn smiled. "Margueritte's quite a woman. I'd like to show her off in New York."

"She'd make a hit with your friends." Oxby took Llewellyn aside. "I hope Astrid has been getting on all right. Has she gone up to the galleries?"

"I asked Pourville to give her a tour."

"I have friends in Provence in the event she is interested in antiquing."

"I don't think she's up for that. In fact, she's become skittish the last few days."

"Still bothered by the Paris episode?"

"Some, perhaps. She continues to insist that I'm in some kind of danger."

"And still worried that the painting is going to be stolen?"

Llewellyn nodded. "She blurts it all out, then becomes quiet. I try to relax her."

"How?"

"When—" he paused—"when we're in bed."

"Spare the details. Recently?"

"Last night."

"What happened?"

"She was cold, like ice. I had no interest in sex, and certainly she didn't. I thought it was best for her to be with me where I could take care of her. I told her that nothing was going to happen to me, that I was under twenty-four-hour guard, that I had a gun and knew how to use it."

"Had you told her that before?"

"Not about the gun."

"She said?"

"She began to cry. Then I blurted out that it didn't make any difference—that I didn't have the real painting. That I had a copy."

Oxby reacted as if he had been sledgehammered in the pit of his stomach. He whispered, urgently, "Then what—"

"She asked where the real painting was, and at that instant I felt that our charade didn't matter anymore, that I was safely in Aix, and so was my painting. I told her that Alex Tobias had brought it over, that it was safe with him."

"Wrong, wrong!" Oxby said. "Astrid's in this with Vulcan, sometimes called Dr. Metzger, real name Peder Aukrust—a Norwegian, trained pharmacist, and skilled chemist. He's had all bloody day to locate Tobias. Find Ann, tell her to send Sam Turner to the Nègre-Coste hotel. Tell her it's damned important and to be careful."

Aukrust waited for the night clerk and his friend to return to their books. He considered the elevator but only briefly and went to the stairs. They were wide and carpeted to the second level, after which they narrowed and curled continuously to the upper floors.

At the third level he heard a television and inhaled the pungent aroma of garlic and burnt olive oil. The walls were covered in a brown paper figured with trees and birds. The lights were cream-colored globes, suspended from brass chains. He slipped off the green wrapping from the flowers and cradled them in his arm, continuing to room 28. From his pocket he took a three-inch-long aerosol can and uncapped it. He rapped lightly on the door.

A pause, then a male voice. "Who is it?"

"I know it's late," Aukrust began in his smooth baritone, pronouncing each word in an accented English he had practiced repeatedly, "but I have flowers for Mrs. Tobias, a gift from Mr. Llewellyn and also Gustave Bilodeau, who is my friend at the Granet." He cupped the aerosol can in the palm of his hand.

The door was unlocked and opened. Helen and Alex Tobias stood in their bathrobes, side by side. Helen Tobias was embarrassed that her hair was full of curlers, as she was plainly preparing for bed. Aukrust stepped into the room, closing the door behind him. He held out the flowers to her. "These are especially for you."

She took the flowers and smelled them appreciatively. Then Alexander Tobias stepped beside his wife, "Who the hell are you?" he asked. "This is no damned time to deliver flowers—"

Aukrust pulled his hands from under the bouquet, and as he did, he released the valve and a puff of white mist spread out from the flowers and into two startled faces. With the burst came an intensely sweet floral scent that Helen Tobias was able to enjoy for exactly two seconds before the flowers fell from her hands and she and her husband collapsed to the floor. Aukrust put a mask over his mouth and nose.

"I'm happy you approve, Madame Tobias. Jasmine and rose mixed with my own blend of enfleurane and nitrous oxide."

He went directly to the closet and found clothes on hangers, small packages of gifts, and two pieces of luggage, which he carried to the bed. The one tagged with Alexander Tobias's name was locked, its scruffy appearance perhaps a bit too deceptive. Aukrust opened it with pliers and a knife, then slashed at the lining until he discovered the false bottom. There he found the flat metal case wrapped in a sheet of black plastic.

From the Musée Granet to the Hôtel Nègre-Coste was three blocks, or five hundred yards, or so Oxby guessed it to be as he ran along Rue Frédéric Mistral, the Cours Mirabeau directly ahead. Lights shone from three of the six rooms on the third floor of the hotel, and he computed that the room farthest to the left was the one occupied by Alex and Helen Tobias. At the entrance he looked back for Ann and more hopefully for Sam Turner, but neither one was in sight.

"Are the Tobiases in their room?"

"Yes, I'm sure they are," the young receptionist said.

The girl looked up from her book. "A friend came, a doctor, for Madame Tobias. She is not feeling well, he said."

"When was that?" Oxby asked.

"Ten minutes, maybe a little more."

"Is he still with them?"

The young man shrugged, "We can't tell from here . . . sometimes they go out the back door to the parking area."

"Call the room . . . quickly, then the police!"

Aukrust was at the door when the phone rang. He glowered at it then set the lock and pulled the door shut behind him. For a precious few seconds he stood motionless, eyes closed. At the stairs he heard footsteps coming toward him. He about-faced and started up to the floor above. At the turn of the staircase he stopped and was able to see a man's legs coming up the stairs and running in the direction of room 28. Aukrust started down, slowly at first. Then when he was past the second floor, he took the steps two at a time to the lobby. A silent television picture flickered in the lounge. Coming from the reception desk was a man's loud voice demanding Alexander Tobias's room number. Aukrust crouched in front of the television, twisting dials as if he were a guest trying to sift static from the picture, but his eyes never strayed from the lobby. The man hurriedly ran past him and up the stairs

It was quiet again until the student receptionist and his girlfriend began chattering in French about all the strange people who had come to visit the Americans in room 28.

Oxby lifted Helen Tobias onto the bed and covered her with a blanket. Then he helped Tobias into a chair.

"Describe him, Alex, and stop wincing that he got the best of you."

But Tobias did wince; his anger at being outsmarted wasn't about to go away quickly. "He was tall . . . light hair . . . a mixed accent I couldn't place . . . late thirties—that's most of it, Jack. He came in the room and poof—I'm out!" He looked at his wife. "Helen's all right?"

"You're both fine," Oxby said as he ran his hand across the bottom of the empty suitcase. "Bloody bastard got it."

Sam Turner was at the door. "What happened?"

"Tell you as we go." He nudged Turner back through the door.

Aukrust ran to his car, angry that he had parked in the tourist shopping zone. When he reached the wide boulevard he was met by a crowd of university students gathered outside a popular cafe. Several formed into an obstreperous mob and circled his station wagon. They tapped on the roof and stared insolently through the windows at him. Aukrust pushed his door against one of them and leaped from the car, roaring. They quickly retreated.

He entered the Cours at the midpoint of the half-mile-long boulevard. To his right, the west, automobile traffic thickened and circled around the Fontaine de la Rotonde, a garish display of water splashing over snarling lions and giant geese that was brilliantly illuminated with blue-white lights.

Aukrust's hesitation was infuriating; his vaunted decisiveness deserted him for the moment. Then he sped ahead, turning sharply to the left, nearly scraping against one of the thermal fountains. He patted his medicine case reassuringly, his eyes concentrating on the road ahead that would, in two hundred yards, shrink to the width of a single car and lead beyond to the sanctuary of the city's suburbs.

From behind him, as if catapulted out of the black void, a car without lights raced past, then all of its rear red lights blazed at once as the car braked abruptly and spun a precise 180 degrees, coming to a stop with its high beams shining directly at Aukrust. Aukrust reacted by jamming on his brakes and turning hard right, but as he did, the car opposing him turned in the same direction and sped toward him. As Aukrust turned sharply to the left a sharp sound erupted inside the car, as if the windshield had been struck with a rock the size of a fist. The headlights on the other car blinked high then low. At the same time there were two more loud cracks against the windshield. With the fourth came a different sound, a sharp, metallic snap, and the rearview mirror shattered. In four seconds, the entire windshield became glazed like ancient pottery, and in the middle of a million tiny lines were four bullet holes.

Aukrust came to a complete stop, backed up until he hit a parked car, then turned and pressed hard on the accelerator. The other car came at him again and as he continued forward he recognized the silver Porsche lurking next to him. Immediately he processed several thoughts, none in his favor. The driver was behind the wheel of a Porsche—a car that was faster and more agile than his old station wagon; the driver had a gun and was using it; the driver was LeToque.

Escape meant reaching the fountain and the busy streets beyond where he could meld with the traffic. But his car was not a sprinter, which suggested to him that if he weaved erratically he would force LeToque to stay behind him. But that strategy failed after a hundred yards when the Porsche drew alongside. Aukrust glanced to his left; at the instant he did, the window was shattered by two bullets. One tore away the end of his nose, amid a shower of fine glass shards that blasted against the left side of his face, blinding him in that eye, causing half his face to erupt in a mask of blood.

Anger overwhelmed his fright, and pain overrode all. There was no way to reach the agony inside his eye, no way to wash away the tiny bits of glass that burned with such excruciating intensity. Desperately he forced himself to drive forward, trying as he did so to steer into the tormenting car to disable it or get past it.

He straightened and aimed as best his vision allowed toward the blur of lights shining on the big fountain. His foot pressed hard to the floor, and it seemed he had broken free when he was a hundred feet from the fountain . . . then fifty feet. . . .

The last bullet entered the rear window and lodged high in Aukrust's back in the soft flesh in his shoulder. It wasn't a fatal hit but a lucky one, which caused him to turn the wheel sharply, aiming the car over the sidewalk and into the carved stone wall surrounding the fountain. The front of the station wagon rose up as if trying to climb over the wall then teetered and fell back.

The door opened and Aukrust tumbled out onto his knees. He struggled to his feet and walked on stiff legs to the fountain. When he reached it he continued to walk, his legs churning futilely against the waist-high wall. He fell forward, his face submerged in cold water that would soothe the cuts and wash the bits of glass from his eye.

But neither eye would see again. Aukrust was dead.

Oxby and Sam Turner had witnessed the entire, bizarre chase, had heard the gunshots, and had sprinted after Aukrust's station wagon on its final, desperate run. After pulling the body from the fountain and confirming that Aukrust was dead, Turner started for the car.

"Stay away from it, Sam! Put your head inside and breathe just once, and you'll be as dead as this poor bastard."

Chapter 63

January 23 was a wintry London day, and on the Thames the wind swirled doggedly—cold, penetrating, rippling the water that was the color of the thick scraps of purplish clouds beginning to drift in from the northwest. Aboard the duty boat were Sergeants Jennings and Tompkins of the Thames Division. From the Metropolitan Police were Sergeant Jimmy Murratore and Detective Chief Inspector Jack Oxby. The men from Scotland Yard had been picked up at Westminster Pier, and the black-hulled boat was now seven miles east of Tower Bridge and three hundred yards astern of Alan Pinkster's converted tug *Sepera*. Ahead of the tug, four hundred yards farther east, was another duty boat. Both were in continuous radio contact with each other by way of a scrambler on a high-range FM frequency.

"Ten before two," Jimmy said and lowered his binoculars. He pointed at the south bank of the river. "That's Woolwich Ferry. Two quid says Kondo comes out of there."

Oxby pulled the wool tam down across his forehead. "On time, I trust."

"Suppose he's not," the young detective said. "What's your plan if he doesn't show at all?"

Oxby patted the pocket of his peacoat. "I've got warrants for search and arrest. I want Kondo, too." He eyed Murratore severely. "Don't give me a problem I don't want, Jimmy. Any doubts about your information?"

"We heard right, didn't we, Jeff?"

"It's on tape," Sergeant Jennings said.

Jimmy said, "They meet today, right out there."

A tone sounded, high pitched. Tompkins answered, "Come in."

"Small craft entering the river from vicinity of Woolwich Ferry. We'll assume patrol duties. Confirm."

"Confirmed."

"I see him," Jimmy said. "Movin' at a turtle's pace. But he's movin'."

"Can you confirm that it's Kondo?" Oxby said.

"Another two quid?"

Oxby shook his head. "No one took you up the first time."

They turned in a tight circle then cruised slowly toward the south bank of the river, assuming for all appearances that they were a duty boat on regular patrol. The four men stared across at *Sepera* and at the small cruiser approximately a half mile away. Now it was lying still in the water, as if anchored.

"He's not moving now. Not until he thinks it's clear," Oxby said.

They waited.

"Inspector?" Jimmy Murratore said. "We've barely talked since you got back, and I've got a few curiosities to add to the list you put on the chalkboard a while back. Like, who or what killed Vulcan?"

"A little Frenchman named LeToque tried his damnedest, but Peder Aukrust took a whiff of his own medicine. The same poison gas he used to kill Clarence Boggs spilled loose from his medicine case when his car crashed."

"Ann said they didn't find Llewellyn's painting in his car. Where was it?"

"They took his body to the morgue and found it when they stripped off his clothes. It was between two undershirts he had sewn together. No harm done to the portrait. In fact, it's on display as if nothing ever happened."

"And the girl? Llewellyn's friend?"

"A sad problem for her, but Astrid was in over her head. I had the first inkling the morning I met her when she was going off to Johnny Van Haeften's for a desk. One in light colors, she said. Van Haeften has first-rate porcelain and fine silver"—he shook his head slowly—"but not a stick of furniture. Of course, Jimmy, you knew that."

He raised his binoculars, looking first at *Sepera* then at the cruiser. "It's moving again. Slow, but moving."

He kept the glasses trained on the cruiser as he talked. "Astrid's being held in Marseille pending extradition. She may be complicit in the murder of Boggs, and the Americans want to question her about the Boston portrait. Llewellyn took it badly."

Oxby scanned back and forth between the two vessels closing in on each other, then panned the binoculars over the water to pick up the duty boat, which had turned and now was on course for *Sepera*.

"And Pinkster?" Jimmy asked.

Oxby shifted his angle and had *Sepera* in clear view. "In the beginning there was Alan Pinkster, and now, at the end, there is still Alan Pinkster."

Oxby smiled. "But not for long."

Acknowledgments

Paul Cézanne painted twenty-five self-portraits—notwithstanding any statements to the contrary in this story. He painted dozens more portraits of friends, relatives, and ordinary folk, many of whom were asked to return for sitting after sitting while the artist continued his unending quest for a personal expression of the shapes and colors he saw. Such, I suppose, is the nature of genius.

I chose to tell a story about Paul Cézanne's self-portraits because those pictures are the essence of Cézanne and because Cézanne has recently gained the recognition and respect that is long overdue. The thought that a dreadful disaster might befall one of Cézanne's masterful self-portraits presented an irresistible storytelling opportunity.

Acknowledgment is one of those long, dusty words that lacks warmth and does not convey the gratitude I feel toward my many friends and colleagues, who were always ready to share their knowledge and give their support. Having said that, I extend my deepest appreciation and thanks to the following:

The Metropolitan Museum of Art, New York: Herbert Moskowitz, Registrar, Gary Tinterow, Englehard Curator, European Paintings.

The Boston Museum of Fine Arts: Cornelius Vermeule, Senior Curator; Barrett Tilney.

Courtauld Institute of Art: Aiden Weston-Lewis.

Musée Granet, Aix-en-Provence: Denis Coutagne, Conservateur du Musée.

Frick Collection: Edgar Munhall, Curator.

Frick Reference Library: Helen Sanger, Librarian.

Westminster Abbey: Emma St. John-Smith, Press Representative.

Metropolitan Police Service, New Scotland Yard, London: Jackie Bennett and Judy Prue, Press Office.

Interpol, Lyons; Miguel E. Chamorro, Executive Assistant Secretary General.

To my friends: Gene Atkinson, Florence and Bob Campbell, Walter Klein and Mary Eddy Klein, Frazer Sedcole, Jim Soderlind, Stuart Stearns, Keith Way, and Peter Wood.

A special thanks to Greg Tobin and Oscar Collier. Both know a thing or two about the craft of writing.

By naming some, I risk not naming many who I trust will accept my apology for a leaky memory.

This is fiction; however, the self-portraits of Paul Cézanne are real. All except one or two.